LEOPOLDO GOUT

PIÑATA

NIGHTFIRE

Tor Publishing Group

New York

PIÑATA

Copyright © 2023 by Leopoldo & Co.

A Nightfire Book
Published by Tom Doherty Associates / Tor Publishing Group
120 Broadway
New York, NY 10271

www.tornightfire.com

Nightfire™ is a trademark of Macmillan Publishing Group, LLC.

The Library of Congress Cataloging-in-Publication Data is available upon request.

ISBN 978-1-250-78117-8 (hardcover)
ISBN 978-1-250-78118-5 (ebook)

Our books may be purchased in bulk for promotional, educational, or business use. Please contact your local bookseller or the Macmillan Corporate and Premium Sales Department at 1-800-221-7945, extension 5442, or by email at MacmillanSpecialMarkets@macmillan.com.

First Edition: 2023

Printed in the United States of America

0 9 8 7 6 5 4 3 2

"Tikahki in tlatsotsonalistli itech tlahtoltsin inik amo polihwi ipan ilnalmiki."

Listen carefully to the rhythms of your tongue so that they don't get lost in memory.

—Translated into Nahuatl by Gustavo Zapoteco Sideño

PIÑATA

PROLOGUE

Thunder claps from above with a violence that could rupture the very heavens. It is like the booming strokes of an immense teponaxtle drum resounding in an endless funerary procession. People say the ancient gods are trampling and crashing against the new celestial firmament above, trying to smash their way back into the world. But their old temples are hardly more than rubble, their displaced priests fighting over crumbs among the wreckage, and the believers—the ones still able to walk—are begging for food with outstretched, soiled hands. Tenochtitlán, like the Aztec empire of which it was the crown jewel, is in ruins. News of the city's destruction—the subjugation of its people, the massacres, the futility of resistance—reaches the borders of Nahua territory.

When the storm ends, the worst part is the absolute drowning silence; the silence of graves, of the defeated gods, of the broken musical instruments, of the mute poets. The tlatolli and the cuicatl, the poems, stories, and songs that preserved traditions, memory, art, beauty, and magic have all disappeared. A small town by the name of Coicoshan has already been decimated. Many of its citizens died in combat with the invaders, but most of them were killed by disease.

And then, suddenly, noise. A sound so loud it bursts the eardrum. The town has been breached by soldiers, friars, and bureaucrats of the Crown. The air is unbearable. The warriors were captured, most of them executed, and survivors are locked in makeshift jails, bound by shackles on their feet, hands, and necks. This vile wind is decimating the population. Most of its current inhabitants are new arrivals, refugees escaping from famine and the new caciques, both Spanish and native collaborators, in their own territories. Only a few of them actually know the name of this town that, as a last resort, they've turned into their home.

The friars—miraculously immune to the contagious diseases killing the locals, as if the divine protection they spoke of is really achievable—are officiating mass in Latin. The locals don't understand a word, but are forced to attend nonetheless. With most of the material riches already aboard ships back to the Old World—galleons filled with gold, jewels, and artifacts—the only thing left to exploit are the people and the lands themselves. The friars often show up at Nahua homes alongside soldiers without warning, taking children away to be saved through knowledge of a God that hates them.

Several friars force a dozen or so children between five and twelve, still young enough to be indoctrinated, to recite the Ave María again and again. Whenever a child makes a mistake or refuses to sing, they are struck with branches. Welts mark their hands, backs, and necks. The children are shown the Nahua ritual relics of their ancestors—statuettes, masks, weapons—and are told by the holy men that they are the devil's work.

From a table overflowing with sacred objects looted from temples and homes, Friar Melquiades chose a round clay pot covered in feathers and animal hide. He rotated the object in his hands before tearing open a small opening he found near the bottom of it. He recoiled from the tanned flesh he now held at arm's length, as a look of disgust contorted his face. It was filled with bits of flesh, cartilage, and dried organs. The origins of the viscera weren't clear, human or animal both were equally likely to the friar. It seemed to him a work of the Adversary himself—Satan must have had a deep hold on the people of this land, driving them to do such perverse things. The pot had a clay ring on the top, through which he strung a length of rope. He asked one of the solders to tie the other end to a fence-post. He held on to the other end of the rope, raising the object five feet from the ground. Another friar, Simón, handed a stick to a younger child. They had piñatas in Spain just the same as they had in this godless land, but the friars knew that context would make all the difference.

"Tell them to strike it," Melquiades said to the interpreter, "and whoever breaks it gets a prize."

The other friars snickered, amused by the child's realization of what he was being asked to do.

"Tell him it's a game."

"Tlapalxoktli," the boy said anxiously.

The child turned to the clergymen, wide-eyed, then turned back to the rest of the children. Not daring to look at the pot, he grit his teeth as his shoulders heaved and began to cry. Melquiades pushed him toward the pot, trying to make him hold the stick. The interpreter followed suit, yelling and telling him in Nahuatl to strike it. The children shrieked.

"I can't. I shouldn't. It's an offering. It can't just be spilled," the boy holding the stick repeated, again and again.

The interpreter translated. The friar slapped the boy's head and called another child, older than the first, forcing the stick into his hands.

"Hit it, dammit, or I'll have you beaten dead right here," Melquiades yelled in his ear.

The boy swung and connected with the pot, immediately dropping the stick, hoping that he had fulfilled the request. But the friar continued to shout, and grabbed the stick from the ground, shoving it back into the boy's hands, pressing firmly so he wouldn't drop it again. The boy hit the pot once more, weeping between shallow, shaking breaths. He shut his eyes tight, but Melquiades guided his hand, rendering him unable to stop. Suddenly, with a final strike, the pot, the piñata, cracked and broke. Flesh, entrails, and a deep burgundy syrup of coagulated blood poured from the shattered base of the piñata. The shrieks of the children grew louder, watching and wailing in their hopelessness. Their ancestral ceremonies were very similar, cracking the pot at the feet of the god as an offering to Huitzilopochtli, but even the children knew that their old ways were being perverted by the friars. These conquerors made them waste the offerings, spilling them to the ground in the process of forgetting.

It was the end of the world and the end of the gods. These men would see that the gods died along with the priests.

Melquiades turned back to the group, the interpreter relaying his words to the frantic children, "Soon I'll make you see the error, the disgusting nature, of your old misguided ways. No god worth any worship would ask for this . . . filth," he kicked a piece of flesh around in the dirt. "You'll find that God doesn't ask for blood and viscera, none of these barbaric offerings your ancestors gave."

Melquiades grabbed another offering pot and set it up again using the fencepost, "The Almighty only wants your soul. You, boy, come here. It's your turn. Destroy this awful piece of idolatry."

Father Simón pushed the young boy forth, but he refused to break the pot. He wouldn't even hold the stick, still stained with the blood of the last offering jar. Melquiades, fed up with these heathens refusing the call to repent, hit the child to the ground and kicked him in the ribs. The interpreter tried to intervene, but the friar pushed him away and he fell, rolling across the ground. Melquiades continued kicking, the rest of the missionaries only restraining the shouting children as they all watched. The screams died down as the children became stunned by their inability to stop any of this, rapt in the horror their lives had become. Only the thud of Melquiades's foot against the boy's side and his grunt with every kick could be heard until the boy stopped moving entirely. Blood was dripping down his ears and he remained motionless, an example made. A girl freed herself from the friars as they all stood shocked by the brutality on display. She fell to her knees by her dead brother, shaking him and calling his name only for a moment before she was dragged to her feet by the man who'd just beaten him to death.

"Don't worry, child. The dogs will eat him, so he will finally be of some use. He'll return to the arms of one of your horrid gods," said Melquiades.

"Tie her up," Father Simón instructed.

"Her name is Ketzali, Father. She's quite the troublemaker," the interpreter said.

Ketzali leaped away from him as he tried to hold her down. There were more "piñatas" on the table awaiting the same fate as the first. She grabbed a tlapalxoktli and ran, cradling it in her arms. The friars, caught unaware, tried to catch up with her.

"Catch that little bitch! Soldiers, soldiers, she's getting away!" Melquiades yelled.

Ketzali slipped between the guards, running into what had once been a temple whose sacred stones were now being torn away to construct the halls of an abbey. She darted through the corridors, listening past her heartbeat for the steps of approaching clergymen, searching for an exit or hiding place. Hugging walls and narrowly avoiding being seen, she finally found the entrance to a small open crawl space between two chambers under construction.

Sliding herself and the tlapalxoktli underneath a rudimentary tower of shelves, she lay still in the dirt, panting and waiting. Eventually the sound of footsteps coming from the corridors faded away. They assumed she had already made an escape. Thinking it was the right moment, she left the tlapalxoktli behind in its hiding place and sprinted through the doors of the abbey and into the fields.

"There she is!" a soldier yelled.

He ran after her, followed closely by another soldier, but she was already far across the field and nearly in the tree line. They gave up, exhausted and ill-equipped to chase a small Nahua girl through the forests. Soon, Melquiades caught up with them, equally out of breath.

"What do you think you're doing? Look for her! If one Indian escapes, it'll set a precedent for everyone else," he said. "They'll start making for the trees just like her!"

The soldiers composed themselves and kept running after Ketzali as Melquiades headed back to the abbey, cursing his luck. He entered his cell-like room and closed the door. Sweating profusely after their fruitless chase and looking to get some air, he began to remove his robe when he felt a slight breeze.

"Would you mind knocking?" he started, assuming someone had opened his door, but when he turned nobody was there.

In fact, where the door had been there was only an impossibly dark shadow. The light of the candles in Melquiades's room seemed to skip that section of the wall. He now wrapped his robe tightly around himself as the air in the room turned frigid, a kind of cold he had not felt since the oceanic voyage to this land. As he pulled the fabric to his body, his hand involuntarily began to wrap itself around the cross hanging from his neck and he muttered a prayer.

"H-hello? Who is there?" he stammered.

A terribly pale face, skeletal and eyeless, emerged from the shadow.

Near skinless, what flesh it maintained hung tattered and decaying from its visage like ribbons. It's body unrevealed, the face drew nearer to the friar as its neck extended farther and farther.

Melquiades stepped back horrified, his breath catching in his throat as he attempted to appeal to the Lord for protection. Only inches from his own, the face grinned, opening cracks in the diseased flesh and revealing black and jagged teeth. In the flickering candlelight they shone like the obsidian daggers he had seen soldiers take from the native warriors. Its breath smelled like the mass graves the soldiers had piled them in.

Gagging from the stench, Melquiades opened his mouth to scream for help from a guard or an angel, but only blood sputtered forth. Releasing the cross on his neck, he now clutched at his stomach and solar plexus, tearing at the robes as he felt something under the fabric ripping at him. Lifting his frock, the shadow cast by the faint candlelight showed a jagged mass moving under his skin. He was being shred from the inside. Choking Gagging on blood, he sucked in a stuttering, choked breath and tried again to scream for help when pirul branches, just like the ones he used to hit the children, erupted from his mouth tearing apart his lips and esophagus, shredding his trachea before bursting through his heart, lungs, and intestines as his rib cage split open.

The friar fell to his knees, convulsing as a tree grew from within him, gore dripping from its leaves and berries. Only blood spewed from his lips, his last noise not a scream but a desperate gurgle as he beheld what he assumed to be the face of the devil himself sinking back into the darkness from which it came, leaving him to bleed out in the silence of his windowless room.

1

Carmen kept an eye on Luna's bright orange backpack, almost larger than the eleven-year-old herself, as it bounced between stands in the market. Luna stopped to talk to almost every fruit and vegetable vendor she could find. Asking for samples and counting her pocket change out loud in Spanish, she'd retrace her steps to buy trinkets and produce from this and that vendor after being sure she found a good price. She would come back to her mother, Carmen, and older sister, Izel, and breathlessly report on which vendor had the nicest produce, and what price she'd gotten on a pepper that another vendor wanted to charge her ten pesos more for, and why she chose the papaya in her hands over another, before stuffing the haul into her bag and running ahead. Luna would spare no detail as to who was the kindest vendor, the one with the most reasonable prices, the one with the highest quality products, how to know if a mamey was sweet and tender, and which mangos to choose.

Carmen knew her youngest daughter had been anticipating this trip for months—improving her Spanish and learning about Tulancingo from her room back in New York through Wikipedia pages and Google Street View tours of the town—but was shocked to see her little girl so seemingly acclimated. Looking around, even the vendors of the market were entertained by the excitable little girl attempting to haggle in slightly American-accented Spanish. They didn't even seem to mind how harsh of a lowballer she was.

Behind them though, Izel dragged her feet, avoiding the eyes of men, children, and women alike, but mostly the men. As a sixteen-year-old, feeling like everyone was staring at her was hard enough, but knowing they actually were was almost hellish. A couple of the men sitting on produce boxes around the market even dared to wink or blow her a kiss when Carmen wasn't looking.

"Son unos brutos todos," she said, her Spanish dripping with her American accent, hoping to be heard, thinking it would discourage them. The effect was quite the opposite: the men felt seen, recognized, as if they'd achieved something by eliciting a reaction; they persisted and grew bolder, shouting at her back in Spanish to come over and chat.

"Just ignore them, Izel," Carmen said, turning her head without taking her eyes off Luna, "You know how men in the cities are. They're the same here as they are in New York—maybe a little bolder at the markets around here, but the same. You can't give them a reaction."

"But they're so fucking annoying."

"Hey! Language! Believe me, Izel, I understand how it feels, but don't let them ruin your time. That's letting them win, you know?"

"Men are pigs no matter what language they squeal in, huh?"

Carmen laughed a little bit, "Unfortunately, yes. I know you're in a bad mood, but at least don't swear like that around Luna too much, alright?"

Luna, young enough and too far from earshot to be a part of the conversation, was simply thrilled to be in charge of the groceries, piling onions, green tomatoes, parsley, cilantro, and serrano peppers into her backpack. That night they were planning on having dinner with Father Verón. He was the caretaker of the abbey Carmen was renovating for an architectural project and had been the one to welcome them at the airport. For a man of the cloth, he was a surprisingly fun guest to have around the house. A competent chef as well, he'd taught Luna how to make Mexican dishes and lent her some books about Mexican culture and history.

Even though Carmen told Izel to ignore the men, she watched everyone around them in her peripheral vision. As much as she wanted her advice to be all a woman needed in the world, Carmen was acutely aware of the humming, imminent danger that lurked in the background for a woman and two girls in a foreign land. She knew Hidalgo was one of the safer states in Mexico, but living in America for so long had unavoidably altered her perception of the country. So often the only headlines to make it across the border were the horror stories: exchange students ransomed, people found beheaded, the police and the army colluding with cartels, unmarked mass graves—stories of a lawless and brutal land. Even when she tried to think of Tulancingo's relative safety, it reminded her it was only *relatively* safe.

On their way down to the municipal market they had passed through a busy plaza where Carmen had seen all the flyers. Covering nearly every surface were the same DIY advertisements found anywhere. People were offering English tutoring, rooms and apartments for rent, music lessons. But among them she began to notice the faces. Pictures of women and girls, pulled from their social media pages and family photo albums, stapled or taped among the cacophony of ads. Eight-and-a-half-by-eleven-inch pleas for help stapled to every telephone pole. Appeals to God glued to electrical boxes; appeals to the authorities were long abandoned. At first, Carmen didn't give them a second glance, but there were so many: on the streets, inside the market, on the light posts. Finally, she relented to her morbid curiosity and began to read them.

> _Mariana Saldívar Escobar_, sixteen years old, medium skin, black hair, disappeared on July 8 in Progreso district. She was wearing a white blouse and black skirt. She's a student at Preparatoria Técnica 21. **Call if you have any leads**.
>
> _Esther Ángulo Sáenz_, left her home on December 5. She's fourteen years old and a student at Santa María. She was last seen wearing a yellow dress. **Help us find her**.
>
> _María del Refugio Ramos_. Light skin, black, straight, long hair. She has a beauty mark on her right cheek. Last seen wearing a black Adidas sweatshirt and jeans. She works at the fabric shop, Esponda. **Reward: 50,000 pesos**.

Her eyes began to look straight through the ads and shot from one faded face poking through the clutter to the next. There was a nauseating curiosity that made her unable to keep herself from scanning every post for the same faces. She continually checked ahead of her to make sure her girls hadn't noticed the posters and that, more important, they were still where she could see them. There were so many—she could tell by the worn paper that several of them had been there for a long time, while others couldn't be more than a few days old. Carmen wondered whether the yellowed, rain-smeared, sun-bleached ones had been left up because their subjects were found, or the families had finally given up.

She almost jumped when she noticed Luna looking at her and tried to feign interest in a traditional dress on the other side of the window a flyer had been taped to.

"Those girls are lost, huh?" Luna asked.

"Um," she hesitated, unsure of how much a girl Luna's age should know about the world and its dangers, "I'm not sure, maybe they're the graduating class from their high school," she replied. Heat rose in her chest at how stupid a deflection that had been.

"I can read."

"I know." Carmen realized there was no question of how much Luna should know. She was clearly old enough to understand, even if not entirely conscious, what it meant for a girl to be missing, the inherent risks of womanhood. The terribly uncomfortable time was dawning when Carmen would have to tell her how to avoid those risks.

Carmen tried to the push it all from her mind—the flyers, Luna's comment—but now, in the market, she kept a hawk's eye on her youngest daughter as she walked on ahead of her and Izel. Knowing Luna's curiosity often led her to rush off on her own, Carmen was greatly comforted by her purchase of the gaudy, safety orange backpack flagging Luna's presence in the crowds.

Every now and then, as they walked through the stalls, a vendor interrupted and cut them off, showcasing some mamey, apple, or peach.

"Here, try this!"

"No, thank you, no," Izel replied, recoiling from the offered produce and its seller. Even when they had lived in New York City she'd never experienced such aggressive salesmanship from street vendors. She had difficulty grasping how people in a market dared to invade her personal bubble, wasting her time to offer her products she had no interest in. A smile crept across Carmen's face as she watched her daughter grapple with the social conventions of a new place. She'd been excited to expose her daughters to the culture she'd grown up in, even if it made them a bit uncomfortable at times.

"Don't be rude, try it. It doesn't bite," Carmen said.

"What? I don't know what that is! What if I'm allergic or something? Is it even washed properly? The knife looks so dirty."

"When did you become such a hypochondriac?"

"Okay, I have everything on Father Verón's list," said Luna, adjusting her backpack on her shoulder and rejoining her family. "I'm only missing the huitlacoche. I know it has to be around here somewhere."

"I don't know. You're the little expert, Luna," Izel replied without taking her eyes off the phone in her hands and, within nearly the same breath, asked, "Mom, do you have a portable charger? My phone is dying."

Carmen gave her a look and said, "You know I don't. Maybe you can let it die for a whole hour or so, though. I know you miss your friends back home and all, but you could at least try experiencing your first time in Mexico with the rest of us."

Izel sighed and looked up into the sky, pointing her nose to the sun as she slipped her phone back into her pocket. It dinged and she immediately took it back out and looked at the notification.

"Father Verón comes for dinner all the time. I guess he doesn't have anywhere else to go," Izel said quietly.

"That's not nice. He's fond of us, he likes having dinner with us and, yes, I imagine he leads a lonely life. That's the life of a priest," said Carmen. "At least I think it is."

"My phone is at seven percent. I need a charger."

"Let it die. It'll be for the best, for all of us."

"There it is!" yelled Luna, running ahead toward another stall.

"What?" answered Carmen, startled. "Luna don't run off so far ahead!"

"Huitlacoche," she called back from in front of a stand that had basketfuls of the corn fungus. Carmen pulled Izel along to keep up.

"What are we going to do with that?" asked Izel, grimacing with disgust.

"Tamales! But we can make them into quesadillas, tacos, or stuffing for some chicken breasts. So many possibilities!"

"I'll eat something else. Not interested in deformed, rotten corn," and upon seeing a basket full of reddish crickets, Izel stepped back, more fearful than nauseated. "What the fuck is that?"

"Language!" Carmen yelled.

"Mom, look at those things. Are they alive?"

The old vendor standing behind the baskets laughed, "They're fried chapulines. They're not alive. They're snacks to some around here!"

"What? Snacks? For whom? For the toads and lizards?"

While Luna was having an actual fit of laughter, the old lady working the stand pinched a couple of crickets with her bony fingers and offered them to her, so she put on a brave face and crunched into them with little hesitation. Her scrunched-up face soon broke into a big smile and she turned to Carmen and Izel.

"You guys should try them too! They're tasty!"

The old woman held another pinch of chapulines out to them.

"No thank you, señora," said Carmen, as Izel pushed her hands forward as to protect herself from the fried creatures while she looked somewhere else.

"I thought you told me to be polite. Try them, Mom, come on," said Izel with a sly grin.

"Yeah, Mom, try one!"

"No, thank you. Not today," said Carmen with a nervous smile.

Meanwhile, Luna was still laughing and asking the vendor where the chapulines came from and how to cook them.

"How did I end up with a bug-eating alien for a sister?" Izel asked her mom.

"Sometimes I wonder how the two of you ended up so different from each other too."

They watched Luna discuss the prices of the chapulines and the huitlacoche with the old woman, holding out bills and coins and stuffing the fungus and bugs into her bag.

"We've got everything," Luna announced, proud.

"Thank God. Can we just leave now?" said Izel.

"Maybe we could buy a portable charger for your beloved phone," suggested Luna.

"That would make this agony worth it."

"They have electronics and stuff in that aisle, I think."

They looked through one of the aisles and reached a stand selling toys and piñatas. The three of them stopped to look at the dizzying variety of piñatas of different shapes and sizes.

"Come on in, come on in. We have *Frozen*, Spider-Man, and Trump. We also have donkeys and all the classics."

"Thanks, but we're just browsing," said Carmen.

"For your birthday, for your party, for your name day, for any celebration."

"No, thank you."

Luna looked at them in wonder, one by one, from the rudimentary reproductions of Disney characters and Pokémon to the classic round colorful piñatas with seven spiky cones.

"Mom, I didn't know piñatas came in so many different shapes," said Luna.

"They sure do. These are the traditional Spanish-Catholic ones," Carmen drew upon the depths of her early Catholic childhood and the memories of her mother, "If I'm remembering correctly, the seven points are supposed to be the seven deadly sins, so it's like you're smashing apart your sin or something like that. Some of them are still made with a clay pot inside."

"Why?" asked Izel. "That sounds dangerous. Shards of ceramic flying everywhere, mixed in with the candy and stuff."

"That's just the way it was around here. Nothing more normal than having one or two kids end up slightly concussed when you break a piñata at a party, huh? *Barbarous Mexico*, right?" she said, deepening her voice and raising her eyebrows.

"It's still a terrible idea."

Carmen thought Izel might catch her ironic name-dropping of the John Kenneth Turner classic in this context, but moved right along after her joke flopped. "Well, lucky for you kids, now they're made almost entirely out of papier-mâché rather than just a thin layer of it on top of hard clay."

"They're very pretty," said Izel, putting her hand inside one to feel the clay pot.

"Take one for the little one, señora," the shopkeeper said.

Carmen shook her head and waved her hand.

"There's no way they have the rights to copy Donald Duck," said Izel, pointing at a fun-house knockoff of the beloved Disney character hanging from the ceiling.

Carmen sneered at her with a look that said, stop it with the stupid questions. "Are you really that invested in Disney's copyrights?"

"This is so unfair, Mom," Izel said, as Luna ran back and forth.

"How come?"

"This is heaven for Luna. Everything excites her. I don't care about this. What I care about is theater and I can't do that here."

"You'll be able to enroll in theater next school year. I know it was important for you to go with Tina, Halley, and everyone else to that camp, but this trip is important too."

When they eventually went on their way, Luna kept turning around to look at the stand, while the vendor yelled that he'd give them a good price. "Come on, take whichever you like!"

They found a cluster of electronics stands where people sold phones, radios, video game consoles, and every type of accessory, most of them knockoffs of usual American name brands. Here you could get the cheapest charger if you didn't mind it lasting only a few months, even a few weeks. The vendor didn't look at them once during the transaction, his eyes were glued to a screen at another stall where someone was playing a violent video game. Izel finally smiled upon seeing the battery icon on her phone turn green.

"Girls, speaking of piñatas. I forgot to tell you that we were invited to a party tomorrow. One of the worker's little boys is turning ten and I think we should go. We'll have lots of fun, maybe you'll even smile and enjoy yourself, Izel."

"Invited us? What do you mean? They invited you, not us," answered Izel, the sudden smile now completely wiped from her face.

"No, the three of us have to go. How am I supposed to go to a children's party by myself?"

"This is for you, for your job, and you want to drag us there."

"There will be a piñata. The food will probably be delicious, and you'll get to meet some of the local kids."

"I don't care. Take Luna. She would love to eat mushroom cake, and fungus cookies, and slime treats, and insects, and larvae, and whatever else they feed the guests."

"Izel, stop it. You're coming, and that's that."

"It'll be my first Mexican party, the first authentic piñata I'll get to break," said Luna enthusiastically.

"How lucky," said Izel, typing faster and faster on her phone.

"Keep this attitude up and by the end of this trip, I'll use you as a piñata, Izel," said Carmen.

"Great parenting, Mom,"

They didn't talk for the rest of the walk back home. Once in the kitchen, Luna took out the groceries from her backpack, asking how to prepare some of the things they bought as Izel shut herself in her room. Carmen was disappointed, but knew Izel was just being a teenager. She wasn't a kid anymore like Luna, who had yet to exit her tweens. To Izel, the idea of going to a party full of strange kids sounded absolutely abhorrent, mortifying even. In the best-case scenario, they would go unnoticed, but that was unlikely.

Izel *was* right, Carmen was using the kids a bit. The first weeks at the abbey construction site she was overseeing hadn't gone entirely without incident. Ever since she'd arrived, the workers looked at her with distrust, like an ignorant foreigner who wanted things done her way and, of course, they were less than thrilled to be taking orders from a woman. From day one, she'd made every kind of effort to create some amiability, but nothing ever seemed to pay off. Her being invited to a family birthday was important. It was a chance to turn her reputation around, to be seen as a person and part of their community and not as some upstart boss, an Americanized hag, here simply to exploit them.

A wave of anxiety turned Carmen's stomach over as she began to question the decision to take the girls with her. Her mind was stuck in the plaza reading those flyers: the phone numbers and descriptions of girls written by parents begging to see their daughters again. Bringing the girls to Mexico with her felt like a mistake, but there hadn't been a choice. She couldn't ask her mother, Alma, to take care of the girls for such a long time, she worked nights at Saint Francis hospital and often ended up having to cover her coworkers' shifts for extra cash or just to be nice. Her mother was of the traditional mindset that a family should all live under one roof and, while Carmen wasn't happy that her mother was still working, the cost of living was too high for Carmen to support three people all on her own, even after the move upstate to Newburgh. Leaving the girls behind with Alma would have just been too much, not that she'd have admitted it. Her mother always tried her damnedest to not act her age and would have insisted on it being no bother, making a big unconvincing show of how she actually *wanted* Carmen to leave the girls with her. *I'll finally get some time to talk with the girls without their mom listening in!*

But Carmen knew Alma was tired, too tired to handle Izel and Luna for more than a few days. As seventy grew ever nearer, the deepening lines on Alma's face marked a body which could simply no longer keep up with the spirit within.

The girls' father, Fernando, had been a good and attentive dad for the most part when he had been around, but that hadn't been the case for a while now. Even after the initial breakup, he had at least looked after the girls when Carmen needed him to. Once he found a new girl-friend, though, he decided he wanted a fresh start, to begin another life without any of the baggage of his last. "Baggage" was the term he had used. She knew he hadn't considered the weight that word carried when he said it, but when Carmen heard it, the final embers of her affections for him were stamped out. She realized he had always been a man with the capacity to close his heart almost at will. It was warm inside and the doors were wide, but she saw firsthand how easily they were slammed shut. Izel and Luna. *Baggage.* She sometimes wondered if the new woman even knew Fernando already had children. Last she had heard, a mutual friend had mentioned he was on the West Coast now. So, where she went the girls did too.

"Luna, honey, I'm going to lie down for a moment, okay? Can you put away the groceries?"

"Yes, Mommy," she replied, setting down her pencil. She had been drawing little piñatas in her journal. Carmen glanced at them as she passed the table, all different colors and sizes, some were shaped like animals but others had human faces. Luna hadn't exactly mastered the art of rendering humans yet. The faces looked to be in pain.

Carmen left the door to her room slightly ajar and fell on the bed listening to Luna open and close the cupboards in the kitchen. Warm air blew through a gap in the windows. She turned on the bed to look out at the vast landscape of empty, undeveloped land—one of the more arid pockets of Tulancingo. *Almost nothing can grow here with the sandstorms,* she thought as she imagined the wind dragging dust and everything else from one side of the moor to the other. She worried about the mistakes she was making with the girls, unpleasant truths she'd let slip and the accidental lessons she'd taught them too young. Being a mother is about making mistakes, there was no doubt about this, and being a single mother often felt like playing Russian roulette, having to pick the lesser of two evils. On the one hand, she always wanted to look strong and independent, to lead by example and never show her fear of the world, but on the other, she worried they'd become too independent, so headstrong that they wouldn't consider the outside world's dangers, imagining life as a walk in the park. *Miel sobre hojuelas,* as the Spaniards used to say.

Carmen saw a lot of herself in her daughters, recognized her own small gestures and moods. The strong will bordering on insolence her mother, Alma, always chided her for had taken root in Izel while Luna was full of the near-blinding optimism she'd had as a younger woman. How could she not blame herself for passing along those traits? It was inevitable, of course; the lessons imparted on children are often taught subconsciously, in her passing remarks and unconsidered actions. But when she thought of the unnecessary conflicts and the blindsiding disappointments sure to visit her daughters as they had done with her, she wished they could have a slate clean of her own idiosyncrasies. They were already too sheltered in America, not entirely used to keeping their head on a constant swivel. Izel was smart enough and had spent at least some of her teenage years in the city before the move, but even that was pretty safe. Throughout their trip to Mexico, a country sadly infamous for alarming levels of femicide and general crime, she never lost sight of them. How could she not be afraid after seeing the news and what people post on Facebook and Twitter? It wasn't that bad here—or so she was told. Not too many criminals, only the wind blowing the dust back and forth and maybe ghosts longing for a better time, when this was a fabulous pre-Columbian city or when the region had a booming agriculture economy and the abbey was still an abbey.

Izel was sometimes difficult, but who wasn't at that age? She never got herself in trouble. With all the drugs readily accessible at her school, she'd never tried anything—well, if she had, nothing had ever happened—and she didn't get involved with bad boys. She didn't even *have* a boyfriend. So, as rude and hurtful as she could be sometimes, Carmen couldn't be so harsh, strict, or short-tempered with her because, really, she was a good kid. After all, being there with her instead of at the beach or theater camp with her friends must feel like a big sacrifice at Izel's age. She couldn't pile more responsibilities on her, at least not during that summer. In a few years, Izel would be headed off to college and Carmen would barely get to see her. She thought about how this was, with any luck, their last or second-to-last trip together and felt immense sadness. It was like losing something very dear to her. Losing that intimacy—conflicts, fights, and tantrums included—would be painful.

Someone knocked on the bedroom door.

"Come in," she said without getting up.

It was Izel.

"Mom, I'm sorry. I know I was being a little bit mean to you earlier. I don't want you to think I hate being here with you or anything."

"It's all right, sweetheart. Don't worry. I was your age once too. I know a trip with your mom and little sister isn't a sixteen-year-old's idea of a great summer. I'm sorry you couldn't go to theater camp with your friends, and I know it feels like the end of the world to be missing out, but I promise I'm trying to make this trip fun for you too.

"Thanks, Mom. I love you," Izel looked at the ceiling and sighed, "And I'll go to the stupid piñata party."

Carmen smiled, "Thank you very much."

Carmen stretched out on the bed as Izel closed the door, returning to her room. Brief moments like this one made her feel she wasn't doing too bad of a job raising the girls after all. She closed her eyes and fell asleep for a while.

2

The rental house didn't have a dishwasher. Not that Carmen minded washing a few glasses, plates, and some cutlery by hand. It was simply the absence of the appliance she'd grown so used to in her everyday domestic life that made her feel mildly alien in the space, like there was something slightly off. But perhaps what bothered her the most was what it meant for her to give such unwarranted attention to a machine. Their kitchen at home was modern—nothing too cutting-edge or magazine sleek, but it was efficient and tasteful. It was the first thing she noticed when they arrived, carrying luggage after a longer than expected journey marked by endless delays: two layovers and Mexico City's unrelenting day and night traffic. The whole rental was perfectly unremarkable, it worked—except there was no damn dishwasher. It was a quotidian disruption, but when she caught herself reaching down to the space next to the sink where the dishwasher handle was at home, it was enough to make her feel she had been thrust back into a simpler time.

And that's what this was. Coming back to Mexico always meant rediscovering that past that she'd left so long ago, the life she abandoned two decades ago to pursue her master's at Cornell. She had promised people at the time she'd be back, but she never did return, not really. A handful of visits over the course of twenty years hadn't been enough to maintain her connections to the place. She'd even moved her mother to the States with her when Fernando left.

The house had three bedrooms. It was spacious and its high ceilings made it feel full of air, fresh and pleasant. The paint could've used a touch-up, but honestly it was very well kept. The furniture had an air of old-fashioned elegance. There were plenty of houses nearby, but it was a quiet area, perfect for working in silence and focusing on her project. She'd been told it was supposedly a safe neighborhood with a good enough reputation, but girls and women often disappeared from the larger region, just not from here. The posters from the market were a terrifying chronology of an epidemic of people going missing and, more often than not, found dead.

They were close to the city and to plenty of the attractions she'd want to show the girls, but far enough away to offer a view of the surrounding country as it stretched toward the distant hills. Through the windows, she could see the same volcanic mountains and plains—dry and forlorn—that she'd seen during a childhood country visit, a trip she remembered nothing from save for that image, somehow seared into a part of her subconscious. That was years ago, though. Intensifying droughts over the interceding years had ravaged the countryside, starving the land as the lower tentacle of the Chihuahua Desert seemed to creep farther south into central Mexico. Now, the blanket of greenery that had once covered the mountains had retreated up the slopes like a receding hairline. The country had aged alongside her.

As a kid, it seemed if one wandered into that vast landscape, no matter what any map showed, you could walk forever and never find a road again. Once you lost sight of the path you had diverted from, the landscape would swallow you and shift under your feet with the dust blowing at your ankles. Even as an adult, she sometimes had dreams set out there, nightmares of isolation in which there's nothing around her but the low shrubs and dry earth moving back and forth in the winds under the moon. Nonetheless, the region still retained a certain magic, a pastoral, primal beauty that moved her deeply.

She didn't exactly feel at home, but she was comfortable. The house was a sort of reflection, aesthetically, of what a Mexican house should be. It wasn't suffocated in folkloric excess and its decor wasn't kitschy or quaint like other rentals, but it still felt staged to meet the visitors' expectations, most of whom were Americans. It had the traditional wall moldings with a bright blue ceiling; mirrors framed with stained glass; a stone Aztec calendar; and the quintessential heavy, dark furniture and white, woolly cushions. It was all a bit too predictable; Carmen knew this, and even though she was mildly ashamed about having qualified as this category of tourist, she couldn't deny she was comfortable and charmed.

Doing the dishes, Carmen's mind bounced between all the problems at the abbey's construction site: the new issues she had to fix before she could face the old ones, mix-ups with materials, the quantities, the procedures, the contradicting orders she received from the firm and the client. It was chaos worthy of such an ornate abbey, and she sometimes wondered if a job this extensive was a bit over her head. Most irritating of all, though, were the human relations: the actions and inactions of the workers, the suspicious delays on deliveries, the way the bricklayers looked at her and immediately back to the foreman, Joaquín, whenever she gave an order, as if to make sure "the Lady" actually had authority over them. Quite honestly, it was humiliating having to repeat her orders to workers who she knew had understood her the first time but had been directed differently by the foreman. Despite being in charge of what the foreman actually built, she was effectively below him when it came to the construction of something she had designed and engineered.

It had become a daily battle for her dignity.

A wave of humiliation burned her cheeks and Carmen felt a sudden urge to smash a plate against the wall as conversations with Joaquín played in her head on a loop and she wondered what she should've said, which tone she could've used. She thought about the carpenter, Román, and one of the younger bricklayers, Bernardo. She fantasized about firing them on the spot next time they chose to listen to Joaquín over her with a "You're leaving this construction right now." Setting the example with two sacrifices. But in her heart she knew she wasn't about to put two men out of a job; she believed in reason and dialogue, and she often resented herself for this, feeling an impotent pacifism she thought akin to a substitute teacher. Surely that's what they thought of her as, someone who was here now with alleged authority, but who would be gone soon enough. There were hardly consequences in their mind of being on her bad side. As if having to hold together a rowdy crowd of workers wasn't enough, she had to continually argue with Joaquín, who was always on the lookout for a way to undermine her.

It's a construction site, she said to herself, *it's not exactly the most feminist place around. Not only is a woman on the job site, I'm an American to them.* She forced a smile out of herself with that thought and suddenly became aware of how unfair it was for her to be cleaning the kitchen by herself after cooking the girls breakfast. They were so used to having her and their abuela around to take care of everything that they didn't even show the slightest shame hanging out in the living room playing Animal Crossing or choreographing TikToks or stalking their friends posts on Instagram or any number of things that weren't helping their mother while she did everything for them.

That wasn't going to fly while they were here. Carmen was still working a full-time job and now Alma wasn't around to give her another set of hands. Carmen had always believed in giving the girls plenty of free time. School in America was clearly different than it had been for Carmen in Mexico. Luna wasn't even in middle school yet and was already coming home with pamphlets about college planning. Without downtime at home to explore their interests, Carmen was paranoid they'd end up without passion for anything but taking standardized tests. Izel had brought a stack of play scripts with her and Luna had been regurgitating facts about the Aztecs she'd found trawling the internet since their arrival, but it was about time the girls learned to pitch in around the house. They were on vacation, but Carmen needed time to herself just as much as they did. She couldn't always be their mule.

"Luna! Izel!" she yelled. "Girls, can you come and help a little with the dishes from breakfast?" She restrained herself from going on an unnecessary tirade about not needing any extra work to do.

"I can't now. I'm in the middle of . . ." Izel's voice faded into a mumble, too lazy to invent and vocalize an actual excuse.

Carmen stood there silently, picturing Izel flicking her finger across her phone, mildly shocked at her daughter's indolence. She would've never gotten away with doing that to her own mother. It was a different time, a different world—Mexico in the twentieth century. Growing up as a woman during that time had come with heavily domestic implications, more expectations of being. That word, "domesticity," slithered through her mind. Being physically back in the country had been sending her into continual reverie about those days, old emotional memories seeping back into her skin under the sun. She interrupted her own train of thought.

"As if things were any different now."

"What's different now?" asked Luna, suddenly standing next to her mother.

Her eleven years of age had her knowing it all, or trying to. If anything was brought up around her which she didn't already grasp, she had to learn more about it.

Carmen was startled. She didn't expect an answer to her mutterings and, lost in thought, hadn't noticed Luna come into the kitchen.

"What's wrong?" Luna asked, as if it were an extraordinary thing to be called to help her mother out.

"Nothing's wrong, I'd just like you to help out a little."

Luna looked astonished by the strange request; regardless, she smiled and grabbed a kitchen rag and started drying the dishes. She didn't protest nor did she complain about Izel not helping. The little one looked like her father: her hair was straight, long, and black; her nose was pointy and her eyes brown; and she was wearing a red T-shirt and shorts.

"Mom? How long 'til your work here is over?"

"I'm not sure. We're just getting started. We'll be here until the end of summer and then I'll have to come back in the fall, probably. It's a pretty ambitious renovation. Rome wasn't built in a day, you know."

"So why would they want to turn an old church into a hotel?"

"We've talked about this. I think it's an interesting idea to revitalize it. I showed you the drawings, right? The church is actually the old St. John the Baptist Cathedral . . . or it used to be. It was once considered a jewel of colonial architecture here, but now it's fallen from grace, like a lot of buildings from that period. It's been abandoned for a very, very long time and a few more decades of neglect would eventually swallow it up. So, well, the church authorities decided to sell it."

"But can churches even be sold?"

"Of course, it's still a property. It can be sold like any other place, just with more paperwork and government processes."

"Which processes?"

"Too many to get into. People go to school just to learn about all the different forms and documents that have to change hands to make a sale like that official. But they're basically arrangements between the church and government authorities, and the private investors. But that part isn't my job. I don't buy the land, I just design what goes on it."

"Is Father Verón the owner of the church?"

Carmen chuckled. "No, he's just an administrator from the church. Part of the purchase of the land was that we'd keep certain parts of the church intact so people could still appreciate them."

Luna remained still for a moment, as if thinking how to formulate her next question or how to say something without it coming across as an insult.

"And do you think it's okay for them to make a church into a hotel? Aren't churches holy or something?"

"Well, I think of it as giving new life to a very beautiful building. Think about it, those walls, those columns, those ceilings will be admired by lots of people. Remember how the Huitzala estate looked after I remodeled it? It was in ruins, and I think we gave it back its—how can I put it?—its dignity and beauty. I like doing these types of jobs, more than working on malls or parking lots or supermarkets."

"I wouldn't wanna sleep in an old church. I bet it has ghosts."

The interrogation was over as Luna turned back to the dishes in the sink. On the whole, Carmen was proud of how inquisitive and autodidactic her youngest was, but sometimes forgot how sharp the point on Luna's curiosity could be until it gave her a slight jab. It could become off-putting at times.

When Luna turned seven, she'd asked for a telescope for her birthday, and not some little tube for bird-watching either—she wanted something that would allow her to do some real stargazing. Fernando, still living with them at the time as a full-time father, tried his best to convince her otherwise offering a litany of alternatives: dolls, Easy-Bakes, video games. Carmen even offered her an iPad, trying to convince Luna she could look at star maps all day and night on an interactive astronomy app whereas the telescope would hardly even work at night anyways as they still lived in the city at the time. Luna hesitated, but then stood firm: She wanted the real deal. Carmen and Fernando thought that she wanted to see UFOs or aliens or who knows what, but as her birthday approached, they finally got an answer from her as to why she wanted it so bad:

"I want to be able to see into the past, and the only way to see it is when it's really far."

Somewhere, she'd learned that starlight had been emitted millions of years ago and the light that we could see was older than humans all together. Carmen tried to convince her it was better to have something to play with than looking at ancient lights in the sky.

"I think being able to look at the past is way cooler than any of that other stuff."

"Why the past?" Fernando chuckled and lifted Luna up into his arms, "I think I'd much rather be able to look into the future, wouldn't you? Far more useful!"

"I'll be able to see that when it happens, though!"

Carmen and Fernando worried about their youngest. As much as Carmen hated the New Age terminology that was constantly floating around, she couldn't think to describe Luna as anything but an old soul. Every now and again, in the midst of a perfectly average day, Luna would say things like that with a calm and surety that couldn't possibly belong to a girl her age, things that suggested a deeper understanding of being. Carmen would never admit to being a little creeped out by it, but moments like the telescope conversation did send a shiver up her spine.

Izel, by all accounts, had been a perfectly normal little girl and budding teenager, not to say she was boring or unremarkable but, to Carmen, she was at least traveling down a somewhat predictable path. She'd fallen in love with theater at a very young age and dreamed of becoming an actress and going to see all the plays they could. After Fernando left, Carmen had an awful time. The idea of being a single mother to two girls had been impossibly daunting to her. Izel tried to avoid the topic, not wanting to talk about it, and locked herself in the bathroom to cry. Luna, on the other hand, took it calmly. She asked her mother and father separately for an explanation as to what had happened and asked them if there was any space to sort things out like adults. Carmen and Fernando listened to the then seven-year-old without interrupting her, mesmerized.

In the months after the split, when she could manage some free time between work and the girls, all Carmen could do was visit her friend Sofia and cry on her sofa over their future.

"How am I supposed to raise them if I'm just focused on keeping us afloat all the time? At least with that asshole around I could afford to spend time with the girls!"

Luckily, Alma came to end the months of tears. Without her mother around Carmen thought she'd have to open a new line of credit for takeout costs alone. But with another head to keep a roof over, rent in New York became pretty expensive and it seemed like the economical choice to head north. When Carmen moved the girls away from the city to Newburgh to afford a four bedroom for them and Alma, Izel had been furious. She was ripped away from easily accessible playhouses and Broadway musicals and stuck in a town with only one shambling community playhouse.

Carmen pulled her mind back from the past and put aside the plates she was holding. She dried her hands and walked toward the dining table where she'd left the blueprints and digital renderings for the abbey's remodeling and called Luna over.

"Look, here we'll put some very pretty fountains, some more over here, and right here is where we'll have the pool and the Jacuzzi and all that stuff. What do you think?"

Luna smiled, looking her mother in the eye.

"And all that water for the pools and the fountains, where are you bringing it from?"

Through the window, they could see the dirt lifting like a curtain of smoke and dancing among the weeds with every gust of wind.

"That's a very good question, but that isn't my job either. Someone else takes care of that."

"Father Verón?"

"No, I don't think he needs to handle that either."

"Remember when we saw those men, who were very angry, shouting and carrying protest signs in front of city hall, asking for water? Will they be able to use the water for their animals and their corn?"

"I'm not sure about that. I could ask. I just do the architecture, re-member?"

"But you could help them. You're, like, the head of the construction."

"I'm not really the head of the construction. I'm in charge of the project, and that's more than enough"

"I would love to go to a hotel with goats, and cows, and mules, and hens coming to wash themselves and drink from the pool."

"I would love that, too, but I think if animals got to this hotel—"

Carmen was about to say that if the goats, cows, and chickens got to the hotel, it would be as dinner, but of course she didn't. Luna wouldn't find it funny. She ran to the table and came back clutching her notebook to show Carmen.

"Look, Mom, I made some drawings of how the hotel is going to look."

Luna showed her the notebook that she carried with her everywhere. Inside she'd drawn an imitation of the plans and mock-ups of the hotel Carmen left around the house. Carmen took the notebook and leafed through it. There were sketches and notes on everything they'd seen since they'd arrived, animals, plants, buildings. There were some that were quite juvenile, crude lines and notes about misremembered events, but others that were honestly pretty good. The pencil sketches reminded her of the ones she made when she was a girl. Her passion for copying buildings and urban landscapes planted the seed for her love of architecture.

"Have you thought about studying architecture?" Carmen was surprised she'd never asked this before.

"Yes, but I think I'd rather work with animals."

"Of course you would," Carmen smiled, "You care more about living things than buildings, huh?"

Luna nodded as Carmen continued leafing through the journal and stopped on a drawing of a hummingbird. She was surprised by how well Luna had captured the movement of the bird. On another page, there was a wave of butterflies, flying by the dome of the local church.

"This is amazing. Your drawings have gotten so much better. Did you learn this in school?" Carmen was giddy with pride and excited by her daughter's talent, but her delight was tinged with guilt at not having noticed Luna's budding artistry until now. Maybe she didn't check in on Luna's day-to-day life as often as she thought.

Luna ignored the comment and kept talking.

"These butterflies we saw seemed very mad."

"When? How?" Carmen laughed. "When have you seen angry butterflies?"

"I don't know. They just seemed angry at the buildings. Maybe it used to be a field of flowers or something."

Carmen felt a familiar chill run up her spine. The drawing had a threatening, ominous feeling to it. While the form was still juvenile, the way the crudely drawn butterflies lifted like a wave over the church, casting a shadow over the dome, struck a chord of impending catastrophe. It looked as if the little butterflies would crash down on the church like a mighty tide. Carmen shut the journal, not ready to interview the artist on her intention behind the composition of the piece, and turned back toward the remaining dishes.

"Izel, what the hell are you doing? I think you can at least help with your own dishes!" she hollered over her shoulder.

"What's going on? What are you yelling for?" Izel asked, finally reaching the kitchen in her pajamas.

"We're working and we need your help."

But the kitchen was already clean, and everything was organized. Carmen's hands had been moving independent of her thoughts. Only one dish remained in the sink.

"What do you want me to do?" she said, rolling her eyes.

"It's too late. Luna and I already finished up. All that's left is your plate from breakfast. You could've gotten here sooner."

"No, I couldn't. I was busy," she waved her phone around.

Carmen raised her hand to her forehead in a dramatic, exasperated gesture. "Talking to your friends doesn't count as 'busy.'"

"When are we going back home?" asked Izel.

"That's the only thing you care about. If you weren't so eager to go back, and enjoyed a bit of Mexico and Tulancingo, and the ruins and everything here, you could have such an amazing time. When we visit

Huapalcalco, you'll see cave paintings from literally twelve thousand years ago. Who do you know back home who can say the same?"

"I don't even know what Wapalaco is."

"Izel! It's a privilege to be here," Carmen said in exasperation.

"Izzy!" she replied.

Izel didn't like her name and often insisted on being called Izzy, especially in arguments as a cheap shot to remind Carmen of her disdain. Carmen and Fernando wanted to give her a pre-Columbian name, one that was pretty but would still be easy for Americans to understand and spell, without too many *x*'s and *tl*'s. They thought it was the perfect name. Sadly, when she started school, her classmates made her feel like her name was weird and bullied her for it.

She once told them she wanted to change her name, "to something more normal, like Lisa, or Mary, or Veronica!"

They tried to convince Izel her name was the prettiest in the world, but at that age, reason doesn't particularly work, and being different is dangerous. Teachers spelled it as Essel, Isela, or Azil, or a dozen different ways that were ridiculous for such an easy name. Izel, at sixteen, was now nearly as tall as her mother. Her skin was very light, with a few freckles, and she had green eyes and light brown hair. More than once she'd been asked, quite bluntly, if she was truly Luna's sister. When Carmen heard that for the first time, she was made apoplectic by the blatant colorism.

"Privilege? Really?" said Izel.

Carmen threw her hands in the air. She knew there was no use in continuing this argument, trying to convince her daughter of her good fortune, and how special it was for someone her age to be able to travel to other countries and interact with other cultures. But during these weeks, she hadn't even managed to get her to speak Spanish, other than the occasional phrase, and saying gracias and hola. To be fair, there weren't many people with whom she could engage in riveting conversation, but she certainly didn't have the slightest interest either.

Izel let out a long sigh, turned around, and headed toward her room. Luna left the rag on the counter, smiled at her mother, and without another word, hurried away to catch up with her sister.

"Izel, want to play Animal Crossing with me?" she yelled, but her sister ignored her and slammed her bedroom door.

Carmen felt guilty again for denying Izel her dream of going to theater camp. Most of her closest friends were going. They were a group of Broadway-obsessed girls who participated in every school play and swore they wanted to be actresses more than anything else in the world. Carmen tried to take the girls out as much as she could, first to the Disney and Broadway blockbusters, but Izel was also interested in off-Broadway plays. One day, while discussing *The Lion King* and *Cats*, Izel told her that her favorite author was August Strindberg. Carmen found it unbelievable but didn't question her. Izel had seen a production of *The Father* from a small Lower East Side company with her friends, and everyone left the theater utterly impressed. Although Carmen didn't know much about theater, she recognized that play, and she wasn't sure how much those girls could've truly understood it, but they were shocked by the author's pessimism and Swedish humor. She was proud that her daughter's taste in theater wasn't limited to *Wicked* and *The Phantom of the Opera*, but found her fascination with a hopeless, dark author strange. Though if Jorge Luis Borges thought of him as basically a god, who was she to convince her daughter otherwise?

Carmen could hear Luna still begging her sister to open her door and play. She thought about her conversation with Luna, and how conversations like those were the silver lining to not having a dishwasher. She kept organizing the glasses on the dish rack. When she was done, she looked around and said out loud, "Fucking dishwasher."

3

"Señora Sánchez!" he shouted as he answered the door, as if to make the whole neighborhood aware of her presence. More likely to warn the workers already inside the party that they should silence any trash talk about the architect.

Joaquín, the foreman, opened the laminate door and welcomed her into his home.

"Please just call me Carmen. We're not on the worksite, Joaquín."

Carmen had told him at least three different times to just use her first name, or at least to drop the "señora" from her last name. This was apparently impossible for him. She'd even settle for just being called "Architect" or "Boss."

"Of course! Of course! You're right, we're not at work are we," Joaquín replied as the girls came inside, "and these must be your daughters!"

"Yes, this is Luna and that's Izel. Thank you again for inviting us," answered Carmen, handing him the present they'd brought for his son. A Lego set Luna had picked at a toy store in the city shopping center.

"Thank you for coming. How brave of you to dare enter this neighborhood."

"Brave? Why wouldn't I come? You invited me, didn't you?"

"Well, I sure did. Come and have drink with us. The girls can go over there with the rest of the kiddos."

Izel looked at her mother with slight panic, not ready to be relegated to the "kiddos," but Luna was already pulling her toward the backyard.

"Come this way, señora. The mezcalito is on me. Father Verón over there has had more than a few already."

Carmen could feel the guests staring at the new faces in town, intrigued and politely standoffish in the presence of unfamiliar foreigners. She felt the need to win them over, prove herself to be more than just a professional American here to lord over the working men of the area, some gringofied expat. Patience and charisma weren't traits that Carmen often associated with herself, but she'd need them here. Looking around, Carmen couldn't help but inspect Joaquín's home with an architect's eye. It wasn't shabby or poor looking by any means, but it was certainly modest. She could see many structural seams, places where she could tell the walls had been demolished and rebuilt to expand the house. Joaquín had clearly been building out his home over many years with his experience as a contractor. From outside she had seen they had a good bit of land on which the house still had only a small footprint.

The vast backyard where the large celebration of Joaquincito's birthday was being held was teeming with local kids. She had never put together a party like this for the girls, most of their childhood birthdays had happened in public parks in the city. By the time Carmen had moved them upstate and they actually had a backyard for the first time, Luna didn't want to simply invite every name in the new school directory, she just wanted her friends from her old school to come up and visit. By that time Izel claimed she was too old to throw a birthday party in the backyard like some little kid.

Through the sliding doors Carmen could see Izel staring at her phone off to the side, away from the throngs of younger kids, with her shoulders raised, looking anxious and defensive, her eyes out for Luna who was already mingling. Nineties reggaeton played, crunchy and distorted, through a pair of well-worn PA speakers along with cumbias, rancheras, and a few ballads Carmen swore she hadn't heard since she was Izel's age. Luna was being characteristically talkative, having already inserted herself into a group of kids her age, nodding emphatically along with their conversation before contorting her face in a visible attempt to summon her rough Spanish to respond, sliding her backpack from her shoulders and pulling out her sketchbook. A small huddle of older girls stood at an angle to Izel, their conversation clearly revolving around the new girl in town as they glanced over every now and then. Carmen's eldest, noticing her observers, struck a relaxed pose which just made her look like a statue of a cool person. A mild unease came over Carmen as she remembered those feelings of otherness instilled in young women by their peers, the clear lines of in-group and out-group her daughter was very visibly attempting to navigate in the sun-drenched backyard. The statuesque cool-girl leaning against the peeling fence now took the shape of a frozen rabbit being eyed by foxes. Yes. That's how it so often felt. Izel peeled herself from the edge of the space and dragged her feet over to the side-eying group of girls and Carmen just barely caught a glimpse of her daughter's lips mouthing, "Hola. Izel," before her name was called behind her.

"Carmen, so glad you came!" Verón cried, approaching her as Joaquín wandered off to talk to family.

"Hola! And how are you, Father? I've heard they have some really good mezcal here."

"It is splendid, indeed." The father's cheeks were a bit flushed. "I'm so happy you made the effort to be here. It's good that you're trying to make friends with Joaquín."

"That's what I've been trying to do ever since I got here!"

"Sometimes we must be accommodating," he said, lowering his voice and whispering in her ear. "Things are different around here. Not like the States, you know?"

"I know, Father. I'm painfully aware that I'm a bit out of my cultural depth. I can't help but feel it's not about how I do things more than the fact that I'm the one doing them."

"Yes, yes, I know. I'm sure he will warm to you though. You are at his son's birthday after all. Anyways, enough workplace politics. Come over here, the barbecue is great," Father said, trying to change topics.

Joaquín looked at her from the other side of the backyard. She pretended not to notice. Even if he had reluctantly invited her, being friendly here wouldn't mean much if nothing changed at work. Then, an indigenous-looking man approached her.

"Afternoon, Arquitecta. How do you do?" Carmen nearly dropped her glass in surprise, shocked that someone at this party both recognized her personally and professionally. And it was the first time she had been referred to by her profession since she had arrived in Tulancingo.

"Good afternoon . . ." she stumbled over her greeting, realizing that she couldn't exactly place the man's face. She looked at the priest and smiled at him, expecting an explanation. Verón simply smiled back motioning his glass to the man and letting him introduce himself.

"I work at the abbey. I restore the carvings on the rocks," he mimed a little chiseling motion in the air. He was wearing a loose linen shirt, jeans, a blue-and-red woven belt, and sandals.

"Yes, of course," she said.

"Quauhtli," he extended his hand.

"Carmen Sánchez," she replied, extending her hand. "Pleased to meet you"

His hand was rough and rugged. He wasn't squeezing her hand very much, but she could feel it had the weight and strength worthy of a mason. It was a hand made older than its owner by years of work.

"Oh, I know who you are," he smiled.

She laughed nervously. "La mujer mandona, no?" she said, trying to own one of the nicer names she'd heard tossed around by some of the contractors: the bossy lady.

"No. No. I don't think you're too bossy, but there can be very . . . delicate sensibilities around here," he said, glancing at the host across the room drinking with a few of his underlings, "At the end of the day all that matters is that the requests are reasonable, though. People talk, but the work gets done regardless."

"Quauhtli here is a very skilled artisan. And perhaps a little more educated than his workingman facade lets on," Verón grinned and took a sip from his glass, "Despite our initial differences I'd say we've become close friends since he started at the abbey."

"I'm aware! I've seen your work taking shape in the abbey and have been impressed. It's nice to put a face to the craftsmanship," Carmen said.

"It's nice to be introduced. You brought your kids along?"

"Oh! Yes," Carmen turned and briefly scanned the yard full of children. Izel was still standing stiffly among the group of older girls, but one next to her seemed to be trying to bridge the language barrier, coaxing her into conversation. Luna was running around with the rest of the young ones closer to her and Joaquincito's age, she was even getting some time in with the birthday boy himself. Carmen found herself more at ease thinking maybe Verón was right and she wouldn't remain an outsider here for too long as she turned back to her conversation with the priest and Quauhtli.

Luna was fascinated by the other kids. Not that they were particularly fascinating themselves, it was simply that kids her age were practically no different here than they were thousands of miles away back home, playing the same games and talking about the same things. For a moment Luna stood still among the currents of running and chattering children in the yard and just watched them move around her, listening to the snippets of Spanish she could catch which sounded so much like the conversations she'd have with her friends back in New York.

She had lost herself in thought and didn't notice the girl walking through the crowd toward her until she'd already grabbed Luna by the hand, pulling her back into the present moment. The girl's dark eyes looked intensely into Luna's as they were momentarily silent. Luna was transfixed by her. Something in her face seemed older than her physicality let on, and despite their apparent similarity in age, this girl had a gray streak running through her jet-black hair. The girl spoke before Luna could say anything.

"I'm Ketzali. You're the new girl in town, huh? Come on, I'll show you the house since you've never been here before. If we play hide-and-seek later, you'll wanna know the best hiding spots!"

Luna nodded automatically as the gray-streaked girl pulled her along through the rest of the children and began pointing out all the different parts of the house. She showed Luna the dog, the cats, the cake, and the food, explaining every basic little thing in that proud way children often do, as if nobody else in the world is privy to the things they know. Luna, for her part, gave her personal opinions on everything Ketzali decided to point out and explain.

They meandered through the house, passing through the small rooms of the first floor and the kitchen, where Ketzali pointed to another back door leading out to the somewhat neglected side yard of the house. As the screen door wheezed shut behind them, Luna looked around at the stacks of discarded wood from various construction sites piled into disorganized heaps of varying sizes. Huddles of tools leaned against the wire fence, left out in the open but free of any rust. Sounds of the party floated around the corner, the shrill laughter and shrieks of the other children punctuating the dull murmur of the adults' conversations and the low thumping of the reggaeton bass coming from the speakers. But out here, there was nobody else. It was only Luna and Ketzali. This was surely where the best hiding spots for hide-and-seek would be. A clatter drew Luna's attention to the rickety doors of an old shed as they were dragged open by Ketzali.

"Come with me," she waved Luna over as she disappeared into the shaded darkness of the old wooden structure.

Luna stepped down from the small stairs leading back into the house and felt uneasy. She realized that she was still a stranger to the owners of this house and felt like she might get in trouble for poking around in their shed. In truth, she couldn't identify the strange feeling coming over her, not its cause anyway. All she felt was a vague sense of trespassing, as if she was entering some area in which she did not belong. She cautiously approached the shed, hesitant to enter.

"What's in there?"

Despite the brutal sun overhead, the searing brightness landing on the Tulancingo suburbs seemed to shy away from the shed. Perhaps the difference in light played a trick on her eyes, but within the shed seemed to be nothing but inky blackness. Ketzali's laugh echoed from inside.

"It's just some old shed! Come *on*, there's a really good hiding place under some of the old shelves in here."

Luna stepped forward and felt a change in temperature. The shed seemed to be emanating cool, damp air that sent a shiver across Luna's skin as she edged toward the small opening of the shed doors. When Luna placed a hand on the side of the door and slipped in, an unpleasant chill came over her body. It felt as if she'd slid through some unseen membrane at the opening that spread within the shed. Her eyes did not adjust.

Within the limitless dark, she heard Ketzali's voice utter the words, "We've been waiting for you to arrive for so long."

As she spoke her voice shifted in pitch and tenor. With each word the bright chiming voice of a young girl slid into the low rasp of an old woman.

The air inside the shed was stale and stagnant. Luna's legs shook in the frigid darkness and, turning her head slightly, she noticed that the bright sun was no longer visible through the gap in the door she had come through. All she could make out was the same darkness she now found herself in. Suddenly, the dim, cold light of the moon illuminated the void. Luna could faintly see her own body in the dark and, in front of her, the frail body of an old woman whose face remained obscured behind a greasy mop of silver hair shining in the mysterious light.

Luna responded in a daze, "For me? Did Joaquincito's dad say we were coming?"

Suddenly, Luna felt her pulse pounding in her ears, muffling her own words as if she were underwater. Between the rush of blood and dizziness, Luna sensed she was about to faint, her vision narrowing to a pinhole as even the dim outline of her body in the dark began to fade into the pitch blackness. Turning her eyes upward, the roof of the shed had been silently ripped away and above them now shone not the sun, but the starry night sky.

From the penumbra emerged a round, copper-colored object like a blunt ball caved in at the top and bottom. It gleamed under the moon, wet and smooth like bloodied flesh. Luna no longer felt the dirt floor of the shed underneath her feet as she and the strange object seemed to float between the earth and the stars above. From the top of the ball opened a powerful stream, a geyser of thrumming darkness within which Luna could just make out the shimmering forms of insects—the buzzing of flies, grasshoppers, and fluttering wings under the pale light of the moon. They flooded up into the sky above where they spread outward and down on all sides, creating a sphere around Luna and the strange object. The stars flickered out of existence and the moon became obscured by their vibrating crepuscular static.

Among the buzzing of the alluvion of insects, Luna heard the muffled sound of chanting breaking through the sound of her own thundering pulse. The old woman in front of her, slipping back into the blackness, rocked back and forth, heel to toe, mumbling a chant in a language unrecognizable to Luna. The face before her was impossibly wrinkled, as if draped over the vague shape of a human and Luna couldn't even see the eyes within their sockets, only a small, flashing glint of green as the words rang in her ears:

The time has finally come for time to end.

Luna sank deeper and deeper into the buzzing sea of shadows. She felt hundreds of small wings beating around her as she was swallowed totally by the swarm. Then, all at once, sunshine, silence, and the warm air of Tulancingo summer returned.

Light filled the shed from the open door and Luna could hear the noise coming from outside again. When her eyes adjusted to the bright Mexican sun, she was alone in the dusty old shed with nothing but tools, planks of wood, and shelves of rusted-shut cans of paint. She looked up at the ceiling, where a dry-rotted hole in the wood leaked beams of sunlight through the dusty air. The only other living creature in the shed, a black butterfly, fluttered around in the arid, hot air. Looking over her shoulder to see who had opened the door, she saw no one and stumbled out into the light. She walked back toward the sound of the party, her heart racing, desperate to find her mom and tell her about the terrifying experience. Across the yard she saw Carmen and broke into a run, only making it a few steps before Angel, one of the other kids, grabbed her by the shoulder. Luna yelped, turning to him startled and wide-eyed.

"Hey! Where have you been?" Angel said, "We're breaking the piñata! Come on, you gotta get in line!"

Luna let out a heavy breath and looked over at her mother, sure she had to talk to her about something. But like a dream that fades immediately after waking, Luna couldn't remember what about. She shook her head and followed Angel toward the tree where they were stringing the piñata.

"You think I'll get a turn?"

"They're breaking the piñata soon," said Verón.

"Are your girls around here?" asked Quauhtli. "Tell them to be careful. They sometimes let the kids loose and they get too vicious, and some of them end up getting hurt."

"Yes, I've prepared them for it. I don't know if I did it well enough, but it's just a piñata. Do you know my daughters?"

"Around here, everyone knows them."

All of the children and several adults started singing.

> Dale, dale, dale.
> No pierdas el tino.
> Porque si lo pierdes.
> Pierdes el camino.

The birthday boy, wearing a hastily tied blindfold, struck the piñata shaped like a cartoonish pig.

"What do you mean, 'everyone knows them'?"

Quauhtli shrugged. "Everyone knows each other around here, people talk about the new faces they see around. It's normal."

Maybe she had no reason to worry, but she found the idea of everyone in town talking about her girls uncomfortable.

She looked around, trying to find them, but only saw Izel. Realizing she hadn't actually seen Luna for a while, she started nervously scanning the whole party. Just when her anxiety was about to send her pacing around the property in search of her daughter, she saw Luna running across the yard with Angel toward the piñata. She let out the breath she had been holding and admonished herself for letting her anxiety take hold of her like that. They were at a neighborhood birthday party, of course Luna was going to run around and explore things out of her sight. She wanted to stop feeling like danger lurked everywhere, as if she was just another American tourist who thinks Mexico is nothing but kidnappers and cartel thugs. Carmen tossed back the remaining mezcal Verón had given her and he quickly poured her a second drink as they watched the piñata being pulled up and down by Joaquincito's laughing father.

"I think what we like the most about the kids hitting the piñata is watching them transform into little monsters, how they enjoy breaking something into pieces. They're in a fit of laughter but also brimming with violence. The piñata is a cathartic thing for kids," said Quauhtli next to Carmen.

"Now that you mention it, it's true. Precisely what makes this tradition a little disturbing is that it's staging the loss of innocence," said Carmen, but immediately felt her words were too pretentious. She didn't want to be condescending, but she was afraid Quauhtli might see her as a crazy old lady.

"I figured you two would make a good fit. You've known each other for five minutes and you're already philosophizing about breaking a piñata," said Verón

"It's such a strange thing, even perverse, to make children break something pretty to eat its entrails," said Quauhtli.

"Well, that's just how everyone in this country is raised," replied Carmen.

"The rich and the poor," said Verón. "Did you know that the tradition of the piñata had its origins in China?"

Quauhtli and Carmen shook their heads.

The guests kept singing:

> *Ya le diste una,*
> *Ya le diste dos,*
> *Ya le diste tres,*
> *Y tu tiempo se acabó.*

"It's a bit similar to how the Chinese burn fake money, paper houses, clothes, and cars to attract good fortune. Or is it maybe a symbolic way to break a spell?" asked Carmen.

"There you go, exactly like that. It made its way back to Italy with Marco Polo, if you believe that kind of telling of history. Eventually it became part of Spanish Catholicism; breaking a seven-pointed piñata was a catechism for banishing the seven deadly sins," said the priest.

"The ancient Nahuas had piñatas as well, and would use them for their rituals. When the Spanish came to Mexico, the two traditions found themselves somewhat at odds," added Quauhtli.

"I didn't know that," said Carmen.

"Well, we all know whose piñata tradition survived the conquest, eh, Father?"

Joaquincito was furiously swinging the stick, his frustration increasing more and more the longer it took him to connect with the piñata. A woman, who turned out to be Joaquincito's mother, Raquel, got closer, risking a whack to the head trying to snatch the broom stick from her tornado of a child as he kept whaling the air around the piñata. She finally disarmed him and he took the barely tied blindfold off by himself. Disappointment was apparent on his face. It was his party and yet he was not the one to break the piñata. The rest of the children didn't believe that was a privilege he should have, so they broke away from the line they'd been waiting in, nervous and impatient, and lunged at Raquel, trying to snatch the broomstick from her. Luna seemed very entertained. Izel, on the other hand, couldn't hide her disapproval. Among the pushing, shoving, and occasional elbow, the parents were finally able to pacify the children.

"The little monsters really can't contain themselves, eh, Quauhtli?" laughed Carmen. "Hungry for blood and candy."

The kids kept taking turns, some clipping the piñata a few times, but not breaking it, until Luna was up, and she wasn't going to lose her shot. She hit it a few times, getting an idea of its location, shoving all of her weight into nothingness in search of the piñata hanging from the string, maneuvered now by one of the workers. She looked like an expert; she had no fear, as if she'd been doing this her entire life. When her turn was over, one of the mothers called Izel.

"It's blondie's turn!" she yelled, and a chorus followed her.

"Blondie, blondie, blondie!"

Realizing they were talking about her, Izel tried to hide behind a column of the portico, but there was no escape for her. They went after her, even as she explained that she couldn't and didn't know how. Within seconds, they'd already blindfolded her and were spinning her in dizzying circles while they started the song from the beginning. Now everyone was looking—the parents, the priest, and the children. Izel tried to find the piñata in the air without daring to strike it. Suddenly, the piñata was lowered too much and grazed her head, making her lose her balance and nearly fall over. Everyone laughed. She bent her knees slightly, took a deep breath, remained still, and with the broomstick high up, she seemed to be listening to the wind. All of a sudden, she unleashed such a precise strike, it left everyone speechless, especially Carmen. The stick hit the pig right in its belly, and it was enough to break the pot and tear through the paper. The kids leaped toward the center to hoard the candy, fruit, and plastic knickknacks, not even caring that Izel was still waving the stick around. Izel took off the blindfold and, upon seeing all the children tossing and turning around her, she smiled. She looked vindicated.

Carmen clapped excitedly, and Luna jumped around her sister with her hands full of fruit and candy.

"Your daughter seems to have channeled her pent-up rage," laughed Quauhtli.

"So it seems."

"She's very spirited," said Joaquín who joined them for another mezcal.

"Apparently," Carmen replied with a smile.

They clinked their glasses of mezcal and cheered.

"Just like her mother, eh?" added Joaquín.

"I don't think of myself as being particularly spirited. But I like things done well, like everybody else. Who built this house?"

"I built it myself," answered the foreman.

"I figured. The additions are very nice."

The construction was very bare but solid. It was missing the finishes and stylings, but the balcony on the second floor was looking good. It wasn't like most of the houses in the area, where people added floors and rooms erratically and used painfully bright colors of paint, which they seemingly ran out of halfway through.

"I can see you also like things to be done well, Joaquín. I think you and I could get along."

"We'll see, señora. Your demands can be difficult to manage."

"But Joaquín, everything I've ever asked for is in the blueprints. Also, you can drop the 'señora,' we're not at work and I'm not married."

"Yes. We'll see, Carmen. We'll see."

There was nothing to see. There were things that had to be done as agreed, as the owners had requested, and as she'd clearly marked. She drank the rest of the mezcal, which left a smoky flavor in her mouth.

Arguing was pointless. The guy would never be happy until she acknowledged that he knew best. She headed to the table and poured herself another round. She drank it, smiled at him, and said:

"Excuse me, I'm going to check on my daughters."

"Go ahead, Carmen." He emphasized "Carmen" sarcastically.

Either way, she was euphoric, maybe partly because of the mezcal, but also for the girls and her conversation with Quauhtli. The party hadn't ended her rivalry with the foreman but it had managed to give Izel a new relationship with Mexico and herself. When it started getting dark, Carmen said an affable goodbye to Joaquín, and thanked him for his hospitality. She hugged Father Verón and told him she'd see him at the site on Monday. Then the three of them smiled and headed outside, feeling lively. Izel hardly checked her phone, watching the scenery go by on their way back to the rental.

4

Yoltzi watched Luna as she walked down the street. She looked care-free, excited about the strange novelties sitting on the main street displays—the businesses, hardware stores, textile stores, and school supplies. Yoltzi was drawn to the rhythm of her routine. It was like the young girl was continually discovering the world over and over. She would skip ahead of her mother and sister, stop, look, and point at something holding her attention for only a moment before she ran to the next display that caught her eye, finally jogging back to her mother and sister to tell them about the wonders she'd seen just feet away from them. The girl approached people openly, asking questions, making conversation in her mix of Spanglish, and laughing earnestly as if everything were magical and fun. Again and again. Yoltzi couldn't take her eyes off her. That girl gave her the chills. She couldn't help but feel that carefree walk of hers hid something disturbing, that the lightness with which she walked reflected an emptiness within. Not that Luna was an empty person, devoid of emotions or inner life, this emptiness wasn't something so malicious. Yoltzi just felt that behind the girl's enthusiastic curiosity and hunger for knowledge of her world hid an empty vessel, an open, innocent box that could hold something—something out there, lurking, looking for an opportunity to make that space its home. An emptiness that could be occupied, a body that could be possessed.

She'd seen it before, but perhaps without as much clarity and intensity. She couldn't put a finger on it, she could just see it, as clear as she saw the restless eyes and gestures of happiness emanating from the girl. There weren't any words in Spanish to describe it. She followed the girl for several streets, increasingly tempted to get even closer, to warn the mother of a danger she wasn't sure the child could even understand.

But maybe it was the other way around. Perhaps it was the mother who'd be incapable of understanding what she was talking about, but the girl would get it before the words even flew from Yoltzi's mouth.

They are few and far between, the people capable of understanding or appreciating a stranger's warning, someone coming to them and saying, *You have a void, right there in your chest, you know? A warm expanse of innocence in your heart. If you don't protect that, your self, something monstrous can make its nest there and transform you into something you never wished to become.* Yoltzi didn't want to get her hopes up imagining the child would listen to her.

Yoltzi was twenty-four and quite slim—they nicknamed her "Flaca" growing up—and her long hair always flowed freely past her shoulders. Her dresses were knee-length and plain. Foreigners often looked at her like they looked at everyone else with indigenous traits—with curiosity, condescension, or plain disdain. If not disdain, it was that savior-like attitude people adopt when they want to be clear that they're not prejudiced, softening their faces and voices to make sure anyone can tell they're empathizing with an indigenous woman, the insistence of their awareness doing nothing except for elevating their prejudices to plain narcissism. Five hundred years of oppression were still at work. It is nearly impossible, sometimes, to communicate across the borders of class, ethnicity, and nationality.

Yoltzi squinted under the punishing sun. The air and color of the city were blanched under the harsh white light of the cloudless sky as its people came and went, continuing to perform the everydayness that had been broken for Yoltzi when she saw Luna. Little Luna shone among the masses of people, luminescent in a way only Yoltzi could see. This is what concerned her enough to prolong her lunch break and follow the family from a distance like a stalker or cheap private eye. Because if she could see the vast innocence of the young soul meandering down the promenade, then something else could too.

It had only been a few months since Yoltzi first noticed it, but there was something slithering just under the surface of the town. The relative peace of Tulancingo had been slowly eroding over the years and the kind of stories one would hear from the state of Guerrero and other places where violence was the norm were beginning to be told more and more in the restaurants and bars of her town. Cartels passing through Hidalgo seemed to be making more frequent pit stops in Tulancingo, bringing with them all the violence their name evokes. Girls went missing; men were found tortured and dead in the roads, makeshift graves, and even behind bars. An atmosphere of fear had been creeping in over the cloudless skies of Hidalgo.

There was, within people, an understandable instinct to deem the heinous acts of brutal men as "inhuman" or "monstrous." Recently, Yoltzi had begun to understand these words as being bandied about all too lightly, because the people who uttered them didn't know how right they were. Inhuman. That was the only way to describe the presence she had begun to feel within the city. There was a current running through every shadow, a pulse with no heart, just a rhythmic thrumming. It couldn't even be said to be living in the darkness because Yoltzi could feel it wasn't alive. It simply moved.

And Yoltzi knew that, sooner or later, they'd notice Luna shining like a beacon. She had no choice but to keep her distance and wait, even if she didn't have much time. She had to get back to the office at city hall, where she'd been working as a secretary since college. She didn't like her job, but considering her options, it was the best one. At least she had benefits, and her boss was respectful, which was sadly uncommon in her experiences with the working world. He'd never tried to fondle her or drag her away to a cheap motel. He hadn't even asked her for money in order to keep her job, as many others had.

Yoltzi came from one of the oldest families in the area, though the true origins of her ancestors had been lost to the dark abyss of a history trampled by the conquest. When the Spaniards arrived, her people had to concede, pact, negotiate, and withstand. The only possible strategy of resistance was hiding, lying, and pretending. They didn't have the weapons or the men to face the invaders, thus much of their family history and language had to be concealed, hidden in the deepest reaches of the family home where it slowly collected dust and was forgotten by most. Yoltzi spoke Nahuatl, though, and had gotten a bachelor's degree in history. Two small victories in reclaiming a past considered by many to be so long forgotten as to be inconsequential. She had always believed the most buried aspects of the past often held the secrets of present issues, though. When one could not understand why the world was as it was, the answer, to Yoltzi, must be in some overlooked part of the path which brought them there.

As a girl, she wanted to become an anthropologist or an interpreter for her mother tongue, or even a lawyer who would defend her people from the cacique's and the government's abuse. Her father had been a farmer. He had a little bit of land and had hoped his children would be educated and have a career, but he lost everything during the 1980s crisis. The state subsidies he depended on as a small-scale farmer dried up, and they went bankrupt. Not that they were rich while working the land; they had a humble lifestyle, but their needs were met. After the crisis, though, they had to reinvent themselves and find different ways to make money. Many in the same situation fled, some to Mexico City and others to the United States. Her brother, Martín-Nelli, crossed the border to try to make a living, sending them money every now and then. Her mother found a job as a housekeeper. Her younger siblings stayed home with their abuela, who made a few pesos selling aromatics and various Nahuatl crafts near the market's entrance.

A gift manifested itself within Yoltzi at a very young age, which she could only describe as an ability to see inside people. Growing up she realized she was able to understand a person, to know exactly what they were like without a word passing between them. For the longest time she had assumed that this shroud she saw around others—which, to her, reflected their soul—was visible to everyone. But as time went on, she realized this sight was unique to her and began to see it as an unfortunate curse. It was almost as if she could see people in their nakedness, in their shameful and beautiful vulnerability. This brought upon her many disappointments in life. In her eyes, love and friendship were built on the slow discovery of all the mysteries and secrets that lie within a person, a building of mutual trust between people as they revealed their souls inch by inch. She would always be pretending to discover others, having seen them in their entirety when they first met. All the mystery and benevolent secrecy of love were revealed to her. How was she supposed to establish a romantic relationship if she could read her partner's heart before they said a word?

Her gift didn't stop at the unseen world within others. She could also see . . . things. Shadows and the shades of spirits not of this world populated the streets Yoltzi walked. These, too, she came to realize, were invisible to others.

One night as a teenager, she had been walking home when she saw a woman walking in the middle of the road. In the dark streets she wouldn't have even noticed her presence save for her feet scuffing the pavement with every slow, aimless step. The off-kilter gait of the woman and her meandering path made Yoltzi assume there was something wrong with her. As an otherwise generous person, Yoltzi would have normally never hesitated to approach the woman and ask if she needed help. But something had been deeply unsettling to her on that dark road. She couldn't see the shroud around the woman, she couldn't see the woman's soul. Yoltzi had been walking behind her at a distance, watching from the sidewalk, fascinated by the first person she'd ever seen whom she could not read, when she noticed the two small stars of head-lights appear at the crest of a hill in the road. The woman did not get off the dark road and Yoltzi stopped moving. As the car approached, Yoltzi simply watched. Only in the final moments did she begin to call out, but the car had already passed. The woman remained on the road, shuffling toward some unknown destination, and Yoltzi ran all the way home.

It wasn't rare for specters and ghosts to cross her path. Most of them she wasn't interested in. A lifetime of encounters had accustomed her to their presence, like that of strangers who ignored her and whom she ignored, as they lacked the ability to interact with the living, but every now and then, along came beings who could influence and affect people, even harm them.

The situation in Tulancingo had already been dire, but when the new mayor got elected, he brought a whole new wave of violence with him, and everything went downhill from there. Then came the foreigners, armed to the teeth and fond of humiliating people, demanding payment in ex-change of protection and threatening those who dared to oppose them. They put together a small army of young boys, lured by the promise of money and women in exchange for their loyalty, selling drugs, patrolling the streets. Many of them were taught how to kill. Some might have been sixteen or eighteen, but others were literally children, as young as ten or twelve, transformed into brutal hit men by organizations that made them believe they were part of something, part of a family that promised them the world.

But the evil that permeated the air, the one you could feel, smell, and almost touch, went far beyond a few scared children, beyond conceited criminals and arrogant politicians. The evil was everywhere. And the most painful and concerning part of it was the missing women, the murdered girls whose story wasn't even breaking news anymore. One after the other, women, girls, young and not so young, had been kidnapped, raped, tortured, and murdered. Across the country, the numbers kept going up, so much that people had lost count, a real epidemic. They would catch some unlucky man from time to time, a scapegoat, and accuse him, torture him, declare him guilty or trick him into confessing, lock him up, and soon after, another woman would disappear—and another, and another. Another number no one was keeping count of. They'd capture some other poor bastard, and the cycle would repeat itself one more time, again and again. Never ending.

The first case was four years ago. Not that women weren't killed before, but this time was different. Virginia López was her name. She was no older than eighteen. Yoltzi knew her. They weren't friends exactly, but they would say hi from time to time; they ran in the same circles; they walked down the same streets. Their stories weren't that different: Virginia worked in a factory; her family had worked the land as well, but ultimately had to go in a different direction. The father scraped together a bit of money and opened a store. One day, Virginia wasn't back home by bedtime. They found her mutilated body in a ditch seven miles away from her town. They blamed her boyfriend— but she didn't have a boyfriend or even any suitors for that matter. They blamed her for being out on the street so late at night, for dressing provocatively, for not going to church often enough. They hadn't captured the perpetrators yet. They probably never would. Virginia was followed by another girl in a nearby town, and then another from San Melquiades and then a neighbor of hers. These crimes remained unpunished. People speculated whether it was a single killer, a serial killer, or a crime of passion, a boyfriend, a family member, or an out-sider. But the silence remained deafening. Some thought it was a web of human traffickers, or organ harvesters, or a satanic cult, or who knows. It didn't matter. No one was doing anything about it. But with this many dead women, someone had to know. With such a high number of crimes, it was simply impossible to have no witnesses, killers regret-ful of their crimes, or even someone willing to cooperate in exchange for money or getting their own crimes pardoned. These things didn't happen without context. There must be something that can be pointed at, reported, followed through. But there was nothing, the deaths kept coming and the secret remained protected.

Yoltzi stopped at a newspaper stand from where she could look dis-creetly at the mother and her two daughters. The eldest sister spent most of her time looking at her phone, evidently sick and tired of a little adventure that didn't interest her in the least. While the youngest seemed to enjoy every step, the eldest surely saw in her surroundings a lame, dingy town. Yoltzi chuckled, amused by the contrast. It reminded her of her brothers, of a time when something like a trip to the market was a wonderful adventure.

She hid behind the stand, pretending to look at the covers of maga-zines and the newspapers. Her eyes stopped on the front pages morbidly showcasing mutilated bodies, gunshot and knife-wound victims. It was so common that the grotesque had lost its ability to shock, to move, to anger. Women, so many murdered women, up to ten in one day across the country, people said. It seemed more and more unbelievable, the brutal-ity of their murders. This much hate had to come from somewhere. All that resentment, animosity, and frustration the country and the world had been hoarding for so long, it had to come from somewhere crueler, more sinister, more ancient—a sweeping force that planted the desire to leave everyone motherless, sisterless, daughterless. A homicidal force set on ending women altogether.

Suddenly she felt dizzy. A drop of cold sweat flowed from her hair-line down her forehead as her body was gripped by a chill. Goosebumps prickled against her skin as the light of the world dimmed. That inhuman presence she had felt humming beneath the shadows was materializing and swallowing the world around her in the process. The ground vanished beneath her feet in the growing darkness of her vision, and she shot out a hand to grasp the newspaper stand to steady herself—only for her hand to pass through more nothingness. The milling people had all vanished, save for one figure slowly trudging through the sudden night that had fallen on Yoltzi's world.

It was grotesquely proportioned, a parody of human form. A skirt of seashells jingled around its skeletal legs as it moved toward a small fluttering light where the small girl had been. The skeletal figure had no visible soul, an apparition. Yoltzi's heart pounded in her chest and, as if it heard its beat, the figure snapped its head around to look at her. A thick froth dripped from its mouth, all teeth. Its tongue was a flashing blade, darting in and out between the bones, and around its neck swung a necklace of beating human hearts. Its eyes seemed about to pop out of their sockets as it stared at Yoltzi. She tried to cover her eyes, but the face remained, growing as it drew nearer.

Yoltzi couldn't move. She felt the face pulling at her. She was losing herself, sinking. She knew she couldn't let go. She inhaled that incandescent breath exhaled by whatever was in front of her. In her head, she could hear behind the cacophony of noise, a faint tune—every note forming a familiar song she couldn't quite place. Her body was filled by an intense heat, nearly solid, like jelly, filling her up from her nose to her limbs. And once she couldn't hold it any longer, she expelled that substance with all the strength her lungs granted her, throwing it forcefully against the skeletal, twisted body.

The darkness subsided and Yoltzi could once again see the people of the square in the sun. Everything was back to normal. No one had seen anything. As Yoltzi looked around, regaining her bearings, she found herself humming a tune, just loud enough for only her to hear. It was something familiar yet so deeply buried in her memory that she hadn't the faintest idea where exactly it could be from. Some song she had heard performed on the street, perhaps, or some song she had forgotten from her childhood.

The newspaper vendor looked at her with curiosity. She was hunched over, and when she tried to straighten up, she felt her spine seize and a sharp pain pierce her chest. She rose as an old lady would, pretended to look at her watch, and then glanced in either direction as if she was waiting for someone. It wasn't her first time experiencing an apparition, but this thing was not a regular benign ghost or the kind of harmless specter she would often see crawling through the shadows, harassing the living. What she'd just witnessed was an ancient entity, older than dust. She could swear it was a tzitzimitl, and if it was, she had to wonder what it was searching for. She wondered if the only reason she was able to confront that thing was due to her memory of that tune, that little song that she couldn't put together but was showing itself behind the curtains of her memory.

She needed some time to collect herself. She drew in quick, shallow breaths as the air seemed to burn her throat. She caught her reflection on a display: her face was bright crimson, as if she'd spent the day sunbathing or popped her head inside an oven. The ground finally felt solid once more. No one looked at her; everyone kept going along with their day and errands as if nothing had happened. Everyone except for the girl, the girl's eyes had been following her. She, too, had been paralyzed and looked at Yoltzi intently. She recognized something had happened, something unexpected and disturbing, but Yoltzi had no way to know what or how much she'd seen. The danger was perhaps even greater than she thought if the girl could see what she'd seen. The mother got closer to her daughter. Yoltzi knew she was asking her what was wrong, even if she couldn't hear the conversation from where she was standing. The girl didn't answer; she remained fixated on Yoltzi. The mother then tried to follow the girl's gaze. Yoltzi reacted and tried to hide herself from the maternal eye, moving behind the stand, almost as if she felt guilty.

"Need some help finding what you're looking for, my friend?" the vendor asked her.

"Yeah, found it. You should really cover up all of those beheadings. Have you no shame?" she said and walked away, following the girl from afar again.

She saw the girl looking for her among the people, but preferred to remain hidden, at least for a while, at least until she came up with a plan to get closer and help somehow. She didn't have the slightest clue how. She saw them walking farther away. The little one had stopped skipping and running. Now she walked, holding her mother's hand, with her head hung down. Yoltzi followed them for a couple of blocks and saw them stop to chat with Quauhtli. There was her shot, her opening. She'd known Quauhtli since she was a child. He was her best chance to get closer to the mother and her girls, close enough to warn them of the darkness that threatened to envelop them.

5

Later in the day, Yoltzi found Quauhtli sitting in the square by himself with his elbows on his knees. The broad shoulders of his frame were hunched over the shadow cast by the afternoon sun at his feet. He was mindlessly turning a clay Nahuatl figurine over and over in his hands. His eyes squinted against the bright light reflecting off the plaza's paving stones. What most people often mistook for a simple grimace, Yoltzi knew to be the face he'd always made when in contemplation. It was like he thought he could put new wrinkles in his brain if he furrowed his brow hard enough. Yoltzi drew closer and stopped a couple of feet away from him, but it wasn't until she called his name that he jumped from his trance and saw her.

"Hola, Quauhtli. Aren't you supposed to be working?"

Quauhtli bolted upright as he was pulled from thought. "You almost gave me a heart attack!"

"How was I supposed to know you were so jumpy? What are you doing here?"

"Who knows? I finished early at the abbey today and sat here to let my mind wander. How about you?"

"Looking for you, actually."

"What for?"

Yoltzi glanced around the plaza to see if anyone else was within earshot, then cast her gaze to her feet, hesitant to tell Quauhtli about her surveillance.

"Well, I saw you talking to that woman. The one with a blond daughter and a younger one. You know them, yeah?"

"Yeah. Carmen is the architect from the States working on the abbey. The girls are Izel and Luna. Why?"

"I need to speak to her. Do you think you know her well enough to introduce us?"

Quauhtli furrowed his brow. "How come?"

Yoltzi sighed deeply and sat by his side on the bench, struggling to find the best way to communicate what she had seen earlier in the day. Her face darkened and she covered her mouth as if afraid of someone reading her lips from afar. "I think the young girl's in danger."

"Luna? What kind of danger?"

She knew Quauhtli would understand, that he wouldn't mock or discount her words as silly superstition, but it was always a little difficult to vocalize what she saw. "Her heart's exposed."

The family ties between Yoltzi and Quauhtli ran deep. They descended from the survivors of the colonial invasion and the near destruction of indigenous cultures. Their two Nahua families had weathered the endless storm of it all, passing myth and language down the family tree even as its branches were pruned by the brutal passing of time and the Christianization of the land. These two families were nothing short of a miracle in so many ways, long stories of quiet and heroic resistance. As a result, their families were incredibly close, sharing bonds of blood and lasting friendship over all that time. The two of them were only distantly related, but they were brought close by the intertwining roots of those ancient family trees. They both grew up being taught the myths and the beliefs kept alive by their ancestors, but Quauhtli was admittedly less devout, for lack of a better word, than Yoltzi in his personal acceptance of them. He considered himself more of a secular inheritor of their ancestors' stories. Nonetheless, he was never one to discount Yoltzi's spiritual convictions.

"Exposed? How?" he asked.

"Do you know about tzitzimimeh? The goddesses of the dark sky. They'll supposedly come down to end the world at the end of the fifth sun."

"I know the tales. You don't have to explain them to me."

"They're tales until they're not."

"So you think that a tzitzimitl is going to . . . what? Eat Luna? What are you proposing to do if you talk to them? I know you see things, Yoltzi, and I trust that they *are* real in a sense."

Yolzti pursed her lips and looked away. *In a sense.*

Quauhtli continued, "I've known you a long time, though. These are strangers! Americans! What would you even say?"

"I don't know, but I have to say something! There's something happening. You can't even feel it a little bit?"

The air chilled in an instant as the square was covered in shadows. Gray clouds had blanketed the sun, but the darkness which fell was closer to the dead of night or a total eclipse. Among the shadows Yoltzi could feel something moving, something pushing up against the surface of the plaza's stones from a realm unseen. Her grip cinched around Quauhtli's hand like a vice, communicating to him without speaking that they were currently surrounded by the very spirits that she had been talking about. They were being ambushed by murmurs, as if a thousand dark serpents slithered around them in the murky depths beneath, like eels in a lagoon, all while they were surrounded by people completely oblivious and moving on with their days. Seeing her expression and feeling the grip she had on his hand, Quauhtli took Yoltzi's lead and remained quiet and still.

Waiting for the light to return and the spirits to disperse, Yoltzi, in her fear, receded into herself. Her pulse quickened and her head swam as her vision darkened. She fell into an ephemeral, boundless space that felt warm and familiar, like the thoughts of another were stored within her, someone reminding her to be unafraid of what she saw at the plaza. Her fear dissipated and was replaced by the comfort of an old, matronly presence. While she couldn't hear anything, Yoltzi was positive that the darkness was speaking to her but only pieces of Nahuatl came through: *Yehua . . . xiquiyehua ipan . . . pampa ni mitz tlazohtla, pampa ni mitz tlazohtla . . . noyollo.* Yoltzi tried to solidify this presence in her mind, attempting to bring a face or a voice to it, but Quauhtli was shaking her shoulder. Her eyes fluttered open and the light returned to the plaza.

The two of them remained still and silent among the movement and sound of the crowds for a moment before Yoltzi spoke softly, "See?"

Quauhtli's face had softened and it seemed as if he did indeed see what she had been talking about, but responded with a question, "What was that song you were humming?"

"When?"

"Just now, when the shadows surrounded us! You were singing something, muttering under your breath and humming some kind of tune."

"I don't know. I didn't notice myself doing it if I was."

"It sounded so familiar."

Quauhtli tried to repeat the refrain he'd heard her humming, but soon lost his train of thought and couldn't remember much more. Yoltzi said nothing. She hadn't realized she'd been humming again. Both knew the power of the specters relied on scaring the living. They can't intervene in the physical world, can't move anything or materialize. Their strength lies in making people hurt themselves. Yoltzi figured that for whatever reason that tune she hummed unconsciously must bring her some comfort, enough to keep her composure and sanity in the face of the tzitzimitl.

"So when are you introducing me to the architect?" Yoltzi asked.

Quauhtli's face went back to a grimace. Yoltzi watched the lines form on his forehead and at the edges of his pointed nose while he sat silently contemplating. She knew it was a big request to ask him to approach what was, in fact, his superior at work with something like this.

"I don't know her well enough for that. We're friendly, but it's not like we have the kind of rapport that I can say, 'My childhood friend was watching you and thinks your daughter is under demonic threat. Would you care to meet her?'"

"Are you trying to make me sound insane?"

"No, but that's how it will come across. Think about it. I don't even think they're religious, they'll think it sounds like *The Exorcist.* I have a better idea. You should come to the site whenever you can get away from work under the pretext of your job. Say you have to talk to her about some permit that didn't get signed or something, paperwork that slipped through the cracks."

"And then warn her when we start talking."

"No. You'll already be a liar then, pretending to show up under false pretense, and on top of that you'll blindside her. Just introduce yourself, say you're a friend of mine, and then maybe I can convince her to have coffee with the two of us or something."

"But this is urgent. What if—"

Quauhtli cut her off, "Then it's important not to immediately make her wary of you. It'll only make it harder to talk to her."

They remained silent for a moment, listening to the sounds of the square, the people speaking, the balloon vendor, the lotería vendor, the children out from school laughing and yelling, the traffic by the avenue. None of it had been interrupted by the appearance of the specters, but only now did Yoltzi become aware again of all the life happening around them. It seemed the world of those shadows was always churning beneath the baked streets of Tulancingo, boiling it from below as the sun scorched it from above. The nightmares of that world were leaching into the world of the waking, the living. Quauhtli stood up and turned to Yoltzi.

"Have you had anything to eat? I'm on my way to the market, to Don Lucas's pozole. Lunch is on me if you want it."

"No, I'm not hungry. Thank you, Quauhtli. I must get to work. I was supposed to be back at the office a while ago. I'll get myself a torta or something like that."

They hugged goodbye and Yoltzi walked away toward city hall. No one would mind her being a bit late, like she'd said. The boys club that was her work environment, despite her slim figure, apparent frailty, and delicate features, didn't mess with her. They knew that underneath her face, hid a tenacious strength. As she walked, she wondered if that strength would be enough to confront a threat like this one. Just the thought of the apparition she had seen earlier froze her blood solid in her veins. She had not felt strong or powerful in that moment, but when she imagined the little girl she had seen, Luna, facing something like that, her blood began to move again, determined to stand between them.

6

The heat was brutal that day. The morning haze was shattered by the aggressive sun before work at the abbey had even begun in earnest and by noon the old church was a sweatbox. Even the breezes blowing through the openings of the construction site only brought with them hot dust. It was unforgiving weather. Carmen was in the nave of the building, wiping sweat from her brow trying to walk some of the contractors through the blueprints and mock-ups of the section of the walls they were renovating. If they thought her bossy already, Carmen wasn't sure how they'd handle how bad a mood she was in sitting in the oven of the church. Just as she felt her temper about to boil over, explaining what she thought were simple concepts over and over, but hampered by some language barriers, one of the workers tapped her shoulder from behind.

"What?" she snapped. Hearing her own voice come out with such aggression gave her pause. She took a deep breath and regained her composure, resuming with a calmer tone, "Is there something you need me for?"

The worker simply pointed to the church entrance where a young woman holding a manila folder was talking to the grounds' security guard. Carmen left the blueprints in the hands of one of the contractors, telling them to ask Joaquín if they needed more information, and walked to the entrance. The young woman, slight of build with bright eyes, turned to look at her as she approached.

"Can I help you?" asked Carmen, as no one else seemed inclined to say anything.

"Hi! Yes, I'm here from city hall," said the woman.

"Ah, sure. What is this about?"

"Can we speak privately?" she asked.

"Of course, right this way. My 'office' is over here. I hope it's nothing serious," Carmen said jokingly, but upon seeing the woman's earnest face, she started to think that maybe it was.

They entered a room that had been converted into a temporary office. It had some desks and a pair of drawing tables with blueprints. The smell of dust, cement, and plaster permeated the air. Carmen pulled two lukewarm cups of water from the cheap watercooler in the corner of the room and offered one to the woman before sitting down.

"So, how can I help you?"

"Thank you. I brought some paperwork from city hall for you to sign off on. I could've sent a messenger, but I could use the fresh air, so I brought it down myself. My name's Yoltzi, by the way," she set the documents down on the desk next to Carmen and paused for a long while, swallowing hard before adding, "I also wanted to talk to you about something."

Carmen opened the folder and looked through the papers. "Talk to me about something?"

Yoltzi shifted her weight, looking uneasily around the office like she was watching something else in the room other than Carmen. Her initial bright demeanor had become stilted and uncomfortable as her words stumbled over one another. "I saw you the other day. Uh, in the plaza. I saw you talking to Quauhtli. I'm an old friend of his, Quauhtli's, and thought I'd introduce myself."

Carmen glanced up from the girl's restless feet and looked at her intently for the first time: her bare face, her hair reaching her midback, a spotless white shirt, a light blue jacket, and a knee-length skirt. "And you knew to find me here? I don't get it, but okay."

Carmen's eyes narrowed ever so slightly as she contemplated the possibility that this was an attempt at a shakedown. She'd already had to deal with many who had come asking for extra money to deliver materials, so "things didn't get complicated with the permits," so the inspector would give an approval, so the engineer of so-and-so department provided their signature, anything. She was beginning to get used to it and was learning to read which of these blackmailers she could ignore and which ones she had no choice but to pay. Her bosses back at the office knew that was how things worked in Mexico and they'd considered it for the budget, but that didn't mean that she had the full liberty to pay any shameless scoundrel who came by asking for money.

She was especially wary of those from the local government. Now city hall was sending a girl down to the site with some paperwork that, upon a closer look, Carmen was positive she'd already seen approved copies of, and she "wants to talk"?

"And what did you want to talk about, exactly?"

"It's just . . . not easy to explain," said Yoltzi, "So I hope you'll forgive me if it sounds a little outlandish."

She couldn't even maintain eye contact with Carmen as she spoke. Looking up at her, Carmen watched those bright eyes darting around the room, restlessly fixing on seemingly anything that wasn't her. Carmen turned around for a moment to see what was so transfixing to her uncomfortable guest, expecting to see some buzzing gnat or fly. Nothing. A white wall. Carmen turned back to Yoltzi, her already suspicious eyes boring into the nervous girl who refused to look her in the eye.

"Listen, miss, if you're here to ask for something, just ask. I'm pretty busy, as I'm sure you're all aware of over there at city hall. If you're about to tell me there's a 'processing fee' or some crap for this paper you've just brought then you can—"

"Señora, you're going to find this very strange," Yoltzi blurted out, "but you might be in danger."

"Danger?" Carmen asked quietly. "What are you talking about?"

"Around here, there are unexplainable forces capable of causing a lot of pain."

"Are you threatening me?" Carmen's voice remained quiet, but she rose, furious. She wanted to shout Yoltzi out of the room, but calmly walked to the small window in her office from which she could see the piles of building material and parked trucks of the workers.

"No! I'm only trying to warn you." Yoltzi frantically stumbled over her words, "They're very old forces. They've been here since, I don't know, forever."

"How much?" Carmen sighed, still looking out the window, away from Yoltzi.

"How much . . . ?"

"Yes, just tell me. How much is it going to cost us this time around? You come from city hall, telling me that there are some papers that slipped through the cracks or whatever—papers I know I've signed before, I recognize the document code at the top—and say that I'm in danger. How much is it going to be to make sure that these documents get 'properly processed'?"

"No, no, it's not like that. This, what I'm talking about, it's not for sale, or up for blackmail."

"Then what is it you want?"

Yoltzi looked at the floor, her eyes staring straight into one of the old cobblestones visible under the thin layer of sawdust which covered every surface of the jobsite. Carmen briefly softened seeing the young woman shrinking away from her. Even if it was a particularly egregious attempt at a shakedown by the local government, she couldn't be more than twenty-five. She probably was just some poor secretary they sent down here to deliver a message. Carmen spoke her next words calmly and clearly, but there was an unmasked brittleness to her voice, an actively suppressed rage.

"We are working with a very limited budget. I know you think gringos are like bottomless wells of money, but that's not the case. You're making our lives impossible. You go back to city hall and tell them they're going to bankrupt us if they keep this up. And if that happens, every single person working out there will be unemployed. We can't work this way. We've paid the mayor's office plenty by way of permits and work orders. If they've so thoroughly run out of ways to drain us that they're just sending the same paperwork again, I honestly don't know what to say. No more, miss. No more."

"No, you're misunderstanding me. This has nothing to do with the construction."

"Then what is it about?" Carmen was dumbfounded.

Yoltzi finally lifted her gaze from the cobblestone and looked directly into Carmen's eyes as she said the first clear words since entering the office, "It's about your daughter."

Carmen hadn't lost her temper in a very long time. She took pride in maintaining a level head on a jobsite, but this was too much. The brittle, cold calm in her voice shattered and it rose to a bellow with every word.

"Wh-what? How dare you come here and threaten my family?" She stepped away from the window and toward the young woman in her office. "Get your ass out of my office before I get security in here. Get off of my jobsite!"

"No, señora, I'm not here to threaten you."

Carmen snatched the paperwork Yoltzi had brought with her from her desk and shoved it into her hands. "Leave now. Tell them to just send an invoice like everyone else does. For lumber or something. But get the fuck out of here."

Carmen was livid, but she was also afraid, afraid like she had never been before. The horror tales—the kidnappings, murders, femicides, and other atrocities—she'd heard about for so many years yet felt so distant, as if they belonged to another world, not hers, materialized themselves in this young woman with indigenous features, unarmed and humbly dressed. She never expected this fear to manifest itself in such a way. She thought she must surely just be a messenger for someone else, someone who could hurt her and her family.

"Señora, you've misunderstood me. I don't mean to scare you or harm you. I come to warn you about these forces."

"Leave, now, please. Before I call the police. I'm going to research who you are, and if anything happens to me or my daughters, you'll be held responsible."

Yoltzi stood up.

"I'm sorry about this misunderstanding. Trust me, I came bearing no ill will."

Carmen walked toward her desk, grabbed her phone pretending to ready herself to call someone. She followed Yoltzi's movements with her gaze while she realized she had no clue whom she would call. The police? If this was a government racket like she assumed, they'd only hand wave it away. The workers who hated her? Father Verón, who was even less intimidating than she was? She felt more alone and far away from home than she'd ever realized since arriving.

Carmen clenched her hands to stop them from shaking as she watched Yoltzi disappear beyond the door of the abbey, she didn't want anyone to see how shaken the encounter had made her, didn't want to give them yet another reason to talk about her. Carmen's gift as a professional woman had been, for many years, her ability to remain calm no matter the situation. Compartmentalizing. That was the way to survive the competition within the American corporate world as a Mexican woman. If you show too much emotion, you're considered either vulnerable and weak or a volatile drama queen, neither of which belonged in a budget negotiation. If you show nothing, they don't trust you and brand you an outcast, incapable of being a team player, a robotic bitch. Architecture was still a boys' club and she could feel it. No one said it outright, but she knew the second she slipped and let her temper flare, people would quietly label her whether they were conscious of it or not. She walked back to the workers and resumed her explanation on the wall finishes without showing any distress. Unscathed. Even a bit more severe.

But her fist was still clenched at her side to stop the trembling. She couldn't quiet the thought that people were stalking her, people who knew she had girls at home. Perhaps she shouldn't even be leaving the girls alone. They were an easy target; all anyone had to do was stop by and take them. How was she supposed to remain calm under these conditions? She would have to report what happened to the central office in New York, but they might go into hysterics and bring her back immediately along with the girls, and she would lose the direction of the construction. Or worse, they could think that she was blowing it out of proportion and use it as evidence that she was not ready to manage a construction in a foreign country, never mind that this was her own country, confirming the racist stereotypes and anti-Mexican prejudices that some of her bosses—and the executives at the office—held. Right this moment, Mexico was going through a particularly negative phase with the international press. She had to be careful with what she said.

When she was finished speaking to the workers, Carmen decided to head home, quickly, to check on the girls. She called Izel on the phone as she gathered some of her things from her desk.

"Izel? Are you alright?"

"Uh . . . yeah? What's up?"

"Is Luna alright too?"

"Yeah, Mom she's fine. She was just in here trying to show me her sketchbook."

"Go check on her for me, please?"

"Mom, I literally just saw her. She's fine."

"Izel!" Carmen pleaded over the phone, "Please. For your paranoid Mama, just put your eyes on her for me."

She heard Izel groan as she stomped down the hall, "Ugh! Fine. What are you all worked up about? Is something going on?"

"It's fine, Izel. Don't worry, I just wanted to call and check on you guys while I was away, that's all."

"Luna! Mom wants to know if you're alright." Carmen heard Luna's voice chiming on the other end of the line, muffled by her distance from the receiver.

"She said she's fine. I told you it's all good."

"Thank you, Iz," Carmen finally breathed out, "I'll be home in a little bit. Text me if you want me to pick anything up."

Carmen couldn't tell them what had happened either.

She walked toward the exit, imagining herself buying a gun, a small one, a .38 or a Glock, or a semiautomatic rifle, an AR-15, something powerful. A lot of architects from the firm had weapons and loved talking about them. Carmen couldn't remember ever holding a gun, even a toy gun. She thought maybe she could call Fernando. She could talk to him, although he did have the irritating tendency to tell her she was imagining things, he was the gaslighter-in-chief. Either way, she had no choice at the moment.

Yoltzi left the office panting. When she was a teenager, they found a heart murmur, and at this moment, she felt a sharp pain in her chest that barely let her walk. Not only had the confrontation with Carmen rattled her, maybe even more so than confronting a tzitzimitl, but also the shadows manifesting themselves on the walls had filled her with anxiety and grief. She found herself in a very complicated situation. It was highly unlikely that she'd be able to have another conversation with the architect. If she wanted to protect Luna from her terrible fate, she would have to come up with another plan. But at the moment, she felt ashamed, regretful, and hurt, and she couldn't think about anything else.

She was amazed by the irreparably disastrous way she'd presented her case. She'd always felt gifted with the ability to read people and anticipate their reactions, and this time around she'd gotten everything wrong. She let her anxiety and impatience get in the way of treating this as the delicate matter it was. Quauhtli had warned her not to tell Carmen anything right away, but when she saw those moving shadows on the cobblestones, she couldn't stop herself from trying to alert Carmen, who took her vague warnings as a physical threat. Stains on Carmen's improvised office wall had come to life and twisted like messages from a remote past, and the recent pain of her people—their sacrifice upon being converted and forced to build that abbey, exploited until death in the name of a god that was venerated—was clearly marked on the walls.

As a girl, in school, they would call her Yolanda, Yolandita, Yolo. That would always put her in a mood. She would always correct them.

"My name is Yoltzi."

Sometimes a few of them listened to her. Most ignored her, though, and kept calling her whatever they wanted. She thought, understandably, that they meant to belittle her, giving her a Spanish name that redeemed her from her indigenous one. It was a way to show her that they thought of her as less than, that they couldn't even respect her name. She hated that name so much, it was the one she used whenever she felt she'd done something wrong. Whenever she scolded herself, instead of calling herself an idiot or stupid, she'd call herself "Yolandita."

"Ah, Yolandita, you really screwed this one up," she told herself out loud while passing by the security checkpoint, where the guard was having a Coke.

7

After leaving work, Yoltzi liked to sit at the plaza. The heat was less intense than during the day. There were people, children, and you could breathe more of that fresh, idyllic air of peace that's supposed to reign in a small town like this. Sometimes, she'd buy herself some ice cream and enjoy it slowly by herself. People often saw this as a call for company, and men, old and young, drew near to start a conversation. Sometimes they were pleasant, and others disgusting. She didn't mind much. She usually ignored them, or, if needed, used that special talent she possessed to reveal embarrassing truths about themselves, things she read in their faces, the way they talked or walked, dressed or flirted. Rejecting them was like a sport. She didn't find them desirable in the least.

She particularly liked twilight, when light started to recede. Sitting in silence, she saw how the shadows became longer until they slowly conquered everything, like a dark liquid spilling over the plaza, the streets, the whole valley, to flood the town in the blackest of oceans. She liked watching how the glints, reflections, and glares disappeared, only to be replaced by the artificial illumination, in a relay of light and contrast. Likewise, the sounds changed, and the heat gave in. It was a time of ghosts, in which she herself felt part of their history, of the living and the dead, the pilgrims, the victorious and conquered troops, of the markets, of the families and the children. Sitting down on her bench, she could see the days go by, the years and the centuries, with a fascinating cadence. Ever since she was young, whenever she came to the plaza at twilight, she could see the difference between the living, coming and going, worried about getting back home, about having no money, trapped by the desire of having something or someone, and the dead, careless, without pressure or interests, moving ritually, leisurely.

But today, the shadows and specters didn't pass through like they usually did. They seemed confused, and she couldn't feel the harmonious flux that marked the transition from day to night. They were disturbed, moved in disorder, changing their rhythms and directions. Something was happening, or was about to happen, something that had shaken the diaphanous beings, the sleepers, the transparent ones, the gone, the spirits. Yoltzi remained seated, watching restlessly. It was one more sign that the danger was real, that there were forces capable of altering the order in the reign of the immaterial, and it could probably affect the physical world. She could see a giant flock of birds in the sky moving rapidly side to side as the sky grew darker. Yoltzi wondered if people around her could see what was happening, or if they were at the very least bewildered by the bird's erratic movements. The flock seemed to contract and expand, as if it were a giant, obsidian heart. One could hear the screeches and squawks become louder and louder. The sky was nearly pitch-black, but the birds with their synchronized movements throbbed, getting closer and closer to land, as if they wanted to crush the buildings, devour everything in their manic and gigantic pulse. Initially, between the darkness and the distance, the flock seemed nothing more than a uniform mass. Suddenly, she could see that those were not birds, but butterflies, millions of them, a gigantic colony drawing strange figures against the background of a black sky.

They were so near they began to swallow up the power lines and church towers and still they drew closer. People started to run, scared at the sight of so many of them. The butterflies descended like waves, like an invading army, layers and layers of wings flying at top speed among the people, the benches, the kiosk. All those tiny wings, the delicate bodies, swallowed sound like a black snowstorm. Hiding under a bench, Yoltzi could hear people screaming, children crying, but they were muffled by the mass. The beating wings made a nearly imperceptible roar, like white noise, whispered screams. She couldn't believe what she was witnessing, and wondered whether this was another illusion, an apparition. Thousands of wings and bodies comprising a single, massive tentacle brushing against her head, her back. A man was waving a stick trying to scare them away, swatting as if to break a piñata. From the ground, she saw the shadows sliding down the air, threateningly. This was too real for it not to be true. There was no way these creatures had simply lost their way or become confused into a swarm like this.

Paralyzed with fear and perplexity, her eyes shut tight, she heard howls of pain only a few steps away. Kneeling under her meager protection she rocked back and forth, finding herself muttering and humming a song. *It must be the one Quauhtli pointed out last time we were in the plaza together,* she thought. While she still didn't recognize it, she somehow knew the melody. It was unclear whether or not she was making up the words she muttered, they felt like near gibberish to her, but as she sang, the noise began to subside and she no longer felt the wings beating against her back and neck.

When she opened her eyes, she saw the man with the stick drop to the ground and cover his bloody face. As suddenly as the tempest began, the colony disbanded, the butterflies flew away erratically, some remained perched on trees and cables, and many more carpeting the asphalt with their dead bodies. The plaza was now bathed in darkness and a brief moment of stunned silence was soon broken by the confused words, scared voices, and weeping of the few people that hadn't yet fled. Yoltzi stood up, shaking off the dust and little bit of the shame in having been so afraid. She ran toward the man who was now bleeding and screaming.

"Sir, let me help you. What happened?"

Crying, desperately wailing in fear, the man dropped his hands and revealed his skinned face. Flayed flesh framed his bones made shapeless and obscured by the amount of blood painting them, the deep, black holes where eyes used to be, and a jaw holding his teeth like little marble blades. The sobs wracking his body choked together, knotting in his throat as they gasped out of the lipless mouth and twisted into a deranged, roaring laughter. Yoltzi lost her balance and fell on her backside. The man covered his face again, crying and begging.

"Help me, please. I can't—I can't see. I felt one on me and I was just trying to get it off my face."

Yoltzi stood up again and walked toward the man, grabbed him by his shoulder and helped him stand up. As she helped him up he once again dropped his guarding hands. His face was normal, save one eye socket which was bleeding profusely. The wound was deep and ragged. Looking at the hand, still trembling in the air near his chin, the shivering fingers were covered in blood and the nails had clumps of raw, cleaved skin underneath them. She tried to calm him down while they walked, telling him it wasn't that bad, that they would probably bandage him and send him home. She walked him to Juárez Hospital, left him there, and went home.

She had so many questions. Between the meeting with Carmen and the butterflies in the plaza, it had been a terrible day. It seemed like everything was happening too quickly. A sort of vortex was taking over her life, as if the specters were knocking loudly on the doors of reality, trying to come in. But for what purpose? She'd never felt anything like that. With the ability to traverse the land of the living and the dead, she'd never felt there were forces trying to tear down the barrier between worlds. What could they possibly want?

As she walked along the road back to town and home, she watched dusk fall over the clouds as twilight began setting in and whistled to herself. It was a comforting tune. Maybe Quauhtli was right about it being from their childhood. It made her feel safe in this uncertain time.

After calling the girls, Carmen's anxiety had not settled in the slightest as she left the site—piled stacks of paper, binders, and folders in her arms—shuffling out the cathedral doors to her car. There wasn't much more she was needed for around the site today anyway. It was a perfect day to work at home with the girls, where she could watch them, and make sure she knew they were safe. When she got outside, the blazing sun briefly blinded her and when her eyes finally adjusted, Quauhtli was standing right in front of her. Startled, she jumped and dropped her hastily gathered pile of documents to the ground which Quauhtli quickly stooped to pick up.

"Afternoon, how are you, señora?"

It took a few minutes for Carmen to organize her thoughts. She took a deep breath, and put on her sunglasses, coming up with an excuse.

"I-I think I'm doing alright, Quauhtli. I'm just going to finish the rest of my work at home today. It's just so hot here I can hardly think."

"You seem in quite a hurry. Did something happen?"

Carmen had crouched to help pick up the documents but shot bolt upright when he asked that. Her body felt very cold as she remembered the woman saying she was a friend of Quauhtli's. Had the friendly carpenter tipped her off that the architect working on the abbey was a little skittish, someone easy to put the pressure on?

"What makes you think that?" she said, looking at him with surprise and glancing around.

"You practically jumped out of your skin just now. You're on edge about something."

Carmen shook her head but couldn't bring herself to outright deny what Quauhtli was implying. She took the documents from him.

"I just have to go home."

"Are you sure everything is okay?"

"Yes." She stopped and took a deep breath. "No, actually, it's not okay." She lowered her sunglasses as if to discern within the artisan's eyes whether she could trust him, looking for a sign of honesty, even if her intuition was telling her that this man might be part of the people who were stalking her, of those who wanted to hurt her or take something from her. She had no evidence as to whether she should trust him.

"What's wrong?"

"A young woman, who said she worked for city hall, came to threaten me." Carmen filled the next words with venom, "A friend of yours."

Quauhtli placed his hand on his chin and grimaced in contemplation before shaking his head in frustration. "It was Yoltzi."

Carmen froze, looking at him with newfound suspicion. So he admitted it!

"Yes! You know her then! Why are your friends coming to harass me, Quauhtli? She came here and told me I'm in danger and gave me some phony documents to sign? Is the local government trying to squeeze more money out of us or something?"

"I'm sorry, señora," said Quauhtli at last. "I don't expect you to accept my vouching for her as much, but she is a good person. She was not here to blackmail you as one of city hall's foot soldiers. She came of her own volition. Yoltzi had asked me to introduce the two of you and I suppose took this route to warn you."

"Warn me about what? Do you know about the threats? Are you a part of this?"

"I'll take it Yoltzi didn't explain herself very well. She isn't the best communicator at times."

"I don't know if that was the case. But she never said what or how much money she wanted."

"She wants none of that. Don't worry about that. She's just worried about you and your daughters."

"And where does that concern come from?"

"True, she doesn't know you, but she is an honest and, uh, how do you say, a sensitive person. You may not believe this, but she has a gift, a very special gift."

"Quauhtli, I don't know what you're talking about. Frankly, I have to go. I need to see my daughters, just for my own peace of mind. You and that Yoltzi are making me nervous." She thought about threatening to call the police, but she knew it was as absurd as it was useless.

"I understand. Yoltzi is a firm believer in the old Nahua tradition. Call it being spiritual or superstitious, but she has a strong connection to the old legends and, to be honest, I've often been inclined to trust the things she says. It must come across as some ridiculous ignorant native superstition."

"Please, don't say that."

Quauhtli laughed and then became earnest.

"It's hard talking about our beliefs with other people, especially when such beliefs have been portrayed as ridiculous bloodthirsty cults. I don't mean to convince you to believe in something, but Yoltzi truly believes that you are in danger. She's being sincere in trying to help, there was nothing malicious about her warning. I promise."

"Listen, Quauhtli, I don't mean to belittle anyone because of their beliefs, but I don't think it's right for anyone to come and scare me with superstitions."

Carmen was kind of surprised by how eloquent Quauhtli was, and simultaneously because he seemed to be a believer.

"You're right, señora. Scaring you with old legends is the last thing I meant to do. Please, I just beg you, don't think of Yoltzi as a bad person who wants to get something out of you. I've known that girl for forever. Please, give her a chance to explain herself and why she's so worried"

"Well, we'll see," replied Carmen, meaning to sound decisive, feeling relief flood her chest. She didn't know why she trusted Quauhtli, but she didn't mean to show it or let him know in any way.

Carmen walked toward her car and tossed her paperwork on the already chaotic backseat. Quauhtli handed her the rest of everything he'd picked up. She wordlessly accepted it and threw them next to everything else. She got in her car and lowered her window.

"We'll see what that woman wants. If you say she means no harm, then I'd be willing to hear her out if it was important enough for her to come to me like this."

"Go peacefully, Miss Sánchez."

She grimaced, showing her disbelief. She started her car and left without saying another word. The distance between the construction and her home wasn't much, and in less than ten minutes, she was pulling into the driveway.

As she started to gather her things from the backseat, she glanced up and froze in fear. The front door was open. Carmen abandoned the car as is and sprinted toward the house. She stood in the threshold of the doorway for a second, full of more fear than she thought possible. What if there was someone inside? Someone waiting for her, someone with the girls. Cautiously, she poked her head into the living room, seeing nobody in the home.

"Izel, Luna! Where are you?! Izel!" she shouted, racing through the living room to the kitchen then to the windows facing the backyard. As she was running to check the girls' rooms, Luna came around the corner.

"Hey, Mom! Look, I have a new villager," she said while trying to show her the screen of her Switch game console where she had been playing Animal Crossing.

Carmen dropped to her knees and hugged her tightly. She was sweating and her heart was beating out of her chest. Pulling away from Luna, Carmen held her by the shoulders and looked up at Izel who had come out just behind Luna.

"Why did you leave the door open? How many times have I told you to lock the door?" she asked.

"I thought you'd locked it. We haven't even been by the door," said Izel.

"Look, Mom, his name's Apollo. He's a bald eagle. I upgraded my house and caught a whale shark," Luna continued.

"Then why is it open? The door was wide open when I pulled up just now," she motioned toward the still open door, "Listen carefully, you two. That door needs to be locked, completely locked, when I'm not around. And if you ever see anything suspicious, you must call me immediately. I don't mean to make you think you're in danger or make you scared, but I just don't know what I'd do if anything happened to you. Make it a little easier on your paranoid old mother."

Both of them nodded and Izel went back to her room. Luna was still trying to show Carmen her screen, but she was too anxious and paid no attention, looking past the game and straight at Luna.

"Luna, are you sure you didn't open the door? I won't be mad. I just want to know why it was open."

"I didn't open it."

"How about Izel?"

Carmen knew she'd locked the door in the morning. She roamed the house, looking everywhere, for a footprint, anything missing or out of place. For any sign of someone being there.

"I don't think so. I didn't see anything. Are we in trouble?"

Carmen released her grip on Luna's shoulders, smoothing the fabric and patting her on the head. "No sweetie. It's fine. You can keep playing your game now."

Carmen sat at the dining room table as Luna returned to her room. Too wound up to get any work done, she went to close the car's door but didn't bother to retrieve the paperwork from the backseat. Instead, she simply sat and played the entire day's events over in her head. She was sure she had locked the door this morning on her way out, but if the girls hadn't opened it and someone else had, why was nothing amiss? She paced the house several times finding nothing missing or out of place.

During dinner, Carmen brought up the door one more time.

"I know you already said you didn't open the door, but neither of you saw anything weird? Nothing out of the ordinary today while I was away?"

"Where?" asked Izel, rolling her eyes.

"At home, outside, I don't know. Something, anything that caught your attention."

"No, nothing, nothing at all. We're in the most boring place on earth. Nothing ever happens," said Izel.

"I saw that lady who walks by every day. She stops in front of the house and waves hello. She says stuff I don't understand. Sometimes she stays there for a while, lights a cigarette, waves around, and leaves."

"Which lady?"

"I don't know, a lady, an old lady."

"But what does she want? Is she selling something?"

"No, she just walks by and waves kind of funny, moving her hands around." Luna started to flail her arms, up and down, in circles, pointing to the ground, and then her chest.

"Do you know about this, Izel? Who is that woman and what does she want?"

"I don't know. Luna talks to everyone, every person, every animal, and every thing. I'd rather not ask."

"Why haven't you mentioned this before?"

"I don't know. It didn't seem important," said Luna.

"For real, Mom? You're gonna worry about an old lady walking by and waving?" asked Izel.

Carmen crossed her arms so as to stop herself from compulsively asking more questions. She rose from the table and began stacking dirty dishes. She was letting herself get carried away. Leaving the girls by themselves for most of the day hadn't worried her before, she didn't have to start now. She told herself she was losing control over her emotions, or maybe just losing it. If she let herself get shaken at the building site with her workers, it seemed the feeling followed her home. The hot water from the kitchen sink ran over her hands as she centered herself. She laughed at her overreaction, at how terribly she handled the situation with Yoltzi. The girls picked up their dishes and wiped the dining table.

As Carmen did the washing, she tried to calm herself down. There had to be a reasonable explanation for the door being open. She thought about the interaction she had with Yoltzi earlier in the day, something that was at first inexplicably terrifying, but after talking to Quauhtli, had at least some kind of explanation. This must be the same. Perhaps the stress of everything had just clouded her head that morning. It wasn't impossible that she had forgotten to lock the door that day; maybe the latch hadn't caught. She set the knife she was washing aside and went to turn off the water when she saw it.

A roughly woven and frayed bracelet with six green stones sat on the kitchen counter next to the faucet. Her hand now slightly trembling, Carmen grabbed it and held it up to the light. She had missed it in her sweeps of the house. There wasn't anything missing from the house because something had been added. Her pulse began to race again. All of that rationalizing she had done while washing up went down the drain as she became sure she had locked the door that day.

"Girls, where did this bracelet come from?"

Both of them came over to see the stones she held up.

"No idea, I've never seen it before," Izel said.

Luna examined it carefully.

"It looks like the old lady's," she said.

"And how did it get here?"

"I don't know," the two of them answered.

Carmen told the two of them to go back to whatever they were doing. She took the bracelet with her to her room and tossed it into the bedside table's drawer. Whatever it was she didn't want to leave it out in the living room. Some suspicion, its origin unknown, made her want to keep the thing away from her daughters. Carmen was convinced that it must be some kind of sign. Yoltzi's visit happening the same day couldn't have been a coincidence. Either she was the one who did it, knew the people who had put it there, or this had something to do with her bizarre warning. Carmen rolled over and tried to get to sleep, beginning a fitful night of insomnia.

9

By around seven in the morning Carmen gave up on sleep and rolled out of bed. She picked out a pair of large sunglasses for the day to cover the bags under her unrested eyes and put coffee on to brew in the little Italian Moka stovetop maker that she took everywhere. The girls hadn't woken up yet. The bracelet still sat in the bedside drawer back in her room, caged like a dangerous animal. All night she had considered tossing it out onto the street or in the trash, but she thought it was better to leave it be. She thought it might be a test from whoever was stalking them, someone who'd broken into her home and instead of taking something, had left something behind: a threat, a mark, a sign.

Pouring a cup of bitter black coffee, Carmen considered just calling her boss back at the firm and requesting a replacement and going back home to New York. She could forget about the nightmarish construction. Her career would definitely take a hit, a failure she might or might not recover from. She would probably lose her job, but her life and the girls might be in danger. If any of her male coworkers abandoned a job like this, they'd be questioned and possibly reprehended, maybe even reprimanded. But for her, a woman in her home country, she would most likely be the object of scorn.

"Things haven't changed, let's not fool ourselves," she said to herself. "My failure is every Mexican woman's failure." She knew she was exaggerating, but she couldn't help but to imagine her coworkers laughing behind her back, laughing at the little Mexican who couldn't even finish a simple renovation in her own country.

Someone wanted to scare her away, and they were succeeding. Quauhtli's words floated around her head. They didn't make much sense. Did he really mean something supernatural was happening, or was it meant to be a metaphor? Specters and monsters were often a reflection of the horrors caused by human ambition, hate, and selfishness. *Nothing more*, she said to herself. She had a headache. The last thing she wanted to do was go to the site and continue her daily struggle for control over the workers, especially Joaquín. But she had no choice. She finished her coffee, woke up the girls, and insisted that they shouldn't open the door under any circumstance, that they should keep their phones with them, and that they should call her if they saw anything out of the ordinary.

"Even if it's a kind of crazy old lady waving at you. If anyone gets near the house, let me know."

"Okay," the two of them replied, still half asleep.

"I'm double locking the door. The moment I'm out, put the chain on."

"Mom, can I keep the bracelet with the green stones?" asked Luna.

"No. I don't know. Let me think about it."

After checking multiple times that every door and window was latched and locked, Carmen finally allowed herself to leave. The wind was blowing and the clouds were gray. It was a terrible day for rain. They would be delivering very delicate materials, and some parts of the roof hadn't been totally waterproofed yet, meaning they'd have to wait another day to let it dry out before actually sealing it. Upon reaching the construction, they were already delivering some marble and a large piece of carved wood, a restored antique that would go by the entrance behind the lobby. She was happy to see something had finally gone according to schedule. The workers were unpacking the marble for the lobby and the dining area. Carmen was satisfied, smiling, until she drew closer and noticed that the stones hadn't been polished or handled the way she had asked.

"Stop! Everybody stop! This is not what we requested."

The workers froze, uncertain.

"The wood stays, but this marble isn't what we ordered from the supplier. They must have sent the wrong shipment. Load it back onto the trucks. I'll call the company."

Joaquín rushed over, drenched in sweat and furious.

"This is what was requested, señora. Don't mess with my men's heads on some power trip."

Carmen pointed to the slabs of material and said, "Joaquín, these stones aren't polished nor sealed. They're not what I asked for, so we'll be returning them immediately so we can get it right."

"We unloaded them, and we're installing them. We'll polish and seal them later ourselves."

"You are not understanding me. I specifically asked for that to be done by the distributor, who has access to industrial-grade sealant I know will last. Even unpolished you can see they aren't the right color. Look! If you did polish and seal them, they simply wouldn't be what the design is supposed to look like."

"Well, we'll see what Father Verón says."

"Verón has no authority in this or any construction-related decision. This isn't even *my* choice really. I designed the structure, the company who bought the land in the first place has their own designer who chose the materials. It's my job to make sure that their choice is honored so here, we do what I say, and if you don't like it, well . . ." she simply raised her hands.

Joaquín was bewildered. He was used to putting his foot down, and he didn't expect a firm reply, much less a threat in front of his men. Carmen was at risk of an uprising, and if she lost the workers, things would go very wrong. Aside from the delays, she'd seen how easy it was for Joaquín to make things difficult for her, and she knew of the possible consequences if there were a personal retaliation.

"Can I speak with you privately?" asked Joaquín.

"Yes, sure. As soon as this crap is back in the truck. We can't have any more delays. My door is always open, Joaquín. But right now, I want everyone returning this."

"It's just that I got these at a discount. Instead of rejecting them, you should be thanking me."

Carmen quickly realized what had happened: once again, the foreman had gone around her, getting an acquaintance to deliver the goods in return for a cut of the money.

"I appreciate the effort. Thanks, but no thanks. It may have been discounted, but the labor of polishing and sealing gets added back to the budget anyway. I'd rather just have the materials that *I* requested."

She turned around and told the workers one more time to hurry up.

She was afraid they would ignore her. That's when her authority would collapse. But surprisingly, the workers—even the most stubborn ones like Bernardo—started to carry the stones back to the parking lot. She went to check on the wooden piece. It was perfect, a magnificent baroque carving, elegant and filled with wonderful details.

"Careful, this is fragile," she said to the workers in charge of taking off the padding.

"Sí, señora," one of them answered.

Joaquín remained frozen in place with a crumbled paper in his hand, as if this defeat had been personal. Ironically, Carmen's small triumph translated into more delays and possibly more costs, but she was perfectly happy sacrificing a little money to establish who was in charge. She headed toward her desk and sat behind the tower of paperwork, realizing in the dim light of the small room that she hadn't removed her sunglasses yet. Smiling, she imagined what a queen bitch she must've looked like out there, sticking it to that arrogant man.

Leaning back, in a daze of sleeplessness and adrenaline from the encounter, Carmen laughed and said to herself, "Just what I needed: to make more enemies."

The stone bracelet weighed heavy on her mind, but she couldn't help but smile at the absurdity of everything happening around her. She felt deranged for a moment as anxiety and euphoria mixed into a bizarre flash of mania. When her heart stopped racing, she snapped herself back to reality and got to work, floating through the rest of the morning until Father Verón knocked on the frame of her office door.

"May I come in?"

Carmen waved him toward the seat across from her desk and set a cup of coffee in front of him without a word.

"Thank you, my child."

"Of course. What can I help you with, Father?" Carmen did not raise her eyes from what she was writing.

"Well, I just wanted to check in. I heard you had a confrontation with Joaquín this morning. I thought you two were beginning to see eye to eye."

Carmen finally looked up from her work, "He was pocketing money and trying to tell me I should be thankful for it. I know you wanted us to get along, and I think I'm being pretty nice not firing him for what he tried to pull today."

Verón frowned. "I suppose. Well, I came here to see if there was anything I could do to help smooth things over, but it seems I am not needed."

"Father—," Carmen started, but Verón raised his hand.

"It's quite alright. I very much understand your view on this and I don't think hearing yet another person say, 'It's how things are done around here,' will appease you. I respect you wanting this site run how you see fit. I just—."

"Father, it's not that. I want to ask you something," Carmen finally cut him off at a lull in his speech. "A more personal matter."

"Oh? Of course, I'll try to answer my best."

"I think someone is messing with me, trying to intimidate me, I don't know. I don't mean Joaquín. Someone from city hall came by yesterday and said I was in danger then, when I got home, my door was open and someone left this."

Carmen pulled the jade bracelet from her bag and held it out for Verón, who took it into his hand and turned it over a few times.

"Jewelry?"

"I just wanted to ask you if it meant something. Why was it left behind in my house? I know it wasn't there when we moved in. It was in the kitchen next to the sink. You've been over to cook before and didn't see it either, did you?"

"No, I didn't," Verón looked at the bracelet, perplexed, before handing it back to Carmen. "But if it has any meaning, I don't know it. I've lived here a good long time and don't recognize it as anything but handcrafted jewelry of some kind. All I can say is that it looks similar to some old Nahua crafts I've seen sold around Tulancingo."

"That's alright. Thank you, Father."

Verón set his now empty coffee cup down on the desk and got up to head out the door when he turned around and added, "I didn't mean to defend Joaquín. I hope we can still have our dinners."

"I wouldn't hear the end of it from Luna if I deprived her of your mole."

Verón smiled and nodded before heading out of Carmen's office, leaving her to finish her day's work in peace. As she got back to it, her shoulders loosened for what felt like the first time in years. Even though he hadn't been that helpful, Verón's visit at least reminded her there was someone around who was looking out for her. The jade bracelet, though, still bothered her. The more she tried to put it out of her head, the more it intensified. She tried to imagine who put it on the sink, but could only conjure up a shadowy vague figure placing the thing on her kitchen counter. The harder she tried to visualize who could have done it, the larger the darkness grew, becoming monstrous and inhumanly large.

Verón had said while he didn't know what it was, it looked Nahuatl, so maybe a Nahua would know if it had any sort of meaning. Carmen left her desk and went into the nave of the abbey and found Quauhtli working on the carved wooden piece that had been delivered earlier in the day.

"Hi, Quauhtli. How's everything coming along?"

He turned from his work and rose from his hunched position to greet her, "Arquitecta, things are going well, just working out the details as to how we'll be suspending the piece you got us."

"Good to hear. Come with me for a moment, I want to talk with you about that."

The two of them left the sculpture and Quauhtli's tools behind as Carmen led him outside and out of earshot from anyone else before she turned to face him. She spoke with intentional decisiveness, taking an authoritative tone she had not before struck with the friendly carpenter.

"You need to explain clearly to me what you meant yesterday. I don't want to hear about the various possible interpretations of what your friend was talking about. I want to know why she came here to talk to me and I want to know what this means," she brandished the jade in front of him.

He held out his hand, politely gesturing that he'd take a look at the string of beads. Carmen dropped the bracelet into his hands.

"All I was trying to say yesterday is that Yoltzi doesn't mean to threaten you at all, but believes you are under—for lack of a better term—spiritual threat," he said, holding the bracelet up to the light. "If you're asking if this bracelet has anything to do with her, I doubt it."

Carmen's stomach dropped. The answers she was so sure were a firm question away were in fact much further.

"But I do recognize jade when I see it."

"Does it mean anything?" Carmen asked.

"Our ancestors used to put jade beads in the mouths of the dead, since they thought it could collect the breath, the soul, or the spirit. It was also a symbol of rebirth. But that's just what comes to mind. It could be something else. Why?"

Carmen explained the providence of the bracelet, how it had appeared in her home.

"So someone's trying to put some sort of Nahua voodoo curse on me or something?" Carmen asked in disbelief, unconcerned with her framing of Quauhtli's culture.

"Well, like I said, it could mean a few things. If you're wondering about Nahua 'voodoo' culture," Quauhtli responded, giving her a look, "while I'm indeed a Nahua, I don't know all there is to know about my people. I know you're not thrilled to meet Yoltzi, but if you gave her a chance to explain herself, she could maybe shed light on what the bracelet might mean."

Carmen furrowed her brow, her whole face communicating to Quauhtli how deeply uninterested she was in meeting the woman who just the previous day had seemingly come to threaten her. The desire to know just what, exactly, this strange omen that had been left for her to find burned hotter than her unease at meeting Yoltzi. She held out her hand to Quauhtli, who placed the bracelet back in her palm.

"I suppose the two of you could come over tomorrow afternoon."

The two of them exchanged information and she gave him her address before Quauhtli excused himself to finish working. Carmen, again, decided she should go home a little early that day. Leaving her paperwork on her office desk, she walked to her car and drove back to the Airbnb.

That night Carmen did, however, do work, pulling up tab after tab on Nahua myth and tradition, searching for mentions of jade stones and bracelets. The more she researched, the more conflicting information she found. Any claim to the meaning of jade in Nahua culture was only met with counterclaims and counterclaims of the counterclaims. Each region of the old Aztec empire had different rituals and uses for almost every symbol they seemed on the surface to share. It was all muddled and confused, papered over by centuries of Spanish evangelizing and history's tendency to condense everything into a unifying narrative.

Her sleep-deprived eyes grew heavy and she soon closed the laptop, finally falling to her pillow and into another fitful slumber.

10

Carmen spent the entire next day, Saturday, in the house with the girls. As much as she'd talked about going to see ancient ruins and the sights of the country on her days off, the previous few days had left her in dire need of some rest and relaxation. The three Sánchezes drifted around the house for most of the day. Luna played video games, drew in her journal, and looked things up on Carmen's laptop. Whenever Carmen glanced over Luna's shoulder, she saw yet another Wikipedia page on Aztecs or Nahua. She'd always been a knowledge sponge, but she was apparently doing some homework before their guests came over later that afternoon.

Izel mainly stayed in her room, but when she finally graced Carmen with her presence for lunch, Carmen pounced on the opportunity. She leaned across the table as they ate and began the interrogation process known as getting Izel to share even the smallest detail about her personal life.

"I notice you've been smiling at your phone a lot lately," Carmen said with a smirk, pushing some food into her mouth.

Izel stopped eating for a moment, a brief pause before carrying on, "And? Sometimes my friends send me funny stuff."

"No, no. I know that smile when I see it. You don't think I'm watching, but I'm your mom I see it *all*," Carmen opened her eyes wide to give a visual aid of her maternal vigilance. "What's his name?"

Izel's light complexion turned red. "Who?"

"The boy you need portable chargers to keep talking to all the time. I'm your mom, but I was a girl too."

"Oh my God, literally, what are you talking about? I'm actually just texting Halley and Tina."

Luna joined the conversation from the couch, shouting, "Josh! I saw it on your phone the other day!"

"What the hell? Luna! I told you not to snoop on my phone," Izel snapped back.

Carmen turned to Luna and said, "She's right, Luna! You need to respect people's privacy. And nobody likes a snitch either! No more going through your sister's stuff, okay? But," she turned back to a blushing Izel, "I told you! I see it all."

"Whatever. You only knew because Luna ratted me out!"

Carmen's smile scrunched around her eyes. "No! I knew because I'm your mama. Is he in your class?"

Izel finished her lunch, blatantly sidestepping further interrogation by her mom. Carmen was satisfied letting the rest of it go. She'd already learned more than she expected.

As the sun sank in the sky, hanging low and orange over the hills of Tulancingo, at around five o'clock, the doorbell rang.

"Coming!" Luna shouted, bouncing off the couch and bolting for the door.

Carmen rose from her seat, trying to stop Luna. "What'd I say about answering the door! Do you know who it is?"

"You're the one who invited them, aren't you?" Luna was already undoing the lock and swinging the door open.

Carmen joined her at the entrance in time to see before them a relatively composed Quauhtli and, beside him, Yoltzi, who looked frozen with nerves. Pushing past her reservations about having her come into the house, Carmen put on a pleasant smile and waved them inside.

As Yoltzi passed Carmen, she sheepishly presented a bottle with a handwritten label across the front.

"Sorry about the other day and thank you for inviting us over so I could explain," Yoltzi pressed the bottle into Carmen's hand. "It's just a nice local mezcal. Not much of an apology, I know, but I figured it was something."

Carmen took it into her hands and managed an uncomfortable smile, nodding and saying, "It's a fine apology, thank you."

The two Nahua made themselves at home, taking seats around the dining room table. Quauhtli was looking around the room, his eyes landing on the same points of construction and design Carmen had noticed herself scanning the space when she first stepped inside. It made sense: they were somewhat in the same profession. Yoltzi, though, was only looking at one thing in the room and that was Luna. The slight Nahua woman was gazing intensely at the young girl who, unnervingly, did not seem the least bit interested in breaking eye contact. It looked like they were studying each other. There was certainly an energy between the two, a taut line drawn from one's eyes to the other's, but Carmen was far from convinced that there was anything supernatural about a staring contest. Luna did, after all, have a tendency to stare at new people she deemed interesting. Carmen often found herself needlessly apologizing to people in checkout lanes for her daughter's intense curiosity about others.

Desperate to break the strange silence among the four of them, she called for Izel to come out of her room. "Come say hi, Iz! We have guests."

"Wasn't Father Verón here just the other day?" Izel asked coming out of the hallway before seeing the two new faces and stopping in the arch of the hall.

"This is my older daughter, Izel. Izel, this is Yoltzi and Quauhtli."

Yoltzi finally stopped staring at Luna to look at Izel. She was beaming. "Oh! You have a Nahuatl name!"

"It's a name like any other. People always mess it up and call me Isabel or Itzel. I just go by Izzy with my friends"

"Do you know it means 'unique'?"

"Yeah," Izel studied the floor tiles, "my mom reminds me all the time."

"We're actually Nahua ourselves" said Yoltzi, pointing to herself and Quauhtli.

"Luna, your mother told me you're an artist and a bit of a history buff," said Quauhtli, "Do you know anything about Nahua culture? Your sister has one of our names after all, right?"

"Yeah! I read a book my dad gave me once about the Aztec Empire, but I've spent a lot of time looking stuff up since I got here."

"And what did you learn?"

"The author was talking about how, long ago, there was a place named Aztlan, where the Aztecs lived. And that, one day, some of them decided they weren't treated well, and decided to go somewhere else, somewhere better, where they weren't forced to work so hard or starve.

They believed in a god named Huitzilopochtli, and when they left, they started calling themselves 'Mexicas,' and they walked for many, many years, looking for an eagle eating a snake, on a cactus, in the middle of a lake."

Carmen remembered learning that in elementary school. She'd always found it unbelievable that the sign they were looking for was so specific. She reached for the mezcal and started opening the bottle. She'd already accepted she would probably need it.

"Do you also like reading history books, Izel?" asked Quauhtli.

"Not really, I like reading scripts and manga."

"What's the difference between the Nahuas and the Mexicas?" asked Luna.

"Us Nahuas speak Nahuatl. There are Nahuas all over the country and Mesoamerica. The Aztecs, Tetzcocatl, Cholultecas, Tlaxcalteca, other heirs of the Toltecs—all Nahuas. Mexicas and Aztecs spoke Nahuatl, but not all of them were Nahuas. We call people Nahuas depending on the region they settled in. In their exodus, the Aztecs, or Mexicas, settled somewhere named Coatepec, pretty close to where we are. There, they broke into two groups. Some believed in the Coyolxauhqui, the serpent-skirted goddess, and wanted to stay there. And others believed in Huitzilopochtli, and thought they had to keep looking for the god's sign. They fought, the latter were victorious, and in 1325 they found their sign and founded Tenochtitlán, a magnificent city on Lake Texcoco."

Carmen was starting to get bored. She'd heard these stories hundreds of times, the origin story of the country full of fantasy, rhetoric, and nostalgia. She took a sip from the mezcal. It *was* good. She gestured toward the guests offering it to them. Yoltzi declined but Quauhtli accepted a glass. Yoltzi gave him a scornful look, but he seemed to disregard it and poured himself a modest sip of the gift she had brought to the house.

"I don't get any of those beliefs and people. I only know that their religion was opening the hearts of their enemies and eating the ones they defeated in war," Izel said suddenly.

"The Mexicas became a warrior tribe," replied Yoltzi. "They attacked their neighbors, invaded, looted, conquered, and kidnapped many to use as slaves or sacrifice. Their economy was entirely dependent on war. Being a warrior was the only way to climb the social ladder, be honored and recognized. They went from being nomads to becoming the founders of a wonderful civilization, but never got rid of the religious obsession of feeding blood to their gods nonstop, especially Huitzilopochtli, who developed an insatiable appetite." Yoltzi looked at the girls and realized her descriptions of war and sacrifice might not be the best small talk. "I'm sorry, this is not a great topic for the girls."

"I've read about this online," said Luna.

"She knows plenty about human sacrifices and cannibalism," said Izel with a grimace.

"Don't worry, these girls have heard everything or almost everything. Well, at least Luna has, for a fact, been looking at plenty of articles online about Aztec sacrifices and the like. It's hard to discount something when it is technically educational," said Carmen with a shrug.

"You hear a lot about the wars, the military greatness, and the cruelty of the Mexicas, but people rarely speak about how they were also the people of the flower and song," said Quauhtli.

"And despite being obsessed with war, with what they called death by the edge of the obsidian—meaning the pride of dying in battle or sacrifice—they were defeated by a bunch of Spaniards with some cannons, horses, and a knack for diplomacy, who managed to gather the neighboring tribes to rise against their enemies and oppressors, the Aztecs," said Yoltzi. "Which happens often with warrior societies."

"You know all of this from your upbringing?" Carmen asked.

"Some of it. But I also hold a degree in history from the state university," answered Yoltzi.

"We can't judge the Mexica culture by today's standards," Quauhtli tried to interject.

"I know, but we can't ignore that they chose to fight, war, and invade over cooperating and harmonizing either," said Yoltzi.

"As far as we know, peace wouldn't have come easy in that neighborhood. And don't forget their economy was based on agriculture and the tributes from wars."

"Yes, but when the Mexicas had already created an unbeatable empire and held extraordinary wealth, they continued their expansionist war race, and for what? To see their culture destroyed in the blink of an eye by a weak and completely unexpected enemy—"

"Please excuse us," said Quauhtli, a bit ashamed of having ignored their hosts while they quarreled, "Yoltzi and I still disagree on these sorts of topics."

"Yes, I'm sorry too," said Yoltzi, who was so tense, she was barely breathing. "I come from the Netzahualcóyotl tradition, from the philosophizing Mexica poets," she said, and forced a smile as if she had delivered a joke only she could understand.

"Don't worry, I suppose this is why you guys came over in the first place, isn't it?" said Carmen.

"I want to learn more about the jaguar warriors, and eagle knights, and the rites of passage they had to go through," said Luna, and asked, "Is it true that there is no other culture in the world as death-obsessed as the Aztecs?"

"Most people only care about the architecture and violence of the Mexicas, as if they'd been a culture that was piling up stones whenever they weren't killing people," replied Yoltzi. "The truth is their philosophical system was complicated, elegant, and rich. They worried about the life of the soul, and had a spiritual dialogue with the medium. Like Matos Moctezuma said, 'Aztecs don't worship death, they worship life through death.'"

Carmen watched them, equal parts fascinated and terrified, asking herself where these people came from. It was otherworldly how such strange, well-informed individuals she wouldn't have given a second glance at on a normal day had somehow entered her life, but she had to interrupt them. She was more concerned about the pressing problems. They could discuss the Nahuas, Netzahualcóyotl, and Huitzilopochtli another day.

"Girls, the grown-ups are going to talk about work stuff. How about you two go to your rooms? It's going to be pretty boring."

"No, I want to stay. I want to keep talking about the Nahuas and the flowery wars," said Luna.

"Luna, I wasn't really asking. Just go to your room for now. We'll talk about anything you want later. Now we need to take care of some work issues."

Izel left quickly, looking at her phone. Luna, on the other hand, left reluctantly, dragging her feet.

"And close that door," yelled Carmen, and with the same breath, she turned to Yoltzi, "Please explain to me what you think is happening."

"Try to forget, for a second, everything you've been taught. Imagine there's a thing such as ghosts, transitory beings, spirits, demons, diaphanous souls like Yoltzi calls them," said Quauhtli.

"And this is coming from someone who studied physics."

"I know it's not easy to believe this, but imagine there are parallel worlds, worlds we cannot see and the people in those worlds can't see us either. But suddenly, there are portals that open up for whatever reason, and the living and the dead can come together. Some of those encounters are meaningless, some are positive, and some can be dangerous."

"That's what half of horror cinema is about," Carmen said.

"And also about myths and legends across the globe. There's a reason for that."

"How is this related to my family?"

"Your youngest daughter," said Yoltzi, "she's at risk of being used as a portal between worlds." She looked down at the floor, as if she were embarrassed to talk about this in front of her.

"Why Luna?" asked Carmen, visibly distraught.

"Luna has a special sensibility. I'm sure as her mother you can see that much, her openness to the world, that hunger to know everything and everyone, it's wonderful, but also a vulnerability. Coming here has woken up ancient forces that see her as a passage, a portal, or a vehicle."

"And what can I do?"

"Protect her from it, from the demons," Quauhtli added.

"Okay, yes, of course. How am I supposed to do that, though? Quauhtli, please understand. I don't believe in apparitions, miracles, possessions, or demons. I don't want to judge your beliefs, but I can't accept that what you're telling me is true."

"I know."

Yoltzi spoke again, "A few days ago, I saw how your daughter has something that attracts the diaphanous beings, certain spirits. I know this sounds odd, but imagine it's like a light that can go through the barrier between two worlds. It's something most people cannot see, but for some reason I can. At first, I wasn't sure, so I followed her down the street for a little bit, and suddenly one of those beings appeared, a tzitzimitl, a demon. It was as if it was marking its territory, like a hunter watching its prey, following it until its vulnerable, and then attacking. When it saw me, it tried to intimidate me."

"Yoltzi, don't take this the wrong way, but what you're saying sounds like fanatical madness. How can you be sure this isn't just your imagination?"

"Oh, it could be, I'm not denying that. I spent a long while questioning my sanity, but I'm past that now. I've seen enough things . . . come to pass."

"But you're talking about satanic forces or demons or whatever it is that only you can see and hear."

"We speak about these kinds of things with the language given to us in school, at church, on the street, or even in movies. When we say 'demons,' we think of religious paintings and film. The words we use don't accurately represent those beings, or things, or whatever they might be. These immaterial beings have always been here, our ancestors and their ancestors knew that, coexisted in different ways, were afraid of them, and asked them for favors. From time to time someone, like me, had the ability to see them. They don't share our values or worries, but they do have ambitions that mirror ours. Are they our dead, our gods, interdimensional beings? I have no clue. Myths and religions try to explain their presence. I just know they're on the other side of a barrier and can only occasionally affect our lives."

"What you're telling me sounds interesting as a theory. But when this appeared in my kitchen," she said, holding the jade bracelet, "it did concern me. I have no idea where this came from. It could've been a coincidence, maybe the girls found it and don't want to tell me, or maybe it was already in the house when we arrived. But the truth is it's a mystery."

Carmen reached out and handed it to Yoltzi.

"I really don't think the girls have anything to do with this," continued Carmen. "And I'm sure we would've noticed something like this if it'd already been here. This appeared suddenly, and the door was open. I don't know, but I don't think the specters you're talking about need to open doors to enter. I thought that since it seemed to be Nahuatl, you two might know if it meant something, had some kind of message behind it, but I wasn't aware that we'd be discussing things like spirits and gods," Carmen added.

"Jade was precious in every culture in Mesoamerica," said Quauhtli, "I did some reading after our conversation yesterday. It might be an offering, a symbolic payment in exchange of something. It might be nothing."

"And the open door?"

"Like you said, I don't think spirits have any need to open doors," said Quauhtli, "But what about the lady you mentioned? You said the girls saw an old woman walking around?"

"I don't know anything else, but I doubt she's much of a risk."

"Maybe she's not an old lady; she just looks like one. Things are not always what we think they are," said Yoltzi.

"Frankly, I'm worried about the living, the ones who exist in this world and dimension, and might have bad intentions, either because of my job, or because they see my daughters as gringas, or simply for being women. Women around here are in constant danger."

"If anyone knows that, it's me," said Yoltzi.

"There are reasons to be careful around here. Joaquín might be dangerous. But he's not mad, he wouldn't mess with an American," said Quauhtli.

"I'm protected by a passport, that's my magic. But I must say, it's terrifying to see the posters of the missing girls everywhere. How can you live like this? Quauhtli, Yoltzi, I believe you when you say you're worried about my well-being and that of my girls. I was perfectly willing to hear you out, but, like I said, I have too much to worry about in the material world to be dallying in the realm of the spiritual. I'm not sure if a talisman or whatever will protect us, but I think keeping the deadbolt shut will," she stood up to signal the meeting had come to an end.

Yoltzi stood up immediately, hanging her head a bit. She looked slightly dejected like a salesman who'd failed to convince Carmen to pick up what she was selling. Quauhtli stood up as well and offered his hand to Carmen.

"I'm here for anything you may need. Help with the living or the dead," he said with a grin.

"Thank you very much."

"And yes, it's awful what happens with the femicides, and not only here, but in the whole country."

"Don't worry, I won't bother you again without warning, señora," Yoltzi added. "And the fact that these crimes happen everywhere doesn't make the atmosphere of fear here any better."

"Don't worry about bothering me anymore. I think we overcame our misunderstanding. I really do appreciate your concern, even if I don't find myself exactly sharing it."

Yoltzi turned around, clutching her bag against her chest, and walked toward the door with short, quick steps. Upon hearing these movements, Luna rushed out of her room.

"Why are you leaving? You said we'd talk more about the Aztecs and the Mexicas."

"Our guests have to leave, Luna. We'll see them again soon."

Luna reached Yoltzi at the door and hugged her firmly. Yoltzi held on for several seconds, without letting go of her bag until Luna broke away.

"Thanks for teaching me."

Luna gave Quauhtli a hug as well. Carmen was confused by Luna's sudden overfamiliarity with Yoltzi. On one hand, it was sweet and by no means out of the ordinary for the sunny Luna to show affection toward someone she'd just met, but Carmen didn't want to extend this visit or this relationship any further than it really needed to go. She just wanted to close the door on everything that had been said and put it in the drawer of absurd memories. She hoped in a not too faraway future, she wouldn't remember anything about the crazy, wise Nahuas who wanted to protect her daughter from ghosts.

She got the first part of her wish and finally closed the door. Luna was already heading back to her room and Carmen sank into the living room couch without answers as to how or why the bracelet had gotten there, but with a much more comprehensive understanding of Nahua culture. So, she thought, at least it hadn't been a complete waste of time.

11

Back at work the next week, Carmen was meandering through the construction site, giving everything they'd completed so far a once-over. Overall, she was happy. Despite some bureaucratic and supply setbacks they were making good progress and she hadn't felt much resistance from the general laborers as of late. Joaquín was doing whatever he could to avoid her, and he'd mostly delivered his materials on time. While her personal life seemed to have taken a bizarre turn, everything at the abbey was actually under control for once. The universe had taken away the stresses of her job and, in its place, dropped the anxiety of the jade bracelet on her kitchen counter.

Her phone rang. It was Izel.

"What's wrong?" Carmen asked hurriedly, without saying hello.

"Nothing's wrong, chill. It's just that we're bored, and sick of being stuck at home, so we decided to come visit you at the construction, at least to get some sunlight."

"Okay, just give me about half an hour and I'll come by and pick you two up in the car."

"It's fine, we're already almost there."

"You went outside by yourselves?" Carmen was already speed walking toward the abbey's bright doorway. "I distinctly remember saying only a few days ago: 'Don't go out by yourselves without giving me a heads-up.'"

"I'm literally giving you a heads-up right now," Izel said, "We'll be there in like five minutes."

"Izel!"

The line cut and Carmen's phone only beeped in response.

Outside of the shelter of the abbey's shade, the heat was dry and intense. With no clouds in the sky, Carmen had to squint hard against the sunlight reflecting off the landscape as she scanned the horizon for the girls. As long as she could see them, she thought, it would be fine. But she could discern almost nothing among the shimmering heat lines rising from the baked earth. Leaving the car where it was, Carmen started walking in the direction of the house. If they were only five minutes away on foot they should be just over the slight hill around the abbey. Dust floated into the air as Carmen began down a faint footpath worn into the brush with the sun beating down on her head. The longer she went without seeing the girls over the rise, the faster her feet moved under her until she was nearly running. When she finally saw something moving up ahead, she broke into a run. But the silhouette, about Izel's height, didn't seem to be moving toward her and Carmen waved her hands over her head, shouting.

"Izel! Is Luna behind you?"

Izel didn't say anything back, but waved her arms in response as Carmen kept running, the heat and panic rising in her chest as she began to feel ill with anxiety. Had something happened to Luna? Is that why Izel had stopped? Carmen pulled her phone out ready to dial 911.

As Carmen's eyes finally adjusted to the blazing sun, she realized she hadn't been running toward Izel at all. The silhouette had been that of an old woman. A mop of dirty gray hair dangled from a tattered shawl over her head, obscuring the haggard, deeply wrinkled face as the old woman muttered in a quivering voice, waving her hands around in the air at nothing. Carmen froze and scanned her surroundings, no longer able to see the abbey behind her, or the end of the footpath leading to the Airbnb the girls should have been coming from.

Unlocking her phone, Carmen turned away from the old woman and dialed Izel—no answer. Dialed Luna. Dialed Izel. Dialed Izel. Her fingers were shaking as imagined scenarios her girls could be in flashed through her thoughts. The posters from the plaza sprang to mind.

The old woman had grown louder, more crazed. From the corner of her eye Carmen could see she was being looked at as the hag waved her arms more frantically. She decided she'd need the car. She had to go look for the girls. Maybe they'd walked along the main road. Carmen finally looked up from her phone and went to run back to the abbey, but her surroundings had changed entirely.

Tulancingo's landscape spun around with her at its center and vertigo sent her reeling. Her anxiety-sick stomach hit its limit and Carmen keeled over and wretched into the dry dirt of the footpath. Straightening back up and tilting her head back for a deep breath she saw the midday sky had turned a deep scarlet and the surrounding hills had been flattened into a vast, barren land that stretched out in every direction. Without any way to find her bearings, Carmen felt her only option was to run in the direction she assumed the abbey had been, the direction she thought she'd come from.

"Oh God, Luna, Izel, where are you?" she yelled.

Stomach acid burned in her throat as she gasped in the hot, dry air. The illusion of control and the good mood of the morning were gone. Carmen felt entirely alone and terrified in the empty Mexican terrain. Alone except for the old woman. The old woman was still there. In all the changing landscape, the barren and empty space that had replaced Carmen's reality, the woman had remained. She could still hear her incoherent ramblings, the sonic backing to this waking nightmare. The more ferocious side of Carmen's nature was bubbling to the surface. Spurred on by paranoia and a deep terror for her daughters' safety, Carmen spun around and shouted at the lunatic.

"Who are you? What the hell do you want?" she asked.

The lady stopped moving and locked eyes with Carmen.

"I'm looking for my daughter," the old woman said.

"Your daughter? Who's your daughter?" Carmen asked.

The old woman's eyes narrowed. Under the wrinkled old eyelids the glassy whites of her eyes turned from bloodshot to a deep, bloody red. Carmen had seen something similar happen in boxing matches on TV. It looked as if the blood vessels in the woman's head had spontaneously popped. Carmen took a step back, catching her heel on a stone and stumbling, but keeping her balance as the old woman advanced toward her, beginning to chant once again.

While she moved her hands in a pattern, her nails cutting symbols and images in the air between them, Carmen couldn't stop watching her face. The skin didn't hang correctly over her features as her mouth moved. The wrinkled visage looked slapped on like a cheap latex mask. She swore she could see it slipping away from the orbitals of the woman's eyes. Her chant got to the part where she placed her hands on her chest and when she did, the shawl draped over her body caved in under her palms. It was as if there was nothing where her rib cage was meant to be, but something began to move and shift under the fabric. An elbow or a wrist pushed against the shawl from within. Something beneath the shawl was pressing outward, like an extra appendage bursting forth from the woman's sternum.

The vertigo was back, nauseating Carmen again. Planting her feet wide apart to keep her balance, she shut her eyes tight and tried to focus on not passing out when her phone rang. Carmen reached for it in her pocket. With her eyes still shut tight, Carmen no longer felt the sun falling on her legs and hands. Something was now blocking it. The old woman's chanting was louder and Carmen could sense they were mere inches apart. Swiping blindly across the screen and raising the phone to her ear, Carmen shouted into the receiver.

"Izel?!"

"Yeah, Mom? What's wrong?"

"Where are you?" yelled Carmen.

"We're super close. Luna forgot her sketchbook and wouldn't stop freaking out about it until we turned back to get it. Oh I see you! Are you okay?"

Carmen opened her eyes and was blinded by the sun before she could look around. The sky was clear and everything was back to normal. She saw the girls walking toward her. Luna, carrying her backpack on her back, waved at her while skipping. Carmen felt such relief that she almost forgot what had happened. She looked for the old woman. She wanted to ask them if she was the one they'd seen by their house. But she was gone. She had disappeared. Carmen swiped the sweat from her forehead and eyes. She wanted to scream at them and scold them for putting her through this, but her encounter with the woman had confused her. Luna ran toward her and hugged her. Izel just waved from where she was. She thought it might have been a hallucination, caused by stress, fear, and the heat. Either way, the woman's eyes were etched in her memory.

"I was looking for you. I called you and you didn't answer."

"You did? I had my phone with me the entire time and didn't hear anything. Look—no missed calls. You probably called my American number or something."

"I'm sure I called you. I called both of you, not once, not twice, so many times. Look!" she opened her recent calls and the last ones showing up were Izel's first call and the one she'd just made. That was it. Her head was a vortex. She had a throbbing headache.

"How about the old lady, did you see her?"

"Huh?" asked Izel.

"Yes! She was outside our house today, a while ago," answered Luna.

"But did you see her here? She was here a second ago."

"No," said Luna.

Izel was already texting. Probably telling her girlfriends about her mother's crazy new incident. Carmen wanted to ask more questions, but didn't want to transfer her paranoias onto her kids. Even if it really was nothing, she knew that one of the most terrifying things to a child is seeing their mother scared. It was one of those instincts kids have no matter how old they get. Carmen decided to not push it any further.

"Why did you come visit me?" she asked, changing the subject.

"To see you and, I don't know, actually do something outside of the house. You wouldn't have let us go anywhere else. What other choice did we have?" said Izel.

"Okay. Well, have you two eaten yet?"

"No, and I'm hungry," said Luna.

"I could grab a bite," Izel said, without even looking up from her phone.

"Great, we could go get some quesadillas from the market."

"Yes!" said Luna, delighted.

"Could we just go to a normal restaurant for once?" Izel's voice dripped with annoyance. "I get that you want us to have an 'authentic experience' or whatever, but I don't think people *only* eat their meals on dirty, uncomfortable benches here."

"Come on. It's just a quick meal and then you can come back with me to the construction to supervise the crew finishing up the atrium and we'll go somewhere after that. You're right, you two have been cooped up in the house a lot lately."

"Yes!" Luna yelled again.

Izel gave a kind of frustrated grunt as she walked in circles, but then followed her mother and sister to the food court.

The quesadillas restored order, as usual. Even Izel, who had complained so much, scarfed down three, forgetting about the hygiene and cleanliness of the little market stall. Luna was delighted, and Carmen managed to eat two cheese quesadillas as her earlier feelings of nausea subsided. When they were done, Luna wanted to check out the produce, food, and curios stands, but Carmen had to get back. She'd left the construction unsupervised in her absence, and she was worried about some finishes and had plenty of documents to sign. Sitting down on the small stools at the food stand amid the afternoon hustle, Carmen felt the otherworldly nature of her fear superseded by the familiar everyday anxiety she felt on the job, as if her earlier fears and concerns had been nothing more than a bad dream, something she'd seen in a movie she hadn't paid close attention to and that she remembered in bits and pieces, disjointed and unbelievable scenes, and the woman's piercing eyes. She was rousing once more to the normal stress of her waking life.

Luna was writing something in her diary, supplementing her words with drawings. Carmen could see she was drawing pyramids, headdresses, and flint. Luna always had a good hand, especially for replicating images, but these sketches were extraordinary.

"Luna, those are such pretty drawings," she said.

"You always think my drawings are pretty."

She almost said that this time was different, this time she meant it, but instead, she asked to see the sketches, and she thought them very mature and precise.

"Where did you get these images from?"

"I don't know."

That was a little weird. Normally Luna had a freakishly encyclopedic memory for the things she tried to replicate in her sketches. She'd ramble on and on while flipping through them for Carmen.

Izel leaned over from her seat and peered into the open journal in Carmen's hands.

"Yeah, they're nice. You're definitely getting a lot better. Can I post them on my Instagram?" asked Izel, pointing her camera at the notebook.

Luna snatched her journal from her mother's hands. "No! I don't want anyone to see it."

Carmen and Izel jumped back, surprised by Luna's vehemence.

"Okay! Don't worry. I'm not posting anything. Sorry for asking," said Izel before returning to her screen.

Carmen rubbed Luna's back from her seat at the table, "It's okay if you want to keep your journal private, but Izel didn't mean to bother you or anything. You didn't have to react so aggressively, Lunita."

Luna closed the journal and held it to her chest.

"I know. I just didn't want her to take a picture of it before I could say anything," Luna looked up at her mother and sister, then down at the ground and muttered a begrudging, "Sorry."

"Well, we have to head back to the construction. I'm already late. You can come with me and wait for a bit. But please don't go too far and don't get in trouble. Izel, do you also want a notebook so you can journal?"

Izel dropped her shoulders and rolled her eyes.

"No. Thank you."

12

They walked under the sun. It was familiarly hot and dry. A breeze was blowing in from the east, bringing with it some cool air, but also kicking up dust. When they got to the abbey, the girls settled down in Carmen's office. Izel video-called her friend Tina to complain about how awful everything had been. Luna kept drawing and taking notes in her notebook. Quauhtli popped his head in to say hello.

"How are you?"

"We're good, Quauhtli. We just had some lunch and the girls are staying here for a bit while I'm working."

"Quauhtli! Look at my drawings!" said Luna, taking her notebook from her backpack.

He leaned in and assumed the face one is supposed to make when looking over the art of a child—an exaggerated expression of concentration. Quauhtli made to look as though he was truly evaluating the art of the young girl when his face softened and he said with a genuine admiration in his voice, "Hey! Those are pretty good, Luna! You've got quite an eye, huh? Impressive for someone so young."

"What?" said Izel from across the room, "So you won't show them to me, but Quauhtli gets to see?"

"Because he gets it."

Izel rolled her eyes and chuckled, "Oh, alright, sure."

"I wanted to see you to tell you that the tiles in the yard are done. Could you come and check them for approval?" Quauhtli asked Carmen with his eyes still watching the pages in Luna's sketchbook as she turned them over for him.

"Perfect, I'll be there in a second."

"And, since the girls are here, I actually had some things I was gonna give you to bring them. Mind if I just hand them over now?" he asked Carmen.

"Of course," she said, intrigued.

"This is for you, Izel," he said, reaching into his apron pocket and handing her a wooden pendant with an Aztec-style carved tiger.

"Thank you, Quauhtli. You carved this yourself?" she asked. Izel set her phone down and tied the pendant around her neck before picking the phone back up and showing Tina the gift she'd just received.

"Sure did. And this one is for you, Luna," he gave her a similar pendant, but with an eagle instead.

"It's the warriors' eagle," she said, excitedly.

"Yes, it's the highest of honors for young Mexicas."

"Thank you, I love it! I'll wear it forever."

"Thank you, Quauhtli. You're very kind. They really are very pretty." Carmen wasn't a big fan of crafts, but she truly liked the pendants. Then she glanced at her watch and added, "Oh! I gotta go start making my rounds. I'm behind schedule and I have so many things to do before the day is over."

Quauhtli turned and started out the door of Carmen's office. "I'll walk with you."

"Sure." Carmen turned to her daughters on her way out and said, "Girls, please let me know before you go anywhere. You're on an active construction site so try and just stay in here if you can. I'll try and finish up early today and we can go out to eat after."

"Okay," said Luna, as she went back to her journal.

Izel gestured with her hand, as if saying, *Yeah, yeah, just go already.*

Carmen walked with Quauhtli. They first stopped to look at the mosaics he'd installed and supervised and then kept making their rounds as Carmen checked in with the staff. The new master carpenter and the painter were already waiting for her.

"Where's Joaquín?" Carmen fumed.

No one replied. Joaquín was supposed to be there for the tour, but he wasn't, and Carmen didn't miss his attitude at all, even if his absence made it more than obvious that things were not okay.

She forced a smile. "Let's get it over with then."

The moment they were entering the main nave, they heard shouting. "Move! Move! Move!"

Pins and needles of adrenaline prickled Carmen's skin as her eyes darted around to figure out what everyone was clamoring away from. She heard it before she saw it, the sound of metal against metal clanged through the vaulted abbey announcing the first rod of scaffolding falling loose. Her eyes finally fixed on the wobbling structure just in time to watch another support rod fall as the section of scaffold began to buckle and sway, its joints flexing and the walkway boards tumbling down. A few workers jumped from it and hit the ground running to get out from where it might fall. One man landed wrong and Carmen saw his knee buckle under him as he crumpled to the ground, struggling to scramble back to his feet as the structure caved alongside him.

The crash was deafening with all those pieces of hollow metal smashing down. A couple workers who had been on the upper levels of the makeshift structure hadn't been able to climb down in time and tumbled down alongside it. The scaffold smashed into a wall, tearing into the brick as if it were mere drywall.

"Is everyone okay?" yelled Carmen before the ringing of the metal had even ceased. Her head swiveled around trying to evaluate the damage as she thought of her daughters. Her blood ran frigid as she spun around, ready to sprint to her office, praying the girls had listened to her and stayed where they were. As she turned, she practically bowled them over. Her nerves and the shock got the better of her, she stopped holding her breath and yelled at Izel.

"What the hell are you doing?! I told you to stay in the office! You could have been hurt coming out here! What if something else fell?" Carmen dropped down and clutched both her girls to her chest. "What if you'd gotten hurt!?"

Izel squirmed briefly before embracing her clearly shaken mother. "We were in the office when we heard it. Luna jumped up off the couch and I was gonna stop her, but we had to see if you were okay."

Luna pressed her face to Carmen's shoulder. "Sorry. We just wanted to see that you were all right."

Carmen gave the girls a tight squeeze and stood up, looking around and once again calling out to everyone in the abbey, "Is everyone accounted for?"

There was no direct reply, just the cacophony of shouts and murmurs as the workers called out for their friends. A few men gathered around the debris of the catwalk and worked together lifting rods and boards off one of the men. Carmen pulled the girls off to the side as Quauhtli went to check on the workers and ask, one by one, if there was anyone missing.

He came back after talking to a few of them. "It seems like everyone is all right. Only one of them got caught under it and he seems to be a very lucky man. Broke his leg and got some bruises by the falling boards, but they are already taking him to the hospital."

Carmen looked on at the scene as the dust filtered down through the light of the church, finally beginning to settle. A wreckage of metal scaffolding bars, wooden catwalk boards, spilled buckets of plaster and mortar, and the ancient stones of the abbey itself were strewn across the floor of the cavernous nave in a massive scrap heap of construction equipment and history. Carmen pictured where her feet might be sticking out from beneath the tumble of bricks if she'd arrived a minute earlier than she did.

The wall which had been smashed open revealed a sealed-off room in the nave of the abbey. It looked as if the wall had been added specifically to section the room away, but there hadn't been anything in the floor plans she'd seen when designing the renovation. This room had been there all along, an invisible growth on the church, like a cyst or a tumor clinging to its internal structure undetected for decades, maybe centuries. Motioning the girls to stay where they were, Carmen moved through the coughing bricklayers, waving dust away from her face as she approached the dim opening of the unknown room. As she got closer to the shattered facade of brickwork, the smell of stale, damp decay wafted out from the darkness. This forgotten chamber in the heart of the abbey had been festering away inside for years. The cold, cave-like air sent a shiver down her spine as she pointed her phone flashlight inside, revealing nothing but a dirt floor, a small worktable, and some shelves.

"What is this? This room doesn't show up in the blueprints."

Quauhtli had arrived by her side and looked in as well.

"Get me some lamps," yelled Carmen over her shoulder.

Meanwhile, she continued to scan the room with the light from her phone. Quauhtli followed suit along with several workers. They entered the small room that had been walled in for God knows how long. The smell was musty; centuries worth of rot, decomposition, and old dust were barely breathable. There were objects visible, clay antiques and rocks stored in boxes.

"I just don't understand how this went unnoticed for so long," said Carmen, still in disbelief. "I guess we should call someone, right? If the church had known about this, it would have been in the floor plans. This must have some kind of historical significance. I mean, how old must all this shit be?"

Nobody said anything in response as she pulled out her phone to call Father Verón. She explained there had been an accident at the abbey and to come as fast as he could, she would fill him in on everything once he got there. In the meantime, the workers continued to peer into the darkness as Carmen instructed them to place the floodlamps to light the space and begin clearing the detritus of the accident.

Carmen and Quauhtli browsed the objects. Luna called out to them from the edge of the rubble pile behind them, "What's in there, Mom?"

"I'm not sure," she bent down and flipped on one of the utility lamps brought over by the workers, "But stay back, okay? I don't know how stable this room really is right now."

"What happened?" Father Verón had arrived in the abbey and was surveying the catastrophic scene. He walked by the girls on his way through to get to Carmen and gave Izel and Luna each a small, affirming squeeze of the shoulder as he passed. "I'm glad to see you two weren't hurt in all of this."

Carmen explained how the scaffold had collapsed and that the crash had smashed open an unaccounted-for room.

"With the suspicious timing that it happened exactly when we were supposed to begin the inspection we'd planned weeks ago," said Carmen.

One of the workers approached Carmen.

"It seems like the room is solid," he said.

"Either way, get the workers out while we evaluate it."

"And what is this?" asked Verón, upon seeing the cracked wall and the access to the vault.

"Another one of the abbey's little secrets," said Carmen. "It seems to be a sort of storage room they decided to close and wall in for some reason."

"But when?"

"Judging by the work, the stone they used, and the cement they used to bind it," Carmen ran her fingers along the rough edges of the newly torn open portal, "this had to have been done a very long time ago, and then forgotten. Look at this concrete. It's nothing like what we use nowadays. I think this might be considered cultural heritage, it's clearly older than any living memory if you didn't even know it was here, Father. We should call the Institute of Anthropology and History."

"If we do that, the construction will be paused for months or years." Verón shook his head. "You've gotten a small taste, but you don't know how bad it can get having to deal with bureaucracy in this country. This is just junk anyway," said Verón. "Look, it's old furniture and broken crafts."

In the corner of the room a few small stones came loose and knocked against the ground as they fell. Carmen turned her head and saw Luna digging something out from under an old shelf, recklessly clearing away rubble and dust.

"Luna! What are you doing?" said Carmen, "Get away from there! We don't even know how stable the walls are in here yet. You can't just throw rocks around. It's dangerous, get out."

Luna stepped away, backing toward her mother and the entrance of the small room, but she couldn't keep her eyes off what she had just discovered, as in a trance. Peeking out from the pile of rocks Luna had cleared was a small, round object. Just barely poking up above the pile of rubble Carmen could swear the thing had eyes as well. Quauhtli stepped forward and picked it up. When he turned it in his hands, he anxiously glanced at the faces in the room as if expecting someone else to know what it was. He blew the dust off the clay pot, revealing it to be coated in leather and adorned with a terrible grimacing face. Its teeth were bared and its tongue was out. It looked like a monster.

"Interesting pot," said Carmen.

"It's a tlapalxoktli," replied Quauhtli.

"What is that?"

"A piñata."

"For children to break?"

"Not exactly, it's a sacrifice, an offer, tlamanalistli."

"Is it valuable?"

"I've never seen one like this. It's rare. But I don't know if it's valuable."

"This is property of the church. I'll have to speak to my superiors," said Father Verón.

"You think everything belongs to you," said Quauhtli.

"It was in the church. It's been here for years. I think the best course of action is to seal the wall one more time. I don't think it makes sense to take anything out."

Carmen looked at the priest in disbelief.

"These are antiques! They're probably priceless."

"We can't get sentimental over every old pot or scribbled rock. I'm sorry. If we take it out and don't report it, we'll be accused of looting cultural heritage. So, we'll just do what many in Mexico City and other archeological areas do: If you find something, put it back, and don't look for trouble."

"Father, I find that irresponsible, arbitrary," Carmen looked at Verón and then at Quauhtli, looking for support.

"I'm not surprised. They've been doing this for centuries," said the artisan. "But in this case, it's not a bad idea to leave everything as it is. And don't touch anything."

"But why? Quauhtli, not you too?"

"There are some things that are better off hidden and far away from people's reach. This is one of them," said the artisan.

"But won't you defend your culture and your heritage? I thought that's why you'd left your scientific endeavors and came back to your town."

"I'm Nahua, but unlike Yoltzi, I accept that I'm a hybrid. I'm also a man of this world too. There are remnants of pre-Hispanic culture everywhere. What do you think the bases of these columns are, and these walls, if not pieces of Aztec history?"

"We have a bigger problem now. Why did the scaffolding collapse?" Verón interrupted him.

"I don't find it very mysterious. Where's Joaquín? Isn't he the fore-man? Isn't it odd that he isn't here today?" said Carmen.

"I'll graciously ask you not to jump to conclusions. This issue will have to be investigated seriously and not going by hunches and baseless accusations. I'll talk to your team, Carmen, to my superiors, and then to the investors," said Verón.

They exited the vault. Izel was sitting on a pile of cement bags.

"We're heading back home. Where's your sister?"

"I don't know. I thought she was with you. I just saw her go over to the hole in the wall."

"Why didn't you stop her? It's dangerous over there. I just told her to get out of there too," said Carmen, hustling back to the annex.

"I thought she would catch up with you."

"Luna! Luna! Where are you?"

Quauhtli saw Carmen calling and looking concerned and joined her as she ran back into the chamber. Luna stood motionless looking at the artifacts in the dark room. Carmen went in running and felt relief from the pain that was starting to throb at her forehead.

"Luna! What are you doing here? You can't just come and go as you please. I just told you not to mess around in there! Don't you under-stand how dangerous it is?"

"I do understand. I was just here with you, looking at this stuff."

"Let's *go*," barked Carmen. "Out! Now! I'm not gonna say it again. You're gonna get hurt in here."

As Luna reluctantly left the dim cave they had discovered, Carmen felt the veins at her temples throbbing. Her blood pressure had probably gone up. The fear of the collapse that could've killed her, the fright of losing her girls, the disappointment of having accidentally discovered what could be an ancestral treasure that nobody wanted to recognize, and the frustration of having lost part of the progress of the construc-tion, putting her job at risk. All these worries swirled together, forming a pitch-dark hole, a tomb as black as night. She had started the day off so full of hope only to now have her heart sitting in her stomach.

After the collapse and the multiple injuries suffered by some of the workers, Carmen sent everybody home to collect themselves or see a doctor if needed. The only thing she had to be grateful for was that nobody died on what would have been her watch, but even still there was a broken bone that might cost her this job. She drove the girls home silently, too caught up in her own anxiety to really engage either of them in conversation.

Upon getting home, the silence remained unbroken. The second they were through the door Luna made for her room with a brisk pace, leaving Carmen and Izel alone in the living room of the rental. Izel turned to her mother and spoke meekly.

"Sorry I let Luna run off earlier. I probably just stressed you out even more than you needed to be."

Carmen was too absorbed in her own worries to properly comfort Izel and simply rubbed her shoulder.

"It's fine. It was chaotic. I'm glad you girls didn't get hurt, but sometimes I just need you to be a big sister and look after her at times like that."

Izel went off to her room and Carmen took after her daughters, thinking maybe she, too, could use a moment to herself. She walked down the hall to her room, passing Luna's, which was uncharacteristically closed.

13

They had leftovers for dinner, some chicken Carmen had made the day before. Nobody seemed in the mood for small talk. Not even Luna. Izel asked about the accident.

"I don't know what happened. Nothing like that has ever happened to me," said Carmen.

"But it wasn't your fault."

"No, but in this case, I'm the one who'll have to suffer the consequences."

"Are we going back to New York?" asked Izel.

"I don't know. But we'll definitely head back earlier than expected."

"But nobody died," said Luna.

"Luckily, yes, but some people got hurt and I'm the one responsible for this job. I'm supposed to know what's going on and be the firm's eyes on the ground to make sure that everything is being thought of."

The girls cleared the table without being told to. They washed the few dirty dishes they had and went to their rooms. Carmen needed a drink. She had the mezcal Yoltzi had brought her. She went to the pantry, grabbed it, and put it on the table. She looked for a shot glass and filled it to the brim. After taking the first sip, she felt a small relief, a soft weightlessness from the bottoms of her feet all the way up to her shoulders. She spotted an orange in the fruit bowl and cut into it. She sucked on a wedge, and took her second, even more comforting, sip of mezcal.

Something made a faint noise from the other side of the room. A light noise like rustling paper, it sounded like something skittering around. Following the sound pulled her attention to the house's front door. Carmen imagined the sound as something that might come from a giant bug, maybe a massive Mexican moth smacking against the porchlight, but the closer she listened, creeping toward the source of the noise, the more it sounded like words, words spoken quickly and repeatedly. It was almost like some sort of incantation. Carmen stopped in her tracks and backed away from the door, running to the window to get a glimpse of what was outside.

The old woman from the footpath stood on their front steps, waving her arms and whispering her chant. She didn't look in Carmen's direction, her eyes seemed to be closed, she just stood at the front door drawing symbols in the air with her outstretched fingers. Carmen looked over her shoulder to make sure the girls were still in their rooms. Pulling a chef's knife from the block in the kitchen, Carmen stormed to the front door, her heartbeat thudding in her ears, as she flung it open.

"Excuse me, what do you want?"

The woman didn't stop chanting.

"Lady, go home. What are you doing? Why are you following us? I saw you outside the abbey."

As if waking up from a trance upon hearing the word "abbey," the woman was paralyzed for a moment. She said something Carmen couldn't understand.

"What?"

The woman kept talking in her high-pitched, shrill voice. Izel and Luna, hearing the shouting, poked their heads out of their rooms to see what was happening. Carmen suddenly noticed the old woman's face molting again, elongating in the darkness. The mask she seemed to be wearing now looked as if it might fall off at any moment. Even in the dim light, Carmen swore she could see the wrinkles writhing on the woman's face like worms. For a second she thought she'd drank too much mezcal. Once again she felt that vertigo and nausea from their previous encounter. Suddenly, the woman's face was just a skull, and her jaw shook as if it were a machine. Carmen slammed the door shut, pressing her back against it to prevent anything from getting inside.

"Did you see that?"

"Yes, the old lady's face was just bones," said Luna casually, as if this was an everyday occurrence.

"What? I didn't see anything," said Izel. "Can I go out and see?"

"No, stay here."

"But I wanna see her," she said, while looking out the window. "There's nobody out there."

Carmen checked the lock on the door, making sure it was deadbolted.

"It must have been a trick of the light. It was just that crazy old woman who walks around the neighborhood. Please, just go back to bed you two."

"But it's not even ten yet," said Izel.

"I don't care," she said, and went to the kitchen. She finished her glass of mezcal and sucked on another bit of orange.

"Can I at least call Halley?"

"Call whomever you want to call. I just want some peace and quiet."

Carmen looked at her phone. She wished she could call someone, find a kind, patient ear among her contacts. She went through the names of friends, colleagues, and family, but she didn't feel a desire to contact any of them. She had a book on the shelf, but no energy or focus to read. She checked out a Facebook post, but lost interest quickly. She wanted to scream. She could hear Izel chatting via FaceTime. Carmen was sure she heard her laughing and celebrating that they'd be back home sooner than expected. She couldn't blame her for it. Luna was playing or something. Carmen could hear Luna's voice and steps coming from her room.

Her head was reeling with scenarios where her bosses screamed at her and fired her from the architecture firm, or fired her kindly, or asked her to resign, or blackmailed her into leaving her job, or blamed her for criminal negligence. She considered reorganizing her priorities, perhaps looking for a new job or venturing into having her own firm. She'd always wanted to do that.

Her head hit the pillow and the toll of the day rushed over her all at once. Her muscles had been in a constant state of tension since she had gotten the first call from Izel and were only now untangling. Before she knew it, her heavy eyelids closed on their own. She was in a field covered in tall weeds. She was walking, a bit disoriented, looking for her daughters. But she didn't want to look worried or anxious because someone might judge her harshly. While she moved forward, the weeds were wilting. She then turned around and saw that the whole field was aflame. It was hell, and the flames were headed toward her. She tried to run but couldn't move quickly enough.

In her room, Luna was standing in front of her bed. Stiff. Her eyes were fixed on her backpack on her bed. She took deep breaths, drew closer, and carefully unzipped it. Inside, wrapped in a sweater, was the piñata she'd taken from the secret chamber while her mother argued with Quauhtli and Father Verón. She put it on her desk. It was a hollow pot, simple, with a bitter grimace on its face. But Luna felt an uncontrollable pull toward it. She assumed no one would miss it. It had been lost for so long, how bad could it be for her to take it? Simply having it near her made her feel good, euphoric—not happy, really, but she felt a certain warmth and tingling in her chest, like when she waited for Christmas when she was younger. At first, she felt like she'd done something bad. She'd taken something that wasn't hers, and that was a terrible thing. But now she knew that this object belonged to her, and she belonged to it. She couldn't give it back. She wouldn't. She could feel how the piñata had a pulse, a will, a hunger. Yes, hunger. And she didn't know how to satiate it.

14

The bad news arrived in the morning. Carmen had woken up early. While she was making coffee in her beloved Moka pot, the phone rang. It was her boss, Michael Harper, who never called her personal phone number, and much less before work hours. He must have something really awful to say. She let it ring three times, and then picked up. He got straight to the point, asking about the scaffold, about the human and material damages, whether she had any information on how long it would take for work to start again. The hotel had to be ready for the winter holiday season, so there were only a few months left to finish the job and start promoting it. The archbishop was unhappy, and the investors were going to no doubt be skittish about the project once they heard there was a delay.

"Carmen, I wanna say first that I really have no doubt in your abilities. You're talented and I trust you and it is precisely because of that trust that you're there," Harper explained, "but these circumstances call for drastic decisions. I want you to come back and I'll send Sam Miller to replace you. We're in the hole now. You did an amazing job designing the renovation, but Sam knows how to do things quick and cheap."

She didn't say anything. She couldn't show her anger, disappointment, or sadness. But Miller? Really? Michael was right, Sam worked quickly, but being replaced in her own country by that dogmatic Republican didn't sit right with her.

"I just want to be clear with you, Carmen. You did a great job, spectacular, but it's time to come back. Our experience tells us that when things like these happen and the clients start getting worried, it's better to make a switch in personnel. That's all."

Obviously, his little speech, the praise, and making the call himself was part of his strategy to prevent a lawsuit. It was the only thing they cared about. Everything else was irrelevant. Instead of fighting for her job or standing up for herself, she thanked him for the opportunity, said she would see him in the office soon, and hung up. She had to get dressed and go to the construction to say her goodbyes even if nobody would miss her. Either way, she'd go now and start packing in the afternoon.

A few hours later, she was in the abbey's nave. They were almost fin-ished cleaning yesterday's mess. She saw they were sealing the chamber as well but couldn't see if they'd taken out the relics. She considered reporting them to the Institute of Anthropology out of spite. But she guessed that even if she did, they would probably just bribe them or the Institute wouldn't dare to do anything out of fear of the Church or guys like Joaquín, who was finally back on site and pretended he didn't see her come in. He spoke energetically with his workers. Carmen pulled him off to the side.

"How nice, you actually managed to come to work today."

"Someone has to, right?"

Carmen wanted to insult him, but she didn't. She kept walking to what, until then, had been her desk. She picked up her things. She didn't have that many. Quauhtli arrived and greeted her from the door.

"Come in," she said.

He walked in, crestfallen, remaining a few feet away from her desk.

"I imagine you already heard what happened," she asked.

"Yes, of course. It was a pleasure working with you, Arquitecta."

"Thank you so much, Quauhtli. The pleasure was mine. You're very talented and dedicated."

"Thanks."

"The only thing I can't wrap my head around is your attitude about yesterday's relics."

"Believe me, there are things best left in the shadows. There are objects that can unleash a terrible power. You might not believe the su-perstitions, but the sudden appearance of those objects makes me think that Yoltzi was right to be worried. It's a very strange coincidence."

"I'm afraid we won't be here to confirm whether she was right or not. We're leaving tomorrow."

"Perhaps we'll meet again."

"Let's hope that's the case."

Carmen often had trouble falling asleep before a trip. But that night her usual anxiety was heightened and compounded by what was surely a mess waiting for her at home. She wondered how she would support the girls if she got fired from the firm, but immediately pushed the thought from her mind. She refused to assume the worst. The gentle thrum of nerves was secondary, though, to the piercing memories of that strange woman, Yoltzi's theories, and the horrible feeling that something was enveloping her. She felt the land attempting to swallow her. The faint silhouettes of the mountains, dimly defined by Tulancingo's light pollution, would surely rise over the horizon and realize her nightmare.

She'd planned on visiting Mexico City when the construction was over, stay for a few days to meet up with some old friends, and travel the city with the girls. She would've liked to have taken them to the Museum of Anthropology, Palacio de Bellas Artes, Palacio Nacional, the Catedral, and Templo Mayor, like she'd promised Luna. All those plans were now canceled. Carmen had imagined future memories of introducing Luna and Izel to their familial culture, a fantasy of Izel letting a genuine smile crack across her face on a day trip out of the city; memories she'd invented and already began to look back on with fondness. Those dreams crumbled away with the scaffolding, joining the droughted dust blowing across the valley floor. The trip had only been worthwhile for the opportunity to show the girls something new that was a part of them, but it had only put them in danger—both physical and spiritual if Yoltzi was to be believed.

¡Cállate! Carmen's inner voice cut off her own train of thought abruptly. *Keep those superstitions out of your mind.*

She tried to convince herself that it wasn't her fault, that it had been a combination of bad luck, blatant sabotage, and her boss's paternalistic and condescending attitude. Even then, she couldn't avoid feeling sorrow. Carmen poured herself a sip of the mezcal from the other night and sank into the couch trying to calm herself down and focus on the days ahead.

She finished packing up later that evening, pacing around the house and collecting her things, erasing her presence from the rented home. Folding the last of her clothes and setting aside an outfit for the trip home, she nestled the small colorful souvenirs she had picked out during their trip to the market into her belongings to keep them safe for the journey. Small figurines and a kitschy shot glass she got for her mother sat atop the clothes in her suitcase like a small casket. Alone in her room, while the girls packed their own things, Carmen finally let herself cry, as quietly as she could manage, over the suitcase, mourning the premature end of her family trip.

She then helped Izel with her packing, knowing she was bound to leave everything to the last minute just before leaving for the airport. She tried to help Luna, but she refused any help, which was fine. Luna was extraordinarily well organized for a girl her age. Carmen went to the kitchen and poured herself another shot of mezcal. The bottle was now only a quarter full. She walked around the house in the dark, trying to make a mental checklist of what she had to do tomorrow morning. They had a long journey ahead of them. They wouldn't be landing at JFK until around midnight.

Someone knocked on the door. The old woman's face flashed before her eyes. Her breathing became shallow. She had to calm down, think. Deep breath in, look for a weapon. She took several slow, deep breaths. She couldn't let her nerves get the best of her. She heard another knock on the door. She stood up, took a broom, and headed slowly toward the door and opened it abruptly, holding the broomstick firmly in her right hand.

"My child, sorry to drop by so late at night," said Verón, stepping into the house, "You don't have to sweep. I believe these rentals have a cleaning staff for after guests leave."

Carmen sighed, feeling the cold sweat on her face. She laughed.

"No, Father, I was . . . getting ready for tomorrow's flight. Come in."

"I'm so sorry about what happened. Seriously, your boss has made a big mistake. I don't think there's anyone more capable than you to finish this project. And the people here were just starting to grow fond of you."

"Thank you, Father, but it might have been just too little, too late."

"That's the way things are. But I wanted to see you personally to wish you safe travels and let you know I'm here for you. Do you need a ride to Mexico City tomorrow?"

"No, Father. It's all right. We're set up with a car."

"And how do you feel?"

"What can I say, Father? Disappointed, tired, but more than anything, confused by everything I've seen."

"What have you seen? The workers' sexist behavior? Crime? Not so confusing around here, sadly."

"That as well, but . . . I'm a little embarrassed, but I've seen, um, apparitions? When we spoke at the abbey, I didn't dare tell you, but they've been happening more often. I've seen them, and the girls have too. We saw an old lady who suddenly transformed into a skeleton. You're going to think I'm mad, Father, but it's been more than once that we've seen things that are . . . supernatural. Do you think I'm going crazy?"

Verón meditated on this for a moment, resting his chin on his left hand. Carmen stood up to make herself some coffee.

"Can I offer you some coffee or mezcal?"

"Both please. Thanks." Verón stood up and caught up with her in the kitchen. "It isn't crazy, what you're telling me. You're not the first to speak of such things."

"What can it be? I spoke to Quauhtli and Yoltzi, his friend, who's like a seer or something. They think it's spirits."

"And what are they proposing?"

"They said I had to protect Luna, but they didn't really seem like they knew what protecting her actually looked like. It was all very vague. Nothing really made sense to me, but maybe that's just the cultural divide."

"I'm not a big believer in exorcisms, but it might be a good time to try something like it to see if it helps."

"We're about to leave, Father. Honestly, I just think it's stress. You know? Since we've gotten here, I've done nothing but work and worry about the girls. At first I was so excited to bring them along with me, but the more posters of missing girls I saw, the more terrified I became day by day. It's no wonder I might've started seeing things that weren't there. Hopefully, this will all be over when we're home."

"Let's hope that's the case."

They clinked their glasses of coffee and a touch of mezcal to good times ahead. Then Verón stood up and said goodbye.

"It's late, Carmen. I should be getting home and you have to rest before your flight. Take care."

He hugged her and left.

Now alone, Carmen let herself drop to the couch and covered her face with her hands. She had a headache, which wasn't surprising considering her anxiety followed by a couple of mezcal shots. She then heard a shrill murmur, like an insect or a faraway phone conversation. She thought it might be the girls, talking to someone or playing some video game. Carmen looked around, but she didn't want to turn the lights on, so she remained on the couch. She then clearly heard a high-pitched voice speaking in an unknown language. She walked toward Luna's door and heard her speaking to someone.

"Luna, who are you talking to this late at night?" she asked through the closed door.

The voices continued, and Luna didn't reply. Carmen imagined her daughter must've been talking in her sleep. Perhaps she should leave her alone. Surely, it was nothing to worry about. But the noise coming from her room didn't feel quite human, like the voice of something singing off-key and speaking at the same time.

"Luna, what are you doing?" she said, quietly but firmly.

The voice grew louder. She heard, clearly, "Lárgate, puta," in a low grumble, as if someone were speaking with their mouth full, followed by high-pitched laughter, like the voices of little girls, the sounds elongated and distorted while saying, "Fuck off, whore," in Spanish.

"What did you say?" Carmen tried opening the door, but it was locked. She knocked twice, firmly but careful not to wake up Izel.

"Lárgate, puta," she heard again, clearly this time. The laughter continued, with a chorus of voices joining in.

The words hit Carmen like a brick. For what had to be the first time ever raising Luna, she was absolutely speechless, her mouth agape. Her sweet little Luna had hardly ever even talked back to her. Suddenly she was shouting depraved insults at her through locked doors? The shock of such words escaping Luna's mouth had Carmen almost tearing the handle off the door.

"Luna! Open this door right now," she struggled with the knob while trying to remember where she kept her key.

"Luna!" she yelled, no longer worried about waking Izel, or even the neighbors for that matter.

The door opened. Luna came out, rubbing the sleep out of her eyes, a bewildered look on her face.

"Why did you lock the door? Who are you talking to? I heard cussing." She couldn't stop asking questions out of nerves.

"I left the door locked by accident. I wasn't talking?"

"I heard it clearly. Someone was cussing."

"I don't know, Mom," she said, and headed back to her bed. The phone was turned on and a video was playing.

Carmen grabbed it as if she were handling a mouse, pinched between her fingers. The screen featured a skinned face, skeleton-like, laughing and saying something incomprehensive, while the shreds of skin moved like papier-mâché.

"What is this?" Carmen asked, nearly dropping the phone in fear.

"It's a TikTok. I must have fallen asleep while watching it."

"Is this the kind of stuff you're watching?" She looked again and saw on the screen two girls with their faces painted like skeletons, saying, "Trick or treat," and then bursting into laughter. The short video would then begin its next loop again and again. The recognizable score from the shower scene in *Psycho* was playing in the background.

"It's a TikTok, Mom. That's it. Can I go back to sleep now?"

"Yes, yes, I'm sorry. It's just the volume was too loud. That's all."

Luna was back asleep. Carmen kissed her forehead, left the room, and closed the door. She took a deep breath and sighed—she knew she had heard something. Even if it was muffled on the other side of the door, it sounded completely different. Her brain felt full of anxious static as she considered the possibility that she was so on edge she was actually beginning to hear things that weren't there. She went back to the living room, looking for her mezcal shot. She picked it up and downed it in one gulp. *Am I drinking too much?* she wondered. As she put the glass down, she saw the same skinned face she thought she'd seen in Luna's phone reflected in the bottom of the glass. Her breath caught in her throat and her muscles spasmed with the shock, the glass falling to the floor.

"I need to lie down," she muttered to herself, "my mind is playing tricks on me. I just need to lie down."

Her hands were shaking, she felt she had lost her balance and could not stand up. Between the mezcal and her terrible nerves, her legs had turned to jelly. She stayed there for what seemed a long while until she was able to finally pull herself to her feet. She didn't know what was scarier, the things she kept seeing out of the corner of her eye or the idea that in the tailspin her life had been thrown into she was losing control of her own mind as well.

Dragging herself to her room she counted her blessings that they needed to stay there for only one more night and would hopefully never have to think about this place again, even if it was because she was being effectively demoted. Collapsing on the bed she realized she was even afraid to turn the lights off.

She swore she heard something move underneath the bed, something hiding from the light, a cockroach perhaps or even a rat scurrying for cover in the dark. She wanted so badly to ignore it, to just have the day be over. All she wanted to focus on now was the flight she had to catch the next day.

Let the owner handle it. Or the next tenants. I don't fucking care, just not me.

But the sound kept going back and forth under the bed like it wanted her attention. Her heart was racing so hard she began to worry it might seize up. Was she old enough yet to have a heart attack? The skittering under the bed continued. Whatever was under there, Carmen was convinced that if she woke up to it crawling on her, she might really go into cardiac arrest with the amount of stress she was already under. She shifted her weight on the bed and started to roll over.

The room was silent. Carmen tried to listen for the rustling.

Nothing.

Finally, she dared to put one foot on the floor, looking around, wishing to have at least a broomstick to defend herself. She walked, tiptoeing out of her room, trying to fly, like when she was a child imagining the floor was lava. Dashing to the kitchen, Carmen grabbed the broom and when she passed the counter, a glint caught her eye, and she once again armed herself with the chef's knife. She couldn't picture herself stabbing a rat, but there was no other choice. She came back, tiptoeing again, trying to make as little noise as possible. She felt a bit silly armed with a broom and a knife, trying to hunt a tiny pest. Squatting, she swiped under her bed with the broom, not hitting a thing. Wiggling the broomstick around, trying to coax whatever had been scuttling around to at least leave her room, she heard something behind her. She stood up and looked around, holding the knife in her hands. She saw something move under the wardrobe. The gap was too small to fit the broom, so Carmen inched closer to get a better look at whatever it had been.

Something looked back at her. An eye opened in the darkness and blinked.

Carmen let out a small yelp and jumped back, frantically waving the broom in front of her.

"Shoo, get away from here, you bastard," she said, forgetting that the girls were sleeping, and she sliced the air with the knife. She then stopped, imagining the rat might catch up with her and bite her hand. She imagined getting rabies, tetanus, or God knows how many horrible maladies, but she was the most horrified by the idea of its tiny teeth sinking into her skin, tearing at a vein or a tendon. She tensed her arm and stood up. She let the broom drop, and it was right then that the animal—the rat or whatever it was—escaped. Carmen couldn't see what it was. She sat on the floor panting. Setting the knife by the broom on the ground, she pulled herself back into bed and fell asleep with the lights on, eager and ready to be done with her day.

15

"Quauhtli, sorry to call you so late at night."

He remained silent, dazed and a little annoyed at being woken up by the ringing of the phone, but recognized Yoltzi's voice.

"I wasn't even asleep. I'm usually clipping my nails at . . ." he looked at his clock, "four in the morning. Excellent timing."

"I'm sorry, but this couldn't wait."

"Go on." He stretched his arm, looking for the glass of water he usually left on his nightstand. He reached it and finished it in one gulp.

"I had a nightmare."

"I didn't know we were waking each other up to talk about nightmares now. In that case, I—"

"Do you remember the butterfly swarm that attacked the square last week?" she interrupted him, not really appreciating his efforts to lighten up the mood.

"I remember you telling me about it."

"Butterflies, Quauhtli, and tzitzimimeh. I can't believe I didn't realize it sooner. I hadn't connected the dots."

"The what? How? Which dots? I don't know if I'm still dreaming or what you're telling me is too strange."

"Do you remember Itzpapálotl? The obsidian butterfly?"

"Of course I do, but why?"

"A tzitzimitl, goddess of war and human sacrifices. Don't you agree that this is related to what's happening to the Luna girl? A skeleton with obsidian blades instead of wings. An apparition with an invisibility cloak."

"What can I say? That's true, but she was also the goddess of renewal, of change. She's the one who transforms and allows us to become better people."

"In my nightmare, I was with Luna at the square when a wave of black butterflies fell upon us, cutting everything they touched with the blade of their wings, like knives. I tried to protect her, shielding her with my body, feeling their wings brush past me, slicing my back open. But I never let go. Until one of the butterflies perched itself in front of me, and transformed into Itzpapálotl, and asked me to hand her the girl, that she was trying to protect her. The other butterflies kept slicing me open—my arms, my face, my legs—the cuts deeper every time. I tried to cover my face with my hands, but they sliced my fingers off one by one. I watched the stubs without pain, only fury at not being able to protect the girl and having to hand her over. Then I woke up."

"It's just a dream, Yoltzi. Don't worry."

"All the signs are there. The gods have always communicated with mortals through dreams."

"I think that's more like once in a blue moon," said Quauhtli, losing his patience. "Most dreams are just that, dreams."

"You don't believe me?"

"I believe you dreamed that, but I'm not sure that's meant to be a message or that there's something you're supposed to do."

"Dreams are often revelations."

"Not every dream."

Quauhtli had a complicated relationship with his culture's myths. He didn't question that the forces that his ancestors recognized as gods—the ones to whom they offered prayers, offerings, and sacrifices—were represented in the real world. What seemed to his early ancestors to be gods were in reality natural and psychological phenomena yet to be understood and, in that sense, the gods were still real today. Quauhtli saw the reality of nature and the movement of culture and the Earth as the movements of gods as real.

Yoltzi was more in sync with the stranger, immaterial side of spiritual manifestations, and knew how to connect them to this or that god, spirit, or specter—as she liked to call them. They sometimes argued when she talked about gods from different mythologies as if they belonged to the same pantheon or tradition. Quauhtli had lost his temper often when she mixed up Chichimeca legends with Toltec traditions, forcing all her interpretations within a Nahua framework. This was an example, in a way, of how she believed in a general theory of Mexican gods. He told her this one day and she didn't respond. Maybe it offended her. It was often hard to discern what Yoltzi thought and felt.

"Just let me think about it then. Let's speak tomorrow. But since you already have me awake, there was something I wanted to tell you. In the abbey while remodeling, we discovered a cellar with ancient objects. There was a tlapalxoktli."

"Really?"

"Yes, I'm pretty sure."

"Do you have it?"

"No, I preferred to leave it there and Father Verón, who's the church's representative and administrates the construction, decided to leave it where they found it and seal the crypt back up."

"That's another sign, Quauhtli. It has to be. Something like that, an old relic of ancient Nahua culture, buried under the bricks of the church resurfacing after all that time? It must be connected somehow to all that I've been seeing. We should destroy it."

"They're sealing it away. Trapping it back where it came from. If it wanted to resurface, it won't get its wish for a very long time."

"All right. I guess. I'm sorry I woke you up to tell you about a dream."

"It's okay, never mind. I have work to do. I'm going to use this time to get ahead on some carvings that I want to finish and deliver this week."

Quauhtli hung up and stood, stretching his legs. His house was small and humble. He had lived by himself for years. He didn't have a partner and wasn't looking for one. He was happy the way he was. The journey back to sobriety, sanity, and stability had been difficult and full of quitting, abandonment, and disillusionment. He'd been focusing on manual labor, on his wood carvings, mosaics, and stonework. They were arts and trades he'd learned from his grandfather. His father, Cuauhtemoc, had also been an artisan—he painted and sculpted with exceptional talent, but as often happens, poverty, injustice, and scarcity got the best of him. It wasn't often that Quauhtli's and his father's skills were remunerated fairly, as there are only a few legal protections for the trade. There weren't many unions to join in the area, after all. A colleague whom his father trusted suggested investing in woodwork machinery to make more pieces faster. Cuauhtemoc withdrew all his savings, asked for a loan, and gave his friend all the money to ship in some shop machines. Cuauhtemoc never saw him again. This con left him broke and emotionally defeated. It wasn't long before he lost his shop and had to work for other people for pennies. He started drinking uncontrollably.

Quauhtli, who must have been around twelve at the time, wanted to help, but his father wanted him to focus on his studies. He didn't want Quauhtli to end up doing crafts like him. Since he was good at math, Cuauhtemoc was hoping he'd become an accountant or an engineer to help the family. Quauhtli stood out as a brilliant student through the years, got accepted into UNAM (the National Autonomous University of Mexico) and left for Mexico City where he lived with a cousin by Azcapotzalco. It was a sketchy area far away from school, but he figured it out, lent a helping hand at his cousin's store, studied, and went to school in the Accounting Department. Meanwhile, the situation at home deteriorated, worsening every day Quauhtli was away. What's more, Quauhtli was terribly unhappy with his major, which bored him to death. Without letting anyone know, he enrolled in the Science Department to major in physics. At first, he thought he'd be able to sustain the double major, but after two semesters he realized it would be impossible to do so while working for his cousin. Plus, he had no interest in punching numbers. So, he dropped accounting and dedicated himself to physics. But things started to go downhill as he increasingly relied on amphetamines, drugs, and alcohol.

Despite his mother's attempts to hide it, he knew his father kept drinking himself to unconsciousness, but wasn't aware he had heart failure. One Monday morning Quauhtli got the call, they'd finally found him dead, lying on the street among the filth with enough booze in his blood for a whole Mexican wedding party. An expected but wholly undeserved death for what was once a noble man. Quauhtli was devastated, and this hastened his own downfall.

Quauhtli took a shower and made himself some coffee, forgetting about his past for a moment. He had some day-old bread in a basket. It was stale, but it was better than nothing. He sat in the living room, turned on the TV, and had breakfast around six in the morning while watching the news. They'd uncovered a scandal in Pemex, a group of senators were punching it out. The air quality was terrible, pollution levels were "sky-high" according to the host, who thought himself hilarious. Local news reported three more women missing. The usual. Everyday tragedies. They showed some photos from a mass grave a few miles from his place. Five bodies, mutilated beyond recognition, and they were blaming the narcos. The camera was zooming in on some small green pebbles as a man explained that all the dead had one beneath their tongue. Quauhtli saw the stones and jumped out of his couch.

"Jade."

He abandoned his coffee, put on a jacket, and left in a hurry. He climbed into his run-down pickup truck and drove until he reached the mass grave. The forensics team were still uncovering the corpses. There was police tape surrounding the area. Quauhtli approached them.

"Epa, amigo," he yelled at one of the technicians who was carefully digging around the human remains with a small shovel.

"Yes?" he replied, pausing his work and walking toward him.

"Did you see the stones that the corpses had in their mouths?" Quauhtli asked.

"Yes."

"Were they green?"

"Yes."

"It's kind of odd for them to put jades in the victims' mouths, don't you think?

"Not really. We've seen it often in this area. We suspect it to be the local hit men's calling card around here, like cutting their index finger or pulling out their liver. Stuff like that, you know? And we usually—um, you're not related to the victims, are you?" he asked, suddenly realizing that he might have been oversharing.

"Fortunately, no."

The man pulled out a cigarette and lit it.

"Thank goodness."

"Could I see one of those jades?"

"What for? That's evidence, compadre. No can do."

Quauhtli pulled out a one-hundred-pesos bill from his wallet. He didn't have much more. He showed it to him.

"I just want to see them."

"Make it two of those and we have a deal. Are you one of those relic collectors?"

"Yes, let's call it that. I collect . . . signs."

The technician discreetly took the money and headed back to the site where they were digging. He looked around, and when no one was watching, he opened a bag and pulled out an object. He walked back toward Quauhtli, offering him his hand with the stone hidden in the nook of his palm. Quauhtli shook his hand and kept the jade, dropping it into his pocket.

"For your collection. We have more than enough. One less won't hurt."

"Thanks, good luck."

Quauhtli headed back to his truck. He turned on the ignition and headed toward the abbey. Upon reaching his destination, he parked, turned off the pickup truck, and took the stone out of his pocket. It was oval-shaped, smooth on one side and round on the other. Someone had shaped it specifically for Nahua funerary rituals, chipping small symbols into the delicate stone. Faces, skulls, crude imitations of the kinds of ritual faces one found on the walls of Aztec ruins or death masks. Quauhtli chipped at the stone with his own fingernail and flaked off pieces of the gem. It was fake.

The ones responsible for this awful massacre hadn't been specters, just men. What Quauhtli held in his hand was nothing more than some kind of sick calling card he figured they left at the scenes of their crimes. He threw the awful thing aside, furious. Furious at himself for driving all the way out here on a hunt for hocus-pocus stones. Even more furious that the symbols of his people had been so reduced to spectacles of death and dismemberment. Even people who lived in the shadow of the Nahuatl culture only saw it as people running around and ripping hearts out. The cartels must think of themselves as some kind of modern Aztec warriors if they leave behind things like that Halloween store crap bracelet.

Quauhtli turned on the engine of his car and drove away, leaving the stone in the dirt.

16

A cabby had his arm around the neck of an airport bellhop, who was elbowing the cabby in the stomach. Carmen watched the fight from the Uber they had taken to the airport, now stuck in the traffic caused by the small crowd that had gathered to look on. The men broke free from each other and tumbled to the ground, grappling amid gum spots and cigarette butts as the onlooking strangers cheered, the airport's sterile monotony relenting to the familiar violence of the streets. Their cars idled on the road, belching exhaust.

"Get his ass!"

"Stop being such a pussy and hit him!"

"Go! Go! Fuck 'im up!"

Carmen didn't see the traffic moving anytime soon and, with their flight time getting closer, she leaned forward and tapped the driver.

"We can get out here," she said in Spanish.

The driver opened the back door of the SUV and got out to help them out with their luggage. Unsurprisingly, there weren't any bellhops available to give them a hand; their many redcaps swam in the sea of people around the brawl. Carmen tried to get the attention of one nearby, but the fight seemed worth more than a few pesos in tips. One of the red hats entered the center of the ring, joining the fray. Already tired and frustrated, she didn't have much sympathy for the collective desire for bloodshed. The men cheered louder. Carmen didn't look to see what had happened, turning instead to the girls.

"Screw this, girls. Izel, you and I just each grab two suitcases and let's get going."

She thanked their driver and started walking toward the door, reminding Luna to hold on to her arm and Izel to stay in front where she could see her as they passed through the crowd. The bodies flowed around them, all jostling for a better view of the fight or to join it themselves. As the shoulders of people parted and closed again, the sea of onlookers seemed to open for a moment revealing a mop of thick, dirty gray hair shrouding a terribly wrinkled face looking away from the center, instead tracking the girls as they passed through the airport doors.

Izel stopped cold for a moment, dropping back next to her mom and sister.

"Is that the same old woman from last time?" Izel whispered in Luna's ear.

"Yes," she replied, without looking back.

Izel felt her skin prickle with a cold fear, "How did she get here?"

"I don't know but I think she's here with us."

"What do you mean? Like she's seeing us off? We don't even know her."

"No, she's coming all the way to New York."

"No way! If I see that woman on our plane, I'm gonna find the air marshal or something. Someone with a gun."

Luna was now too busy wrestling the largest suitcase with its loose wheel to answer. Carmen waited for them to catch up. Izel, seeing the stress and exhaustion on her mother's face, didn't think it was a good idea to mention the old lady. She wasn't even sure it was the same person. *How many old ladies look the same when they're dressed like that?* she thought, recalling the woman's outfit: covered in layers of sweaters and what looked like a shawl. *Maybe even abuela Alma would look the same in an outfit like that.*

"It's crazy, isn't it?" Carmen's voice broke their collective silence, "What a strange way to say goodbye to Mexico . . ."

The girls didn't reply. Carmen was surprised that Luna, usually a chatterbox, didn't have anything to say about what they'd just witnessed. Looking over to Izel, she recognized a glazed and crestfallen look on her face. Sometimes she seemed to forget how old Izel was now, old enough to understand the situation awaiting the family back in New York, to understand that Carmen might be looking for a job soon. The look on Izel's face was so recognizable by virtue of Carmen seeing the same look in the mirror that morning that she began to worry she was infecting Izel with her own worries. She reached over and gave her eldest daughter's arm a soft squeeze.

"Are you alright? You look sad to be leaving when I thought you couldn't wait to go home," said Carmen, smiling to reassure Izel she was joking.

"It's nothing, Mom. I'm okay."

"Are you going to miss Mexico? You've been speaking more Spanish lately."

"Um. Not really. I'm glad to be going back. But I *am* trying to speak more Spanish."

"How about you, Luna?"

"I'm okay, too, Mom. I wish we could stay longer, though."

"I understand. You know I had no say in this. We have to go back, but the good news is you have a few weeks left before school starts. You can go to the pool, hang out with your friends."

"I'm not really in the mood for swimming."

The rest of their time waiting in line was spent in silence, only briefly speaking to the attendant at the ticketing desk as they handed over their checked baggage. The wait in the security line was similarly lacking in any conversation. The three of them stewed in their private thoughts. An officer called them forth with his gloved hand and directed them to one of the conveyor belts. Luna put her orange backpack on it before anyone else and basically dashed through the body scanner, slipping past an older man who was next in line.

"Hey!" one of the officers called out. "You gotta wait your turn, little lady!"

They turned to Carmen, "Keep your kid where you can control her, please."

Carmen was taken aback and ashamed to be one of *those parents* at an airport. She'd never had to discipline her daughters in public and didn't know whether to say something, apologize, pretend nothing had happened, or better yet, pretend it wasn't even her daughter. Izel was also startled by her sister's behavior. It wasn't rare to see her run, skip, and jump full of energy and joy, but she'd never seen her disrespect anyone, or act spoiled. Maybe it wasn't a big deal, maybe it was a reflex, if a bit disrespectful, brought upon by the tiredness and frustration of going back so soon. Luna was definitely at home in Mexico; she was in her element. It might take her a while to accept her life back in the suburbs.

When Luna's backpack rolled out of the X-ray machine, one of the officers grabbed it.

"Whose bag is this?" she asked.

"Mine!" Luna yelled.

"There's something suspicious in it."

"Suspicious? It's a little girl's backpack," Carmen said, catching up with her daughter.

Luna looked uneasy as the officer unzipped the backpack, removing another bag from within containing an object wrapped in newspaper. The other officers looked over at their colleague's hands as she unwrapped it, finally revealing a plastic jar full of what looked like rust-red woodchips.

"What *is* this?" she asked.

Carmen couldn't figure out what it was either. Izel looked down and away, studying her shoes. Luna blushed but watched the officer intently. The officer opener the container carefully and produced a fried cricket.

"Chapulines?" she was perplexed, but quickly resumed her authoritative tone. "This is not allowed."

"Why not? Is it illegal? It's not a liquid and it's not toxic," Luna retorted.

The officer looked at her colleagues, at a loss for words.

"You can't transport something like this in an open container."

"It was a closed container until you opened it."

"They won't let you keep it over there, I promise this isn't making it through American customs."

"Then I'll eat them on the plane. Why can't we take it with us?"

"Airline policies."

"I'm sorry, you're telling me there's a policy banning fried crickets on a plane?" Carmen interjected.

"They're insects."

"That we can agree on. But they're food. They're dead and cooked. Don't you know that insects are the future of human nutrition?"

The officer remained silent. She searched for her colleagues' eyes, asking for backup. One of them joined the debate.

"You just can't, ma'am."

Carmen was tired. The line only seemed to grow longer, and she could sense their annoyance at being delayed over a jar of crickets.

"All right." She took the jar from the officer and turned to Luna. "Do you want to eat them here?"

"I'm not hungry. I want to take them with me. They're mine."

Carmen raised her head and rolled her eyes. Luna grabbed a fistful of crickets and ate them. Several travelers waiting for their turn stared at her in horror, disbelief, and a trace of disgust. Carmen handed the jar with the remaining crickets to the officer.

"What? They're just crickets!" Luna said, practically yelling at a staring traveler.

The officer closed the backpack and handed it to Luna. Izel grabbed her bag and walked far enough ahead that she could pretend she didn't know them. Carmen grabbed her stuff from the conveyor belt and pulled Luna along next to her.

"Thank you very much," she said, resentfully.

They walked until they reached a crowded bench, where they put on their shoes and fixed their bags.

"What's going on, Luna? You practically shoved that man in line out of your way."

"I don't know. I didn't mean to do anything wrong."

"Don't worry. I'm not going to scold you, but I just wanted to ask."

"They took away my crickets. It's so unfair."

"I know. But it's to be expected."

When they arrived at their gate, Luna took a seat on the ground and didn't move the whole time they waited. Carmen watched her daughter stare into the boarding screen practically motionless and thought she should say something, but was unsure how to talk to Luna when she was like this. It felt like she hadn't seen her this upset since she was a toddler. Deciding to leave Luna alone for the meantime, Carmen turned to Izel.

"So!" she said, cheerily. "What's the first thing you're most excited about doing when we get back?"

"Just hanging out with my friends, really."

"You gonna go to the pool? Or are you also not in the mood for swimming?"

"I don't know, maybe? I was thinking we could go to the city and watch some summertime plays in the park."

"That's a nice plan. I just need to check where I'm standing with my job. Hey, if I get fired, we can watch all the plays you want!" She laughed humorlessly. "How does that sound, Luna? Would you want to go to the theater with us?"

"I don't care about theater." Luna didn't turn away from the boarding screen.

They boarded the plane as the last rays of daylight were swallowed up by rain clouds.

"I hope our flight isn't delayed by this storm. We're getting in so late as is," Carmen noted as soon as she heard the thunderclap above.

Rain drummed on the thin metal of the jetway as they shuffled onto the plane with the rest of the passengers and settled into their seats. The sky had been torn open by the thunder and their plane was pinned at the gate for an hour waiting for the storm to ease off. Eventually, they left the gate despite the rain hardly letting up. The city had uneasily relinquished them.

The plane shuddered and jolted as they climbed through the roiling clouds, but smoothed out as they reached altitude. Izel grabbed a book and tried to read, but she was too tired and distracted to focus. Struggling to keep her eyes open, let alone following the words on the page, she noticed that Luna, who she'd assumed was asleep already, was still awake—she just wasn't moving a muscle. Luna had been sitting stockstill in the seat next to Izel, staring straight ahead at the black screen in front of her.

"Luna, did you want to watch a movie or a show? Is the screen broken or something?"

"No."

"Do you want to do something? Play a video game maybe?"

"No."

"What's wrong?"

"Nothing's wrong. I know how to turn on a screen for myself if I feel like it. Just read your book or something."

"Okay, jeez, never mind."

Normally set anxiously on edge by turbulence and flying through inclement weather, Carmen was too exhausted to be afraid for very long. Her head lolled to the side and she dozed off listening to the gentle roar of the wind around the fuselage and the quiet, sibling bickering of her daughters. She slipped into the formless dark limbo between wakefulness and dreams.

Thunder clapped just outside the plane, jolting it violently to one side and snapping Carmen awake. Her skin prickled with adrenaline from the startle, unclear how long she had been out. She looked around the cabin, sure to see the rest of the passengers in a similar state of worry and disorientation, but they weren't. The whole cabin was dead asleep, unbothered by the violent turbulence that had roused her. Lightning sparked outside, illuminating the cabin like a flashbulb. Carmen braced her nerves for another thunderclap, but it didn't come. The lightning seemed to hit just feet away from them, though. On the other side now, it struck again, mute. The roar of the wind outside was gone as well.

A gentle tinkling of seashells and the snapping of twigs were the only sounds to break through the silence of the cabin, coming from Carmen's left. She realized that in all this time, in all her worry, she hadn't even looked across the aisle to see if the girls were all right yet, but the thought of turning her head now, toward the clattering shells, froze her heart with indescribable panic. Motherly instinct began to triumph over her personal fears, though, and she slowly turned her head across the aisle.

Luna lay against the seat, her head snapped back and the veins of her neck bulging with strain. From an indiscernible place in Luna's chest grew a pulsing, metastatic black mass of tar, blood, and branches slipping against itself as it shifted and grew upward into a horrible humanoid form. Carmen was breathless, staring at a twisted and skeletal face from which the skin, gray and diseased, sloughed away like dry leaves. It leaned forward, arching itself over and around Izel while Carmen sat frozen and helpless across the aisle as it wrapped its claw-like fingers around her eldest, looking her in the eyes. Its horrid face cracked, grinning widely, showing jagged black teeth that shone like obsidian as the lightning silently flashed again. Suddenly, bursting from its back, two massive, black butterfly wings unfurled, bringing with them a final, deafening clap of thunder.

She heard Izel distantly say, "Ow! Stop it!"

Another jolt of turbulence shook Carmen from her dream. Groggy and with a cold sweat on her brow she looked around in a panic, seeing other passengers looking back at her and her daughters.

"What the hell's gotten into you?" said Izel.

Carmen snapped her head to check on the girls only to see that their bickering had devolved into violence as she slept. Izel was shoving Luna's arms away from her as Luna kicked at her older sister's legs. Carmen was immediately flooded with embarrassment and snapped at the two of them

"Stop it. Stop it!" she shouted in a whisper. "What happened? Did you take a page out of the cabbies' book? You should be ashamed of yourselves. I never thought I'd have to worry about you two acting like this. Especially in public . . ."

Izel jumped in. "I didn't even start it! I just accidentally bumped her when I dozed off and she started getting all pissy."

"Maybe you should've just apologized and watched where your bony elbows were going!"

"Stop it, both of you! You are not gonna fight on the plane, just go back to reading or whatever you were doing. We can talk about this later."

The girls both pushed themselves into their seats and proceeded to spend the rest of the flight in silence. Carmen couldn't believe the girls had been fighting. They hadn't had a fight in years. Izel usually just ignored her sister, but maybe now, as Luna was getting older, they felt a little more rivalrous toward each other. Things like this were a bit of a mystery to Carmen as an only child. The dynamics of siblings was always something she went to the girls' father about, but maybe Alma would have some insight when they got back home. At the same time, Carmen couldn't help but think it equally funny and disconcerting to have heard sweet, bubbly Luna say something so mean to her sister. Luna had apparently developed a mouth for comebacks Carmen hadn't heard until just now. The girls were probably just stressed from the last few days and would even out once they were off the plane and back at the house.

All three of them were wide awake for the rest of the flight. Izel pretended to lose herself in a movie but watched her sister from the corner of her eye. Luna remained still, as if in a trance, uncharacteristically quiet after her outburst. Carmen tried going back to sleep but found herself wide awake no matter how long her eyes were closed. She stayed like that until the cabin lights came on and their descent toward JFK airport was announced. As the bulkhead opened on the ground, Carmen stood up, caressed Luna's head, and smiled at Izel.

"Is everything okay?" she asked, yawning.

They didn't answer.

"Are you still mad at each other? I don't want to go back home with both of you in a bad mood."

Izel stood up, grabbed her backpack, and turned her back on them. Luna stood up and got ready to get off the plane.

"You're not talking to me now too? What is this all about?"

They left the plane, slowly, went past immigration, baggage claim, and the TSA check. Luna was tense, hugging her backpack against her chest, probably afraid of another airport official taking it away again after the cricket mishap. A TSA officer with deep under eye bags was leaning on a table, as if he couldn't stand upright without the support. He asked them whether they'd brought anything from Mexico.

"Tequila? Food?"

Carmen simply shook her head and the officer signaled them to keep walking toward the pickup area. Standing on the sidewalk, Carmen pulled out her phone to call her mother and let her know that they were ready. Soon Alma pulled up in Carmen's car and shuffled around to give her granddaughters a hug, planting a big kiss on the forehead of her youngest and ushering the three of them into the vehicle. Carmen slipped into the driver's seat.

The traffic was light at that late hour and they were making good time.

"I wish you had just let us take the train back home, Amá. You didn't have to drive all the way to the city for us."

"Nonsense, mija! It's late at night, I'm not such an old woman that I can't pick my granddaughters up from the airport."

"I know, I know. Thank you." Carmen turned her head a bit, talking to the girls in the back, "You girls hungry?" Neither of them had touched the airplane food, the pasta or the chicken. "We can order a pizza or Chinese. What do you think?"

"Ah!" Alma interjected, waving her hand, "I already made food for you before I left. Just have to heat it up a bit when we get back." She turned around in her seat and, seeing Izel deeply interested in her phone, looked at Luna and added, "So! How was your first trip to Mexico? You miss your abuela?"

Luna smiled coyly, nodding her head before the smile fell from her face, "It was fun but . . ."

"But what?"

Carmen's ears perked up.

"Everything changed over there. Nothing will ever be like it was before," said Luna.

Alma turned and looked at Carmen somewhat concerned.

"Everything will be fine, sweetie. I know I joked about losing my job, but we'll all be okay." Carmen said.

"I don't know," Luna replied.

Alma spent the rest of the car ride trying to get Luna to talk more about their trip to Mexico, but, as time wore on, Luna's answers became shorter and more disinterested. Carmen felt relieved when they finally pulled into their driveway, especially looking forward to peace and quiet after unpacking and going back to their usual lives. She wasn't too worried about work right then. Carmen and Izel had a good dinner, but Luna, who still seemed absent and moody, barely touched her food. Alma noticed and tried to ask her what was wrong, but Luna just said she was too tired to eat and carried her bags to her room.

"We had so many adventures. Luna will need some more time to process all of it. She's very tired, and the time went by so quickly it's hard to remember all of it. But the memories will come to her eventually."

Izel soon followed Luna's lead after saying goodnight to Alma. Carmen stayed with her mother in the kitchen, but she didn't want to go into details about their early return. She told her they'd had issues with construction, but her mom was worried about Luna.

"She looks different, no? More mature, maybe?" Alma said.

"I think she's just tired, Amá, and maybe a bit grumpy. She didn't want to come back. You know her, she's Mexican through and through. She was so excited to finally go there and I had to bring her back early."

"I've just never seen her like this."

"Don't worry. I'm sure once she settles back into homelife and gets some rest things will even out. It was a long trip, you know? I think they were just starting to get used to being down there when we had to leave and, you said it yourself, maybe Luna's just getting a little early onset teen angst," Carmen said. Then she opened the liquor cabinet and poured herself a tequila.

"What, no tequila for your mother?" asked Alma.

They drank as Carmen told her about what had happened on the job as well as recounting their dinner with the Nahua.

"Long story short, I think I was sabotaged by that misogynistic bastard of a foreman. But even on top of that, the craziest part of the trip had to be those two coming over to seriously warn me they thought Luna was at risk of being possessed by evil, ancient forces or some crap like that. That aside, everything was normal."

Alma flapped her hand and chuckled. "Maybe the foreman was really just an evil spirit in disguise too!"

"See, Amá? I told you we saw it all. Even paranormal encounters!" said Carmen, laughing.

"Who are those people? Who did you associate with? I spent a lifetime living there and no one ever said crazy crap like that to me. If *your* abuela, mi madre, had heard someone come around our house talking about Aztec death gods and her kids . . . Well, I doubt they'd make it past the stoop before she grabbed a frying pan!" Alma cackled and pointed at Carmen with her glass before taking another sip.

Visions of old women in the desert and monsters on planes *were* truly ridiculous things to take seriously in any way. Carmen was an earnest woman and she had been under a lot of pressure back in Mexico. Part of her was almost a little happy she was taken out of that place if staying there meant more dreams and hallucinations from stress. Carmen laughed it all away and poured herself a final nightcap. Soon she'd turn in and try to get some rest before facing the day already threatening to break the horizon.

Taking the Metro North into the city again felt so extraordinarily unusual to Carmen, she nearly missed her stop after transferring to the subway system. It felt as if it'd been years since she'd last been in the city rather than a couple of months. Nothing felt familiar. Everything had changed, but she couldn't quite put her finger on how. Her days in Mexico had left a disproportionately large mark in her memory, as if she'd been there for decades. When she arrived at her office, she resumed her usual ritual of buying herself a latte and a newspaper before getting on the elevator. Sipping the latte in the elevator it tasted odd, almost greasy. *That overpriced café must have put oat milk or something weird in it*, she thought. She missed the taste of the Mexican coffee she'd make every morning in her old, trusty coffeepot. When she walked into the office, she felt a social chill. Most of her colleagues barely acknowledged her, as if she wasn't even there. Nobody asked how her trip was or how the project went. If word traveled around the office as fast as it usually did, they already knew this information. Sitting down at her desk, she wasn't sure where to begin. What work did she even have to do at this point? She had no project. Right as she was shuffling some random papers on her desk, her phone rang. It was her boss's secretary, Linda.

"Mr. Harper wants to see you now."

Carmen hung up without saying anything. She stood up but hesitated as to whether she should take her coffee with her or leave it there so it would cool down. She decided to take it with her. Maybe by holding a cup of coffee, it would make the meeting less intense than she was expecting.

"Good morning," Carmen said as she walked in.

"Carmen!" he said, feigning surprise and rolling the *r* of her name with exaggeration, a habit he saw as jocular and she felt as passively racist. "I'm so glad to see you. How was your trip back? Everything alright with the girls?"

"Everything was great, thanks. The girls are settling back into US life."

"I'm guessing you're wondering about your new responsibilities and what your job will look like now that you're back."

Carmen forced a smile.

"I want you to take it easy over the next couple of weeks while we assign you a new project. I'll have a meeting with the board in two weeks where we'll decide what that will be. For now, just focus on getting Sam up to speed before we send him down to Mexico to finish the project. You did a really great job getting this off the ground, so if you can make him as talented as you are in the next couple days before he heads south, things should work out fine."

Carmen knew this meant the board would decide whether she'd stay or be fired and her chances might be slim. The rest of the firm probably knew, too, unsure of whether or not to approach her with pity yet. She exhaled deeply, too stressed to hide her frustration, and stood up. Turning to look out the windows onto the city skyline from the twenty-fifth floor, Carmen noticed the strangest cloud she'd seen in her life.

"Thank you, Michael. I'll send Sam all my notes," she answered absently, giving a polite and professional smile as she stared out the window at the black mass hovering above the city. She almost jumped with surprise as it suddenly pulsed, spreading out into small black dots before reforming. Now that she had seen it as a swarm of something, she noticed its edges blurring and shaking like static as the blackness struggled to maintain its form above the city.

Harper followed Carmen's eyes and joined her at the window. "Huh. What the hell is that? They're not birds, are they?"

"Too small . . ." Carmen remembered Luna's drawing of the sky, one full of angry butterflies. "I think they're butterflies."

"I've never seen butterflies do that or moths or god knows what. I didn't know they swarmed like that," said Harper. "Have you seen something like that before?"

Carmen was entranced as the butterflies stretched their swarm into strange shapes in the sky. Harper didn't seem to think they were anything but the random movement of bugs in the sky. Meanwhile, the

black, beating bodies seemed to be speaking to her. Watching the pat-
terns the insects wove in the air, they looked like that of a forgotten
alphabet, a series of macabre ideograms that she couldn't read but could
simply sense were some sort of ominous communiqué, their repetitive
motions a simultaneous chant and ceremonial dance. More than ominous, they seemed to be an omen themselves, thousands of dark omens
cursing the sky and city in an unknown language of hieroglyphs.

"No. Never seen anything like it," she said, and left Harper's office.

When she got back to her desk, she called Alma. While dialing the
numbers, she thought about their conversation the night before, how
they had laughed off any notion of superstitions and curses of the old
country. She sipped her cold coffee and reminded herself that she wasn't
insane, only stressed. One time she had read that stressed people often
search for meaning or superstitious reasons for their dread. Maybe she
searched for her meaning in swarms of bugs. The phone began to ring
and she reigned in her imagination.

"Hi, Amá, just calling to check in and see how you and the girls are
doing."

"It's all good here. We're having breakfast soon. How's everything
with you?"

"Fine! Well, not really. I don't think it's *bad*, but I'm sure it's not
good. God, I don't know." She couldn't tell if she was talking about her
job or her mind. "I'll tell you about it when I see you. Just let me know
if I need to pick anything up on my way home."

Alma said goodbye and hung up the phone, turning back to the sim-
mering pan of salsa on the stove. She turned the flame down and scraped
a spoonful of adobo sauce into the pan. With Carmen already back at
work, Alma wanted her granddaughters to settle into their usual daily
routines with ease. She just wanted to make sure they felt like nothing
was changing too much and that started by filling the house with the
usual smell of Abuela Alma's Original Huevos Luneros. It was actually
just her huevos rancheros, but Luna's odd palate demanded one special
ingredient for her plate.

After Alma set another pan on the stove to heat for the eggs, she went upstairs to wake the girls with a knock on the door. Izel woke up in a bad mood, but hugged her abuela warmly on her way out of her room and downstairs. Alma got to Luna's door and knocked once, twice, before trying the doorknob only to find it locked.

"Lunita? Are you awake? Why's your door locked?"

Luna yelled from behind the closed door, "I'm allowed some privacy, aren't I?"

"Oh! Of course, mi amor. Well, since you're awake, come down for breakfast, okay?"

"Fine. I'll be down in a minute."

Alma joined Izel downstairs, where she fried some eggs for her and set a hot plate on the table.

"Is your sister alright? She seems a little ... I don't know," Alma asked quietly.

Izel just shrugged. "She's been like that since we had to leave Mexico. It's probably just a temper tantrum over the trip getting cut short."

They heard Luna finally descending the stairs. Alma put on a smile and slid Luna her huevos luneros as she sat down, huevos rancheros with a little anchovy on top of both eggs. Izel made a gagging noise and laughed at Luna's favorite breakfast. But Luna barely ate, pushing her food around with her fork, as if trying to decipher the mystery of her meal. She barely lifted her head to look at her sister and grandmother as she gave single-syllable answers to her grandmother's questions.

"Did you bring a lot of stuff from Mexico, Luna?"

"No."

"I thought you'd bring tons of crafts! Not even a souvenir for your old abuela?"

"No."

Alma looked at Izel, puzzled. Izel could only shrug in response.

"Your mom told me you met some interesting people who knew a lot about Nahua culture."

"Yes."

Luna pushed her still almost full plate away from her, then stood up and headed back upstairs to her room.

"Seriously, what's up with her?"

Izel only shrugged again.

The two of them tried to talk about something else as they cleaned up the kitchen, but they were too distracted by the noises coming out of Luna's room above: stomping on the floor, knocks on the wall, something being dragged, bumps, and strange creaks.

"*Now* what is she doing?" Alma was exasperated

"No clue. I heard it last night too."

Izel finished cleaning with Alma and leaned over the counter looking at her phone, swinging her feet off the ground and smiling. She looked up at her abuela and grinned.

"Soooo, I'm gonna head out."

Alma smiled back. "Oh, *really*? And where does my granddaughter have to run off to today on her first day back with her abuela?"

"I'm just gonna walk over to my friend Josh's house is all! I'll leave you his mom's number if you wanna call her and ask."

"Oh, I won't embarrass you. I trust you, but maybe I think that Josh isn't exactly just a 'friend.' You don't smile that wide when you go to see Halley, you know! Just be back by dark so we can all have a proper dinner together when your mom gets home."

Izel blushed and went to her room to get dressed. Even though Alma said she didn't need it, Izel left a note with Mrs. Rosenbaum's number on the kitchen counter as she headed out the door, giving her abuela another hug. The door closed behind Izel and Alma stuck the number to the fridge door with a magnet. Above her, the odd sounds continued emanating from Luna's room, distant and muffled through the ceiling. She figured if Luna was so dead set on having her privacy, perhaps it was best to give it to her and let her calm down a bit. After all, the girl had been through a lot the last couple of days.

Carmen finished out the rest of the day at the office, collecting all the emails and documentation that she had on the Abbey Hotel project and compiling them for her replacement. She was fully aware and even understanding of how office and corporate politics functioned, knowing

that there really wasn't any option but to send someone new to head up
the project on the ground after the scaffolding failure, but all the same,
she still resented Sam. More so, she found herself resenting the idea of
some gringo going to Mexico to help demolish an old abbey. It felt like
one symbol of colonization being refurbished by the new colonizers. At
least when she was involved it felt closer to a process of reclaiming the
land, now it was just the work of a Spanish man being replaced by an
American man giving instructions.

All the same, she cc'd Sam on everything he needed to know and
sent him a file of all the permits he'd have to reference once he got down
there. She also gave him a list of personnel on site with a "rude, pockets
money" note next to Joaquín's name. Carmen left a little bit after everyone else, hanging back to avoid sharing the elevator with anyone who
might ask about Mexico as well as to catch a train home that might have
an open seat.

Casting a premature twilight on the city, the sun had hidden behind
the Midtown buildings by the time Carmen stepped onto a train at Grand
Central. Sliding onto a seat, she got herself comfortable for the long commute back up to Newburgh and was shocked by how few people were
on a train so close to rush hour. It almost seemed unfair that she'd been
charged for a peak-traffic ticket. The train rolled out of the station and of
the city and, as they rumbled farther from Manhattan and the sun sank
lower in the sky, the few people in Carmen's train car slowly trickled out
their respective stations until it was just Carmen with a car all to herself.

She stared out the window at the sun setting over the other side of
the Hudson River as the sky grew increasingly dark. Watching the tree
line drift by, she suddenly saw movement, something flickering at the
edge of the orange sky and the dark silhouette of the trees. Her eyes
widened before squinting into the bright sun, trying to catch another
glimpse of what she had seen. A gap in the trees appeared where a power
line ran from the river's edge into the west and that's where she saw the
buzzing static of a black cloud. Her breath caught in her throat as she
briefly glimpsed the undulating black swarm outlined by the sun before
disappearing again into the dark shadow of the tree line, which now
became blurred and fuzzy.

The train rocked around a bend and an embankment blocked her view across the water. Among the sounds of rumbling machinery, she heard clattering seashells coming from the front of the train car. Yet there was nothing and nobody in there with her. Through the windows into the next car, however, she saw a ratty mop of gray hair peeking above one of the seats. Whomever it belonged to had their back to her, but she could see the layers of wool blankets piled atop her shoulders as she swayed back and forth.

There was no way it was possible, but no way it wasn't her: the woman Carmen had seen in Mexico outside their home and during her stress hallucination outside the abbey. The gray-haired woman raised her hand and, gleaming in the fluorescent lighting of the train, Carmen saw in her grasp a bracelet decorated with green gems. Carmen rose from her seat, ready to run into the next car, but as they passed the embankment the setting sun flooded the cars with light. Her eyes adjusted quickly, but when she could see again, it was as if the sun had erased the old woman. The only people in the next car were two suited men.

A feeling of nausea washed over Carmen. She closed her eyes and pressed her face into her hands, only wanting to be back home with her family, her girls.

Alma climbed the stairs and opened the door to Luna's room. She was used to having a pretty open relationship with the usually sunny Luna and didn't think twice about not knocking. Luna was sitting on her bed, staring at the object on her desk. She turned to Alma in silent anger and stood up.

"What do you want? You didn't think to knock?"

"I just wanted to have a little chat. You seem strange lately, like you're sad or worried. You can talk to me, you know? I'm always here for you if anything is bothering you, cariño."

"I'm not sad or worried," she said, and sat back down.

"Did something happen in Mexico?"

Luna didn't answer. Alma sat next to her and hugged her. Luna's body felt cold to the touch. It was then that she noticed the item on the table.

"What is *that*, then?" she asked, unable to hide her disgust.

"It's a craft I got in Mexico. Mom said I could keep it."

"But it's so creepy! What is it?"

"It's a piñata."

"I've never seen one like that before," Alma said, her fingers reaching out to touch it, drawn in by an instinct to understand the object's strange texture. It looked wet, and almost alive—breathing and pounding. Luna jumped up to shield the piñata with her body and move it away from her abuela's grasp. Alma jumped back, not expecting Luna's reaction.

"Careful! It's fragile!" she said, hiding it away.

"Luna, what's wrong? I just wanted to see it."

"I'd rather you didn't."

They remained silent and still for a few minutes, both recognizing in each other's eyes that something deeper had happened right then. Something had been broken in their relationship and there was a new barrier between them that had never existed before, as if Luna had revealed something unforgivable, something terrible, and quickly sealed part of herself off from her abuela. Luna stood up and placed the piñata in the closet.

"Luna, I really don't understand what's happening with you. I'm trying to understand, but I feel like you're just so far away from me right now."

Luna didn't say anything. Alma stood up and walked hesitantly toward the door. She didn't want to leave without figuring out what had just happened, talking about it. All she wanted to do was break down that wall that Luna had put up. She knew that behind Luna's shell was still the adorable little girl she'd always been. Luna then raised one hand toward her chest, touching the pendant Quauhtli had given her. She touched it gently and yanked it off. She looked at it, open her desk drawer, tossed it in, and, from that same drawer, produced the jade bracelet. She slid it on her wrist as Alma began closing the door. Alma tried to figure out if this was somehow related to what had happened, but didn't dare ask. She paused for a moment before finally shutting the door.

"Luna, you can always talk to me, about anything. Always."

She stood on the other side of the closed door, grappling with the sudden distance between her and her granddaughter. They'd always been so close, yet now it felt as if they were strangers. Turning from this unknown person's door, Alma started downstairs, feeling like she had to talk to Carmen about what had just happened, but she didn't know how exactly. It was normal for kids to grow apart from their elders. What more was there to say than that? After all, Carmen had a lot to worry about already, but hiding what just happened made no sense. The best course of action was to bring it up and figure out what was happening to Luna.

She kept slowly descending the steps when she heard a sound, like seashells knocking against each other. Turning, she saw a large, green grasshopper. She looked at it, intrigued, and when she glanced up, there was a skeleton with insect-like wings, dressed to the nines in golden and gemstone jewelry floating over the stairs. Its skirt was made of seashells, musically clinking against each other. The monstrosity extended its bony hand to her. Alma screamed, and when she did, she stepped back and missed the stair, smacked her head on the banister, and crashed down the staircase until her unconscious body reached the floor, strewn like a raggedy doll where she lay still, a steady trickle of blood slipping through her hair to the floor.

By the time Carmen opened the door nearly twenty minutes later, it had broadened into a small puddle around her head. From above it looked almost like the halos drawn around the saints in the abbey, a broad disk of deep crimson hugging her mother's crown.

18

Carmen's eyes were swollen, aching, and bloodshot from crying and lack of sleep. The three Sánchezes had been sitting in the bright waiting area of the hospital for hours as Alma received treatment. Izel had apologized so many times for not being home when it happened despite how many times Carmen had told her it was okay. Carmen was only thankful that Josh's mom had driven Izel so quickly to the hospital to meet them. It was past midnight now and Izel was finally asleep with her face still pressed to Carmen's side, damp with tears. Luna, however, was awake, dry-faced, and alert. A question was rising in Carmen's throat that she dreaded to ask, everything was still so fresh, but she had to know the answer.

"Why didn't you call anyone, Luna?" Carmen asked quietly. "We've talked about what to do in an emergency, right? You know how to dial 9II and you know you can always call me."

Luna looked down, remaining silent. Carmen's eyes ached more.

"Luna, it's okay to tell me if you just got scared and didn't know what to do. I just wanted to ask . . ."

"I was in my room. I didn't know abuela had fallen," Luna mumbled, still looking down.

"She didn't yell? You didn't hear her falling down the stairs?" Carmen was shocked at how accusatory her voice sounded.

Luna remained silent, still staring at her lap. Carmen followed her gaze and saw Luna fiddling with something around her wrist. Her blood ran cold as she quickly reached over, snatching Luna by the arm and pulling it toward her. Dangling from her daughter's wrist was the jade bracelet that had been left in their rental in Mexico.

"Why is that on your wrist? I told you not to wear it."

"You never said that," Luna replied, covering the bracelet on her left hand with her right, "Let go!"

Carmen went to pull Luna's hand off it, with half a mind to rip the damn thing off right there. It made her indescribably uneasy that her daughter was wearing something that had been so clandestinely snuck into their home. Just then, a nurse interrupted them.

"Are you Miss Sánchez, Alma Calderón's daughter? Your mother's out of surgery."

The voice reminded Carmen of where she was and helped clear her mind. She immediately let go of Luna's arm, embarrassed and ashamed she had laid hands on her daughter like that. She turned to face the nurse.

"Can we see her?"

The nurse led them down the hallways and to a room lit with the same awful, buzzing lights that had been in the waiting room. Under the electric droning, the breathing machine keeping Alma alive wheezed in the corner. Carmen held her daughters close to her as she looked down on her mother's gray face. Alma was so energetic and full of attitude that Carmen usually forgot her age, but now, with a breathing tube in her mouth and bruises blooming under her tired skin, her mother had never looked older, never so close to death. She felt Izel squeeze her hand as the door opened behind them. A thin woman with glasses and seemingly premature gray hair framing her young face stepped in holding a tablet.

"Miss Sánchez? I'm Dr. Müller. I'm the one in charge of your mother's treatment."

"Carmen is fine. This is Izel and this is Luna."

"First, let me say I'm very sorry, Carmen. This must be terrifying for all of you."

"How is she?" Carmen cut through the condolences.

"Still very delicate, I'm afraid." Müller snapped into diagnostic mode. "She has a concussion and a fractured skull. She also sustained some hairline fractures to her hip and shoulder on her way down the stairs, it seems. We don't know what kind of long-term consequences we're looking at yet, but we've put her in a medically induced coma for now due to the swelling in her brain."

"For how long?"

The doctor avoided eye contact, and stretched out her arms, as if to say there wasn't much they could do but wait. "Until the swelling subsides." She gave Carmen her card. "Rest, go home. We'll keep you updated if anything changes. Call me whenever."

Carmen remained still for a second, but she soon realized it was pointless to stay. The breathing machine's pump moved up and down above her mother's head as Carmen stepped over to her and gave Alma a kiss on her bruised cheek before turning to her daughters.

"Let's go, girls. We should get some sleep. We can visit abuela again soon, when she's hopefully better."

None of them spoke much during the car ride home from the hospital. She didn't turn around to see, but Carmen knew that Izel and Luna had probably fallen asleep on the backseat after such a long night. The car radio played quietly as Carmen navigated the dark suburban roads toward their house, struggling to keep her focus. Her head swam with anxiety and thoughts of the omens she saw earlier that day. Each thought of omens and visions was immediately met by the same awful question in her mind, *Am I going crazy?* She wanted nothing more than to get home and pour herself and her mother a tequila and talk like they had the night before. She wanted her mother to joke about the hocus-pocus of superstition and laugh away Carmen's worries with that warm chuckle, but she worried she wouldn't hear that laugh again for a very long time—if ever.

When they pulled into the driveway Carmen's face was wet with new tears. She shook the girls awake and the three of them walked back into the silent house. Luna ran up the stairs as soon as they were inside. Carmen listened to her feet pound up the steps and the door to her room shut and looked at Izel, but the two of them were too tired to make another comment on Luna's attitude. Izel went to the bathroom to wash up before bed and Carmen walked to the kitchen where she pulled down the bottle of tequila and poured two glasses. She tossed the first one back and set the empty glass back down on the counter next to the second shot. Carmen simply stared at the shallow pool of booze. After standing silently in the kitchen for a while, Carmen finally picked up the glass, raising it up above her head and tapping it back down on the table before lifting it to her lips. A small sip was all she took before setting it back in the center of the counter for her mother.

Like leaving a glass of milk out for Santa, she thought, feeling herself smile for the first time all day.

Carmen heard the stairs creak and the door to Izel's room click shut upstairs. The house was once again silent as Carmen sipped her mother's glass of tequila. Then, from somewhere she could not discern, she heard buzzing. It sounded almost like a cicada, but more consistent and sustained. Gulping down the last of the liquor, Carmen grabbed a newspaper off the counter and rolled it up as she walked toward the source of the noise. Playing a game of hot and cold with the droning insect lead her up the stairs where the sound grew louder as she approached, shockingly loud. Sitting near the top of the stairs was a grasshopper rubbing its sickly yellow legs together, whining louder and louder until Carmen smashed it down with her newspaper.

But the sound persisted, quieter, now coming from somewhere else in the house. Carmen crept toward Luna's room, where the buzzing was clamours. Looking down, she saw the yellow leg of a grasshopper emerge and disappear under Luna's door. She tried the knob but the door was locked, something she'd never encountered in their house before. She knocked gently and the sound halted.

She didn't have the energy to deal with this, to wake Luna up and scold her for her locked door. Even her tongue felt too heavy in her mouth to talk. She dragged herself down the stairs and to her room collapsing on her bed, panting as if she'd just come back from a run. She closed her eyes and when she opened them, she saw a grasshopper. It was huge, nearly dog size. She couldn't scream; she couldn't open her mouth. Her fingers were intertwined and she couldn't summon the strength to untwine them. She began to cry softly, while the grasshopper looked at her with its lifeless eyes, blacker than obsidian.

Izel woke up on top of the covers the next morning, still wearing her clothes from the day before. She looked at her phone and saw it was already nine. Half-stuck in the haze of sleep, she felt like she was still dreaming. Everything looked like her house, her room, but something was off. It was the silence. The silence of the house was uncanny, a familiar environment made alien by the absence of clattering pans and a crackling radio echoing from the kitchen downstairs as Alma cooked breakfast. The remnants of sleep vanished as Izel remembered she might not hear those noises for a very long time. She needed someone to talk to, to tell her friends about the strange situation in her house. She called Halley. It rang and went to voicemail. Izel didn't leave a message. None of the girls had answered her texts the last few days. The distance that Izel worried was going to form while they all went to camp together and she was away in Mexico had continued to grow. Hugging her knees to her chest on her bed, she looked out the window.

Outside, there was a black cloud of butterflies forming strange shapes. Izel pressed her nose to the glass for a better look before taking several photos and videos with her phone. They were beautiful, it was like they were dancing around each other, orbiting an invisible point in the middle. The butterflies slowly began breaking from their swarm and approaching her window in small groups. Izel started recording a story, zooming in on the undulating mass of butterflies hovering in the summer heat. They were fluttering close by, too close, nearly touching the wall and windows. Suddenly, one of them crashed against the glass with a shocking amount of force, leaving a crack as it fell. Izel stumbled to the floor, startled. She kneeled, lowered the curtain, and remained still, not sure what to do next. The butterflies' light, almost weightless bodies bouncing off her window sounded like hail or a sudden summer downpour. Izel was convinced that, at that rate, they'd break the window, but the storm slowed to a patter, then to a few bumps. Cautiously, she stood up and opened the curtains again, seeing nothing but darkness—the mass of butterflies blocked her entire window. When she blinked, however, they had all vanished save for one, which fluttered just outside the window, its wings shimmering a darkly opalescent purple in the gloomy morning light. She ran her finger along where she had seen the first butterfly crack the window, but nothing was there.

She fell back into bed, taking a deep breath and wondering if she was still dreaming. She quickly pulled her phone back up and opened her camera roll. The thumbnail of the video showed the black mass in the sky, but when she clicked it, the video only showed her recording an empty sky before jumping back from the window for no apparent reason. She swiped through the photos of the blank morning sky and deleted them all. Opening her texts she noticed there was one from Josh.

"Are you okay? You were really freaked out yesterday. I'm sorry about your grandma. Is she gonna be alright?"

"I'm okay. I don't know. They don't really know how she's doing yet, you know? I feel like I'm fucking losing it a little, if I'm being honest."

"I hope she gets better soon. And I'd probably feel like I was losing it, too, you know? What you're going through is, like, super intense."

Izel hesitated for a moment, and typed another message, "I just saw the craziest thing though. Outside my window."

"What was it?"

"It was, like, thousands of butterflies or moths or something swarming around in the sky like a big blob."

"I didn't think butterflies flew in swarms like birds do."

"These ones do I guess."

"Well . . . I know you're probably busy with family stuff, but if you want, we can hang out again soon?"

Izel didn't know what to think. She'd always thought Josh was cute, but she thought having to leave their first real hangout with a crazy emergency would make things weird between them. It was nice to see he still wanted to meet again and that he seemed so concerned about her, but she couldn't help but feel like he was kind of obligated to be nice to her right now. A boy can't exactly ghost the girl he's been talking to when she's just had a traumatic family emergency. She didn't really care, though. A pity shoulder to cry on would do just fine. Now more than ever, she just felt like she needed someone to talk to, someone she could trust now that her friends seemed too busy for her.

"Yeah! I'd like that. Maybe after school sometime since it's starting kinda soon?"

She heard her mom knocking on Luna's room next to hers.

"Luna, honey, are you there?"

Izel hopped out of bed and poked her head out of her room.

"Yes, Mom," Luna replied from the other side of the door. "What are we having for breakfast? I'm starving."

"Uh, I don't know what we have but I can whip something up."

Luna opened the door with sleepy eyes, but a sunny disposition, walking right past the two of them and toward the kitchen.

"I hope we have orange juice."

They all climbed down the stairs together, with Luna skipping down the steps like she always did. It was like the girl had entirely forgotten about the events of the previous night. Izel almost thought she had to remind her that it was weird to act so chipper with a loved one in the hospital.

Carmen made the three of them fried eggs, bacon, and toast. At the table she realized Luna wasn't wearing the jade bracelet anymore and made a mental note to look for it and get rid of it as soon as she could. Even if it was just some superstition she had picked up from Quauhtli and Yoltzi, she would feel better without it in the house.

"I would've preferred some huevos luneros," Luna said, "but these are good too!"

Carmen pulled the business card from her purse and dialed Dr. Müller's number to see if there were any updates on Alma's condition.

"Hello, ma'am. I'm sorry, but nothing has changed. We'll call you if there are any updates."

"Can I visit her today?"

"We'll let you know when she's ready for visits. I know you just want to see her, but I'd really like to keep a close eye on her for a while until I'm sure she's stable. A woman of her age receiving a head injury like she did," the doctor paused, "I'm just playing it as safe as possible. But I promise, you're my first call the moment we think it's safe to wake her up."

Carmen hung up and sighed.

"I'm sorry, Mom," Izel said.

Carmen caressed her head. Luna watched, eating her breakfast.

That night Carmen climbed the stairs and made her way down the hall as quietly as she could. Setting her glass of wine on the floor, she hopped up and reached to grab the pull cord to the attic stairs. She yanked the old wooden ladder down. Years of sloppy paint jobs and warp from humid summers made it quite an effort, but she managed. After picking out some stray paint chips that had rained down into her wine glass, Carmen climbed up to the attic. Making her way through the clutter, she opened the attic window and stuck a leg out. When she found a stable spot on the sloped roof, she slid the rest of her body out of the window and sidled around, out of sight from anywhere the girls might catch a glimpse. Laying down with her glass of wine in hand, she gazed up at the stars. It was an exceptionally clear summer night without a cloud in the night sky.

Sitting up there and stargazing always helped her clear her mind when nothing else would. The small joint in her pocket would probably help too. The August night air was comfortably muggy now that they were out of the dog days of July. Soon, fall would come and cold nights would arrive with it. She had to seize these last summer days. She took the joint out from its little plastic tube, lit up, and took a deep pull, patting her pocket to make sure she had her phone in case the girls or Müller called. She couldn't entirely escape the world like she usually liked to up here. It had been weeks without any progress or word from the doctor, but Carmen couldn't allow herself to believe her mother's condition was such a part of her life that she'd get used to it. She was always waiting for the call saying they were ready to wake Alma up.

The gravelly texture of the roof's shingles pulled at her hair as she leaned forward and sipped her wine. The joint was slowly relaxing her body and allowing her to relinquish some of her anxieties. Looking up at the sky she attempted to see some of the good that had come from the past few weeks. The girls at least seemed okay. Izel was in a good mood and couldn't stop talking about what Josh had texted her that day or the plans she and Josh were making. She was far from the sullen girl she had been in Mexico, so worried about her friends leaving her behind. Luna wasn't exactly back to normal, but that was to be expected of a girl on the border of her adolescence. She was still having her mood swings and Carmen couldn't get her to leave her door unlocked for the life of her, but Carmen could think of much worse acts of rebellion she had put her mother through.

She was still on paperwork duty at the office. No new projects were thrown her way, but she hadn't been fired either. Whether it was out of pity for her mother's condition, some kind of diversity requirement, or just the fact that she was good at her job didn't matter. She wasn't thinking about going freelance anymore.

Carmen watched one star in particular, contemplating how far away it was. She tried to imagine how small her worries must be in the scheme of all that was so far above her.

Suddenly, the stars she was contemplating disappeared. They blinked out of existence as if a large, black mantle had swallowed the sky. She was taken aback by the darkness; it almost felt like floating into the void. She took one last short drag and stubbed out the joint.

"This strain is strong," she said out loud, as if to confirm that she was awake and hadn't fallen into the black hole, "or maybe it's just been a while."

She then heard a noise coming from the depths of the sky, like thousands of flags whipping in the wind or hundreds of birds flying in a frenzy. Lying back, she closed her eyes and relaxed, letting herself slip from the dark skies into the darkness of her mind, trying to deduce whether the flapping was real or just the sound of her own heartbeat. From the inky black of her thoughts emerged a figure coming into focus. Carmen concentrated on it and suddenly saw the skinned face she'd encountered by her fence in Mexico. It was cackling and showing her some sort of stone knife. Carmen opened her eyes, but remained in darkness, still seeing the creature as if the image had escaped her mind's eye and became reality. The awful creature cackled, its hanging jaw moving out of sync with its words.

"We're no more than bones in the end, my child," it said in a deep voice pounding against the inside of her head.

"No! Go away!" Carmen yelled, trying again to open her eyes.

The darkness was all enveloping. Opening her eyes made no difference. She tried to reach for her lighter but couldn't find it. She got down on all fours to find her bearings, patting around for something to ground her in reality, but she couldn't even see her hands. This couldn't be real, she wanted to blame everything on the weed.

"What the hell did they sell me?"

Antidrug horror stories of weed spiked with PCP and research chemicals came to mind, filling her with a realer kind of fear. The flapping sounded closer now and, even if she couldn't see it, she knew it was the black butterflies. The ones she had seen in Manhattan, the ones from Luna's sketchbook. Angry, Luna had called them, angry at humans. They flew lower and lower, circling her and touching her softly with their wings as she waved around in the darkness trying to scare them away. One grazed her forehead and she let out a deep howl, unable to control herself despite being aware she was not in the best state of mind, and she didn't want the girls to find her like this—high and hysterical. The entire block would probably look out their windows to figure out what the hell was going on, but she was still unable to see the lights from the houses or the streets. She kept hearing the skeleton's voice in her head.

"We're all the same in the dark."

"Help!" she yelled.

Pelted by small, furry bodies, she was surrounded, enveloped in butterfly wings brushing against her clothes, skin, and hair. She shut her eyes tight and turned over, covering her head with her face against the rooftop. Trying to commando crawl away, she could barely move; she could've sworn the butterflies had a hold on her, ready to pick her up and take her away. The flapping noise became deafening, swallowing up her screams. It was like being drowned in a viscous liquid that restrained every sense, even movement. She had to get out of there. She kept trying to crawl out, reaching for anything to arm herself. She suddenly felt the edge of the roof, and pulled herself toward it using all her strength, as the butterflies pressed against her, forcefully, as if trying to crush her.

Finally able to move, she dragged half her body over the edge. Light returned to the universe and she was finally able to see the fall awaiting her if she didn't hold tight, if the butterflies made her lose her balance, if the weed she'd smoked fooled her senses. Her head felt heavy, and her legs couldn't keep their balance. Her body was like a plank, adrift, sliding little by little toward the ground. Vertigo threatened to pull her over, but the fear of falling was suddenly replaced by a sense of weightlessness, of immateriality. The flapping and buzzing had become an intoxicating, hypnotic drone; she felt part of the black cloud of wings, as if the butterflies were part of her body. She felt that if she just let herself slide forward a bit more, she would take flight over the town rather than fall to the sidewalk.

Luna was sketching in her journal, a habit she'd forgone since her return. She suddenly stopped copying the photo of a cat on her screen and started flipping through her journal to look at her other drawings. She stopped when she reached the butterflies. She stood up and looked out her window, seeing thousands of black butterflies flying around the house, their bodies brushing past the roof. She opened her window and reached out to touch them. Hearing the intense flapping coming from above, she looked up and saw her mother surrounded by butterflies, hanging from the rooftop, seemingly ready to let go. She screamed like she'd never screamed before.

"Mom!"

Luna's voice shook Carmen back to reality and she looked down at her daughter's face leaning from her window.

"Luna!"

Luna frantically shouted back to her mom, "They can't hurt you, Mom! They can only scare you, they aren't really here!"

Carmen's head spun, trying momentarily to understand why Luna would say such a thing, before simply trusting it. She closed her eyes and realized that if she focused, then she no longer felt the butterflies touching her. Opening her eyes and telling herself they weren't really there, the butterflies began to disperse, fading away back into the night and letting her see with clarity again. Carmen's head began to clear enough for fear to take hold again. At the sight of the ground below, she yelped and held on tight to the edge. Her eyes wide with fear, she looked to see Luna's head poking from her window.

"Are you okay?" Luna yelled.

Carmen couldn't answer, but pulled herself back onto the safety of the rooftop and rolled away from the edge, lying on her back. The stars were bright again, just like before. Standing up, she saw her arms were covered in a strange black dust. She tried to brush it away, but it seemed to sink in further the more she rubbed it off.

Luna closed her window and made toward her door. She wanted to know what had happened and how her mother had gotten there. Her hands were shaking as she moved to open her door, but when she walked past her wide-open journal displaying her butterfly sketches, she stopped. She looked at the drawing intently, as if the answers were there instead. She opened her drawer and pulled out the jade bracelet. She put it on, closing her eyes with something like pleasure or relief and saw her mother strewn against the pavement, her legs creating unnatural angles as if they'd been broken in many different places, a lake of blood by her head, a red stain on her chest as if her heart had burst or been torn from her body. Luna stayed in her room. Instead, she grabbed a pencil and drew her mother in the same pose as the famous image of the goddess, Coyolxauhqui, torn apart after being decapitated by her brother, Huitzilopochtli, and thrown off a cliff.

Luna took the piñata from its hiding place in the corner of her closet. It seemed larger than the last time she'd seen it. When she touched it, her fingertips were stained with a red liquid, something like blood. As she watched the liquid drip from the tip of her finger, she felt a sharp pain come from her abdomen. She touched her groin through her underwear with her right hand, and when she saw her fingers were covered in blood, she tried again with her left hand.

Images of the black butterflies flashed before her eyes, thoughts of them flooding into her by the thousands between her legs, tearing her body open from the inside, splitting her in half like a flowing river, taking her skin and turning her into one of those obsidian skeletons. The pain grew greater as she fell on her knees trying to muffle a scream. On the desk, the piñata swelled and moistened, beating softly as Luna cried, rolling on the floor in pain as she covered her groin with both hands. She thought if she moved her hands, all of her organs would flow out of her body in a great gush of blood and black butterflies.

Carmen entered the house, feeling faint. She didn't know whether she was still high anymore. Confused, anxious, and shaking, she walked toward the stairs. She felt she was somehow at fault, as if drinking and smoking made her an object of scorn. Her Catholic education had loaded her with enough guilt to drag around for the rest of her life.

Nothing made sense. Luna had saved her.

She then turned and headed to the kitchen to wash her hands and her face. The black dust was hard to remove. She couldn't figure out how she'd remove the stains from her clothes, which seemed to be covered in soot. An animalistic howl came from inside the house, but even if it was real and not another insane hallucination, she was too dizzy and weak to deal with anything. Her body ached and her head felt like a volcano about to erupt. Digging around in the drawer for some aspirin, she heard, very clearly now, a howl of pain.

"Luna!" she screamed, and ran upstairs despite her aching.

The door was closed. She knocked with her full fist.

"Luna, open up!"

No answer. Only the screams of her daughter. Carmen, disoriented and terrified, began to cry as she pounded the door. This might be a nightmare, another awful hallucination, but she couldn't bear the sound.

"Are you okay? What's wrong? Sweetie, cariño, please! Please just say something to Mommy, okay?!"

Finally, Luna reached the doorknob from her position on the floor. Carmen burst through the door and fell to her knees next to her daughter, horrified by the blood on her hands, face, and clothes. She tried to figure out what was happening.

"Luna, what did this to you?" she asked, still thinking about the butterflies that tried to push her off the rooftop.

Luna cried and covered her groin with both hands once more. It was then that Carmen realized what could be happening. Even then, it felt like too much of a coincidence. She tried to regain her composure and be a mother in the face of her daughter's fear, suppressing the shaking of her voice.

"This is perfectly normal. We've talked about this before, remember? And your doctor talked about it, and at school too. Don't worry, everything is okay."

"I'm broken inside," Luna kept repeating.

Carmen was dirty from the butterfly or moth dust, felt self-conscious, and didn't want to touch anything, but she didn't dare leave Luna alone. She took her to the bathroom and explained that this was a normal thing every woman went through. There was a disastrous amount of blood, nothing like any cycle Carmen had ever seen. Maybe this happened to some girls on their first period? Whatever was happening, Carmen felt her priority was making Luna feel safe and normal.

"Every woman? Even Izel?"

"Yes, Izel too. Izel! Come to the bathroom for a minute!"

Izel ran down the hallway and nearly crashed into the bathroom as she looked around in a panic. "What?! What happened?"

She saw the blood on Luna's hands and her eyes went wide, but Carmen cut her panic short, quickly interjecting, "I was just telling Luna that everyone freaks out during their first period. I figured you could corroborate."

"A part of me is being torn off," Luna grunted, curled into a ball on the floor.

"Oh . . ." Izel looked puzzled, "That's why you shouted for me like that? Don't they teach that stuff in school still? She should already know this stuff."

"Izel, more respect please. It's hard to go through it for the first time. Or have you forgotten how scared *you* were when you came to your abuela and me? There's a big difference between knowing and feeling. Also, where have you been? How could you not hear me shouting earlier?"

"I mean, sure, it can be painful but it's not like it's *that* bad. And I was in the house. I didn't hear anything though."

"I was screaming bloody murder and you're saying you just completely missed it?"

"I dunno. Maybe I had my headphones on or something! You need me in the attic to get all covered in dust too?"

Their back and forth was interrupted by Luna, speaking through gritted teeth with her forehead pressed to the bathroom tile, "The butterflies are inside me."

Carmen's gaze snapped back to Luna. "Butterflies? Why butterflies? Luna what are you talking about?"

Luna looked at her firmly, the veins pulsing against her temples, and said, "They came for me."

"What are you talking about?" Izel asked.

"Something really strange happened on the rooftop. I nearly fell off. There were some black butterflies or moths all around me. Disgusting creatures. This isn't from the attic," Carmen explained, opening her arms and motioning to the smears all over her clothes.

"Butterflies?" Izel responded.

Both of them looked at Luna, who had pushed herself up from the floor and was now standing, motioning toward the door. "Could I have some privacy now? I just need a second to myself. Thanks for making me feel better, but I think I can manage the rest alone."

Carmen and Izel nodded uncertainly before stepping out into the hallway as Luna began to shut the bathroom door behind them. Just before closing it, Luna peered through the crack.

"It's not dust, by the way. They're scales. Butterflies and moths have scales. Some can even be poisonous."

And then she shut the door. Izel shrugged and went back to her room, but Carmen stayed up in the hallway for a while longer. Luna stayed in the bathroom all night or at least late enough that Carmen couldn't remain awake any longer. She checked on Luna once more, knocking on the door and receiving a response.

"I'm still okay in here! I didn't know privacy meant having someone stand right outside the door. I'm learning a lot today, I guess!"

Carmen was too tired to get into it and just said, "Okay."

Then she descended the stairs and collapsed on her bed.

20

Carmen woke up and checked her phone as she did every morning, looking for any missed calls or texts from Dr Müller. Almost a month after the accident, the swelling had subsided, her body was healing, and the medical team had finally pulled her out of her induced coma, but she had yet to regain consciousness on her own. Despite not wanting to return to normal yet, Carmen was due back at the office now that her paid leave after the tragedy was over. Bills still had to be taken care of and they had more than ever now with Alma's many hospital charges. She dragged herself out of bed to put a pot of coffee on the stove.

After some breakfast—Carmen had been getting better at cooking the dishes her mother usually made—she took the girls to school. The ride was mostly silent. Izel rarely spoke in the mornings, too engrossed in her phone to pay any mind to Carmen or her little sister. She'd been spending more and more time with Josh since school had started up again and didn't seem to have time for anyone else. Carmen was a little hesitant to so quickly accept that her eldest little girl already had her first boyfriend—lord knew that Carmen hadn't been a saint with her first few boyfriends at that age and the boys she brought home were hardly ever saints themselves—but Izel was happy and, in truth, Josh seemed the closest to a saint a sixteen-year-old boy could be. Weighing everything that the poor girl had been going through with her friends ignoring her and her grandmother's accident, Carmen couldn't think that a boy who kept her mind off all of that could be that bad. Izel could be prickly and sometimes downright mean to her mother, but Carmen knew that she was a better daughter than she had been to Alma. Carmen thought that her mother would've laughed at that revelation. She'd have to be sure to tell it to her over a drink when she was out of the hospital. If she ever left. Carmen's breath caught in her throat.

Luna, too, sat in silence on their car rides to school lately, but not due to her older sister's same private giddiness. The bright, sunny Luna had become mainly sullen and disinterested. The mood swings that had defined their relationship after Mexico, where the happy-go-lucky Luna Carmen had raised would suddenly plunge into despondence and detached anger, had inverted. Nowadays Carmen found herself lucky to catch a glimpse of the daughter she once knew and Luna's new normal state of being was one of near-constant morose silence. In fact, lately, the emotional whiplash Carmen experienced when Luna snapped from her depressive state back to the Luna that ran around the markets of Tulancingo almost made her more uneasy than just seeing Luna mope around the house all day. It felt like she couldn't tell who Luna really was anymore.

They pulled up to the girls' school and her two daughters grabbed their bags and slid off their seats and out of the car.

Carmen rolled her window down and yelled out, "Bye girls! Have a good day!"

Izel raised her hand in acknowledgment that she'd been spoken to, but neither of the girls turned to respond. She let out a long and heavy breath, one she felt she had been holding during the whole silent car ride, then watched the girls ascend the steps to school. Josh was leaning on one side of the main entrance, waiting for Izel. He saw Carmen's car and waved to her. Izel finally turned around to see who he was waving at and quickly grabbed his hand and walked him into school. Carmen smiled to herself knowing she could still embarrass her little girl.

Some boys were waiting for Luna outside as well. They smiled when she walked by them and said something before following her inside. Carmen was relieved that she had some evidence that Luna had friends at school considering she couldn't get a word from the girl about how her days went. She'd begun to worry that Luna was just as quiet out of the house as she was in there but seeing her interact with some people at school made Carmen feel like Luna was maybe just fixing to be an angsty one in her coming teen years.

She turned the car radio to a station she liked and pulled away from the school, getting on the highway to the city.

Luna kept her head down and walked through the front door without looking at any of the three boys who had been waiting for her, even when one of them stuck his foot out to try to trip her. She stumbled forward a bit and almost lost her balance but steadied herself.

"You should watch where you're walking," commented one of the boys.

Luna looked up from the ground and glared at the one who had spoken, a boy named Lester a couple grades ahead of her. She turned her head to where Izel and Josh had been, hoping that at least one of them might stick around to see what was happening, but only saw the back of their heads as they headed in the other direction down the hall toward the high school lockers. She could swear she saw Izel turn to look at her for a moment before continuing on with Josh, who himself was none the wiser.

"What are you looking over there for? We're the ones talking to you, beaner" he said, advancing on Luna.

"She's probably looking at her sister over there," responded the other. His name was Albert and Luna had heard from one of the other girls in her grade that he had been held back twice already. He was Lester's older cousin, but was still stuck in the same grade as his younger relative.

"That's her sister?" said Lester, turning back to Luna, "Why's she so much lighter than you? Your mom used to like White guys or something?"

Luna didn't respond and just kept walking. The three of them had been doing this little routine since the first week of school when they first laid eyes on her. Even in elementary school she had dealt with her fair share of mean little White boys in her grade, but had never let them get her down. Teachers had commented to Carmen all through Luna's first five years of school how she seemed to kill everyone with kindness and never bow her head in shame. She had never hated any-one before. But these boys were older, meaner. Years of quiet acqui-escence from teachers and parents to their behavior had led to them getting away with almost anything and now they were aiming all that terrible privilege down on this little Mexican girl in her first year of middle school.

The three boys watched Luna walk away from them and Albert shouted after her, "Where you goin'? The cleaning closet's the other way, Consuela! Don't you need some Fabuloso to start the day?"

Luna spun the dial on her locker, ignoring the boys' overexaggerated laughter as they walked away. The music teacher, Miss Moore, stuck her head out of her classroom and shouted at the three to come into her room that instant, to which they quickly walked away.

"Hey! Get back here!" she shouted, quickly giving up and turning to Luna. "Sweetie, are you alright?"

"Yeah. I'm fine." Luna didn't look away from her locker.

"Do you know those boys? Want me to send them to the principal's office?"

"No. It doesn't really matter."

"Well, I for one don't think—"

Luna slammed her locker shut and Miss Moore stopped talking as little Luna tucked her sketchbook under her arm and walked away. The rest of the students in the hall had started moving again. They had all seen what had happened and had stopped to watch the show. Some snickered under their breath. Others avoided any possibility of eye contact with Luna. Another middle school girl, though, walked next to Luna.

"Why didn't you get them sent to the principal's office? Those three suck so bad," she said.

"It wouldn't do anything," answered Luna. "I'm sure they'll get what's coming to them, though."

"What? Like you think karma's gonna get them or something?"

"Yeah. Or something."

Luna stepped out of the hall and into her homeroom class where she began her now daily routine of sleeping through school, drifting from class to class and keeping her eyes open just enough to avoid being called out by her teachers.

Sitting in history class that day, Luna kept her glazed eyes forward. She wasn't ever actually focused on her teachers, only looking in their direction, watching their blurred form at the front of the class drone on and on about fractions or iambic pentameters. Her history teacher, Miss Alpert, grabbed a whiteboard marker and drew a rudimentary map of South and Central America on the board.

"So we've already been talking a little bit about what European settlers found when they came to America as we know it, but now we're going to focus more on what was happening in southern America at the same time," she circled a large chunk of Mexico, "So who knows what the Spanish who came across found when they got to Mexico?"

One of Luna's classmates, Tasha, raised her hand and responded, "Aztecs?"

"Very good. Yes. As you all would have read in your textbooks over the weekend, when the Spanish first arrived in Mexico in 1519, they came into contact with the native Aztecs."

Luna finally came out of her self-induced trance to audibly groan. Miss Alpert turned from the board where she was crudely outlining the limits of the Aztec Empire, surprised to find that it was Luna who had not only spoken—if a groan counted as speech—for what seemed the first time all semester, but had done so to interrupt class.

"Yes, Luna?"

"What's the point of teaching this if you don't even know anything? 'Native Aztecs?' This is going to be what you taught on indigenous American tribes all over again."

"Do you not think learning about those who lived here before us is important? Don't you have Mexican family, Luna? You might have Aztec blood in you! You should want to learn about that."

"Not from you, gringa. I don't have 'Aztec blood'," she emphasized. "I have *Nahua* blood. Even while trying to pretend you want to focus on the cultures your ancestors crushed, you can't help but further trample on their history. You teaching this is stupid."

"Luna, please settle down," Miss Alpert couldn't believe an eleven-year-old girl would speak like that. She thought, of course, that someone was feeding her such ideas, indoctrinating her in hatred. It was crystal clear and something had to be done about it.

"It's not a farce. We're sensible people and we're interested and curious about these tribes who are a part of our melting pot."

"This melting pot was created by stealing, raping, killing, enslaving, and exploiting our native people."

"What you're saying is unacceptable, Luna. It only shows your ignorance."

"The system that wrote all the crap you're trying to teach us about native people all comes from the same place. America and Spain destroyed their culture and now wants to teach kids what that culture was to make everyone feel better."

"Who's telling you this stuff? They've taught you to hate your country."

"This isn't even her country," Hunter said. He barely knew her.

"Stay out of it, Hunter," the teacher said, and turned to Luna. "I'm not planning on arguing with you. It's preposterous. Go to the principal's office."

Luna stood up. She walked toward Hunter and gave him a steely glare.

"What is *your* country? Because it's definitely not this one."

"You have to be kidding me," the teacher said, as she walked full-speed among the desks to intervene. She grabbed Luna's hand and dragged her out the door. The children started yelling and insulting Luna. The teacher left the classroom, pulling Luna with her.

"Stay quiet, nobody leaves and nobody move. I'll be right back."

Everyone in the room continued to yell chaotically.

"Luna, what's wrong? Why are you trying to provoke everyone?" the teacher said while she held the girl's wrist in front of the classroom door.

"What's wrong with you? You've taken everything from us and now you want us to be docile and obedient," said Luna.

"Who are you talking about? I haven't taken anything from anyone.

I'm sorry if I got some things wrong, but I assure you I'm just trying to teach about—"

Miss Alpert stopped speaking abruptly. She was still holding on to Luna's wrist as she tried to reassure her, but what she had gripped in her hand suddenly felt ice-cold and hard as stone. Her first instinct was that there must be something medically wrong with her student. Miss Alpert was filled with concern for Luna, but when she looked from Luna's sickly gray arm to her face, that concern quickly became fear for her own well-being.

Looking into Luna's eyes was like looking into two deep, dark caverns stretching endlessly into a mountainside. Deep within Luna's hellacious face burned an ancient fire, whose flickering light was all but smothered by the thick darkness within. Miss Alpert couldn't look away, as if she was being drawn into those depths. Time froze and flickering on the walls of the two caves on Luna's face were the shadowy visions of death and dismemberment, a terrible ritual taking place by the fireside within her. Miss Alpert's stomach began to turn, the blood draining from her face, leaving her as stone-gray as Luna. In the shadows of the cave, a figure was held by the arms as another plunged something into their chest, spraying blood against the cavern's walls. Down the hallway someone slammed a locker closed, and Miss Alpert was kicked back into reality, a reality in which Luna now looked at her crying out.

"Ow! Miss Alpert! You're hurting me! Let go!"

The teacher, stunned and dizzied, saw her hand around Luna's wrist, the knuckles white with strain as Luna tried to pull away. Miss Alpert had been crushing her student's wrist. Still in a daze, she let go of Luna, revealing red finger marks and a rapidly blooming bruise.

Luna looked at her, clutching her wrist, and asked, "Why did you do that? I'm sorry for talking back in class."

The other students had gathered at the door after hearing Luna yelling.

"How did you do that?" Miss Alpert asked in a daze.

"Did you hate the story of my people so much?" Luna responded, glaring at her through tears, before running down the hall toward the principal's office.

The teacher put her hand against her chest. Her heart was beating furiously as if it were about to burst. She took a deep breath. She had a massive headache. What she'd seen had been so real, so tangible, so impossible. She wondered how she could explain what had just happened.

Carmen was still fighting her way through morning rush-hour traffic crossing the Bronx when the radio cut out, replaced by her phone's ringtone. After a brief delay the console on the car's dashboard revealed the caller ID: Doctor Müller. The immediate rush of blood to Carmen's head almost made her rear-end the sedan in front of her. Her pulse raced and she instinctually rolled down the window of her car, letting in the cool autumn air, hoping to keep herself present. She was frozen, knowing the call was either good or crushing news. Her finger trembling, she tapped the green phone icon.

There was long pause on the other end of the line as it connected, leaving Carmen to listen to the sound of her heart beating in her ears.

Müller's voice came through the speakers, "Miss Sánchez?"

"Yes," Carmen's voice was faint.

"Don't worry. It's good news. You're mother has woken up."

Air finally returned to Carmen's lungs. She hadn't realized she had been holding her breath. She quickly blurted out, "Can I come see her now?"

"Of course. I'll fill you in on the details when you arrive, then."

Carmen pushed her way over multiple lanes, calling her boss and explaining she would need an extra day before coming in as she tore toward the northbound side of the highway.

Getting out of the car in the hospital parking lot, she texted her old friend Sofia that she wouldn't be making it into the city that day after all and would have to get lunch together another time. Carmen made a beeline through the automatic door to the front desk at the hospital and filled out her visitor form so fast it must have been some kind of record. The woman at the desk pointed her toward the elevator and paged the doctor to meet Carmen at Alma's room.

Müller was awaiting Carmen when she arrived at the door and held up her hand, stopping Carmen.

"Before you go in, I just wanted to give you an update on your mother's condition and temper your expectations a bit."

"Temper my . . ." Carmen's heart sank a bit at the realization that of course her mother wasn't fully recovered yet. In her haste to make it to the hospital she hadn't even considered what Alma's condition was now.

Müller continued, "She's awake—a bit in and out of consciousness. It's possible she's still a little shaken up by the concussion, but due to her multiple fractures from the fall, we still have her on a good number of painkillers. It's got her in good spirits, but she is essentially intoxicated so she isn't making much sense. I just wanted you to know that if she sounds a bit loopy, it's more likely the drugs than anything else."

Carmen nodded in agreement and motioned her hand toward the handle of the door, looking to Müller for a cue that she could go in now. The doctor nodded back and Carmen turned the handle with a soft click, carefully opening the door. Her mother very slowly, with a dreamy look of serenity, turned her gaze from the room's window to Carmen as she entered and gently closed the door behind her.

The haunting gasps of the breathing machine Alma had been on last time Carmen saw her were gone along with all the horrible tubes they had needed to shove down Alma's throat to keep her fed and breathing. In the silence, Carmen's heels clicked against the sterile linoleum floor. Alma raised her frail and deeply bruised old arms toward her daughter.

"Mija," she practically whispered.

Her smiling face and the faint call to her daughter made Carmen's eyes tear and she caught a shuddering sob in her throat as she grabbed her mother's hands with as light a touch as possible. Alma's hands felt as delicate as the autumn leaves, like they might crumble between Carmen's fingers if she held her too tight. Foregoing a possibly painful embrace, Carmen leaned down and gave her mother a light kiss on the forehead.

"Hola, mamá," she said.

Alma looked over Carmen's shoulders. "¿Dónde están mis nietas?"

"They're at school right now, but they miss you a lot. God, I'm so glad you're all right. We were so scared, Mamá."

"I was scared as well."

"It must have been terrifying when you fell. If I hadn't come home when I did, I don't know . . ." the sob stuck in Carmen's throat threatened to break free if she continued to imagine what the consequences would have been if she hadn't gotten home on time.

"I don't mean the fall, mija. I saw something. Do you remember the crickets in Tepoztlán? How we used to hear them sing when you were a child? They're so loud. They're here now."

Carmen looked around the hospital room, briefly forgetting that her mother was still in a state of mind somewhere between dreams and reality. "Here?"

"I remember putting you to sleep and listening to the sound of those crickets and grasshoppers all night as they sang under the moon. You would ask me why they made so much noise out there in the dark and I would always tell you that they were gathering to sing you to sleep, that they were the spirits of your grandmothers and grandfathers trying to keep you company through the night despite no longer being able to speak."

Alma's eyes were looking right through Carmen at the ceiling and beyond as she fell into reverie about the past.

"But to tell you the truth, I was always terrified by their lonely sound."

"Did you dream about them when you were asleep?"

Her mother's eyes became clear as day as she looked into Carmen's, an urgency took hold of Alma's frail and weakened voice, "I saw one in the house. Large as a dog. A cricket staring with its obsidian eyes and singing that droning song before I saw death rise from it. It was Luna's. She summoned it."

Carmen's hopes of being reassured by seeing her mother conscious again drained from her heart along with much of the blood in her face. Inexplicably, she found her hands trembling as they held her mother's.

"We threw out the crickets. They wouldn't let us take them back with us," Carmen responded thinking of the only crickets she could remember.

"It brought them with it. She has it." Alma's eyes were fluttering. The

IV bag hooked up to her arm dripped above them silently. "Covered in skin and leather. I saw its face. I saw inside it, saw what it was."

Alma's eyes were frantically darting around the empty beige room.

Carmen leaned over her mother. "Saw what? What was it?"

Alma's glassy old eyes finally stopped moving, locking intensely with Carmen's and she responded, "Tlapalxoktli."

Her eye finally closed, her hand going limp in Carmen's grasp as she fell asleep. Carmen immediately rose from Alma's bedside and opened the door, calling to Dr Müller to check on her mother who, after a brief look at the EKG confirmed she was fine.

"Like I said, she's still drifting in and out. She sounds like she's in some kind of dreamlike state. I hope at least you got to talk to her a little."

"Yeah," Carmen said weakly, "I did. Thank you. I have to go now, but please let me know when you think she's ready to come home."

"Of course."

Carmen made her way through the hospital decidedly slower than she had come in, moving through the halls like a ghost. The only thing that confirmed to her that she was in fact moving her legs was the steady click of her heels against the tile as she wound through the fluorescent hallways. Finally, in the safety and privacy of her own car, she set the sadness in her throat free. Her face flushed, filling with fire as she sputtered and gasped for air between body-wracking sobs. There she stayed, in the cold, gray of the concrete parking structure, weeping in her car, feeling more alone than she had in a very long time.

Her mother's words had come out as nonsense of the unconscious, but Carmen wasn't worried, as Doctor Müller had assumed she would be, that her mother had suffered such grievous head trauma that she was now a crazy, demented old woman. No, what terrified Carmen, on top of everything that had happened to her mother, was that her rambling meant something to her. Within the dazed, meandering reverie her mother had delivered, Carmen felt there was some kind of indiscernible truth. Her mother's words, "She has it . . . tlapalxoktli," rang in her head. Quauhtli had said that word while they were in Mexico, but it was Nahuatl, she never knew her mom knew any word in that language apart from the very common terms that have been assimilated into Mexican Spanish: tlapalería, mecate, chocolate, nopal. Just the night before her fall, Alma had even poked fun at the superstitious beliefs of the Nahuas. Carmen's fear had less to do with the medical calamity and her mother's injuries and more to do with being scared of her own daughter. Those omens and the events of Mexico had followed them all the way back home.

As her tears dried on her face, Carmen started the car and drove out of the hospital parking structure with no direction. She had already called out of work and it was pointless now to drive all the way to the city just to try to meet up with Sofia for a late lunch. Carmen meandered aimlessly through the streets, pulling over to have fast food alone in her car when the sound of a ringing phone once again filled the car. Her heart skipped a beat and she almost choked on her prepackaged salad thinking it could be the hospital again, but after a brief pause the name of Izel and Luna's school appeared on the car console's screen.

Carmen answered, "Hello?"

"Hi, Miss Sánchez. Your daughter is currently sitting in my office. I hate to do this but is there any way you could come pick her up? I have an urgent matter to discuss with you regarding an incident between Luna and one of her teachers."

"Oh, for fuck's sake." Carmen blurted out. "I'm sorry. Today's supposed to be my first day back at work after a break."

"I understand it's an imposition, but I really insist we should have a conversation before I send your daughter home."

Carmen leaned over the steering wheel and sighed deeply. "Okay, I'm actually pretty close. I'll be there as soon as I can."

Carmen tossed the plastic container onto the floor of the backseat and threw the car in reverse, pulling out of the parking lot she'd been sitting in and headed toward the school, her mother's words about Luna and that Nahuatl word still ringing in her ears.

When she pulled up to the front of the school, most of the kids had already gone home on buses or in their parents' cars. Among the remaining stragglers, Carmen saw Izel waiting for her with Josh at her side. From a distance Carmen could tell Josh was trying to raise her daughter's spirits. The two of them were so engrossed in conversation that they didn't even notice Carmen approaching them.

"I'm sure it's fine, Izzy. You know she's just having kind of a hard time fitting in," Josh said to Izel, "It's just normal stuff to go through when you start middle school. I know I didn't get along with everyone when I was in the sixth grade."

Izel lifted her head from her hands. "I mean, it's not normal though, is it? This is fucking crazy. She's already so different and it's not even starting school that did it, I think. She was acting out even before my grandma fell. You don't know her well enough to notice, but I think something's wrong with her or something. It's like she's a whole different—"

She turned to look Josh in the eyes and caught sight of her mother approaching them from behind, "Oh, fuck," she briefly stuttered. "Uh, hi, Mom."

Carmen looked at the two of them for a moment, almost wanting to join in on the conversation, hear everything Izel had to say about what was going on with Luna, but now was not the time. Not in front of Josh, especially. Instead, Carmen smiled at the two of them.

"Hello, you two!" She turned to Josh and added, "Sorry we seem to only catch glimpses of each other in the middle of family drama. I supposed this might be my chance to introduce myself to the boy my daughter's been texting so much all the time!"

Izel grimaced, "Mooom . . ."

"Oh, I knew you weren't always texting your friends while we were away. You don't smile at your phone that much when Halley texts you."

Carmen was relishing this brief moment of suburban normalcy, embarrassing her daughter as she met her little boyfriend from school.

Josh was relatively unphased though, he held out his hand and said, "Well, it's nice to really meet you too! Sorry I've been such an enigma. I guess Izel's just been too ashamed of me to introduce us until now."

Carmen looked at Izel. "He's funny, too, huh?"

"Oh my God, Mom. Seriously, you gotta go to the principal's office and get Luna." Izel's tone undercut the whole jovial interaction as her face shifted from embarrassment to seriousness. "I think it's pretty serious."

The look on Izel's face wasn't lost on her mother. Carmen excused herself and told them she'd be right back to take everyone home, but could sense from Izel's comments that it might not be a brief visit. When she arrived in the main office of the school, the woman at the front desk directed her to the frosted glass door at the back, through which Carmen saw three silhouettes, two large and one small—Luna. She knocked twice and came in to find Luna, her principal, and Miss Alpert. Luna turned to face Carmen as she came through the door with puffy eyes. The principal, Thomas Anders, motioned for Carmen to have a seat.

Carmen did so, but spoke before anyone else, "Just before we start, you called to tell me I needed to pick up Luna, but didn't say what was going on. Is she in trouble?"

Thomas took a deep breath, looking at Miss Alpert and then at Carmen before sighing. "Well, it's slightly complicated. It's a very delicate matter."

Miss Alpert, white as a sheet, broke into the conversation, "I really didn't mean it. I don't know what happened, but please believe I didn't mean it. I'm so, so sorry, Miss Sánchez."

Carmen looked from face to face, finally seeing Luna holding her arm where a bruise in the shape of a hand had now fully shown itself on her thin wrist.

"Please, explain," she said to the principal, who obliged her detailing what the story seemed to be after listening to both Miss Alpert and Luna.

It ended up being a rather short discussion after all. Carmen was incensed that Luna's outburst was even included as part of the story.

"I mean, we can talk about behavior another time, sure. But this?" Carmen motioned to the bruise on Luna's arm, "*This* conversation begins and ends with you being glad I'm not ready to sue the school and her specifically," she said, pointing to Miss Alpert.

"And we are glad it seems you're willing to not take this to court, we really are," Thomas responded. "I only mean to, while you're here, discuss some concern other teachers have expressed about Luna at school."

Carmen stood from her seat and motioned for Luna to join her as she opened the door. "Then maybe I'll come back another time. I won't hear it right now. Goodbye."

Luna followed Carmen out of the office and down the hallway to the front of the school, where they joined Josh and Izel.

"What happened?" Izel asked before seeing Luna's wrist. "Oh my God. Did those idiots do that to you, Luna?"

Carmen was about to tell Izel that they would discuss the situation in the car but latched on to that question.

"What idiots?"

Izel shrank away from the question, looking slightly ashamed as Josh spoke up, "We've noticed some older kids picking on Luna sometimes in the hallways."

Carmen looked at Luna, who averted her gaze, and back to Josh and Izel.

"We'll . . . we'll talk about it in the car."

Josh said a nervous goodbye to the family and gathered his things to walk home. The three Sánchezes drove home in silence.

21

A bright, full moon hung in the sky, illuminating the waxy leaves of the forest as Yoltzi drifted through the humid night air. The only sound she could hear was the gentle rustling of the leaves in the slight breeze. Through a gap in the trees, Yoltzi noticed a soft glow in the distance, surely a city or small town just over the rise, but more than that she recognized the hills she had grown up seeing. The landscape was unmistakably that of Tulancingo, but if that was the case, the forest she now found herself in had long since been developed into housing.

Deeper into the forest, she saw the faint flickering light of a campfire. She moved instantly and without effort, pulled toward it like an omniscient spectator, passing with ease through the trees. Next to the fire was an old woman. She was hunched, haggard, the deep lines of her face showing not only her age, but also an extreme fatigue. It seemed as if her skin was barely clinging to her bones as she sat by the fire muttering quietly to herself and caressed a string of beads in her hand like a rosary. Yoltzi got closer, trying to hear what the woman was saying, trying to find out why she had been brought there to find this tired old woman. She drew nearer, the old woman unaware of her presence, until she could finally hear what the woman was muttering under her breath, finding that she was not muttering at all. She was softly singing to herself in Nahuatl, the same refrain on a loop, repeating it like a prayer or a chant.

> *Yehua in Xóchitl*
> *xiquiyehua ipan moyollo*
> *pampa ni mitz tlazohtla*
> *pampa ni mitz tlazohtla*
> *ica nochi noyollo.*

The old woman was trembling. As close as she was, Yoltzi could now see the woman's arms covered in cuts and bruises, her feet were bare. The woman stopped chanting abruptly, staring into the distance before snapping her head to look directly into Yoltzi's eyes. The old woman's face was stricken with a terrible fear. Yolzti's heart stopped beating almost entirely but soon realized that the woman wasn't looking at her, rather through her. Turning her head to follow her gaze, Yoltzi saw other faint lights moving through the jungle from the direction of the town in the distance. The woman began kicking dirt over the fire, trying to smother it before moving deeper into the forest, but had to let the embers remain smoldering. At the extinguishing of the light, voices from the direction of the other lights started shouting and they moved rapidly through the trees heading straight toward them.

The woman attempted to run into the dark trees, but collapsed. She was too weak. She was old. She was so tired. She had made it farther than any old woman ought to through such brutal terrain. So there she remained, panting on the ground and clutching her string of beads until the lights from the forest finally emerged from the trees, revealing the torchbearers. A small group of soldiers in Spanish uniform surrounded the woman and, bringing up the rear, a man in Catholic garb approached her.

The missionary priest bent down and looked at the old woman before speaking, "I'll give you credit: I didn't expect to have to chase you this far. We thought we'd be back before dark."

On the ground, the old woman continued muttering her prayer to herself. The priest stood up and kicked the old woman hard in the ribs.

"Let's get this over with. Maybe if I bring your head back on a fucking pike, your idiotic people will give up on the spiritual poison you seem so keen on feeding them."

He called one of the soldiers over and took the sword from his belt. The woman continued her prayer.

"I'll wipe your despicable religion from the land and make a new holy empire from the rubble of your satanic temples. You savages believe in blood sacrifice, do you? You think the blood of your people carries the same weight as the blood of Christ?" He kicked the woman onto her back, raising the sword above his head. "Then this should be a great honor to your gods."

Yoltzi tried to close her eyes but couldn't help but watch as he brought the sword down on the old woman. He pierced her stomach and wrenched the blade across her abdomen, spilling her blood onto the dirt, where it pooled and shone black under the moonlight. The old woman writhed in pain as the priest lifted the sword from her body. She stopped her prayer but did not cease to speak. Blood pouring from her lips, she spoke to them in Nahuatl. The soldiers and the priest hadn't brought an interpreter, so they had no way of knowing that her prayer had shifted from one of protection to a vile curse.

Sputtering with every guttural word of hate, the old holy woman cast the sanctity of her soul aside as she rose from the ground. "You spill my blood to try and erase our gods, our language? You think spilling blood will see the end of us? We've been bleeding into this land since the first sun rose over the world. Our gods live in the dirt as they live in our blood, we're in the food your bastard soldiers will eat from the crops and the water you befoul."

Grinning, her teeth black with blood shone like obsidian in the night. Yoltzi and the soldiers watched in horror as the old woman plunged her hand into the gaping incision the priest had inflicted on her. Continuing to curse the priest and all his people as she dug around in her own chest, her severed entrails began to fall out along with many large pieces of clay. Chunks of shattered pottery clattered to the ground into the dark pool around her feet as she cackled, finally done rummaging around in her chest. Her eyes rolled back, becoming black, as she released a horrible, prolonged rasp of breath that grew to deafening volume and ripped her hand from her gutted body. Nobody uttered a word or even breathed.

Under the cold moonlight, they saw in her grasp her own heart, still spasming. Her body, though now naught but an empty vessel of skin and bone, spoke.

"My rage is the rage of my gods, the rage of my people, the rage of my blood you've spilled. It will last as long as my heart."

The old woman lunged forward, falling dead, as she cast her heart into the remaining embers of her makeshift fire, where it continued to writhe and spasm as it was consumed by the heat of the charcoals.

Her blood had sunk into the dirt, making a thick mud from which small lumps began to emerge, squirming toward the surface like maggots in the flesh. These nodes finally broke through the thick plasma, their wings spreading. Black moths emerged from the dirt, thousands of them, draining upward into the sky like blood from a wound until they covered up the very stars above, swallowing the moon and all light with them.

As Yoltzi felt herself being suffocated along with the light of the night sky, she began to lose consciousness and awoke in a cold sweat. Her entire bed was damp with perspiration and her head throbbed like she had been struck with a hammer. It was still dark outside and the clock on her bedside table read 5:35 a.m. She could not fall back to sleep.

She helped her mother make breakfast, as she did every morning, before taking a shower and heading to work, stopping by a pharmacy for some aspirin along the way. Autumn was later than ever and the heat was already unbearable despite how early in the morning it was, the breeze barely even swaying the branches of the trees. Though, when Yoltzi emerged from the pharmacy, painkiller in her bag, even the gentle breeze was gone. Wind now roared past her ears, carrying with it litter and leaves from the street. It could have been the fall finally announcing its arrival, but Yoltzi felt something in the wind that betrayed this. Something foul and unnatural.

The gray clouds seemed to be watching her from above, cracking an occasional whip of thunder as she made her way to city hall. She greeted the guard and climbed the stairs. Sitting at her desk she tossed back the aspirin with a gulp of coffee, trying to ignore her throbbing head as she began to scroll through her inbox. As she scanned the screen her head only throbbed harder and she began feeling faint. Screens could sometimes sting her vision in the morning and her headache probably wasn't helping, so she stood and went to refill her mug, but barely caught herself on the edge of the desk when a dizzy spell hit her. It was intense, acute, and blinding. She had to hold on to the table so she wouldn't fall. One of her colleagues, Edmundo, headed toward her as soon as he noticed her stumbling.

"Are you okay? What's wrong?"

"It's nothing. I'm just light-headed."

"Are you feeling sick?"

Yoltzi held up her hand. "No. No. I think I just stood up too fast. I'm fine."

Looking up from where her hand had caught the edge of her desk, she met Edmundo's eyes but found only empty sockets looking back into hers. Wounds bled from where the crow's-feet of his smiling face once were as he held Yoltzi by the shoulders, trying to steady her.

"Well, just let me know if you need to go home for the day."

Her pulse thrumming painfully in her head, Yoltzi blurted out, "I'm going to go to the restroom," and quickly, unsteadily, made her way to the women's bathroom.

Not daring to look into the faces of her other coworkers, Yoltzi stared at the floor and thought of the old woman in her dreams, her chant of protection. Her hand trailing against the wall of the hallway for balance, she finally made it to the bathroom door, which she promptly locked behind her.

She washed her face, drank some water from the spout, and felt a little more grounded. Over the running water and beyond the door, she could hear the muffled voices of office chatter. Underneath the murmuring voices, she began to hear the incessant chirp of crickets. They slowly grew from background noise to a cacophony, their horrible droning crashing against her throbbing skull, bringing her to her knees. The pain was so great that she held on to her head for fear that it was truly splitting open from the pressure within. With her blurred and watery vision, she saw shadows swimming beneath her feet. They were pushing against the floor, stretching the thin membrane between their world and hers and impressing the bared teeth and writhing snakes of their death masks against the bulging tile.

Shutting her eyes against the horrifying faces, hoping the visions might go away if she simply denied them her sight, only showed Yoltzi new terrors. She saw a pre-Hispanic piñata, a tlapalxoktli, being cut open from the inside as if something within sought to free itself. The leather skin of the tlapalxoktli parted, bleeding as it shed its insides—a few drops at first, and then a steady stream of crimson. Yoltzi remembered the woman from her dream cutting herself open and disemboweling herself. Unwilling to watch, she opened her eyes, but the vision had manifested before her in the bathroom alongside the swarming shadows and deafening insects. Blood gushed forth from the object, splattering against the walls, the mirror, and the porcelain in a crimson waterfall. The ceiling of the restroom was gone and from the night sky hanging above her descended a pair of tzitzimimeh. One was carrying Luna between its bony arms. It was followed by a wave of winged skeletons bringing with them an entire army armed with obsidian blades and the jaws of beasts.

Yoltzi tried to scream, shrieking at the top of her lungs, but could not even hear her own voice over the force of sound coming from the crickets and beasts before her. Desperate she tried to repeat the old woman's chant, but only pulled fragments from her dream.

"*Yehua . . . xiquiyehua ipan . . . pampa ni mitz tlazohtla pampa ni mitz tlazohtla . . . noyollo.*"

She realized as she strung together these ancient words that she could actually hear herself. Her mind felt clearer and, beyond the illusions, as if looking through a thick fog, she could make out the door handle of the restroom. She continued humming and muttering the fragmented chant as she slowly made her way through the fog to the door. Gripping the handle, she flung open the door and fell out into the hallway back into the quiet murmur of the office.

Standing up, Yoltzi immediately scrambled to the wall opposite the bathroom, but saw nothing. Looking around for anyone who might have seen her crash onto the floor, she tentatively opened the door to the restroom to look in. It was the same bathroom it had always been. Her headache was now gone as well, but the voice of the woman in her dream now reverberated in her head. The quiet muttering, a whisper, scratched at the back of her mind repeatedly.

She headed back to her desk. People were working, talking, and wandering around the hallways as usual, acting as though nothing was wrong. Edmundo approached her once more.

"Yoltzi, I have something for you."

Edmundo's eyeless face once again looked into hers. His features began to blur as Yoltzi was looking not only at Edmundo but someone with traditional Nahuatl tattoos and jewelry. As skin flayed from the eyeless face, the other face became clear. It was like the two images were superimposed over Edmundo, flickering in and out of existence, speaking in Nahuatl, Spanish, and something else entirely as he extended his hand to her. She tried to focus on the black object he was holding, and suddenly noticed it was an obsidian blade. She looked at him, bewildered.

"What's this?"

Edmund's features continued rearranging themselves: his skin turned gray like disintegrating cardboard blowing away in the wind, exposing the bones of his face. She heard the chimes of a tzitzimitl's seashell skirt knocking together as well as ceremonial chants and the crackling of fire. With an open palm, he wasn't threatening her with the carved blade. Instead, he seemed to be offering it to her.

"This is so you can open your heart and cut off your head as decoration for a beautiful tzompantli." The three mouths—Edmundo's, the tzitzimitl, and the Nahua moved out of pace with each other, his voice a horrible mix of the three that seemed to come from deep within his body. "I trust you can find a way."

Yoltzi walked backward, slowly. Edmundo, transformed into a tzitzimitl, followed her with his arms outstretched.

"Stay right there!" she yelled as loud as she could, but nobody in the office seemed to hear her. She continued backing away, humming to herself, until she had a comfortable enough distance to turn her back and run. One corner of the office on the third floor had huge windows. Through them, she watched a massive black cloud of insects, the same butterflies she'd seen in the town square weeks ago, roiling in the sky. From the indistinct cloud she saw figures form in relief as the shape of many tzitzimimeh seemed to emerge from the mass. It was the same army she had seen moments ago in her vision.

Yoltzi crashed through the door to the stairwell, sprinted down to the first floor, and burst into the lobby. Heading for the front doors, she passed small groups of office workers and citizens chatting among themselves, indifferent to Yoltzi or her visions. In their faces Yoltzi noticed the same indeterminant features. It was as if almost every person she saw had a second person superimposed on top of them, bodies with many spirits all blossoming forth like the petals of a carnation. She'd never experienced anything like it. Throughout her life Yoltzi had managed to see the specters of the dead on their own and the vague energy of a person's soul, but now she could see the dead that still lived on in the living. Blurred masses of Spanish, Nahua, and proto-Aztecan features swam around the heads of everyone she passed, all speaking the same words but in different tongues. Many faces, many images of people fighting to be seen in the same figure. When she reached the entrance, she looked at the building's courtyard: a dozen tzitzimimeh had landed. The guard looked at Yoltzi.

"Miss, are you okay? You look very startled. What's wrong?"

Unable to understand his garbled speech, Yoltzi wordlessly pointed at the winged skeletons. The guard looked toward the direction she was pointing at.

"What? I don't see anything."

His words, too, were a confusing jumble of Nahuatl and Spanish being spoken over each other. Two voices from the same mouth fighting to be heard.

Yoltzi left the building without saying a word. She didn't know where to go. The faces of all she passed shifted and spoke to her as she hurried down the street, so she stared at her feet as they took her toward Quauhtli's house.

22

Verón wasn't a fan of phone calls. He had very few friends and wasn't interested in reaching out to the ones he had left. If they ever gathered face-to-face, he was happy to hear about their lives and their families, but he was very private, so he didn't have much to share. But over the weeks since Carmen's departure a weight had been pushing down on him. The night before she left he had meant to apologize to her for not being enough of a mediating force. He hadn't protected her from the workers, from the Church, or from the owners of the land. He felt somewhat responsible for her being sent back home and had been constantly thinking about what he could have done to counteract the undermining she had faced on the jobsite. This was all made worse by the new architect running the construction, Miller. In Verón's eyes he was an arrogant man with no respect for the abbey, the workers, the Church, or for him. In Carmen, Verón had sensed an admiration for the abbey as a piece of history and a delicate touch that sought to keep it alive even as it was renovated. This new Miller seemed to be the embodiment of foreign real estate investors: a precise tool purposefully built for efficient, clinical commodification of land. He was here to build a hotel, plain and simple. They'd had a few conversations, but they usually communicated via memos and through his assistant. Furthermore, Verón missed the girls. He'd grown used to visiting, cooking meals, and having long conversations with them, particularly Luna. When they left, he realized they'd made him feel a little less lonely.

Calling Carmen's number should've been easy enough, but he found himself hesitating. He hadn't spoken to her since their flight and even that was just a short nicety, asking if they had made it home safely. Verón took a deep breath and dialed. When she picked up, he said, "Hi, Carmen. I'm so glad to hear your voice."

"Father, what a nice surprise! How are you?"

"Same as ever. You know how it is around here, at least for me. Life moves slowly unlike over there in New York, huh? How are the girls? Luna's just started at a new school, hasn't she?"

Verón kept asking pleasantries, stalling for time as he searched for the words to start the apology he had wanted to give to her those weeks prior. Carmen obliged, seemingly happy to field the questions. She told Verón that, yes, Luna had started at her new school and she mentioned Izel's boyfriend.

"Ah . . . *the boy*. I recall you telling me about your hunch that she had been talking to someone."

"Yes, his name is Josh. He's quite nice."

"I'm glad to hear everyone is well."

"Yeah."

Verón heard the melancholy in Carmen's voice over the phone.

"*Is* everyone well?" he asked.

Carmen paused on the other end of the line. "I didn't want to ruin a pleasant phone call."

Carmen dropped the cheerful tone in her voice entirely and confessed to him that all was not, in fact, well with them back in New York. Verón listened intently, taking a seat in his office at the abbey and covering his other ear against the noise of the construction. He listened to Carmen's worries about her mother in the hospital and about what had happened to Luna at the hands of her teacher. The thought of apologizing over what had transpired between them professionally dissolved, giving way to a desire to help her through her times of trouble in his capacity as a priest.

"Carmen . . . I'm so sorry to hear what you and your family have been going through. I feel awful for not calling sooner. I know when you were here, we didn't discuss topics of faith and I know you aren't exactly a practicing Catholic, but," he paused, "have you given any consideration to prayer? If not as a means of calling on a higher power, then at least as a way to come to terms with these things."

"Sometimes I consider it, but . . ." she trailed off.

"Yes?"

"Do you remember what I told you on our last night in Tulancingo? About the apparitions?"

Verón sat up straighter in his seat and found himself leaning forward with interest toward the disembodied voice of Carmen on the other end of the line. He had thought about those visions quite a bit when he considered his role in Carmen being sent back to New York. If they had been caused by the stress of her job at the abbey as she thought, then her being reassigned was all in all a good thing. He had considered it the silver lining of the whole situation.

"The ones you saw while on the job here?"

"They've followed me home."

"Well, if they were caused by stress, it sounds like your life didn't get much calmer on your return to New York."

"I know, but I feel like I'm going insane. I mean, what else can I call it at this point? I'm seeing things that aren't there. The other night I almost fell off my roof because of a bunch of butterflies. I hear crickets all over the house and see this . . . this *woman* everywhere. Father I . . ."

"Yes?"

"I feel like I'm even believing what Quauhtli and his friend told me that one night. I'm beginning to feel like it's Luna," Carmen's voice wavered on the other end of the line as she held back tears. "What kind of mother can I be like this? She's probably just having a hard time at school and with Alma in the hospital, but when I look at her, something in her eyes is different, like it's not really her in there. I'm losing it, Verón."

The line was silent as the two of them sat stewing in Carmen's confession, the soft static of the international call ever so faintly popping with the background noise on the other end of the phone. It wasn't out of the question that, between her job and her mother's accident, the stress of her life lately really was eroding Carmen's sanity. But her voice was clear behind the tears. He could hear how desperate she was to not believe the things she was saying. He thought of how alone Carmen must be feeling to have told him all of this. His heart broke for her imagining her suffering these thoughts silently, not daring to vocalize any of this for fear of being seen as someone losing touch with reality, someone who might not be fit to take care of children.

"I do not think you are crazy and I know firsthand that you are a good mother, Carmen," he said. Leaning back in his chair, Verón looked out into the nave of the abbey and saw Quauhtli helping with an installation. The next words he spoke came softly, tentatively, and with great apprehension.

"You think the two Nahuas were onto something?"

"I don't know. They seemed to be able to put words to what I had been . . . have been seeing."

"Then I will look into it, if only to assuage your fears of the supernatural. I will pray for you as well, Carmen."

"Thank you, Father. For listening. And for not judging my state of mind."

The two said their goodbyes and Verón promptly headed into the nave to get Quauhtli. Joaquín approached the priest, no doubt to complain more about Carmen's replacement, but Verón simply ignored him, not having time to entertain yet another story about how "that gringo doesn't know what the fuck he's doing."

He tapped Quauhtli on the shoulder and beckoned him to follow him back to his office where he shut the door behind them. Verón explained the phone call he had just had with Carmen, emphasizing his concern for her from both a spiritual and psychological perspective, but made it clear that he believed that the symbolic shape that Carmen's hallucinations or visions were taking seemed to be Nahua in nature.

Quauhtli grimaced. "Crickets and black butterflies?"

"Does it mean anything?"

"Not entirely sure, but I don't take Miss Sánchez as being the type prone to hysterics. If she's in as bad of shape as you seem to make out, it might have something to do with what Yoltzi had been warning her about."

"You mean about the spiritual threat? Carmen mentioned that you had gone to her house, but didn't get into more detail before she left. How much of that kind of stuff do you really believe, though?"

Verón realized from the scornful look that flashed briefly across Quauhtli's face that his question was taken as an underhanded questioning of Nahua belief but didn't feel it was the time to be apologizing. Despite their difference of faith and respect of the Church, he always saw Quauhtli as a reasonable and levelheaded man and needed to know, point-blank, whether Quauhtli saw any veracity in his friend's claim that Carmen was facing some kind of spiritual threat.

"It's hard to say. I believe apparitions and visions can represent something real, pieces of reality that can't be registered by the conscious mind, and to make any sense of them, they have to be related to us through symbols. But if you think I'm about to put on a headdress, burn sage, and dance to scare the spirits away, well, I won't. That's not my thing.

"Do you remember, Father, all those horror movies with spirits and angry ghosts visiting vengeance on an otherwise innocent family? Have you noticed that most times they're set in homes and towns built on sacred Native burial grounds? They're expressions of a culture who is ever aware of the bloodied ground on which they stand. Even if that guilt isn't present in their daily lives, it lurks on the edges, coming to them in fantastical stories of the dead seeking vengeance. It's not just one plot of land like the movies make out. Mexico is built on makeshift cemeteries, thousands of mass graves, the headstones of countless dead: young women, girls, native people, innocents, and poor suckers. We're cursed. We live on a massive burial ground. Not only is there no justice for the dead but no respect for their remains, no homage to their memory nor rest for their souls."

As Quauhtli spoke, Verón couldn't help but feel the comments were aimed at him indirectly. The walls that they stood in now, the vaulted ceilings of the church being renovated for a foreign investor seeking to squeeze yet more money from the building's old stones, must've seemed like a massive sepulcher to Quauhtli. The collar had never felt quite so tight around Verón's neck as it did in that moment, imagining the blood that had been collectively spilled to build this place from the dusts of Tulancingo. Even in Catholic tradition, the sins of the father are visited upon the children. It had been laid out for Verón since he was a child in the very first book of the Bible, the story of creation and the introduction of death into the world, the seed of man and serpent forever bruising one another.

Quauhtli went on, telling him what Yoltzi had relayed to Carmen, giving Verón a mild sermon of his own on the myth of the tzitzimimeh and the underworld of Mictlan. At the end Verón stood up, nodding repeatedly as he processed the mass of information.

"It seems I have my homework cut out for me. I'll consult the Church's archives. There are many recollections of Nahua practices and myths as learned by my—" he paused, looking at Quauhtli with some guilt in his eyes, "my predecessors."

Verón took leave of the abbey and left Quauhtli to return to his work.

Quauhtli helped finish the install of one of his largest pieces for what was to be the main lobby of the renovated hotel that would soon take the abbey's place. It was a light fixture of carved wood taller and wider than Quauhtli himself. He had found the knotted remains of a drought starved pepper tree on a hike months prior and hauled it away in his truck. Hung upside down by the thick trunk of the tree, the bark was stripped and the branches shaped through carving and the grafting of other spare woods into five tendril-like appendages that held the main light source in its palm. Smaller lights dripped down from between the fingers of the pepper tree, escaping what looked to be a hand about to close around the larger light source. Miller came over, on site for the first time that week to see the finished install. He clapped Quauhtli on the back.

"Looks great, Cottle."

Quauhtli turned to thank him for the compliment, but the architect was already off to another part of the nave telling one of the laborers that he was doing something wrong. His work for the day more or less finished, Quauhtli walked to his truck and started the engine hoping to get home before sundown for the first time that week.

Rumbling down the ragged roads around the edge of Tulancingo, he watched the sky molt over his home from the pale orange of the golden hour to deeper shades of red and purple. The days of summer weren't much longer there than any other time of year given how close to the equator they were, but the color of the sky always marked the beginnings of the seasons. The fall sky above Tulancingo bloomed blue and purple like a bruise and Quauhtli barely got his wish as he turned onto his quiet road with the sun just beginning to disappear behind the hills. Pulling into his driveway, though, he stopped short. A light was on inside that he had not left on in the morning. He reached under the passenger seat for the cold handle of his revolver.

His house had been burglarized in the past when he lived nearer the city center and when he moved out of the metro area, where there were even fewer people and police, he finally found himself taking after his old man and learned how to shoot.

Leaving the truck idling in the driveway with the headlights on, he approached the house slowly and quietly, keeping the headlights to his back. He crept up to his living room window and peeked to see a hunched figure crouched under his dinner table, rocking back and forth. It was small, he thought, and there didn't seem to be anyone else in there, so he went inside. His guest didn't seem to notice or care as he walked in, revolver tucked into his waistband. Rocking back and forth, muttering under their breath, Quauhtli noticed that they had wrapped themselves in a throw blanket he kept on his couch.

"Hello?"

They did not respond. Quauhtli left them for a moment and did a quick sweep of the rest of his home for other people, but the lump under his table seemed to be alone. Coming back into the living room, now convinced he was dealing with one of the zombies wandering the roads from time to time, gone out of their minds on the heroin that ran through the veins of the southern highways, he got as close as he felt comfortable. He spoke slowly and clearly.

"Is there anyone I can call to come get you?"

The lump continued to rock back and forth muttering. As they rocked, a lock of gray hair fell from the blanket wrapped around its head and Quauhtli froze. The old woman that Carmen suspected of having the jade bracelet? Was he now being visited by the same specters that were apparently haunting the Sánchez family? Stepping back, he finally realized that the guest was muttering in Nahuatl. Without thinking, he drew the gun from his waistband, not considering the futility of brandishing bullets against a spirit.

Another lock of hair slipped from under the blanket. Black. Quauhtli dropped the gun and tore the blanket off to reveal Yoltzi. She looked at him with tear-filled, crazed, and bloodshot eyes.

"Ah! Yolandita!" he shouted, "What the hell are you doing? How did you even get here?"

At his words she covered her ears and cried out in Nahuatl, "Leave me be! Leave me be!"

Quauhtli dropped to his knees and held her by the shoulders as she thrashed against his touch.

He spoke in Nahuatl, "It's Quauhtli! Quauhtli! You're in my house!"

Yoltzi stopped struggling and pulled her head back, looking intently into his face, scanning his features over and over, searching for him. Her voice was weak and wavering as she spoke back in their native tongue.

"I keep seeing them. I can't stop seeing them. I can't stop hearing them."

"What? You can't stop seeing what?"

"Everyone."

Quauhtli lifted her up and sat her on the couch, pouring her a drink in an attempt to calm her nerves even slightly. Sitting across from her, he watched as she scanned the room, her eyes darting back and forth before finally settling on Quauhtli, which seemed to calm her down.

"I can see you clearly at least."

"What do you mean? I want to help but I need to know what's wrong."

"Visions," she waved her hand in front of her face. "They've never been like this. They're so clear that they're taking over my head. I can't tell them apart from my present. Everyone is all mixed up now. I thought I couldn't even hear what people were saying until you spoke in Nahuatl to me."

"It started today?"

"It started after my dream last night. I think I was given a look into the past, a look at just one of the things that continues to affect the present, and now the two are merging in my head. Everyone I see has more than one face, looking at me through the eyes of all their ancestors, speaking in the voice of everyone that came before them."

If anyone else had told Quauhtli something like that, he would have assumed they were losing it. Even given Yoltzi's visions and feelings of premonition in the past, Quauhtli had always believed them only with qualification. She was someone very connected to the same past he had told Verón about through her blood and through her studies and Quauhtli saw her sensitivity as an expression of the same kind of subliminal anguish he attributed to works of fiction like *Poltergeist* or something.

Yes, he would assume that Yoltzi had succumbed to some kind of madness, if it hadn't been for what Verón had told him was happening more than a thousand miles away. He leaned in, hoping to further focus Yoltzi on himself.

"Have you seen anything more to do with the girl? Is it to do with Luna?"

Yoltzi's eyes stopped searching and looked into Quauhtli's.

"Tlapalxoktli."

Quauhtli settled Yoltzi into the passenger seat of the still idling truck and turned back down the road he had come. Headlights on, now under the rising moon, he headed back to the abbey. When they arrived there were no cars or trucks left in the parking area save for the truck of the night guard, don Sebas. Approaching the abbey with Yoltzi behind him, Quauhtli knocked on the door and called out to him inside.

"Evening, don Sebas."

After a few minutes, they heard the sound of the night guard coming from inside the abbey.

"Who is it?"

"It's me, Quauhtli. I'm here to pick up a few things I forgot."

"Hello there, Quauhtli," he said as he opened the door. "You're still working this late at night?"

"It's not a big deal, don Sebas. This is my cousin, Yoltzi." Introducing her as her cousin saved him from having to give any explanations.

"Nice to meet you, señorita. Come in. I was just making my rounds. When you're done, just make sure to lock the door."

"Of course."

The guard continued his rounds and Quauhtli guided Yoltzi through the dark hallways until they reached the site of the scaffolding accident. After the wall had been breached, it'd been boarded up while a solution for how to reseal the room was devised. Quauhtli removed the boards with the back end of a hammer lying on the ground. The air that wafted out was cold and stale. Centuries of mildew and dust floated on the current that seemed to wheeze from the hole in the brickwork.

Quauhtli switched to Nahuatl, "The piñata was in here when the wall cracked open."

He swung an electric lantern around searching the darker corners of the room as Yoltzi pulled out her phone, turned on the flashlight, and looked along the decaying bookshelf against the wall. Books rotted away by mold and bugs, small wooden knickknacks, and religious paraphernalia were all that was to be found, though.

They looked for the piñata where Quauhtli said they'd originally found it, but there was nothing but dust and cobwebs. They looked through the shelves and the boxes, in every corner, and in between every item. Nothing.

"Shit! Well, what now?" Quauhtli asked.

"It's already started then. Luna has it."

"There's no way she took it all the way back to the States without anyone noticing."

"This explains everything. The moment I saw that girl I knew she was destined to be seen by Itzpapálotl."

"Then there's nothing we can do."

"Yes, there is. I have a brother in New York. Martín-Nelli. I can stay with him."

"What the hell are you talking about, Yoltzi? You don't even have any papers. You're not planning on crossing through the river, are you?"

"Sometimes one has to take risks."

"And how do you know this is one of those times?"

"Because I know, Quauhtli. People will die if I don't help."

Quauhtli threw his hands up in frustration.

"Girls turn up dead every day right here, in *our* town, on what used to be *our* land, both young and not so young girls. Evil is right here, so why look elsewhere? If you're so sure you can save people from the sins of the past, from curses and grudges, why go so far when you only have to go around the corner?"

"Because that burden that should be our own is pressing down on an innocent girl somewhere. I don't know why, but for some reason I have an opportunity to stop it, I think. I've seen the pain and anger that lives in that piñata the girl took. If I stay here and do nothing, I'll go mad, Quauhtli. I don't think this will stop until the girl dies or is saved. I can't change the history of this country. I can't appease the dead that we walk over every day, the dead whose graves have been covered with asphalt and concrete and steel, I can't lift all that pain from all that land.

"But I might be able to do it for one of them. I saw her in my dream. I saw how she died with hate in her blood. I can save her and I can save the girl."

23

Luna walked straight toward the school, not looking at any of her class-mates pouring into the front doors or back toward her mother wishing her a good day from the open window of the car. All weekend Izel had watched their mother ask Luna repeatedly if she was sure about going to school today, telling her it's perfectly alright to stay home after what had happened with Miss Alpert.

Luna had only responded, "It's not like she'll be there."

There was a cold assuredness in Luna's voice, lacking any innocence or naivete. She was right, of course. The school had quickly called in a substitute while the district investigated whether Miss Alpert would be allowed back on campus. Miss Alpert wouldn't be there that day, but Luna's bruise, blooming from underneath the sleeve of her jacket, was very present.

Izel followed Luna from a slight distance and watched the heads turn. The small barnacles of kids who clung to the walls of the hall-ways in conversation, already having heard about what had happened, tapped one another and motioned to little Luna as she walked alone through the throngs of fellow students.

Josh was up ahead, leaning against the wall just inside the school's entrance. Luna passed him without so much as a glance and Josh turned to look at Izel, raising his hands and gesturing at Luna in confusion. Watching Luna silently walk straight ahead filled her with renewed guilt.

"She's back at school already?"

"Mom told her she didn't have to come, but Luna kind of insisted? Or didn't seem to care one way or the other? I'm not sure."

"That sucks. Everyone's talking about how Miss Alpert's probably getting fired."

Down the hall as Luna walked toward the middle school lockers, Izel saw one boy touch his wrist and gesture to his friends that they could see the bruise on Luna's arm. The halls were full of melodrama. Luna walked with her eyes to the ground until she reached her locker, turning the dial and pretending nobody was around her when Izel saw the three boys come around the corner. Albert tapped Ron on the shoulder and pointed to Luna and the triad swerved to intercept her at her locker, snickering as Lester started talking to her.

Izel's feet moved before she could think, but Josh grabbed her by the arm.

"You might just make it worse."

Izel yanked her arm from his grip and kept walking. As she pushed through the other students shuffling back and forth in the hallway, she heard Lester over the din.

"Oh shit, it's true!"

He was pointing to Luna's outstretched arm as she pulled books from her locker.

"I thought everyone was bullshitting, but she really hit you, huh? What'd you say to her?"

"Can you guys just leave her alone?" said Izel, putting her hand on Luna's back and standing beside her.

"We just wanted to know what she said to make Miss Alpert freak out and hit her or whatever, calm down."

"She didn't say anything to *make* Miss Alpert hit her. Miss Alpert clearly just shouldn't have been a teacher. Why do you even care, anyway?"

Ron, standing next to Lester, spoke up, "I heard that she was yelling about how everyone's a colonizer or something and she didn't wanna get taught history by a White teacher. Maybe we wanted to know how she feels about having a White sister, you know?"

The three boys chuckled and Izel's face flushed with hot anger, but more than rage, what Izel found herself feeling was a piercing shame. These three assholes had been harassing Luna like this since she'd arrived at the school and Izel had been ignoring the whole thing. Her little sister's persistently bright disposition throughout their lives had instilled in Izel the notion that Luna was somehow indestructible. Throughout the many changes in their lives—their dad leaving, them moving upstate, leaving friends behind, Mexico—Luna had put on a braver face than anyone else. Izel realized that she'd not only failed to be a big sister Luna could depend on, but she'd actually learned to rely on Luna. Now, as she looked down at her shaking little sister, Izel realized how deeply unfair that was. Luna wasn't looking at any of them; she was just staring into her locker and shivering. Izel's heart sank like a rock as that initial anger was fully drowned in a lake of pity for herself and Lunita.

"Don't you have anything better to worry about?" Josh had finally followed Izel over. "If you guys know about what happened already, then just leave her alone."

"We were just curious to hear a firsthand account. Why's everyone being so sensitive about it?" Albert responded, a shitty grin on his face. He was clearly enjoying himself.

"Aren't you like thirty? Maybe you should be more curious about a GED than a middle schooler, you fuckin' moron."

Albert stepped toward Josh. "Say that again."

The two boys stared each other down, continuing to insult each other and telling the other to do something. Izel just watched Luna. She hadn't moved from her spot in front of her locker. Izel leaned down and tried to turn Luna by the shoulder to look at her. She needed Luna to turn and look at her and know that her big sister was actually there this time, that the times before were a mistake, that this was how things were supposed to be and would be from now on. Selfishly and selflessly, Izel needed Luna to know all of this. She needed absolution and for Luna to be made aware that she did, despite previous evidence, have an older sister. But Luna shrank away from her touch. As she shrugged her hand off, Izel caught a glimpse of Luna's face: her cheeks were glistening with tears, but the look on her face was not one of sadness or fear. It was one of limitless spite, one which twisted the innocent face into a bestial visage.

It hardly even looked like Luna. Lips curled back over her bared teeth, she snarled under her breath as tears poured down her contorted face.

"Pasty gringo pieces of shit. Their ancestors should have been dashed against the rocks and lost to the sea. Their heads should be on pikes all along the coast."

Izel grabbed Luna hard by the shoulder and could barely move her, but managed to twist her body just enough to peer into her unseeing eyes. Luna's bright eyes had been replaced with a darkness so deep and vast Izel thought she could see stars within her sister's skull. The sound of the boys arguing and the other students gathering fell out of focus, muffled as if they were underwater as she looked into the gruesome face that had replaced Luna's. Between their briefly interlocked gaze Izel swore she felt a border, some inexplicable point between their eyes which, if crossed, one could fall from into that darkness which seemed to inhabit her sister. It was the feeling one gets looking out over a cliff, not quite vertigo, but a bodily recognition of danger. Izel could sense Luna was just past that point where, if she reached for her, she could tell she would fall as well.

Someone slammed into Izel's shoulder and knocked her against the lockers. Josh had been sucker punched by Ron and fell onto her, snapping her back into the moment and sending Luna tumbling to the ground. The look that had been on Luna's face disappeared, replaced by a more human anger and Izel watched in helpless shock as she leaped at Ron, digging her overgrown nails into his cheeks and tearing at his face. Izel struggled to get out from between Josh and the wall, clamoring to her feet as the students in the halls closed into a circle while Luna thrashed Ron. She bit Albert as he tried to pull her away from Ron and Lester's hesitance to hit a little girl was finally superseded by the feeling that what was digging its claws into his friend was more akin to a rabid animal than a middle school girl. He pulled back and threw a wild, untrained punch into Luna's side. She managed to scratch at his arm as the wind was knocked out of her and she crumpled to the ground next to Ron.

Izel shoved the other students out of her way and wrapped herself around Luna in a bear hug both to stop her and protect her from any further retaliation.

"Fucking psycho!" Ron shouted. His cheeks were red with scratch marks, but only a small trickle of blood leaked from the right side of his face where Luna had managed to gouge a nail into his skin.

Josh once again placed himself between the boys and the two sisters, but any further conflict was interrupted. Miss Moore and another teacher had pushed their way through the crowd and split the two parties, reprimanding the violence and interrogating how it began in the first place.

Izel was given the privilege of calling her mother and informing her that she would have to pick them up from the principal's office.

"Again?" Carmen asked over the phone. She was whispering into the receiver, trying not to yell in her office. "What the hell is it this time? Is it Luna again?"

Izel shifted in her seat. "No. Not really, I mean. It's a long story."

"Well, I can't skip work again to pick you girls up, so you'll have to wait there for a little bit after school. I'll leave early to come get you."

"Sorry, Mom."

The call ended. She looked over at Josh who smiled at her, which made his swelling, purple cheek scrunch up unnaturally around his eye.

"I can't believe I tried to stop you thinking *you* were the one who might make it worse," he laughed.

Looking at him now, sitting in that office, Izel was struck by how funny Josh must have looked stepping up to be the tough guy protecting her. She couldn't help but picture him as he was in that moment, with an already swollen cheek adding a little extra cheer to one side of his face. The idea of him trying to glare at someone with his exceedingly kind eyes made her laugh far more than his joke did. She didn't tell him that, though, and just chuckled, letting him feel like he had successfully lightened the mood.

Izel turned to Luna, rubbing her gently across her upper back. "You all right?"

She didn't turn to look at her older sister. "I just wanna go home."

"I'm sorry if we just made things worse. We were just trying to get them to leave you alone. I know they've been bothering you lately and," Izel paused, "I'm sorry the first time I decided to do something about it ended up like this. I just wanted to—"

"Yes, I'm sure they'll leave me alone now," Luna said, cutting her off.

Luna pulled her backpack open, getting out her pencil case and journal. It was obvious that she didn't want to talk to her sister and Izel needed to respect that. Her attempt to assuage her guilt about Luna being bullied had only landed the three of them in trouble. Josh tapped Izel on the shoulder and showed her an Instagram story someone had posted of him getting punched in the hallway.

The two of them went through the various videos and pictures other students had taken of the scuffle, finding at least some entertainment in the whole ordeal. It was kind of fun to see the outside angle of something that had happened so fast in the first person. They passed the time like that for a while, watching videos and texting friends about what had transpired.

As they spoke, though, she saw Josh's attention focus on something just behind her. She stopped talking and he met her eyes, motioning silently toward Luna. The sound of her pencil scribbling frantically on the paper, drowned out by their conversation, was now apparent in the mostly silent office. Izel turned to look at Luna, reminded of what she had seen her doing at her locker when the fight started.

Luna drew with a heavy hand, the amount of pressure on the pencil threatened to tear at the paper as she scratched lines into her journal. She repeatedly scrawled face after face onto the same page. They overlapped, their lines bleeding into one another as the page grew darker and darker. Izel recognized many of them as Azteca, not knowing the names or meanings of any of the images but recognizing the style: bared teeth and facial features that seemed to swirl off the bodies of the creatures Luna drew as their crazed eyes stared out from the page. Each one Luna sketched was different, as though she was either making them up or depicting the entirety of the pantheon. As the vast collection of graphite faces and figures piled up on the page, the edges curled inward and almost all white space had been erased, overrun by mixed shades of gray and black which swallowed all form. The more she drew, the more muddled the lines became; the faces merged and created fusions while still maintaining their distinct forms. One could see how two faces together also created a single, different face.

The page was drowning under the cacophony of figures. But Luna only had one more to go it seemed, which Izel watched her draw with zealous ferocity. Luna pounded into the page with thick, brutal line work, forming a skeletal face—its jaw, teeth, and cheekbones exposed by the flayed skin hanging from its chin. The face dominated the entire composition, the dark lines which comprised it plowed through the rest on the page. All the smaller figures, the minor gods and beasts that had sprung from Luna's fingers, were dashed away by the oppressive, gruesome visage she carved into the paper, holding her pencil like a murderer's knife.

The entire time they waited for their mom, Luna had to sit listening to Izel and Josh, subjected to boring conversations about people she didn't know. What the hell was so important about this to Izel? They didn't even talk about anything interesting. They just talked about what happened time and again. Their voices faded; she could hardly hear them now. If she did, she wasn't processing the noises they made as words. Luna had been having trouble understanding what people were saying to her lately.

It felt like someone was trying to split her head open. It almost felt like someone was burying an axe in her skull, but it was coming from the inside. Her eyes gently teared as the pressure in her head built up. It came in waves, she found, as if there were an ocean spilling over some precipice into her head, each crashing wave building the pressure, overfilling the vessel of her skull, and increasing the pain between her temples.

When she imagined the waves, swirling dimly under the shimmering dark waters were faces, hundreds of them—faces and people and pictures. The pain lessened when she peered into the roiling, shallow sea of images. The sound of each wave blurred together into a dull, throbbing static—a screaming whisper. She took out her journal and tried to pull the faces out of the water, give them definition. This all felt autonomic to Luna, like an exercise she'd been practicing for years and now came as second nature. If she took the faces from beneath the murky waters of her mind to paper, the pressure in her head would lessen. It seemed quite straightforward as far as Luna was concerned.

It was the same with the voices she heard. If she just repeated them, her headaches would go away. She didn't even have to say them out loud, she could just mouth the words and it would be good enough. That's all she had to do to keep the pain away. It was so simple. It was all she had to do. She just had to repeat what they showed her and they wouldn't hurt her. It wouldn't hurt if she just listened. It wouldn't hurt if she just let the waves wash her away.

She remembered going to the beach with her mom and Izel one summer, where Izel showed her how to float on her back. It had been so easy to let the waves pass under her, they rocked her so gently. She didn't even notice that the tide had been carrying her away from shore until she heard her mom shouting over the roar of the ocean. Izel had swum out to get her and grabbed her wrist, pulling her along back to the beach.

When they'd crawled back out of the surf together, Izel turned to her and said, "I know it feels nice, but you gotta make sure you don't let it carry you away, okay, Lunita? Mom just about lost it when she saw you so far gone."

Luna scrawled into her journal, relieving the pressure in her head until her mom arrived. Josh's mom was there too. She was White and looked older than Carmen. Luna sat quietly in the office as everyone talked. She was sure people were asking her questions, but none of them felt real. Everyone was gesticulating while they talked. Josh pointed to his eye and then to Luna and raised his shoulders in a shrug. When the assistant principal explained what had happened in the hallway, how Luna had jumped on that boy Ron, Luna looked at the floor and clutched the side of her rib cage where Lester had knocked the wind from her. At every turn Izel made as clear as possible that none of it was Luna's fault. Josh tried explaining that Luna had only done that after Ron had hit him, but Carmen didn't seem to be listening to him at all, she just looked at Luna and Luna looked back at her mother. In the eyes of her mother, Luna noticed a tumult of fear and doubt and guilt. She could see right through her.

Luna didn't remember the car ride home, but that night at dinner her mother continued to look at her like that. Even as she asked her questions about how she was feeling, apparent motherly concern in her voice, Luna could see the dim light of distrust in Carmen's eyes. She had noticed people treating her differently lately, but for the first time saw that even her mom couldn't look at her the same as before. Was this what growing up was like? Forgetting things and people looking at you differently?

After dinner, Carmen gave her a stiff and distant hug, telling her she'd have to stay home from school for the next couple of days.

"I can't take any more time off work right now, sweetie. I think they'd fire me if I skipped another week to stay here with you." Her mother had never looked more tired. "And I can't pay a sitter right now. Will you be okay here by yourself?"

"I'll be fine alone."

Her mother didn't look convinced, but clearly had no other option but to leave her youngest alone in the house while she went to work.

Climbing the stairs to go to her room, Luna was followed by Izel. Holding Luna's shoulder both to comfort and to stop her, she caught her just outside the door to her room. She wore the same mix of concern and guilt on her face that their mother did as she apologized.

"I know I said it before when we were in the office earlier today, but I just wanted to tell you again that I'm sorry. I don't just mean about the hallway today, but, like, everything. You've probably been having a tough time being at a new school and all and I've just been too distracted to check in with you or even ask how you've been doing. I guess I have Josh to talk about things with like what happened to abuela, but you've been kind of alone haven't you?"

She squeezed Luna's shoulder.

"I think I was trying to show you that I was there for you today, but I just made things even harder for you."

A weight that had been hanging over Luna crashed down on her. The emotional toll of the last month—the fear of losing Alma, the loneliness she felt walking the halls of a new school, the distance of her family—all threatened to pour forth from her eyes as her older sister rubbed her shoulder. The sob that stood on the verge of being released was slammed back down her throat as her head throbbed again.

"It's okay," was all Luna mustered in response as her head rang like a bell full of whispering noise and voices.

"And fuck those guys anyways." Izel smiled. "I shouldn't say this but it was pretty funny how you made those assholes scream."

Luna's head was deafeningly loud. She couldn't hear her own thoughts over the sound of crackling fire and voices that simultaneously screamed at the top of their lungs and whispered in her ears. She wanted to talk to Izel, to say something back, but she couldn't even hear her sister correctly. If she spoke herself, she wasn't sure if she'd be able to hear it over the awful din in her head. Then the voices went quiet and she was finally able to hear herself speak, but she wasn't saying anything. Luna heard her voice talking to her sister, but she wasn't the one thinking or saying the words. Someone else was talking in her voice.

"Yeah, I wish those pieces of shit would just die."

Izel stopped rubbing Luna's shoulder and her hand pulled away ever so slightly. "Well, they definitely are pieces of shit. But don't let Mom hear you talking like that."

"I hope they choke on their own fucking blood."

Luna was trying to tell Izel she didn't mean that. She wanted Izel to keep rubbing her shoulder and know that she forgave her for not standing up for her sooner, but all that came out of her mouth was vile death wishes and Izel had already pulled her hand away from her little sister. Luna felt trapped in a body not her own as her thoughts were overrun with images of those three boys. She saw them spitting blood, being burned to death, having their heads smashed to pulp. The sights made her sick to her stomach and giddy with excitement. Some horrible foreign part of her mind jumped with joy at the imagined sight of outsized revenge against those boys.

"Okay, uh, goodnight, then," Izel said, going back downstairs and leaving Luna alone in her room.

With the door shut behind her, Luna heard her family downstairs talking about her. The kitchen was just beneath her room and she could make out the muffled voices quite clearly.

"I know I'm probably saying the obvious, Mom. Like, I know what it looks like today, but I think there's something really wrong with Luna."

There was a pause before their mother said anything. "Does . . . does it seem like her? When you look her in the eyes?"

Luna stopped listening and opened the closet. Crickets and grasshoppers crawled around the ground at her feet, skittering and hopping out of the oppressive darkness that emanated from the open doors. The hanging clothes were full of holes and moths fluttered around in a small swarm, tapping against the walls as they landed and took off. Luna was filled with fear and joy as she looked down at the shining corpse of the piñata. Its leather casing had grown wet with plasma and a viscous liquid that coated Luna's hands as she lifted it from the floor. In her hands it pulsed in time with the beating of her heart and the throbbing of her head.

The headaches would go away if she just used it, she thought. If she let it out, she'd feel so much better. They only wanted to come out, part of her said, and once they were out, she might not feel as alone. Nobody would have her back but them, couldn't she see that? Didn't she hear her own family talking about her downstairs like she wasn't even their daughter or sister anymore? She sank her fingernail into the wet skin of the piñata. Warm blood flowed down the lengths of her fingers and along her forearms. The pressure in her head surged along with the voices of many. She repeated their words, letting the pressure out, with her eyes shut tight, rocking back and forth with the piñata in her grasp.

24

Albert was on his way back home late at night. He'd been over at a
friend's house where they smoked weed in the garage-turned-clubhouse
and played an old game console hooked up to an even older, clunky
CRTV. Albert yanked the old wooden side gate shut behind him and
strolled onto the sidewalk, pulling up the fabric of his sweater and giving it a thorough sniff to check he didn't smell too much like smoke. It
wasn't that bad. He'd just take the long way home and air-out enough
that his parents probably wouldn't notice the smell, if they were still
awake. They didn't really care about much, but they seemed to relish
any opportunity to give him trouble. It didn't matter to them that he
was a fuckup, it only mattered that they could tell him so.

When he hit Leavenworth, he looked down the direction of his home
and turned the other way, figuring he'd take another meandering lap
around the neighborhood before he headed back. Counterintuitively, he
pulled a pack of cigarettes from his jacket pocket and shook one out.
After he lit it, he traded the lighter into his left hand and turned his
right over, inspecting the faint mark still left behind from where that
deranged middle schooler had bit him at school. He chuckled a bit,
blowing smoke and steam out into the cold night air. That idiot Ron
was the only one of them who actually got in trouble for technically
starting the fight.

Hearing himself break the silence of the night with that small
chuckle made Albert realize just how quiet it was out on the streets.
It wasn't that late. Usually there'd at least be some families still up
watching a movie, TV, kids playing games, people coming home from
a night out; but there was just . . . nothing. He stopped for a moment
and inhaled the cigarette, hearing only the soft crackle of the igniting
tobacco. When he exhaled, something akin to wind chimes or a beaded
curtain sounded behind him, but there was no breeze and, when he
turned to see where it came from, he saw no chimes either.

He shrugged and continued into the eerie night. He couldn't even hear the familiar white noise of the highway bordering the neighborhood, nor did he see the lights of any cars. Not exactly sure why, he sped up his pace. There was an uneasy feeling creeping up his lower back that he couldn't explain, as if his body wanted him to move faster toward home. The wind chimes sounded again. He turned around quicker this time: still nothing. Every house he had passed had their lights off now. He threw the cigarette into the gutter and kept walking, decidedly faster now.

Making the next left onto Plymouth Street, Albert was going to cut his walk short and just head straight home. As he traveled down the block, the chimes followed distantly from behind—from somewhere beyond the darkness formed by the conspicuously extinguished streetlamps. No longer able to attribute his unease to simple paranoia from the blunt, Albert broke into a run. He was racing down the dark street, pursued by that glittering sound from the dark. The low, static hum of the highway was back, the sound of many tires rolling over the rough pavement. It was growing louder too. So was the gentle tinkle of the chimes. Albert made it to the end of the block and saw the sign for Leavenworth again. He made the right toward home.

His heart thumped in his chest. The sound of the highway had grown and now in his ears, over the heavy thuds of his heart and the clattering sound he dared not look back at, was the whispered scream of thousands. A breathless cacophony of tortured souls howled like wind in his head. He reached the end of the next block. The sign read Plymouth Street.

Albert froze, short circuiting, unable to comprehend how he had apparently run in a circle, back to where he'd first took flight from the sound. The sound. It was behind him. The clatter of many small objects grew closer.

There was no spit in his mouth, his throat was dry, and the overgrown high schooler was trembling as he turned around. Empty eyes stared back into his and a dress of seashells swung gently as whatever had been following him stepped toward him. Crickets leaped from its empty sockets, wriggling out from somewhere within the cranium as the skin of an old woman slowly fell away from the bones of her face.

All he could do was run, but the clattering of seashells behind him sounded in time with his own strides, matching his every footfall. It took him only seconds to reach the end of the block. Being a track runner had its advantages. The streetlamps were still off, and he could hardly see more than a few feet ahead under the sliver of moonlight, but the reflective street sign was just legible: Plymouth Street. He ran harder. Plymouth Street again. The sound of the shells continued in pursuit. Plymouth Street again. Tears sprung to Albert's eyes and burned along with his lungs. He was gasping for air, gulping down confused sobs as he tried to keep moving faster. In the dim light he saw something lying in a yard ahead and made a quick move to grab it in passing, picking up a small garden shovel for self-defense.

The hoarse screams in Albert's head were deafening when he finally saw Leavenworth. This had to be some awful nightmare. One that might end if he just made it home to his bed. He turned right and saw his house. Ignoring the pain in his lungs and legs, the blubbering boy leaped over the side gate like an Olympian and wheeled around to tear open the sliding door of his home. Inside, he collapsed over the dining table wheezing for breath. The time on the microwave flashed 3:14 a.m.

The seashells were gone. The screaming had ceased. Over the thudding in his ears, though, Albert heard a floorboard creak from somewhere in the house. He pressed against the wall to hide from view and clutched the shovel in his hands, scanning the dark room, when he suddenly realized that everything looked wrong. A painting of a castle on a hill hung above a couch much larger than the one in his living room. *Just a nightmare.* The creaking was coming down the hall toward the living room and kitchen. Albert kept looking around the unfamiliar space that a moment ago had looked exactly like his family's living room. He felt crazed. His head was still swimming from the lack of oxygen and he saw a silhouette emerge from around the corner, just a formless shadow in the lightless home. Still high off fear and adrenaline, Albert brandished the shovel and cried out as he swung to defend himself.

He connected and sent the man sprawling against the countertop. His gruff voice howled in pain as he clutched at his side and scrambled to grab what he'd just dropped on the counter.

"You fuckin' tweakers! I don't have anything of value!" he cried.

Albert stood there gripping the shovel, his massive frame towering over what he now made out in the darkness to be a wiry, older man. Tears still poured down Albert's face. He had no idea how this dream was supposed to end. He thought this was his house, where it would all stop.

The old man turned from the counter, gripping a gun in his weathered hand. Albert tried to knock it away with the shovel. The muzzle flash illuminated the room just enough for Albert to see the face of the terrified old man. The second and third shots showed the empty-socketed face of the old woman just behind him. Albert was staring blankly at the ceiling now, the old man standing over him shaking as he dropped the gun. The sound of the man frantically dialing 911 and yelling into the receiver faded into a muffled background noise as Albert's vision darkened. Staring back at him from above were those empty eye sockets. The skeletal woman seemed to grow larger as Albert receded deeper and deeper into the black ocean of his fading vision. She was the sole inhabitant of his now pitch-dark world and in the abyss, fading into the dim cold of permanent sleep, he could now see that her eyes were not, in fact, empty.

Lester was safe at home. He had the place to himself for the night while his parents were out at a movie, no doubt they'd stop at a bar on their way back. He bounded up the stairs from the basement with a bottle of cheap rum he'd stashed away down there after snaking it from a party weeks earlier. Tossing himself onto his desk chair, he pulled the lever underneath and leaned the seat back a bit. A Discord notification flashed on the side of his computer monitor. A guy he'd met in a meme server, @ChimpConnoisseur2124, had direct messaged him to hop online and play with him. Lester swigged the cheap rum from the plastic bottle. Warm. His face twisted up and he sucked in air before shaking it off. He slipped on some headphones and hopped into voice chat.

"Hey, Chimp."

"My buddy just hopped off, wanna take his spot and play some duos together?"

"Sure."

They'd never learned each other's names online. There was a tacit agreement on a lot of the servers Lester spent time on that you should never give anyone anything that could somehow identify you. The kind of stuff they shared wasn't even that bad—in their eyes—but there was an understood collective fear of being exposed in real life, classmates, teachers, parents, college admissions taking the things they said out of context and making it look worse than it was. Imagined judgement by others silently haunted the chatrooms. So, Lester was @lurky-murker1592 and Chimp was just Chimp.

The two of them played a couple rounds, Lester taking a drink every now and then. He eventually decided to take a little swig for every head-shot and after a few more rounds, his ears felt hot in his headphones. He'd been telling Chimp all about what had happened at school that day. Chimp kept laughing while trying to talk and it made his crooked teenage voice break, which made the two of them laugh more.

"You just decked her?"

"I didn't know what else to do, man! She was going nuts and I thought she'd like scratch his eyes out or some shit."

"I can't believe you punched a little Mexican girl in the kidney," Chimp wheezed into his microphone, "hard enough to send her sliding across the linoleum of a hallway."

"I don't know, man, I just freaked out and swung."

"No dude. That's hilarious."

Lester lit a cigarette and pulled an empty can of soda over to use as a makeshift ashtray. He took a pull and set it across the lip of the can as the next round started. After a few minutes the audio of the call became distorted and choppy. Lester was having a hard time hearing any of his friend's callouts and there was a bizarre static layered over everything. It sounded like someone was shaking a rattle into Chimp's mic while he was talking.

"Chimp? You have a TV on or something? I can't hear you anymore."

Chimp's voice was entirely drowned out by the static and Lester began fiddling with the cord on his headphones, thinking there must be a wire split somewhere inside. The rattling continued and was joined by a soft chanting. It sounded like a crowd of people, far away, were shouting and grunting in time with the atemporal shake of the rattle.

Chimp's character was still moving and playing normally on the screen. Over the static, Lester finally heard his voice again.

"Oh, yeah it's just on in the corner of my room."

"Okay. Weird. I couldn't hear you for a second, only the sound of whatever that rattling is."

"Rattling?"

"Maybe it was just the static."

"Hey, Lurk, turn around!"

Lester spun his character around to check behind them, but didn't see anyone. He dove for cover and zoomed in on the scope to check if anyone was there.

"Don't see anyone. You see where they went?"

"No, Lurk. I mean turn around, bruh," the rattling had grown even louder, no longer suffering any kind of distortion over the headphones. It was crystal clear. Chimp's voice was calm and commanding, "You still haven't noticed? It's been in here for a while now. She's just been looking at your dumbass waiting for you to turn around."

In the faint reflection of Lester's room from one of the darker corners of his computer monitor something moved. He jolted and flung the headphones off, his head spinning around and knocking the chair over as the wheels caught on the carpet. The cord of the headphones hit the old soda can he'd been using as an ashtray and the lit cigarette tumbled to the floor.

Lester didn't notice the smoldering polyester of the carpet next to his desk, the growing circle of caramelizing synthetic fibers. He was transfixed on the slow encroachment of the woman. Her flayed skin swung with the clattering of her seashell skirt as she slowly crossed the room toward him. In the dim blue light of the computer screen, the tzitzimitl's hollow eyes were voids of pure darkness. Its arms moved around, the wrists and fingers lashing out into the air in an apparent conjuration. The joints moved wrong, like there was nothing between the bones. Her hands spun around repeatedly, turning in circles. The acrid smoke of the burning carpet finally hit Lester's lungs. On the ground behind him the smoldering cherry of the cigarette had grown into a small fire. The house, unrenovated since it's construction sometime in the 1980s had the opposite of modern fire-retardant carpeting and now that it had caught, it quickly swallowed Lester's desk. Consuming the wood like a hungry beast, the flames leaped to the window curtains and painted the walls.

Black smoke billowed from the carpeting and the toxic chemicals made Lester's throat burn and cinch shut as he helplessly gagged for air. He made to break for the door of his room, but she was standing there. The petite figure of the skeletal woman had grown into a towering broad beast of bone and ribboned flesh that charred at the edges along with the rest of the room as she lurched toward the boy. With each step she seemed to grow larger and the room accommodated her. Space bent around the pallid monster as Lester, his eyes boiling in his head and his lungs spasming for oxygen, found himself at the foot of the mountain she became before him. The flames rose into walls of cosmic scale and violent brightness. She bent down, her great empty sockets the size of moons.

Within her skull was a cosmos, full of stars and birthing galaxies. Lester watched as the great multitude of lights blinked out of existence, millennia passing in an instant as the night sky within the woman's cranium was crushed into inky blackness. That darkness, the darkness at the end of all things, of a starless night, reached out from the goddess's eyes and pulled Lester into its hopeless waters. He plummeted into nothingness, his soul consumed by the eternity of the void as his body collapsed into the bubbling plastic tar on the floor of his room to be consumed by his burning home.

The fire burned unreasonably hot. There was nothing left behind to suggest there had been a body in the home, let alone anything to identify Lester as a victim. There was no way it could've happened, they'd said, house fires simply don't burn hot enough. Even his bones had turned to ash carted away among the rubble. The absence of the morbid evidence denied his parents any closure and they would always hold on to the fantasy that he could be alive somewhere, a spiteful, house-burning runaway rather than scattered ash in a landfill among charred lumber.

Ron was tearing down a quiet road in his Jeep. He was bundled up in multiple layers and a parka as the cold tore through the flimsy canvas top of the old, roofless Wrangler. He wasn't headed anywhere in particular. He just needed to be out of the house, away from people. The tires screamed against the pavement as he drag-raced nobody down the empty streets of the once industrial part of town. At an intersection, in the glow of the streetlamps and traffic light, he poked his head up so he could get a look at his face in the rearview mirror. In the dim light he could still faintly make out the scratch marks and the one deep gouge that had been drilled into his cheek by Luna's nail.

He swore and punched the accelerator, taking the entrance to the freeway. This late at night there were hardly any cars on it. It wasn't an interstate, just some lonely old highway through a forgotten corner of the American Rust Belt. Ron sailed through the night finding himself calmed, almost lulled, by the steady sound of the tires against the road. He went to switch the radio on to wake himself up when he saw something crawling out of the air vents. A dark, glistening insect wriggled its way out of the vents and slowly opened and closed its wings before taking flight inside the car. Ron swatted it away and turned up the stereo.

Another bug, possibly the same one, fluttered by in front of his face and he managed to catch it between his palm and the window. Flattened against the plastic of the driver's window Ron saw that it was a black butterfly. The streetlamps passing by on the highway illuminated the squished bug from behind and its tiny scales shimmered against the glass. Initially captured by the novelty of the small creature, Ron shrugged and flicked it off the window somewhere into the backseat to be forgotten.

Then it flew by his face again. He went to swat it, only to miss and see another one on top of the dashboard. Looking over at the air vent, dozens of them were beginning to wriggle free from somewhere in the car's ventilation.

"Ugh!" Ron shut the heat off and slammed the air vents shut. He shivered from the cold and the thought of all those tiny little bugs crawling around and over each other in the depths of his car. Some part of his mind couldn't help imagining being in there with them, like taking a worm bath on *Fear Factor*.

He shuddered and kept going down the highway toward his home. The drive wasn't as relaxing now that he knew his car was infested with bugs, majestic as they may be. Just when he caught sight of the first sign of his exit, still two miles away, the vents shunted open. A flood of shimmering black wings burst out like the night's tide and swarmed the car. They landed on every surface of the interior as well as on him. Ron howled in confusion and disgust as he swatted at them, desperately trying to keep them away from him without crashing the Jeep.

Each time he swiped his hand, more butterflies appeared to block his view again. The interior of the car was invisible now, impossible to see through the thick blanket of teaming wings that enveloped him. He couldn't see his own hands anymore as he tried to swipe them away from the windshield. He felt one of them on his face against the sensitive flesh of the wound from Luna's nails. It was noticeable even in the blizzard of the rest of them. The sensation of it beginning to enter the wound was indescribable and excruciating. The insect wriggled into his skin as he fruitlessly batted away at his cheek. He could feel it piercing the layers of his flesh like an IV as another landed. Ron desperately groped for the zipper on the canvas door to open the car and release all those awful insects when he felt something grope back.

Hard, bony fingers clutched his shoulders from behind. Someone was sitting in the backseat, digging their fingers into his shoulders, and pinning him in place. He couldn't lean forward far enough to reach the windshield anymore. When he strained to try, he felt the fingers pierce his skin. The parka became very warm as the bony claws wrapped around his collarbone, stabbing into the muscle and grabbing the bone like a handle.

He slammed his foot down to the brake but felt nothing. He couldn't feel his foot on the gas either. It was like pressing into air where the footwell once was and Ron noticed that he didn't feel much of anything, not even the warmth from the blood soaking his parka. In the rearview mirror a pair of hollow eyes set in a pale skull of a face looked back into his from the flickering darkness made by the swarming bugs. The world was silent as their gazes locked.

The butterflies vanished and Ron's sight returned in a bewildering instant. He only had a fraction of a second to realize his shoulders were unharmed and that his foot was still on the gas before he finally registered the fire hydrant as the Jeep's front end wrapped around it in a head-on collision.

The crumpled Jeep leaped into the air and the canvas rooftop simply ripped away from the mangled metal frame as Ron slammed into it. He sailed through the night air for what felt like forever in his severely concussed mind, but what was of course only a violent instant. The low, LOADING ONLY sign was waiting for him. The sharp metal cleaved into Ron's abdomen as his body rag-dolled into it, impaling him only halfway and ripping him open like a fish. Looking around, he could see he'd come off the freeway at some point and into town.

I wonder when I did that.

Nothing was registering for him. He tried to lift himself off the sign, but only felt his leg crumple beneath him like a sock full of ground meat. His body involuntarily spasmed from the unfelt pain and caused blood to flood from his mouth. He reached behind him with a limp hand and felt the cold edge of the parking sign poking out from the other side of his back, slick with blood.

The muscles in his neck fully gave out and his head slumped forward, looking straight down at the opposite corner of the metal sign where a black butterfly was perched, gently opening and closing its wings.

That's how they found him. Eyes open, unseeing, and staring at something that was no longer there.

25

By morning the entire town had heard what happened. Calls went out to all the households with students at the girls' school notifying them that classes had been canceled for at least that day to give classmates and the community at large some proper time to process the sudden deaths of three students.

Carmen's body went stiff as she listened to the message over the phone. With the cell phone up to her ear, she looked across the kitchen at Izel as she ate breakfast at the small table where the girls usually had their morning meals. She hadn't woken Luna yet given that she wasn't even supposed to be going to school that day anyway. Carmen slipped her phone back into her pocket and sat down at the table across from Izel.

"Iz, have you heard anything from friends or seen anything on Instagram about what happened last night?"

"No, why? I haven't really checked my phone yet this morning I just woke up."

"Well, you're not going to school today. Classes are canceled."

"What? Why?"

"Those three boys that you said had been bullying Luna . . . the ones that she ended up attacking yesterday . . . they died last night. I recognized their names in the call I just got from the school."

Izel stopped eating and looked at her mom. The two of them stared silently at each other as they both tried to grasp whether or not the other might call them crazy for what they were both thinking. Izel looked over her shoulder, clearly looking for Luna and turned back to her mother.

"What the fuck? Did the school call you specifically?"

"No. No they haven't. I mean why would they? It was just a prerecorded message from the principal."

"What do you mean 'why would they?' Just yesterday your daughter attacked the three of them like a wild animal and they all wound up dead that same night?"

"There's no way they'd actually think a little girl did that. There's no way she could hurt those three boys like that, she's tiny. Do they even live near us?"

"I mean, yeah, they live outside of town, but," Izel looked around, "I don't know . . . I know what everyone around town will be thinking, though."

Carmen grimaced and nodded. It was ridiculous to think Luna had the capacity to physically hurt those boys given her size, but she thought of the butterflies on the roof. She was thinking of Yoltzi's warning back in Tulancingo. She understood what Izel was implying. The kids in town would be talking about how Luna went to Mexico to learn voo-doo or Mayan sorcery or some bullshit. The parents wouldn't be much better. They would simply come up with some "rational" explanation for the whole thing. If they weren't the kind of crazed fundamentalist Christians she'd met around here who think everything is witchcraft, they'd say its gang connections, a bad cholo tío who heard his little niece had a problem with some gringos. She knew what was on the TVs in the bars, restaurants, and homes in this town at prime time. Everyone around here was fed on the kind of informational diet that made them think MS-13 wasn't only already encroaching on upstate New York but was selling weed specifically to *their* children.

Carmen looked at the clock and saw that she needed to leave if she was going to make it to work on time. After all the time off she'd been taking recently she didn't have the option to use any more. She had no choice but to leave Izel and Luna home for the day while she went into the city.

"You'll be all right here by yourself, Iz?"

Izel was already buried in her phone, swiping through stories and texting kids in her class about what they heard had happened to Albert, Lester, and Ron. She looked up from her phone, though, and back at Carmen.

"I'll be fine, Mom. I know you have to go to work. I'll stay here with Luna for the day. We'll be fine."

Carmen sat in her car, letting it idle in the driveway for almost fifteen minutes as she couldn't bring herself to put the vehicle in reverse and pull away. Something wouldn't let her leave Izel and Luna all alone in the house together that day. She wanted to stay with them so badly, but she couldn't afford to get fired right now. She just had to swallow her anxieties and get on the road if she was going to make it through the day. Taking a deep breath, Carmen finally threw her car into reverse and watched the house recede in the rearview mirror as she headed off to work.

Inside, Izel slowly finished her breakfast while learning as much as she could about the deaths of the three boys from school. It had only been a few hours since they were found so not many people knew exactly what happened but all the rumors said that it had been violent for all of them. She heard the house creak above her in Luna's room and a terrible chill ran up Izel's spine as she realized that she was afraid of her little sister.

She remembered what Luna had said the night before as she went to bed: "I hope they choke on their own fucking blood."

Luna would have been left alone at the house anyway if school was in session and Izel didn't want to be in their at that moment. She shivered and headed out the door, texting Josh that she was on her way. When she got to Josh's house, his mom greeted her with a hug and a sorrowful look.

When Izel found Josh in his room, she immediately closed the door behind her. They stood there for a moment, not saying anything, but having a moment of joined shock at the situation that they had awoken to. The whole school had seen the two of them get into a confrontation with those three and they showed up dead the very same night. No matter what the reality was, they could rest assured that they were being talked about in some capacity all around town. Josh finally broke the silence between them.

"What the hell is going on?"

"I don't know, dude! It's fucking crazy right?"

"Do you think people will think it has anything to do with us?"

Izel gave him a look and rolled her eyes. "Of course they will! Even if they don't think it seriously, everyone's already probably getting jokes ready about how Luna finished the job last night."

"Does she know yet?"

Izel didn't answer, but instead sat down on the floor with her back against Josh's bed. She didn't know how to respond. Of course, nobody had *told* Luna what had happened, but she was sure Luna knew. Izel looked into Josh's face, his cheek still red and slightly swollen from where he had been clocked the day before, and didn't know how to tell him what had happened the previous night. Well, it wasn't that she didn't know how to tell him, but she didn't know if she could admit that part of her really thought that Luna *did* actually have something to do with all this. She started small.

"Luna said something to me last night."

"Yeah? Did she hear something?"

"No. No. She didn't hear anything. I don't think anybody told her about it yet, but . . ." Izel paused and let out a deep sigh, "she said she wanted those three to die."

"Well, that makes sense. I mean she was mad at them, wasn't she? That seems like a normal enough thing to say."

"Then she said, 'I hope they fucking choke on their own blood.'"

"Less normal. Much scarier. But she was just an angry kid, you know? It's not like she actually meant it."

Izel couldn't bring herself to say it outright, so she instead started to cry. Deep inside of her somewhere she knew that there was something wrong with Luna and an even deeper part of her really did think that Luna had done that to those three boys, but she couldn't admit it out loud. Not only was she terrified by the thought of Luna doing something like that to her, she was mortified by the thought that she could suspect of her little sister like that.

"Woah! Hey! It's gonna be okay."

Josh slid down to the ground next to Izel and put his arms around her, repeating variations of that phrase, trying to convince Izel that everything would be all right. She cried into his shoulder and shuddering through her tears told him how scared she was.

"Please don't say I'm crazy if I tell you this."

"I promise not to think you're crazy. Given what apparently happened last night, I'm kind of willing to believe anything."

Izel smiled weakly.

"So you know how my whole family went to Mexico together?"

"Yeah."

Izel began telling Josh the story of her time in Mexico, which he had heard before, but this time she didn't leave anything out. She told him everything about the old woman, the scaffolding, and the Nahua who came to visit one night. They sat together on the floor of Josh's room for most of the day talking about what had happened in Mexico and how Izel was starting to think there was something larger at play.

Driving home from work Carmen was full of anxiety. All she had been able to think about that day was the look that Izel had given her that morning when she broke the news about the three boys. They hadn't discussed it point-blank but Carmen needed to know whether Izel thought that Luna could have had something to do with what happened the night before. She hadn't had the nerve to ask her that morning, too afraid to be seen as crazy by her own daughter, but after a whole day of the thought tearing at her mind, she knew she wouldn't be able to let the evening end without knowing the answer to that question.

Pulling into the driveway of the house, she once again sat there and let the engine idle. At the beginning of the day she couldn't bring herself to leave and now a part of her was terrified of going back inside. She shook her head and turned the car off.

Inside, she looked around for the girls, but didn't find either of them. She couldn't hear anyone moving around in the house either. She called out to her daughters, "Izel? Luna?" As she climbed the stairs, she could hear something coming from Luna's room. Izel didn't seem to be home, but Luna certainly still had to be. Something was happening in her room, rustling and fluttering sounds came, muffled, through the door as Carmen got closer. For the first time in a while it seemed, the door wasn't locked; Carmen paused after the knob turned and very slowly cracked it open. It was so dark in Luna's room that Carmen could hardly see the inside even with the light of the house at her back. When her eyes finally adjusted, she could see what the fluttering sounds had been. Hundreds of bugs flew around the room, smacking against the door and flying past Carmen's head as she opened it wider. The light from behind her fell on the foot of Luna's bed upon which the piñata sat, throbbing and glimmering wet in the faint light that leaked in. Carmen was entranced by its terrible appearance.

She swung the door wide, realizing that it was the piñata from the construction site and understanding what Alma had been trying to explain to her in the hospital. When the light flooded the room, movement in Carmen's peripheral drew her eye up. Near the ceiling, above the bed, Luna floated in midair, supported by a flying bed of insects. She turned her head to look at her mother, eyes black as obsidian, and spoke.

"Mictlan in rising. Revenge will come to the land and the dead will steal the sun back for themselves."

It was Luna's mouth moving, but the sound seemed to come from every corner of the room. It was all encompassing and deafening. The only thing Carmen could hear was the terrible alien voice penetrating her mind. She tried to cover her ears as the crickets began to sing, drilling their awful song into Carmen's skull.

"Luna!" she cried out but couldn't even hear her own voice.

The sound was so powerfully painful that she was sure her head was about to implode and out of some survival instinct she slammed the door shut again. The sound stopped and the pressure was relieved from Carmen's head. She slumped to the ground with her back against Luna's door and began to cry, reaching up to feel the door handle which was once again locked.

26

Quauhtli was working at the abbey that night as he often did. He liked working in silence, and the solitude of the abbey among its ancient and tortured sounds were like echoes of eras more miserable than his. He could spend a full night among the creaks of the old planks holding up the roof, the whimpers of the contracting and expanding wood. He thought it impossible that he was the only one who felt the history in the ragged old material of the abbey's walls. Imagining the place populated by tourists, he wondered if they'd hear those echoes of history howling, muffled, from within the stone walls scrubbed clean of the blood which mortared them, but stained nonetheless.

That night, he was trying to finish up some wooden ornaments that he had to repair and paint. He'd promised they'd be finished this week. Miller had no interest in what he was doing. He wouldn't even talk to Quauhtli most days. Quauhtli wasn't too bothered by this. He didn't need his own job or deadlines explained to him repeatedly. No one messed with him and that was one of the things he liked the most about working there. He knew the history of every corner of this abbey, its architecture and decor, what it was missing and what it had more than enough of, the changes in theme and renovations. The statues, the icons, the paintings, the tableaux, the bases of the candles, the reliefs, the carving of the columns that sometimes showed a variety of styles incorporated in different periods, following the trends of the times and without much consideration to aesthetic coherence. He knew how to be loyal to the artistic spirit of the construction, and how to respect the work of the numerous artisans and construction workers, most of them indigenous, who throughout time had added and taken out elements for a variety of reasons.

Quauhtli was up on a scaffold, painting, when he heard a scream, an electrifying howl which couldn't be confused with the building's own sounds. His body went stiff, only his eyes moved, darting around the darkness looking for a source. For a moment, he thought a murder was taking place within the abbey. An instinct toward assuming the worst filled his head with the image of the empty construction site being used by a passing gang to take care of some poor snitch or police officer. It wasn't the most absurd idea. He'd worked on enough construction sites to have seen it before. Once, he'd arrived on a site in northern Hidalgo to a crowd of laborers standing around a blood-smeared drop cloth, hastily wrapped around some unfortunate soul, tossed in among the scrap wood. The plastic tarp was only barely opaque enough to blur the gruesome sight, but not enough to conceal it. Some of the more curious workers had gone to lift the plastic sheet up when Quauhtli decided to walk away.

He climbed down carefully, trying to not make any noise. He slowly walked among the shadows, through a hallway and then another, and suddenly, he heard voices. He hid against the wall until he heard a familiar voice.

"Who's there?"

"It's me, don Sebas."

"What's wrong, Quauhtli? Are you trying to scare me to death? I hadn't seen you and I had no idea you were around."

"I've been here all night." He pointed toward the central nave. "I was working and I heard a scream."

"Ah, sorry about that. That's *Radio Muerte*, the show. Have you heard about it?" don Sebas asked, showing him his old, rackety radio. "I've been listening to it for a long time."

"Yes, don Sebas, everyone has heard of *Radio Muerte*," he replied with a smile. "I'm almost done here. I want to finish a few things on the central nave wall and I'll be out."

"Need to warm up a little?" Don Sebas held out a small pint bottle of mezcal and shook it.

"No, thanks." Quauhtli waved the offer off and smiled. "Mezcal and climbing scaffolding doesn't seem like the best idea, does it?"

Quauhtli headed back to work. He felt a bit silly now, being spooked so easily and laughed at himself as he climbed back to his work. When he reached the top, however, his smile quickly faded and was replaced by an awful cold sweat. He felt ill with anxiety and fear. Looking up at the section of wall near where he was to hang the ornament, he saw something bulging forth. In the darkness it was hard to make out, but the growth slithered down toward him, stretching against the surface as if there were an invisible skin on the brickwork. Reaching him, Quauhtli saw its form pressed against the veil separating his world from that of the dead, a woman. She was skeletal and in her hand he could make out an obsidian club.

He wanted to refuse to believe he was seeing something like this. He even made to pick up his tools like he would keep working, but his hands shook too much to grab anything. There was no way he was going to make his way down the scaffolding like this.

"You're afraid, Quauhtli," the specter said in Nahuatl.

So it was obvious to the ghost as well. Quauhtli's head swam. Even after hearing about spirits from Yoltzi for so many years and growing up with description and stories of the gods, he was wholly unprepared for such a vivid encounter.

"You and your friend should stay away from that which doesn't concern you. It's time for vengeance," the voice continued.

"If you say so."

"You shall be a powerful man. The people will be back from Mictlan to demand what is rightfully ours. The underworld will empty out into that of the living through the girl. She will be the vessel of our vengeance."

"What I see is my people being carted away to Mictlan."

"Many more will die. You and your friend are royalty. You still call yourselves Nahua. You recognize the blood in your veins for what it is, unlike so many others who choose to ignore it. You can live like princes or be devoured like dogs."

The walls were crawling with shadows, moving quickly: silhouettes of men, women, and children running desperately side to side. Then the skeleton disappeared. Quauhtli took out his lamp to check whether it was still there. His hands were still shaking. The shadows were still moving in a frenzy among the white walls. There was a putrid stench. Unable to continue working there, he descended the scaffolding without gathering his things and ran to his truck. It was nearly two in the morning, and he tore down the highway as fast as his old pickup would go.

There was no wind, and the inside of his truck was still stale and hot from sitting in the sun all day. He opened the window to let in the cool night air when another pickup truck with half a dozen men armed with AK-47s on the back caught up with him. Their masks were covering their faces, decorated with pre-Hispanic skulls. Quauhtli kept driving without looking at them directly, only sneaking glances in his rearview mirror. While he was wary of them, of course, at the moment they seemed so similar to the spirits that seemed to haunt the land that he couldn't think of anything to do but ignore them. By denying them his fear, it seemed he could get them to go away like a malevolent specter.

Quauhtli had grown up around enough boys who joined the likes of the men behind him to know just how similar they were. There was a rage within them, a feeling that something had been taken from them, something that should have been their right. Prosperous lives were impossible for them from the moment they were born, it seemed. Even if they had a chance, by time they were teenagers the promise of easy money and power was too good to pass up. The men in that truck behind him wanted the same revenge as the spirits, they just didn't know it. Revenge against history, taken out on the wrong people every day.

They kept pace with him for a few minutes without doing anything. Suddenly, one of them gave an order and the driver sped up, leaving Quauhtli behind. When he drove past Morelos Square, he noticed another group of men had several people on their knees. There was a bonfire over one of the grassy areas.

"Lawless land," he said out loud.

When he arrived home, he found Yoltzi standing in his living room with packed bags and a defiant look on her face. She had said the other day that she wanted to go help Luna, but despite how confident she looked standing there in his living room, Quauhtli knew she was in no condition to travel. She had been staying at his house since he found her under his table and still couldn't understand anything but Nahuatl. How she expected to get to the border let alone to the other side was beyond him.

"I'm ready to leave."

"Think this through, please. You're risking your life for people you barely know."

"You don't get it. This is not about me knowing them or not knowing them. This girl runs through my veins, and yours. I don't know how, but there she is. These forces trying to possess her are the same ones that have broken everything we are and what we live for."

"How can you be so sure?"

"The signs are all there. I've been seeing them everywhere I look. What's happening to the girl is the same thing that's happening here and if I don't stop what's happening to her, I don't think there's any hope for us here either."

"Is that everything you're bringing with you?"

"I don't need anything else."

"It could be a long trip. Listen to me. If you speak to the mayor and explain that you have to go see your brother and make something up so it sounds urgent, he can maybe help you get a visa and go, legally, on a plane. I'll help you with the money for the flight and everything."

"Quauhtli, you know how this is. Even with his help, it'd be hard to get approved for a visa. And either way, it would take weeks, even months. There's no time."

"It's too dangerous."

"It's dangerous *here!*" she motioned around them. "Do you remember when it was unusual for someone to get killed here? Nowadays, people disappear every day and there are mass graves with bodies dismembered and burnt, corpses hanging out from bridges, heads being found in parks. There's an epidemic of raped and murdered women. This is normal now."

"And do you think that's going to change if you confront the specters up north?"

"I don't know. I just know that I've seen the pain of the specter that's haunting the girl. It's so angry, Quauhtli. It's forgotten that there's anything good in the world of the living as it is blinded by revenge. But I've seen it! I know who she was when she was alive. I can remind her that she was among the living too and that it's not all bad here. I can make her understand that the living can live well."

Quauhtli saw in her tear-filled eyes that he wouldn't be able to persuade her not to go.

"You're still seeing and hearing things, aren't you?"

She nodded.

"Then I'll have to buy your bus ticket for you."

Quauhtli carefully drove her to the bus station. He was afraid of running into the same brigade he saw earlier. If they saw him with a woman, there was an even higher chance of getting stopped. Quauhtli tried to keep the conversation going.

"Reaching the border is the easy part. What will you do after?"

"Don't worry about it. My brother sent me a list of everything I have to do, who I have to contact and everything else."

"You know, there are people who stop these buses and kidnap everyone inside."

"Don't worry."

They reached the bus station at a little after three in the morning. There were only a few people hanging around the depressing shack, buzzing fluorescent in the desert night. Moths bounced against the harsh white lights on the outside of the station. At the counter Quauhtli looked around thinking he might be the oldest person there. Sitting around the interior of the station were young men and women with fabric luggage, old coats, and the sparkle in their eyes of the promise of a new life and the fear of not living to see another dawn. He talked to the counter attendant and got Yoltzi her ticket.

"Well, see you . . . someday, I guess," she said.

Quauhtli wasn't very good at showing affection, and Yoltzi wasn't either. He thought of hugging her goodbye, and she wanted that, too, but they just remained still, looking at the floor. He stretched out his hand and she held it. He held her shoulder with his free hand.

"Goodbye, take care," he said, forcing a smile.

"You too."

He turned around and walked out the door, headed to the parking lot, climbed in his truck, and took a deep breath. He put the key in the ignition but couldn't turn it. He stayed there in silence. He saw a black suburban truck drive by, full speed, and behind it, two police cars with the siren on. Behind those came two pickups with a turret.

"Fuck!" Quauhtli beat his palm against the steering wheel.

He grabbed a small backpack from under his seat, put on a jacket, and walked back toward the bus station. There was an ATM, and he withdrew as much cash as it would let him. He went to the waiting room for the bus to Ciudad Juárez. There were a lot of people, a lot of them sleeping on the benches, some of them on the floor. Yoltzi was standing by the window. She looked at the buses and the people in the dark.

"Let's go."

"Where?"

"I'm taking you to the border. My truck can handle the road."

"Don't mess with me, Quauhtli."

"I'll leave you at the border and head back."

"Forget it. It's pointless. I already have my ticket."

"It's not pointless. Screw the ticket."

"Quauhtli, you can't protect me forever."

"You can hardly talk to people right now. I could see in your face back inside the station that you were having trouble keeping up with what was going on. You were just staring at the attendant. I can't let you try and make it up to the border on your own the way you are right now. I may not be able to cross with you, but I can at least make sure you get far enough to make your own stupid decisions."

He picked up her bags and started walking back to his truck before she could even respond. When she rounded the corner of the door to go back outside the passenger door was already open and Quauhtli was in the driver's seat. The engine was running.

27

Verón spent the entire day in the church archives. There was an interesting yet chaotic collection of every imaginable type of document. It was evident that no one had come to do any research since the times of the Mexican Revolution. He found educational manuscripts from the sixteenth century, an 1867 invoice from cattle sales, yearbooks detailing the efforts of evangelists and chronicles on community work. Most of the documents were related to the abbey's finances, the daily administration of the institution, and the property's regime. There were interesting documents on the relationship between the Augustines and the Dominicans, as well as the itinerant missionaries. He found some testimonies and reports on heresy and Satanism in 1715, as well as the crown-ordered measures for the second conquest: the spiritual conquest. He was more interested in finding anything related to piñatas and how they were connected to tzitzimimeh. He imagined it'd be hard to find documents relating the arrival of the tzitzimimeh to Earth, but maybe he could find an indirect reference.

Verón was about to give up at six o'clock. He was hungry, his eyes stung, and the old dust had penetrated deep into his nose. He gathered some of the documents he found interesting, even if they weren't directly related to his research. The lighting was terrible. Right then, Father Saldívar arrived. He was over eighty years old and had been handling the archive for half of his life.

"My child, they've told me you've come in search of some documents."

"That's right, Father, but I couldn't find any."

"May I know what you're looking for?"

"It might sound silly, but I'd like to know if we've documented the presence of indigenous piñatas, tlapalxoktlis, in the temple during the first years of the establishment of the abbey."

"Interesting." The old man studied the shelves of old material. "Any reason for the sudden interest in old clay pots?"

"It's complicated, Father. But have you ever heard about the tzitzi-mimeh?" he asked, laughing nervously.

Saldívar nodded. "End of the world stuff. Demons coming down from the sky."

"You know about them?"

"Yes, of course. I had to learn *something* surrounded by all these old papers. I've always been a little morbidly fascinated with other cultures' versions of apocalypse."

"What else do you know about them?"

"The Nahuas celebrated the fire ceremony every fifty-two years. It was a function of their calendar, which was really two calendars: a spiritual one of 260 days and a solar one of 365 days. Each day of either calendar was dedicated to different gods and spirits, hundreds of different meanings for every single day for fifty-two years! Really makes you appreciate only having to worry about one God and a handful of saints, doesn't it?" Saldívar chuckled and smiled at Verón, "You know it's really rather interesting to me the separate calendars, such a literal and everyday practice of separating the civic and practical life from that of the spiritual. Also, that their spiritual calendar was about the length of gestation. It's always fascinated me how we choose to count time in accordance with our cultural—"

"Father!" Verón cut off the old scholar's rambling. He knew Saldívar was an impressive wellspring of knowledge, but had heard him lecture before. If he allowed him to start pontificating, he'd never get his answer. Verón cleared his throat. "The new fire and the tzitzimimeh?"

"Hm? Right. The calendars aligned once again every fifty-two years. It was their most important celebration of life, the closing and opening of a new spiritual century. It was a time between time, where the state of the universe was uncertain. People tossed out belongings, made sacrifices, and every household hearth was to be extinguished save for one holy fire. From that sole fire from the last century, a new one was kindled to begin the next hundred years.

"In their cosmogony, they were living under the fifth sun. Four generations of the human race had been wiped out before them along with the previous four suns. On these fifty-two-year alignments, they weren't sure if the sun would continue rising. It was considered a dangerous and unlucky time. Massive rituals of prayer, song, dance, and sacrifice were performed."

"To keep the sun alive for the next cycle."

"Exactly. The songs were so intricate and important it's said that a drummer who missed a beat was executed."

Verón tried to encourage the archivist with a little humor of his own. "Fifty-two years to practice a song to stop the end of the world is certainly a very high-stakes performance."

"Well, the last celebration was in 1507. That year, they had the most lavish celebration in the history of Mesoamerica. The lords of Tenoch-titlán, Texcoco, and Tacuba were in attendance. The next one would've been in 1559, but it wasn't celebrated because of the conquest."

"The end of the world certainly never comes from where you would expect, does it?"

"Yes. They spent all their time worshipping hundreds of multifaced gods to keep the sun from extinguishing, only to have a Spaniard with gunpowder and a runny nose bring the sky crashing down. Makes you wonder how wrong we'll be about our own judgement day. We've been waiting on John's Revelation for two millennia now and one has to think about who our snot-nosed conquistador will be."

"Yes, of course." Verón was squirming to pull the answer he needed from the meandering old man. "How did the tzitzimimeh fit in to all this?"

"The tzitzimimeh were the goddesses of the night sky, massive be-ings who lived in the darkness of the cosmos, their very joints composed of whole stars. If a new sun failed to rise at the dawn of the new century, the tzitzimimeh would descend and devour the earth. They were war-rior women who'd died during childbirth, symbols of the death which so closely clings to new life. They're mentioned in the Codex Maglia-bechiano," explained Father Saldívar, referring to the Aztec document that dated back to the sixteenth century.

"So, they were only a threat during this ceremony's eve?"

"Yes, that's supposed to be their only window of opportunity. During the five unlucky days of the new century, if the new fire ceremonies weren't sufficient, the offerings not enough to sustain the sun, the music of prayer played out of tune, the tzitzimimeh would darken the sky and destroy humanity," he replied, and laughed, showing a decaying, yellowing denture.

"And when would the next new fire ceremony take place?"

"I don't know, my child. Do the math."

Verón took out his cell phone. He typed 1559 and kept adding 52. 1611, 1663, 1715, and so on until he reached 2027.

"This year, 2027," he said, part flustered and part amused. "Right now."

"Are you sure?"

Verón double-checked and got the same result.

"Yes, I'm sure."

"What time of year did the celebration use to take place?"

"Some sources say December, but it's hard to know. Many modern scholars have tried to match the calendar up with modern Gregorian timekeeping."

"But the weather wasn't too cold around these areas."

"That's true, but the Aztecs came from the north. They knew winter and used crops and stars to guide their way. For that reason the most apparent marker of the season would have been the equinox."

"Father, what else do you know about these monstrosities?"

"That their favorite victims were pregnant women, whom they'd transform into one of them. Ah, and of course, children."

"Children? Are you sure?"

"Yes, of course. Boys and girls. We could go to the episcopal library in Puebla. There's an eighteenth-century document there about it, if I remember correctly. It's quite the bizarre thing. I read it years ago, so I don't remember much. I believe the author was some Sebastián Melgar."

Verón left in high spirits. He liked the idea of visiting Puebla. It was a short trip and he could be back home the same day. He didn't dare ask Father Saldívar directly whether it was possibly to exorcise such a monstrosity, but at least he felt a little less lost in his search.

Verón woke up earlier than usual that morning. He made himself some breakfast and a sandwich to eat on the go. He was excited about visiting

La Cordial and ordering a nice, steamy plate of chicken mole before heading back. He left early to avoid rush hour. A lot of people who worked in Puebla made the same commute. On the way, he thought about what Father Saldívar had told him. Perhaps he wouldn't find out anything else and what the older priest had shared with him would have to do. He was lost in thought when he suddenly realized he was already in downtown Puebla.

He was greeted by the priest in charge of the archive, Father Antón Juárez-Valdivia, a fortysomething year old man, with a heavy mustache and a bald head. He had a Spanish accent, perhaps Andalusian. Antón took quite a bit of convincing to let Verón rifle through the ancient documents without any sort of appointment or training in handling archived materials. The head archivist was on a sabbatical and wouldn't be back to guide Verón through the materials for at least two more weeks. Verón felt himself on the verge of attempting to bribe his fellow clergyman when Antón finally relented making Verón swear on their faith that he'd put everything back exactly where it was, which he, of course, agreed to do. Verón wriggled his hands into the nitrile gloves he was given as he was led into the belly of the ancient library and left there by Antón.

Verón walked to the bookshelf, figured out how it was organized, and found the part of the archive he was interested in. He pulled out his notes from the day before and focused on finding the text from the Melgar guy Father Saldívar had mentioned. He checked the codex and manuscripts, fascinated. He would've loved to have more time to simply read leisurely. It didn't take longer than a few minutes to find the Melgar text. He knew immediately it was the document they'd been talking about. It was a deposition on some evangelical processes, written for the cardinal in order to integrate a trade that would be presented to the viceroy.

It spoke of indigenous customs and the educational programs for children. In passing, it mentioned how they'd instructed the children to break their parents' idols, aiming to free them from the enchantment of the demons they'd served. The objects they'd broken were the piñatas, the tlapalxoktlis. Apparently, they were repulsive objects made of blood, hair, clay, entrails sewn with fibers and shaped like demons. Melgar hadn't understood the symbolism of the piñatas: on the one hand, they claimed to venerate them; on the other, they broke them to free spirits. Verón wasn't clear on what the punishment was, considering that those objects had been made to be broken.

Was the transgressive part to break the piñatas without ceremony? he wondered.

Evidently, the friars were iconoclasts. They dedicated themselves to turning statues into construction stones or statues of saints and crucifixes. Verón thought of how many of the stones they had been moving at the abbey as part of the remodeling had once been sacred artifacts, pulverized and reset as bricks for the construction of the church's oppressive structures. The clay figures were broken, buried, or thrown into the river. He and Quauhtli would often make small comments about the history between their two cultures, but reading accounts like that of Melgar made Verón feel terribly guilty. He knew that his predecessors had not been true saints, but the wanton destruction of the Nahuatl culture was sickening. It wasn't enough to make him question his faith, but certainly the roof under which he practiced it.

Either way, the author pointed out that breaking those piñatas unleashed the fury of the tzitzimimeh. These underworld demons ascended from Mictlan seeking vengeance. They had the power to make anyone who laid eyes on them go mad or be driven to suicide. Once they reached the Earth's surface, they metamorphosed into black moths and great grasshoppers, although sometimes they'd show themselves as old crones. The old Nahuas claimed that when the tzitzimimeh showed up, the end of the world was near.

If they weren't stopped, they could destroy all of humanity. Melgar described how these beings had made six guards dismember each other, how three clerics had died under suspicious circumstances: one had been impaled, another incinerated, and another beheaded, apparently by his own hand. The deaths made several friars flee. They searched for the only surviving Nahua priest to demand his help and defeat the tzitzimimeh, who were ravaging the abbey and the convent. When they finally found the old shaman and dragged him to the site, Melgar only vaguely described the priest as "performing a Nahua ritual of prayer and song," and the plague of death ceased. That was the end of the document. The codex didn't explain how they'd stopped the plague back then.

Verón said goodbye and thanked Father Antón. The way back was certainly more exhausting than the way there. Traffic was intense. He got home as it was getting dark and sat at his dining table to reread his notes.

Verón then settled into his bedroom and called Carmen. He had promised her that he would look into the things she told him about and he had, though he was hesitant to call her without having an actual solution at hand. The best he could offer her seemed to be the beginning to a problem he had no actual way of solving. All his time in the archive had only pointed him toward a way to possibly identify what was happening, but there wasn't any kind of ritual or summoning that he could think of that might help her.

He dialed and quickly heard the line click.

Neither of them spoke for a moment, but Carmen broke the silence.

"Father?"

"Yes, Carmen, it's me. I've just come back from the church archival libraries. I've been looking into possible spiritual reasons behind what you described was happening to Luna and I'm not sure if I've exactly come up with anything conclusive."

He could practically hear her breath seizing up on the other end of the line.

"Even if it's not conclusive, please, just tell me you at least know something. I know when I called you the other day I was unsure of what was happening and maybe thought I was just a little bit paranoid, but..."

Despite the fact that Verón had gone all this way to look into the claims Carmen had made, he felt himself becoming increasingly concerned. He wasn't ready for what Carmen seemed so hesitant to say.

"Yes?"

"I know it's true now. I know that there's something inside Luna. It looks out of her eyes but it's not her. I've been pretending like I didn't notice, like I could live with it, but it's already killed three boys in our town and I think it will only get worse."

"Listen to me then, Carmen, I'm coming to New York. I believe this has something to do with the Aztec New Year. There's an old Nahua tradition called the 'new fire ceremony' or the 'binding of the years,' that seems as if it was meant to ward off things like this. I don't know anything about the pantheon of Aztec gods or beliefs, but the timing seems to make sense. The beginning of the unlucky days is set to begin September twenty-sixth, so I believe that is when it will be at its worst."

"Why are you coming to New York then, Father?"

"I can't perform any Nahua rites, but I will try to perform an exorcism. It's all that I have in my power against a spiritual threat like the one you are facing."

"Do you really think . . ."

"I don't know, but it's all I can think to do for you and your family. I'll be there by the twenty-sixth."

They ended the call and Verón went about scheduling his flight to New York for the following week.

28

Sleep had become a stranger to Carmen. She couldn't even recall the last time she'd gotten a good night's rest. Sometime before the trip to Mexico to be sure. God, that had been months ago. All she knew at night since then was the sight of her ceiling. Carmen lay in bed staring at that same ceiling, thinking of how much she missed the time before she'd taken the abbey renovation job. Inside her was the ache of an impossible desire to go back and turn down the opportunity to show her girls where their family came from. She'd even go back and change her entire career if it meant that she no longer had to feel this way.

There she was, a fully grown woman, lying in bed in fear of her own daughter. It felt to her like there was some dangerous animal caged just down the hall behind Luna's locked door.

Carmen thought of the girl she had watched bouncing along the stalls of the Tulancingo marketplace, the bright smile on Luna's face and her shrill giggle permeating the air. Tears filled her eyes as she imagined that same girl tied to a chair and thrashing around while Verón threw holy water at her and yelled in Latin. What the hell was she about to do to her daughter?

Josh came over Saturday morning to see Izel. Nobody had been sleeping well and Josh had received an alarming text from Izel, begging him to come and pick her up. He was nervous.

Izel ran out the front door, and into Josh's car. She didn't want to stay there. Everything was so strange. "Let's go, just, anywhere. I can't be here. This house is suffocating. It's haunted."

She never thought she'd use that term to refer to her own home, but reality was a concept that didn't seem very clear at the moment.

He didn't know what to say. He wanted to be with her and share her anguish and anxiety, but he was incredibly glad to be able to go home whenever he wanted, disconnect from Izel's strange and insane world.

"Are you hungry?"

"Yes. No. I don't know. I just want out."

Josh hadn't yet eaten anything that morning, so he decided to head for fast food.

Josh drove for ten minutes to their nearest McDonald's. It was starting to snow, just a few snowflakes here and there.

"No way it's snowing right now, right?" Josh said.

A frigid wind met them as they opened the doors into the parking lot. Izel looked up at the sparse flakes falling from the stone-gray sky and caught one on her sleeve, looking at the undeniable evidence before it melted into the fabric.

"It's snow," she said, her voice flat and dull as the cloud ceiling above.

"I'm sure it's just the planet reminding us that it's dying. The jet stream bending out of position, trying to reach down and freeze us while we're unprepared," Josh chuckled. "We're so fucked."

She stared at the sky over the town as they walked through the parking lot, the cold air stung her eyes and nose. Normally she'd join in with Josh, make a joke about how the boomers left them a dying world, something like that, but she could feel the same dread in the parking lot she'd been feeling at home. It was escaping into the real world now, outside their house. It wasn't the planet reminding them of the changing climate. It was whatever was in Luna reminding Izel that it was waiting for her at home, that it was unavoidable.

Josh ordered a Big Mac, McNuggets, a large order of fries and they both ordered vanilla milkshakes. She couldn't understand what had happened, but she'd accepted just then that she didn't have to look for an explanation. It would come sooner or later. They sat next to the window. It was mostly empty; it was not the usual time for a hamburger. Or that's what Izel wanted to think. Josh ate voraciously. Izel stared down at the molded plastic table between them. She wasn't hungry.

"Hey . . . Hey, look!" said Josh, pointing out the window. "Didn't you say that a black cloud like that was outside your window a few weeks ago when things started to get weird?"

Izel looked up and saw at a distance thousands of black butterflies fluttering about, like waves, cresting and dissolving, only to multiply like Mandelbrot's fractals.

"Jesus . . . first this freak freeze and now . . . They probably thought they still had a couple weeks or something to migrate." Josh kept biting into his food, "They're all gonna die, huh?"

He finished his meal. Izel had barely taken a few sips of her milkshake. The butterflies were getting closer by the minute. Izel began to shake. The dread she felt in the parking lot grew with the advance of the butterflies, pulsing and flaring up into a body-seizing terror. Her skin felt like it was trying to peel itself from her body, yelling at her to get out, to run.

"Something is wrong. They're coming our way," she said

"Okay, okay, but look at their movements, the precision. I've never seen anything like that. It's almost like a performance. It's like they're doing a dance or spelling something out. They keep moving in the same cycles."

The flood moved quickly, and before they could say anything more, the swarm was crashing against the large McDonald's windows, thumping against the safety glass with a shocking amount of force. The employees came out from behind the counter to see. Izel yelled at Josh, who seemed hypnotized contemplating the spectacle.

"Josh, let's go!"

The drive-thru window had been left open and the insects poured into the restaurant through the kitchen. Upon seeing them, Josh finally stood up, grabbed Izel's hand, and ran for the door, but it was already mobbed from the outside. The mass of black wings smacked against the plexiglass from outside, bouncing off and threatening to swallow them should they try to open the door. They couldn't get out, and there were more and more butterflies in the restaurant by the minute. The employees were swinging their utensils and food trays as makeshift weapons trying to swat them away or kill them but there were too many.

Josh and Izel hid under a table, but quickly realized how useless their little cover was.

"Wait here," Josh squeezed Izel's hand and glanced around the restaurant. There was a determined look in his eye. "I'm getting the car.

I can slip through the door really fast and I'll just back it all the way up to the front door."

"No, don't leave me here. I'm coming with you."

"Wait here," he said, and darted out from under the table.

He covered the lower half of his face with his scarf and plunged into the opaque wall of shimmering wings, disappearing into the midnight of the swarm. They surrounded him, rubbing against him. The swarm was impossibly dense. All the small bodies worked in tandem against him and moving through it was like running underwater or trying to walk in a sand dune. He opened the car, got in, and some butterflies snuck in with him. He frantically swatted them down and killed a few against the window. When he had cleared a good amount of them, he finally realized that he was absolutely coated in what looked like soot. He ignored it and threw the car in reverse, whipping the wheel around and sliding up right next to the entrance of the McDonald's where he honked the horn. He couldn't see through the cloud but Izel soon materialized out of the swarm and dove into the car.

"What is this shit?" he yelled. "I'm covered in it."

Josh's tires skidded against the pavement as he whipped out onto the main road and sped away from the cloud behind them.

"Let's go back home. You can shower there," Izel said, her attention on the cloud still in the rearview mirror. She began to notice the car drifting to the left. "Watch where you're going! Josh!"

When she turned she saw Josh slumping against the driver's side door, barely holding on to the wheel. He lurched forward and tried to keep his grip.

"I don't feel so good."

"What's wrong? Josh! Stop the car!"

"I'm so . . . dizzy. . . ." He coughed out, before fainting forward against the steering wheel.

"Josh! Josh!" Izel yelled.

She reached over and grabbed the steering wheel as it slipped out of his hands. His foot was still lightly resting on the gas and the car kept moving forward. Izel struggled to lift his leg and toss it to the side, moving his foot away from the pedals and guiding the car as best she could until it came to rest against a lamppost.

Izel jumped out of the car and ran around to the driver's side, shaking Josh and unbuckling his seat belt. She kept calling out to him, trying to get him to open his eyes, but he just slumped in his seat. A small trickle of dark, opalescent liquid dripped off his lower lip. It appeared to be the same shade as the butterfly scales she had seen her mother covered in a few weeks earlier. Not knowing what else to do, Izel did what anyone would and called an ambulance.

"My boyfriend just passed out behind the wheel. We didn't crash, but something's wrong with him and he's unconscious. We're at the intersection of Havemeyer and Fifth, please hurry!"

The operator told her to stay right where they were and that someone would be there to get Josh. As the sirens approached, Izel could only keep calling Josh's name hoping he might hear her and open his eyes.

During the ambulance ride over to the hospital, Izel had the awful job of calling Josh's mom to tell her that Josh was being taken to the hospital and to get there right away. Holding his cold hand as it hung off the ambulance medical bed, Izel cried, realizing that her family tragedy was now destroying those close to them as well. She then called Carmen and told her she'd be spending the night at the hospital by Josh's side.

"Josh is in ICU. I called his parents. They're here too."

"But what happened?" asked Carmen.

"They don't know yet, but they think he was poisoned by something. A severe allergic reaction maybe? I know it sounds crazy but I think it was those weird black butterflies."

Izel wanted to stay there, but Carmen convinced her to let her pick her up and take her home.

"Why weren't you affected by the butterfly dust that night on the roof?" her daughter asked her as she drove back home.

"I don't know. Perhaps I didn't inhale as much as Josh did."

"Or maybe they were trying to scare us rather than kill us."

29

Quauhtli drove anxiously through the highway heading north. He felt like they were being followed, like they were being watched. Each time he saw a car's headlights in his rearview mirror, he tried to glean their intentions from the speed at which they approached, whether they were keeping a distance or disappearing now and then. Yoltzi knew what was going through his head. She was also alert, but not so much because of the criminals, but because of the specters she saw and felt, even in the truck. It was a long drive, nearly twenty hours to Ciudad Juárez, where Yoltzi would meet up with the coyote her brother had recommended.

They finally stopped for breakfast in Aguascalientes once morning broke. It had been nearly six hours since they'd departed.

"We have around fourteen hours left," Quauhtli said, satisfied after a breakfast of enchiladas mineras and smoked meat.

"It's still a while."

"Or we could be satisfied that we tried our best and head back."

"Why?"

"Because there's no point in moving forward. You know this."

"This isn't up for discussion. If you want to head back, no problem. I'll still be grateful you drove me all the way over here."

Quauhtli thought about it. It wasn't a bad idea, going home. He'd be there early, maybe by noon. He could just go to work and sleep in his own bed. He looked around the restaurant. The only people there were four men with trucker hats, maybe truckers, maybe not. They were eyeing them shamelessly. Yoltzi saw them too.

"What do you think they're looking at?" Quauhtli asked her, whispering.

"They know where I'm headed and what I'm about to do. They don't want me to go but there's nothing they can do about it."

Quauhtli looked at them, unsure. He noticed they were dressed differently from a second ago, and their faces were different from the ones he'd seen. They weren't eating or drinking like they were before. There wasn't a single plate on the table.

"What happened? Those guys aren't the same ones from a moment ago," he said. "How did they change?"

"I don't know, Quauhtli."

He looked at them again and once again, different faces, different clothes, a blue cap, a rancher's hat.

"What's going on?" he asked.

"They're here for us."

"Should I go and cuss them out or pick a fight with them?"

"I don't know, maybe they'll leave you black and blue, maybe they'll disappear. I can see things but that doesn't mean I understand them."

"Let's go, then."

He called the waiter over and asked for the check. He paid for their meal and they left, avoiding the gazes of the four men who kept transfiguring. They climbed in the truck, made a quick stop to pump gas and went back on the road.

"Do you want to stop somewhere and get some rest before we keep moving?" Quauhtli asked.

"We don't have time to waste. You know how sketchy the motels can be around the highways. The last thing we need is the truck getting stolen while we sleep."

"Fourteen hours is a long time to stay awake. Why don't you try getting some sleep and I'll wake you up in a while. We can take shifts driving."

Yoltzi nodded and rested her head against the truck's door, letting the hum of the wheels against the road lull her to sleep.

Far from falling asleep, Quauhtli was alert the entire drive and never woke Yoltzi for her shift. Yoltzi slept for a few hours. They reached Torreón early in the afternoon. They made a pit stop for coffee and a snack. They didn't want to waste any more time. They had less than ten hours to reach the border and wanted to be there as soon as possible. That last stretch of the trip was no easy feat, but it went by relatively quickly amid the escalating heat. Camargo, Delicias, Chihuahua. Over the course of their journey, Yoltzi began to sing, first nothing more than a hum, but eventually she was almost singing to herself.

"Where did that song come from?"

"It's been stuck in my head. At first it was just the melody, I think you pointed it out some time ago in the plaza. But slowly the words came in bits and pieces until I had a dream and heard the whole thing."

"So that's what you were singing the day the shadows showed up. It's nice. Comforting, you know?"

"Maybe," she said, and she hummed a few fragments she remembered, stopped, and started again, in a different key.

"I swear I've heard it before, though. Not just from you." He began to imitate the tune, louder.

"By God, Quauhtli, you might be tone-deaf, you know," Yoltzi said laughing. "But go on, let's see if you can remember it."

They kept singing in a chaotic back and forth, sometimes inserting words in Spanish and sometimes in Nahuatl. They reached Ciudad Juárez a little past eleven at night. They'd never been there before. They traveled the streets in silence for a while. They were both starving. Luckily, by then the mind-altering heat was beginning to subside. She told him to head downtown. They could find a diner and call the coyote from there, some guy named Patricio. They found a modest restaurant next to the Santa Fe Hotel. Quauhtli was tempted to rent a room and take a nap. They ate and Yoltzi texted Patricio. She told him where they were.

"You're really going through with this then," Quauhtli said, back in the truck.

"I didn't have you drive me all the way out here for nothing."

"How do you even know that you can trust this guy?"

"I don't know for sure. You can never know for sure, but he's supposed to be reliable."

Quauhtli leaned back against the headrest and let out a lengthy sigh. Yoltzi had never seen his brow so wrinkled as he stared out at the diner parking lot.

"You're still having trouble hearing and seeing straight aren't you, Yoltzi?"

"It's gotten better. I could understand you and the attendant at the last rest stop we went to. Faces still look strange to me, though. It's like I'm seeing everyone's ancestors and them at the same time."

"Fuck."

Quauhtli put his head against the steering wheel in frustration at what he was about to do.

"Tell him you need to bring your cousin too. Tell him you'll have the money for two people tonight. I'll just be worrying myself to death for weeks if I let you go alone. If anything happens to you on your way there or back, I really don't think I'd be able to live with myself. I clearly can't do anything to stop you considering I'm actively helping you at this point. Tell him you're bringing me too."

They were at the spot they'd agreed on at eleven-thirty, waiting in the truck for Patricio. Quauhtli had the money Patricio had asked for in his wallet after draining his savings considerably and had found a place to park his truck where it'd be waiting for him when he got back across. It was well lit and there were other cars in the lot. He hoped his modest vehicle wouldn't catch anyone's attention and get stolen. After more than an hour of mounting anxiety, Patricio finally arrived far after midnight.

"You're late. We were beginning to think you weren't even coming anymore," Yoltzi said, visibly annoyed.

"Don't worry, chill. I had to handle some stuff because of your change of plans."

He came with four more men, other travelers. They were carrying backpacks, water bottles, and bags with God knows what meager belongings they were willing to haul on their journey to the States. They were all quiet. It was evident they were afraid. Patricio did not introduce them. He approached Quauhtli.

"Where's my money?" he asked.

Quauhtli grabbed the cash from his pocket and handed it to him. Yoltzi was watching them anxiously. Patricio counted the money.

"We're leaving," he said.

They walked in the darkness for a while.

"They rarely check this tunnel. Either way, be careful. Wait for my signal. Don't leave the tunnel until they come get you. That's the most important thing to remember. Those dudes will pick you up there and take you to Las Cruces. The ones who've done this before know the drill over there, and the ones who haven't, well, you'll figure it out. You need to get in the pipes when I tell you to. Don't forget, quietly. Not a word. And don't turn on flashlights either."

Patricio left them to make a call. Quauhtli approached one of the young men waiting with them.

"What's your name?"

"Ramiro."

"Is this your first time crossing the border?"

"Yes. I tried a year ago, in a boat, but la migra caught us and sent me back. But it seems to be easier this way."

"And you?" he asked another guy, who was praying and crossing himself.

"I'm Ángel. I lived in El Paso for two years. I was deported a year ago. ICE caught me and I was locked up in the Winn Correctional Center down in Louisiana. But I can't make a living over here, so I gotta try heading back."

A man with gray hair stretched his hand to Quauhtli.

"I'm Alfonso. I was also deported. I'd been living there for fifteen years. We had a curtains shop. My family is waiting for me. My children were born in Tucson."

Quauhtli wanted to learn more about their lives, but when he was about to ask the last one for his life story, Patricio came back running.

"Now. Move, move. Quietly."

They followed him through some wasteland amid trash, rusty car parts, and dry bushes. They walked quickly, crouching as low as they could. They suddenly reached what seemed like a mountain of metal scraps, gas tanks, and car doors, all piled up. Patricio moved some scrap that was hiding a hole on the ground.

"This is the safest path along the whole border. Well, safest illegal path. So, good luck."

The men climbed down a makeshift stepladder headed toward what seemed to be a sewer pipe. Yoltzi climbed down and, finally, Quauhtli did too. Before going in, he saw Patricio smiling. It wasn't anything out of the ordinary, but he found his smirk suspicious, as if he was mocking them. Quauhtli entered the tunnel. There was dirty, fetid water, about a foot high. They crawled or crouched silently wading in the darkness for a while. Now and then, someone turned on a phone flashlight to see but they remembered Patricio's words and turned it off. Quauhtli guessed he'd been walking for a mile when they felt air blowing in their face. Quauhtli squinted in the darkness, not about to turn on a flashlight so close to an apparent opening, and noticed what seemed to be a sheet of corrugated metal leaning vertically. One of the younger men inspected it and saw it was the exit. The group had been told to wait until someone came to get them and lifted the makeshift door from the other side. If they went blindly opening the tunnel into the United States, they had no way of knowing if there was an ICE patrol coming by or a militia group skulking about. So they sat in the water, waiting. Nobody said a word. Some were shaking from the cold and fear. Quauhtli wanted to ignore the advice and leave, but Yoltzi was still, as if in a trance.

"I don't have a good feeling about this," he whispered in her ear.

"Neither do I, but we have to wait. Suck it up," Yoltzi replied.

"Shut up. They'll hear us," a voice in the darkness said.

Hours went by until someone yanked aside the metal sheet at the tunnel's exit. The bright floodlights of a truck behind the man blasted his shadow into the sewer pipe and blinded the group of travelers. Quauhtli noticed right away that he had an AK-47 hanging from his arm. Not standard issue for police or border guards, but certainly the kind of gun that'd be hanging off a possible militia member. Quauhtli knew that worse than the kind of militant cops one might find behind the wheel of the ICE trucks were the anti-immigration zealots he had heard about near the American border. The kind of civilian paramilitary psychos who shot holes in water supplies used by immigrants or simply shot the immigrants themselves. He imagined his and Yoltzi's last moments running like wild game hunted by some racist bastard, until he heard one of the men yell in fluent Spanish.

"Come on, *hijos de la chingada*. Get the fuck out with your hands up."

That didn't sound like someone who would help them cross over either. Quauhtli looked quickly, checking if they could head back or hide in the tunnel, but there wasn't anything they could use for shelter. He and Yoltzi left the tunnel with their hands up. Outside there were armed men with their faces concealed. They had a couple of pickup trucks with floodlights aimed at the group. It was easy to get disoriented after walking underground for a long time, but considering the distance they'd covered and the direction they were headed in, he was convinced they had to be on the other side of the line dividing Texas and New Mexico.

The gun toting men shook the group down, taking cell phones and all other belongings from them before forcing them into the beds of the pickups at gunpoint and taking them to a cellar about twenty minutes away. There was no way to know where they were or where they were going. It was the middle of the night. The trucks came to a stop in a bare, corrugated steel construction storage house in the middle of nowhere and the migrants were corralled off the pickup beds

"Some of you will die here, but others will be lucky. Whoever has family here, raise your hands."

The older man, Alfonso, raised his.

"My wife is here. Please, don't hurt me. She'll pay."

"That's how it's done, boys," the man with the weapon said to the others.

He approached the man and, smiling, hit him in the face with the butt of his rifle. No reason at all, just to show his power and authority. To intimidate. Another one of the kidnappers grabbed Alfonso while he writhed in pain from the broken nose and took him to the corner so he could call his wife and ask her to pay his ransom.

"How about the rest of you?"

"I have uncles in New Jersey," said the young man whose name Quauhtli never learned.

"All right then. How about you? Or would you rather just die here and now?"

"My abuelita lives in California, but I don't have her number," Ramiro said.

"We'll, you have about ten minutes to get it, son, or we're cutting your balls off."

"I have some friends, but I don't know how much money they can gather," said Ángel, his head sinking into his shoulders.

"Then you're going to call these buddies of yours and figure out how good friends they can be."

They took them to make their calls. Only Yoltzi, Quauhtli, and a few unlucky others remained at the behest of the men with rifles.

"What about you two?"

"I have no money nor family here," Yoltzi said.

"How about you, man? Are you gonna save your girl?"

Quauhtli didn't answer.

"I'll tell you what's about to happen, then," the armed guard with the beard explained. "The rest of you poor sons of bitches without anything to offer us get shipped out tomorrow morning. We have packaging facilities and farms for you to work on until you can pay your own ransom. We can't waste our time on people like you."

Yoltzi had heard of operations like this one. It seemed that either they had found out about the coyote they'd hired and forced him to turn over this group or Patricio just sold people out every time. Groups like these men waited on the other side of the border getting quick cash from ransom and using the stragglers as slave labor on farms both for produce and more illicit substances. As the armed man spoke, Yoltzi focused hard on him.

She watched the swirling faces of his ancestors and family, a visible history of his blood evident in his face. If she could only glean something that might help her. Though, she thought, a man like this likely didn't put much stock in the importance of his ancestors. Without money the only appeal she had was to some other part of his humanity.

"Did you know your mother's cancer can be cured?" she said to the armed man.

"What are you saying, you whore?" he said, holding his weapon, pointing at her with his finger on the trigger.

"What you heard. Her cancer isn't terminal, despite what doctors say. They're quacks. I can help her. That's what I do, in Catemaco, where I come from."

"What the——? Are you a fucking bruja?"

"I can tell you more about your family. But you'll choose whether you want to waste any time. I'm actually pretty good at healing people."

The man was unnerved. He took off the ski mask and dropped the rifle. He looked around to check on what his colleagues were doing with the other immigrants. Some were making phone calls, others were beating their captives and yelling insults at them. Right now, it was he who was anxious.

"How am I supposed to know you're not fucking with me?"

"Well, by trusting me. If I save her, you let me go, if not, you can just pick up where we left off."

Quauhtli was studying the man's movements, waiting for him to slip up. The kidnapper left the weapon on the floor and took a phone from his pocket. He dialed and turned around to make sure the others weren't listening. Right then, Quauhtli saw his chance and he took it. He jumped up and charged, striking him square in the back and knocking him over. Quauhtli picked up the weapon with a swift movement. The man on the floor tried to stand up, but Quauhtli stepped on his chest and pointed the rifle between his eyes. The other kidnappers realized something was going on.

"Help me, you shitheads!" he yelled, staring up the barrel of the gun.

As they turned to help their partner, Quauhtli shot one, then caught the second in the face as he turned around. He pointed at third who was running back with a gun in his hands. Quauhtli shot and the guy fell, writhing on the floor. He shot another one who fell, but was still moving. He searched for the other two.

"Behind you!" Yoltzi yelled.

Quauhtli turned around but it was too late. A bullet tore into his left side. Quauhtli kept shooting and dropped the final one. He walked toward Yoltzi and they both ran out of the cellar and climbed onto one of the trucks. The keys were in the ignition. He twisted the keys and drove away. He thought about shooting the motor and tires to render the other vehicles useless, but the other men had finally recovered from their initial confusion and were shooting at him and he didn't want to push his luck.

"How the fuck did you know about that guy's mom?" Quauhtli asked.

"I don't know. It was like what's been happening with people's faces and hearing Spanish and Nahua at the same time. It was like I could see his mom inside of him, like I was following the history of his blood up the family tree and quickly found her."

"You know how to drive, right? I don't know how much longer I can keep this up," he said, touching his bullet wound. His shirt was soaked through with blood.

"We need to go to a hospital," Yoltzi said.

"It'll be complicated, explaining what happened. And finding one will be even harder."

Quauhtli was losing blood quickly. Yoltzi didn't know what to do about a hemorrhage like that. She wished she actually had healing powers. In an unfamiliar country, they had no idea which direction to go; luckily the gangsters drove older trucks and the one they had grabbed had an old GPS in the console.

"I can't do this anymore," Quauhtli said. "You drive."

They shuffled around in the front seats and Yoltzi kept talking to him, while she looked at the rearview mirror, expecting to see the truck behind them at any moment.

"I'm going to rest for a while." Quauhtli said. "Let me know when you want me to wake up."

"Quauhtli, don't go to sleep. Hold on for a bit," she said, knowing that he would never wake up if he did.

"Just for a little while. Sing that song for me? I don't know what it was about it, but when you hummed it in the plaza that day, it really made me feel so safe."

Yoltzi watched him slip into unconsciousness and knew she wouldn't be able to keep him awake. She hadn't cried in a long, long time, but now she wept next to him as she hummed and tried to sing him the song.

On the verge of sliding forever into the darkness, Quauhtli reached up with his bloodstained hand and touched Yoltzi's face, whispering faintly, "You know, I think your grandmother used to sing that song to us when we were kids. She used to say her little song would get rid of the fears hiding in your room."

"Quauhtli? Please, please, stay awake for me, okay?"

He smiled. Blood trickled from the corner of his mouth and he chuckled. "Here I was thinking I needed to come along to protect you and I'm the one who ends up getting hurt."

"Don't go, Quauhtli, hold on, I can't do this alone."

He smiled and his lips filled with blood as he coughed. "I already left. I can't go back anymore. Tell Luna and the rest that I'll be looking out for them."

"Tell them yourself! You just have to stay awake! Wake up!"

She pleaded with him to stay awake, shoving and yelling at him, but after minutes of silence she knew she was driving with a corpse in the passenger seat. Regardless, she hummed and sang her grandmother's song for him, hoping he could hear it wherever he had gone.

Soon enough, the truck made a horrible grinding noise, and the speedometer wouldn't go up no matter how much she revved the engine. It was probably hit by one of the bullets fired at them as they sped off. The gang was still, no doubt, in pursuit, and she'd be a sitting duck in this busted down truck. She climbed out, looking at Quauhtli for the last time.

"I'm sorry, but I can't carry you on foot," tears ran down her face as she was forced to abandon the only other Nahua she knew. "Thank you, brave Quauhtli. I'm sorry you had to protect me again."

Panicked, she ran toward the road. There was a town not far from there according to the GPS. Maybe a few hours walking distance. She had to risk it. There was nowhere to hide in the desert.

After only a few minutes she heard the rumbling of the vehicles Quauhtli had failed to disable coming up the road behind her. She saw a large rock and ran to duck behind it. There were some bushes and a trench. She lay down as well as she could and covered herself with twigs and dirt, as if to bury herself. Right then, the truck with two surviving kidnappers drove a few feet past her. They were standing in the bed of the truck, searching with lamps and weapons, ready to shoot. It was only a few hours until sunrise. They'd surely found Quauhtli's dead body in the truck already and were looking for her. They knew she couldn't be far off and there weren't a lot of hiding spots in these dunes. She could hear them yelling and driving around, convinced that she had to be close. They called out to her, telling her that if she showed herself, they would kill her quickly.

"But if you don't, we'll pluck your eyes out and dismember you alive, you fuckin' whore!"

She remained there, motionless. The men climbed out of their truck. They walked a few steps away from her. They didn't see her. They weren't willing to let her go.

"She has to be around her somewhere. She couldn't have reached the highway already. She ain't no racehorse."

"Well, she damn sure isn't here. I don't see shit."

"Maybe she headed toward Santa Teresa."

"Don't be an idiot. We would've seen her."

"Let's go look for Jones and his people so they can help us find her."

A while later, in the faint morning light, more of them came and went. The cartel had far more than the four or five people she saw earlier looking for her. She counted at least twenty different men combing the desert, seeking revenge for fallen comrades. Surely they would have just let a runaway go, but she and Quauhtli had killed three of them to make their escape. Yoltzi hadn't moved an inch since night and lay motionless, closed her eyes, and imagined herself floating away. The voices and shouts still rang in her ears, getting closer and then moving farther away. It was like she was in a coffin. It felt impossible that they hadn't seen her. But at the same time, she saw hundreds, thousands of diaphanous men, women, and children, forever condemned to march north. Somehow, they interrupted and distracted those looking for her.

When Yoltzi opened her eyes. It was night again. There were no voices or sounds. She was scared, but a voice kept telling her that this was her chance to leave. *Now, or you'll turn to dust right here,* she heard in Nahuatl. The night was moonless. The darkness was dense and heavy. She began walking toward the highway, afraid to run into the patrols looking for her. She wasn't looking sideways, only ahead. She thought of Quauhtli's abandoned body. She felt like it was all her fault, that there was no point in moving forward or in going back, like she'd failed before she'd even started.

Suddenly, she realized she wasn't alone. Her ancestors, specters all of them, walked by her side. She reached the highway. She walked among a multitude of specters for nearly two hours, singing her grandmother's song as the melody and words became clearer and clearer, rising from the murky depths of her memory. Headlights from the kidnapper's truck became visible, heading toward her, but she didn't try to hide. She just kept walking with her head down. It was impossible for them not to see her, but the pickup drove right past her. She'd become another one of the ghosts. They'd rendered her invisible, faceless among many ancient faces. She couldn't stop herself from fulfilling the purpose of her trip. When she reached the nearest town, she looked for a bus station and bought a ticket north. She hid in the bathroom for hours, assuming the kidnappers would come looking for her at the station. Listening for the sounds of commotion outside, she sat and waited in her stall until it was time for the bus to leave.

Darting from the bathroom into the mostly empty bus, she finally sank into the cheap upholstery of the seat, keeping her gaze from the window. Remaining awake with her family song, she finally dared to fall asleep once they had crossed the Texas state line. Drifting off into the unconscious, she saw the specters that guided her along the highway. Among the luminous, indiscernible faces she saw Quauhtli's grinning face and knew he had been telling the truth when he said he'd be watching out for everyone.

30

Verón hadn't set foot in the States for a few years. He'd had no reason to. Fortunately, his passport and visa hadn't expired yet. Last time he'd visited, he'd gone to the opera at the Met with his childhood friend, composer Oscar Mandel, who had invited him to come over for a few weeks to listen to some of his productions given his recent diagnosis of cirrhosis. They stayed in an apartment on Ninety-Second Street. They went to see Verdi's *Un ballo in maschera*, Wagner's *Die Walküre*, Dvorak's *Rusalka*, and Puccini's *Manon Lescaut*. They traveled the city top to bottom talking about art and discussing the history and nature of religion. Ever since Verón had enrolled with the Jesuits, Oscar, who'd been an outspoken atheist his entire life, had criticized him fiercely. He couldn't believe his lifelong friend was dedicating his life to the Church. They fought endlessly over his vocation but given the diagnosis, Verón flew anyway despite their differences, and his own moments of doubt.

When he took out his passport from its drawer, he was reminded of his friend, his doubts on religion, miracles, and faith. During those moments of introspection, Mandel's words echoed in his mind. How could he be arrogant enough to think that he'd be capable of performing an exorcism? What would his friend think of such nonsense? But he couldn't listen to reason at the moment, not even from the ghost of his dead friend to whom perhaps he owed posthumous respect by forgetting about the madness he was about to embark on.

He bought his ticket using his credit card, without thinking it might be an expense he would come to regret. He boarded the plane at gate 45 and tried to focus on his book, *The Rite of Exorcism, the Roman Ritual: Rules, Procedures, Prayers of the Catholic Church*, by Michael Freze, which he downloaded on his e-reader. He also bought *Basics of Exorcism*, by Ryuho Okawa, but he was unsure about it. Everything seemed eccentric and absurd. He read through the entire flight. People often react very particular to him being dressed as a priest. Some pretend not to see him, like they can hide their sins by pretending he doesn't exist. Others smile excessively, trying to have theirs pardoned.

He landed at five in the evening at JFK, walked past customs, and picked up his suitcase. The officer asked him whether he'd brought tequila or anything to declare. He was about to tell him all he'd brought were a couple books to learn how to do exorcisms, but he didn't think the agent would understand the humor behind it. Even for autumn it was cold, especially coming from Mexico. Verón found his old hands shaking a bit as he dialed Carmen's number to let her know what hotel he would be staying in.

Verón unpacked in his room and spent the evening wondering how he would perform his exorcism when he drove out to Carmen's house the next day. He read an essay again on the theory of placebo by Roger Bartra. Every time he finished reading one piece of his meager research he was again struck with a feeling of unpreparedness and would pick up another. He drank his coffee uninterrupted, pouring himself one cup after another from the room's percolator. "The ritual is what matters," he kept telling himself in order to stop thinking about the content of the ritual, which was meant to be sheer improvisation in the best-case scenario. He took breaks to pray.

He set up the cassock he would use, the texts he would read, tap water which he would bless as holy, a rosary—no—two rosaries. He couldn't think of Luna as a spoiled child who was acting up. He wasn't sure if he was meant to assume a demon had possessed her or if something inside her had broken. *How am I supposed to differentiate between a mental illness and the influence of an external factor?* he wondered. That was the dilemma more than the nature of the external factor, whether it was a demon, ghost, or something else.

He began to read passages from the Bible, which he'd picked among the recommendations he found in the library's texts and books he bought online. He kept glancing at the clock, feeling like a schoolchild the day before a test. The thought brought a brief smile to his face. How interesting it was to relive the emotions of his youth at a time like this. He was having trouble focusing, though. There would be only one chance at doing this right.

He left his room for a walk, hoping the cool autumn air might clear his head somewhat. There wasn't a lot by the hotel in Newburgh. It wasn't going to be an inspiring or scenic walk. Everything was too far away and it was getting cold. The wind was strong and freezing and he was discouraged from having a leisurely stroll. There was a strip mall, a couple of bars, fast food restaurants, and a Vietnamese restaurant just across the road from his hotel. Clutching his thin jacket to his body and looking at the neon sign of the restaurant, Verón realized his last meal had been a paltry lunch served on the airplane and considered eating there. The gusts became stronger and he could see a black cloud on the horizon, moving swiftly, despite the headwind. He found it strange and hurried toward the restaurant.

When he arrived, the dining room was empty. He took a seat in a small booth by himself and pulled out his Bible, continuing to pore over the pages in preparation for what he must do the next day. A waitress offered him a menu, which he took without looking at her, barely tearing his eyes from his verses to study the menu before ordering. After waiting for what felt like an eternity a bowl was set down in front of him. He thanked the waitress without looking up at her again, grabbing a spoon and dipping it into the broth still with his eyes scanning the pages of the text.

With his free hand he lifted the spoon from the bowl and toward his mouth, blowing on the broth. Verón leaned in to smell it and instead of the fragrance of broth and spices, he caught a whiff of decay. He set down his book and looked at the bowl for the first time and saw it had a small bird in it, too small to be chicken. Perhaps a quail? He dipped his spoon and took out a black butterfly, soaked wet, that started to move its wings under the weight of the broth. Verón yelped in surprise and dropped the spoon. He jumped out of his seat, looking around the dining room and seeing nobody. He couldn't see the waitress anywhere, so he picked up his bowl and walked toward what seemed to be the kitchen.

"Hello," he said at first, his voice cracking under the confusion, and he cleared his throat. "Hello?! There's some kind of bug in my soup, I can't eat this."

There was no answer. He pushed the door and looked inside. There was a mass of black butterflies, flying frenetically around the room. Skin littered the floor, flayed from the bodies that now sat, leaning up against the stoves and ovens. Above them, in the uniform of a waitress, stood a skeletal figure, missing its face. Its eyes, lacking eyelids, wide open and rolling around as it stepped toward Verón. The bowl shattered against the ground as he dropped it in fear and backed away. While the skeletal face spoke, its voice sounded like a chorus, and spoke out of sync with the motions of the jaw which hung from its head.

"Looking for your book to save you, Father? You think the dogma of the Church would silence those dead by its hand? We don't fear the fire and brimstone you and yours preach, we've seen what the men of the frock are capable of."

Terrified, Verón ran out of the restaurant and didn't stop until he reached the hotel lobby once more. He walked toward the reception, gasping.

"I was just in a Vietnamese restaurant over there," he pointed in the general direction. "I don't remember the name."

"Yes, I know the one," said the front desk staff member.

"Bodies. I saw two dead bodies inside. I don't know maybe three."

"What?"

"I had just sat down to eat and I went to the kitchen and I think the cooks are dead."

"Wait. What the hell are you talking about? The place has been closed for years. You went in there to eat?"

"I'm telling you I did."

"How did you even get in?"

"I just—"

Pointing behind him at the restaurant across the street, he turned his head and now saw it boarded and chained closed. The receptionist turned around, grimacing.

Verón went back outside. The wind was even stronger. He walked toward the restaurant once more and noticed that the door was closed and taped. There was a big sign that said FOR RENT. The windows were covered up with paper and plywood. It was in ruins. How did he not notice this? How did he even get in? He headed back, shivering. The light jacket he'd brought was no match for this weather. He ran back to the hotel. He'd even forgotten he was hungry.

As Verón splashed water on his face in the bathroom, he looked up in the mirror and was horrified to see that standing right behind him was another skeleton, this time adorned with gemstones, a feather head-dress, and sharp, metallic teeth. It was looking at him and seemed to be smiling. He turned around but there was nothing there. The tzitzimitl was in the mirror, and it stretched out an arm to touch him.

"Damn you! Get away from me, devil's spawn!" he yelled.

The skeleton started crawling out of the mirror. Verón recognized the image before him as one of the tzitzimimeh from the archival texts he had read. It must have been one of the spirits now possessing the young Luna. There was no time for speculation, though, it was a hellish manifestation, and that was that. This being hadn't waited for him to go look for it; it'd come here to confront him at his own hotel. Verón left the bathroom, tripping over a shoe and falling to the ground. He could see the tzitzimitl walking toward him in the mirror, slowly, with an obsidian blade in its hand, showing its fiery tongue. From the ground he picked up another one of his books and flung it at the bathroom mirror, shattering it and the image of the tzitzimitl before slamming the door shut, shaking the walls. Verón tried to put on his shoes, which he'd taken off in his room, but they were brimming with insects. Crickets poured out of them in his hands. He left them on the floor and crawled back against the wall. He started reciting the Lord's prayer, but inter-rupted it with insults and threats as he saw the terrible demon appear now in the full length mirror across his room.

"Our Father, who art in . . . step back, you bitch. You can't hurt me . . . heaven, hallowed be Thy name . . . damned monstrosity, go back to your tomb, you pile of bones . . . Thy kingdom come . . ."

The skeleton had already passed through the glass of the mirror and stepped onto the carpet of his hotel room. He dragged himself scream-ing to his bed and reached for the bottle of water he had blessed himself. He tried to open it, but fumbled with the cap and, in a panic, threw the whole bottle at the demon. Sailing through the air and right through the image of the monster, the bottle shattered against the opposite wall, staining the wallpaper with holy water as the skeleton advanced on him. All the noise he was making prompted a neighbor to bang on the wall between their rooms.

"Quiet! What's wrong with you? What's with all the screaming?"

"Help!" Verón yelled back, "It's here! It's in my room!"

The person behind the door ran toward the lobby to tell them that someone in room 205 was screaming, breaking stuff, and asking for help. The manager quickly dialed the police, assuming it was a domestic violence incident or some kind of robbery.

"¡Holy Virgin of Guadalupe, Queen of the Angels, Mother of the Americas . . . be gone, monster, go back to hell . . . we come to you, your beloved children. We pray you intercede for us with your Son . . . you miserable, putrid demon, leave me alone!" Verón cried desperately.

He could hear a voice in his head, saying, "Is this your exorcism? Is this what you came all the way here for, Father? All that power you priests lorded over the living, the promise of paradise and saviors. You can't even save yourself. You're weak. And you thought your hateful Church was going to save the girl? You thought you'd tamp us back down where your predecessors put us?"

As the beast spoke, it grew in size, towering over Verón as he cowered in fear, praying aloud and feebly defending himself with hotel room furniture. Verón threw the remote at it and shattered the window. He then threw a lamp. He heard someone knocking violently on the door.

"What's happening? Open up immediately!"

"I can't!" Verón yelled, "You're not real. You're not here. Pray for us, doting Mother, and . . . Die, you fucking corpse whore!"

Verón got on his knees. The knocking and yelling by the door increased. He assumed the person was coming in to save him. He reached his hand out, hoping for help. A cop pushed into the room, gun drawn after hearing so much commotion. The first thing he saw was a bony hand threateningly holding a knife. Unable to control himself, he shot once, twice, three times, the bullets flying past the specter and hitting Verón, two in the head and one in the chest.

The other guests and hotel employees were in the hall trying to see what was happening. When they heard the shots, some ran, others dropped to the floor. Upon realizing that he'd shot the man on the floor, no knife, no nothing, the cop panicked.

"He had a knife, a big knife. There was nothing else I could do. He threatened me."

The people approached the scene to look at the dead priest on the floor. They wanted to see what had happened.

"You heard him. He was nuts. I thought he would attack me. I didn't have a choice. I had to shoot."

31

Yoltzi had never left her country before—the farthest she'd ever gone from Tulancingo was Mexico City or maybe Guadalajara to visit relatives—and her English wasn't the best. But she found herself moving without hesitation. What was once a blurry vision of her ancestors was now in sharp focus and she could once again understand the world around her. She took a bus to Albuquerque. Always looking back, not so much because of the men who were out there looking for her, but because of Quauhtli, whom she expected to see any moment. Yoltzi traveled for three days through Amarillo, Tulsa, St. Louis, Columbus, Philadelphia, until she finally reached Manhattan.

The journey had drained her significantly. What little money she had kept hidden from the cartel that had captured them at the border and whatever she could scrounge up begging near the bus stops had barely been enough to get her multiple bus tickets and she had to buy food sparingly. When she arrived in Manhattan, she immediately dropped a few bucks at one of the dollar pizza places near Port Authority before heading toward Grand Central. The delirium inducing level of hunger she had experienced had brought her further clarity about her purpose. She felt like a spirit cleansed by the fire of the journey to get all the way to where she was. That fire had latched on within her and she would now carry it to save the girl.

Spending the absolute last of her money, Yoltzi bought her train ticket north to Newburgh, settling into her seat a filthy wreck of a woman. Covered in dirt and grime and tattered old rags, she looked out the window as the train rolled out on the final leg of her journey to fulfill what she had set out to do. When she stepped onto the train platform across the Hudson River from Newburgh she made for the bridge. She'd have to walk the rest of the way. Despite no longer having the address from Quauhtli's phone, or Quauhtli to help her, she knew where to go. The shimmering afterimages of her ancestors, the ones who had guided and protected her this far, stretched out in front of her, marking the path toward the center of the rift in the two worlds. The ghosts of the dead would lead her to the point where the two worlds were being breached as Yoltzi trudged along the cold autumn road.

When Verón didn't arrive for their scheduled makeshift exorcism, Carmen became increasingly worried. He had called and told her he would be there on September 26 to perform an exorcism. She had been researching the things he mentioned about the new fire festival and the days of bad luck at the end of the Aztec calendar cycle and wasn't sure what she would do now that he hadn't arrived.

Crickets could be heard in the house every hour of the day now. They seemed to be spawning from between floorboards and cracks in the walls. She and Izel didn't try to open the door to Luna's room for fear of what they might find inside. Their indecision and unwillingness to believe what had been happening up to this point now stared them in the face as a visible darkness seemingly emanating from Luna's bedroom door.

Without Verón, Carmen could only think that they would have to perform the festival rites she had read about on her own. Her mind was spinning out of control and she couldn't even tell reality from a nightmare now. She and Izel were curled up on Carmen's bed, whispering about what they would do next.

"Is Verón not coming?" Izel asked.

"I don't know. He won't answer his phone. I could go to his hotel to check on him."

"I'm coming with you, then. I'm not staying here by myself."

The two of them got in Carmen's car and drove out to where Verón said he'd be staying. Carmen pulled into the parking lot outside the small hotel and went up to the front desk with Izel in tow and requested the room Father Verón was staying in. The receptionist started to type his name into the computer but stopped before he finished, his face suddenly pained as he looked back up at Carmen.

"I'm afraid I have some terrible news."

Pushing through the doors out of the hotel, Carmen and Izel rushed back to the car, mute with shock. Carmen started speeding back home. Izel looked to her mom from the passenger seat.

"What are we going to do without Verón? You said he was going to try and fix Luna somehow. Are we supposed to do an exorcism ourselves?"

Carmen had a white-knuckle grip on the steering wheel as she sped back toward their neighborhood. While Izel spoke, Carmen fought to suppress a violent sob from wracking her body. Verón, that lonely old man, had come all this way to help them, to help Luna. Not only had a quite pleasant light just been extinguished from the world, but so had Carmen's greatest hope of saving her daughter.

"I don't know. It doesn't look like his faith did much to protect him, and he was a *priest*," she said. "I doubt whatever exorcism we tried would do much good. I mean, I'd just be working off of what I remember from *The Exorcist* and I haven't seen that in years!"

Carmen burst into laughter. The tension in her body which had been winding up to break into a sob finally escaping as a shrill giggle. Tears streamed down her face while the car's engine revved and the speedometer broke ninety as they approached their exit.

Izel held on to the passenger door and grabbed her mom by the shoulder. "Mom! Mom!"

Carmen could hardly see through her tear-stricken eyes but veered off the highway and down the exit ramp. She couldn't stop laughing. Or crying. She couldn't tell which she was doing now. Her exhausted body was hardly able to register what was happening to it.

"You haven't even *seen* that fucking movie!" Carmen cried.

An intersection was approaching as they launched down the exit ramp and back into town.

Izel closed her eyes and dug her fingers into her mom's shoulder screaming. "Mom! Stop the car! Please!"

The sound of her daughter's voice finally broke the brief spell of hysteria she had been launched into. The tires squealed as the back end of the car slid from side to side and they came to a sideways stop at the edge of the intersection. They watched an old cream-colored Plymouth cruise across the intersection, piloted by an elderly woman, in utter silence. The old woman hardly even looked at the car which had just screamed to a halt before her.

Carmen let her head fall against the steering wheel and continued to cry softly, and Izel rubbed her back. She held her mother firmly by the shoulder and spoke calmly.

"Mom, what did Verón say he was going to do? He wasn't going to just throw some holy water on her and recite the Ave María, right? You said he'd gone to some archive. What did he find?"

Carmen's forehead was still pressed to the steering wheel as she answered, "He told me that we're entering some kind of . . . transition period, unlucky days at the end of the century that have to be warded off somehow."

"Did he say how?"

"He didn't say specifically, but I tried looking some things up. The Aztecs and Nahua would apparently do things like destroy household items, throw their blood into a fire, and cleanse themselves of the last years."

She finally looked up at her daughter. There was a thick red line where the steering wheel had pressed into her forehead. When their eyes met whatever had hardened inside of Izel seemed to transfer to Carmen. Within them both was a recognition that, as far as they knew, they were the only ones who could save Luna now. Carmen put the car back in drive and peeled out of the intersection toward the hardware store.

"So, we're going to try and make a fire?"

Carmen nodded.

"A big one."

The mother and daughter walked quickly, nearly running through the hardware store as Carmen swept an armful of lighter fluid into the cart and the two of them heaved bundles of firewood into the back of the car before speeding back home.

Pulling back into the driveway of their house, the two of them realized whatever was inside was waiting for them. Moths and black butterflies swarmed the home, and the ground surrounding the house all the way out into the street was a moving floor of crickets. Carmen and Izel held each other's gaze for a long moment and squeezed hands, steeling themselves for what was to come. They both hated bugs.

"One . . . two . . . three!" Carmen cried and they flung the doors of the car open and ran to the trunk.

Izel grabbed the plastic shopping bag full of lighter fluid and the two of them piled as much firewood as they could carry into their arms. All the while the crickets crawled over their shoes and up their clothing. Once they had everything they needed, they ran through the teaming blizzard of insects, crashing through the front door of the house, and slamming it behind them only to find it was, of course, no better inside.

A steady flood of insects poured down the stairs to the front door and covered the bottom floor of the home like a wretched, living carpet. As Carmen and Izel made their way to the kitchen and sliding door to the back patio, Carmen noticed that every step felt wrong. Each stride covered a different distance. The interior of the house felt warped, the walls seemed to heave with breath as the space she moved through stretched and snapped back into place. The illusions the demons were capable of creating were beginning to swallow the house itself, turning the whole property into something unreal.

They emptied their armfuls of wood onto the backyard's concrete patio. The sun was beginning to go down as Carmen sprayed lighter fluid on the pile of wood and turned to Izel. She lit a match and threw it into the hastily stacked logs and they went up with a violent *whoosh* as the flames sprang to life around them.

"Start finding things to get rid of."

"Do you really think this is going to work?"

"Izel, mija, I don't know. I'm not even sure if this is real." Carmen could see the bright light of the bonfire flickering in Izel's eyes as she stared into the catching wood pile. "Even if this is some horrible nightmare, it's all I can think to do. Maybe it's just about believing. Maybe that's all any ritual is."

"So you believe this will stop all this?"

Carmen turned to look at her eldest daughter. "It has to."

Even if she wasn't sure it was the right thing to do, she had to believe this would work.

Izel ran inside, scavenging for whatever she could find. As she ran through the rooms, searching for items to cleanse the house of, she found herself getting increasingly turned around. Looking though their living room for anything that would burn, she figured it had to be things important or sentimental in nature, but couldn't think of anything that would suffice.

She heard someone at the top of the stairs and froze. Only one person could be up there and it was the last face Izel could bear to see right now. Luna had been fully transfigured into something horrible, something so monstrous it surely could only be rectified by a holy fire. Izel's mind conjured the most grotesque monstrosity it could manage in the place of Luna, but behind that was what truly terrified Izel.

What if she looks the same as ever?

It was looking down from the banister near the top of the stairs, she could tell from the creak of a board. If Izel was going to save Luna, she would have to look at her eventually. Izel whipped her head around to take the sight in all at once, like ripping off a Band-Aid.

Standing at the top of the stairs, Alma looked down, confused and horrified. "Iz! What is going on? Where are all these awful bugs coming from?"

Izel let the collected items fall from her hands into the sea of crickets at her feet. "Abuela! When did they let you out of the hospital? How did you even get here?"

Alma began to descend the steps. "Nobody was answering their phone, so the doctor gave me a ride home herself!"

"Alma! You need to get out of the house! You don't know what's happening!"

She watched as Alma turned and looked at her, sticking out a foot over the stairs, and then fell straight forward. The old woman hurled her body down the wooden steps, thumping down almost every stair as her frail bones cracked. She fell into a broken heap at the bottom of the stairs, landing at Izel's feet. Izel dropped to her knees and shook Alma's shoulder.

"No! Abuela! Wake up! I'm sorry I wasn't here when you fell, please just be okay."

Izel turned Alma over onto her back and yelped in horror. Her face was gone, her features inexplicably and violently bashed in beyond recognition, reduced to an unrecognizable mush of teeth and viscera. Nausea and guilt and terror filled Izel's chest as she could do little else but howl in agonizing terror and grief, interrupted by the snapping of her grandmother's disjointed teeth.

Izel tumbled backward onto the ground, scrambling to her feet and brushing insects off of her as Alma's mangled body dragged itself forward with its broken limbs. The face, a tangle of twisted tendons and cracking bones, sputtered and wheezed as it approached Izel. She held out her hands to shield her eyes from the sight. Seeing them covered in Alma's blood, she tried to wipe it away on her shirt and sobbed out quavering apologies to the mess of gore which was reaching out for her.

"I'm sorry! I'm so-ho-hu-rry! Abuela, please! Please! Stop! Don't touch me! I'm sorry!"

The one still-recognizable eyeball, sunken into a smashed socket looked up at Izel like a hungry dog as she begged for what was once her grandmother to leave her alone.

"You see what happens when you get in the way? What happened to this pathetic old hag? Soon, you, too, will be held by the returning spirits from below. Mictlan will rise right here, in you. This world will be replaced by that of angry spirits. We'll have our revenge."

At the top of the stairs now stood Luna. She was paler than ever. More than pale—her skin had lost all color. It was as if the very blood had been drained from her body. Her gray skin was visibly decaying like a body in the tomb. Large, translucent patches of it hung off her arms like fins or delicate wings. Her eyes filled with black veins that spread out like a spider's web across her face. She opened her mouth and from her throat called many voices.

Carmen heard the scream of one of her daughters from inside the house as she was building the fire into a steadily roaring blaze. She dropped the stick she'd been coaxing the inferno with and sprang for the handle of the sliding door, shoving it open and darting through the kitchen toward Izel's screams.

"Izel!"

Carmen turned the corner into the living room and saw her daughter cowering in the corner, wiping her hands repeatedly on her shirt, and screaming in horror between sobs of apology. Carmen cautiously crossed the living room and grabbed her by the shoulders. Wild eyes, crazed with fear, snapped around to look into hers and quickly softened as Izel buried her head in Carmen's arms.

"It was Abuela! She—she fell down the stairs again and I kept apologizing but she just kept coming toward me."

Carmen shook her daughter. "Iz! Iz! It wasn't real! It wasn't real, okay? None of it's real, remember?"

Izel looked up from her arms and past her. Carmen followed her gaze up to where Luna stood staring down at them through those pitch-dark eyes, flaying arms at her side. Luna looked diseased, sick. Her Luna was rotting away from the inside, like a termite-infested tree. Something in Carmen, some undeniable instinct to hold her child, drove her toward the stairs. All Carmen could think was, *She must be in so much pain.*

Planting a foot on the first stair, crushing crickets under the sole of her shoe, she tried to keep a hand on the wall for security, but the familiar rough stucco sank away from her touch. The space around her was ever expanding as she lurched through the house while the whole thing twisted and bent like a vertigo episode. Luna dashed away from the stairs and back into her room as Carmen stumbled up the steps.

"Luna! I won't leave you in here again. I want my daughter back!" she cried up the twisting stairway.

Every step felt harder and harder, her breath ran thin and her legs felt like they were made of lead. Her daughter was just up there, in her room. Carmen refused to let Luna remain this way. She didn't care what it was going to take, and she didn't know how she was going to do it, but she knew that as long as she was alive, there was a chance she'd get Luna back. A patch of crushed crickets underfoot caused Carmen to slip on the edge of a step, crashing her rib cage against the stairs and knocking the wind out of her. Gasping for air, she felt like she was climbing Everest as she wrapped her fingers around the banister poles and pulled herself up the stairs on her stomach.

As her head crested the top stair, she found herself face-to-face with the dead, vacant stare of a massive cricket. This is what her mother had said she saw before she saw death at the top of the stairs. Looking up, there it was again, just the same. A floating specter of death, one of the tzitzimimeh Yoltzi had told her about, swaying back and forth in its seashell skirt as it waved its hands in the air. Carmen recognized the movements as those of the old woman from Tulancingo. Looking into the dead, wide-open eyes of the skeletal figure, Carmen found herself falling into the hellish world within. The symbols the tzitzimitl drew before her pulled her deeper and deeper into an illusion as she fell into a world of fire.

She writhed on the ground, screaming in agony as all around her she saw the souls of the dead and the unborn struggling to break into her reality. All of these souls were ready to tear through her daughter, using her as an escape from Mictlan into their world to destroy the living. Carmen was filled with the pain of them all as she was given a small taste of what was scorching through the insides of her daughter.

The wind outside was blowing violently and Yoltzi watched black clouds rolling in from the horizon, carrying faces of tzitzimimeh in their billowing forms as she broke into a run down the street. Above one of the fences she saw the glow of a fire and heard the howling scream of what must have been Carmen. Yoltzi ran to the house and pushed on the front door, only to find it shut tight. She slammed her shoulder into it, trying to get it to budge, before simply picking up a rock and smashing out one of the windows. Running through the house she saw Izel standing by the fire and rushed outside to her.

"Izel!"

Izel turned abruptly and shrieked.

"It's me! It's me! Yoltzi!"

Izel caught her breath. "I thought you were that old woman. Like you followed us from Mexico or something. What are you doing here?"

"I'm here to stop all this."

'Where's Quauhtli?"

Yoltzi sighed and allowed herself a brief moment of emotion within the urgency of the situation. "He didn't make it. He was killed on the way here."

Izel looked at Yoltzi, this tired woman who had lost so much and all to seemingly save her little sister where she herself couldn't. She began to cry.

Yoltzi patted her on the shoulder and then hugged her. It felt nice to share these emotions with someone in a way. She also wanted to cry but couldn't, so she felt Izel was crying for them both. Yoltzi couldn't show any weakness, not here, not now, she had to keep her nerve. She looked at the massive fire they'd built in their suburban backyard.

"You're attempting a new fire ceremony?"

Izel nodded. "Father Verón was supposed to come and do an exorcism, but he also—" she paused, "didn't make it. This is all we could think to do."

"It won't work. That's not what they want, they don't want to be quelled. They aren't waiting for the right steps to be followed and the cycle to start again. The memory of my people's rituals has been lost, if there were any. My ancestors' customs died with the believers. Willpower and spite is the only thing we have left."

They heard Carmen scream from inside again.

"Your mother went inside to face it alone?"

Izel nodded and Yoltzi went into the house, bringing Izel with her.

"Stay close to me. Keep a hand on my back or something."

As she started singing her song, her ancestors who had protected her across the desert materialized all around them, calmly walking toward the storm of demons, dispelled by the song of protection Yoltzi sang. She followed Carmen's shouts up the stairs with ease and crouched over her, singing the song and protecting the three of them as the tzitzimitl howled at her. The shrieks of thousands of vengeful spirits softened and muffled around them as Yoltzi's voice rang gentle and clear through the cacophony.

Carmen turned over, her eyes wild with fear as she was ripped out of her daze.

"Yoltzi?"

"The tlapalxoktli, the piñata. She has it doesn't she? It's here."

Carmen nodded and pointed to Luna's room. The door slammed open, the handle smashing through the drywall as a dark miasma flowed out of the entryway. They were being invited to walk into the home of whatever it was had taken Luna from them. Yoltzi was shaking, holding on to her courage only by virtue of the comfort her song gave her.

> Yehua in Xóchitl
> xiquiyehua ipan moyollo
> pampa ni mitz tlazohtla
> pampa ni mitz tlazohtla
> ica nochi noyollo.

The three of them approached the cold darkness that poured forth from Luna's room. As they pushed through the black fog, they were given dim sight into the room, now pitch-black. Every surface was coated in the slick, raw flesh-like substance the piñata wore on its exterior. The walls dripped and heaved. The whole room had been transformed into something living, growing, and the piñata beat weakly at its center. Luna stood just behind it, the flesh falling from her face as she addressed the new trespasser.

"Traitorous dog. Your people yearn to come back. Your blood wishes for revenge, revenge for the violence you know all too well. And you've traveled all this way to deny them? You've caused the blood of your dearest friend, a fellow Nahua to spill into the tainted dirt of this land, all to stop your own ancestors from rising up for revenge?"

Looking into Luna's face Yoltzi could see past the grotesque appearance it had taken on to the little girl she had met in Tulancingo alongside the many ancestors who had connected with her while she was there, the good and the bad. Among them, the sad old woman she had seen in that terrible dream, a woman motivated by nothing but hatred and yearning for revenge for love and blood lost to history.

Yoltzi yelled back, "You don't want that, Luna! You have family in this world, remember? Look! They're still here. They're terrified and hurt, but all they want is to have you back!"

"Don't talk down to me! She's not here anymore. The little girl is one of many now, she'll come forth with the rest of us soon."

"I saw you that night! The night you cursed those men, cursed the land and the blood of the conquerors."

Yoltzi began to sing the song of the old woman, her ancestors amplifying the chorus of voices. She reached out to her with her spirit, the many ancestors that had followed her this far carried her message through the darkness toward the possessed Luna. In Yoltzi's melody were love and kindness to remind all the dead of the goodness that remained in the world of the living they missed so much.

The air stood still as Yoltzi sang, her ancestors all around her. Both she and Luna seemed to be locked into a trance, looking into each other's souls. Carmen was still weak and gaining her bearings after being pulled from the grasp of the tzitzimitl, but Izel had her wits about her and her eyes were glued to the piñata on the bed. While Luna seemed locked into contact with Yoltzi, Izel broke from the small huddle they were in and plunged herself into the black fog, slowly moving her way toward the disgusting throbbing piñata.

All around her whispers floated past her ears, the screams of those aching to break from the underworld slipping into her head. Tears flowed from her eyes as she reached in front of Luna, looking into the twisted and tarnished face of what had once been her sweet sister. Anger filled her heart and in one swift motion, Izel yanked the piñata free from its perch on the bed. Tendons snapped and blood splattered Izel's legs as she tore the beating heart of hate from its roots.

Luna let out a bloodcurdling shriek, breaking her concentration from Yoltzi, who started yelling her song. Chanting and shouting in an attempt to quell the newly angered and injured demon holding Luna. Izel was knocked back by the awful sound and struggled to get to her feet and to the door.

Luna's body, shaking and screaming, bent backward as a terrible black mass of bone, blood, wood, and tar burst from her mouth. The pillar of sticky material spread out, growing legs and bone claws. Luna's convulsing body was the base, the perch of the seeping cocoon of old blood, mud, and pitch. Its surface shined darkly above as it grew into the ceiling, pulsing, expanding. The blackness of its exterior looked infinite, a three-dimensional tear between worlds. Through the doorway of the cocoon the three of them saw the glowing eyes of the tzitzimimeh, the fleshless faces of cosmic goddesses, their star-jointed bodies lurched through time and space toward the window they now looked through. A deafening crack echoed through the house.

Luna dropped to the bed, landing in the pool of acrid, dark liquid which had formed as the cocoon split open. Bony, fleshless fingers crept out from the vessel and groped for purchase before ripping through and tearing the doorway born from Luna. Only one of them had made it. No longer an amalgam of illusion and fear, it was finally made material. The vengeful spirit of a warrior mother shred through the remainder of her prison and broke free, lunging toward the three of them.

They dove out of the way as it slammed into the doorframe.

"Run!" Yoltzi yelled to Izel. "The fire! Burn the heart and send it back to the gods!"

The three of them ran for the stairs as the tzitzimitl followed them closely. The wind outside battered the house, ripping off roof tiles and cracking the windows. At the bottom of the stairs Izel broke for the backyard and Yoltzi stood fast. Izel turned briefly to look at her mother, who also stayed behind.

"Go! I have to stop Luna!" Carmen yelled.

She and Yoltzi stood in the demon's way as Yoltzi chanted louder and louder, hoping to stop the charging spirit. Yoltzi raised her voice and the wind outside even started to wane a little. Her song was loud with a deep resonance, joined by the echo of a thousand voices reminding her the words and melody to her grandmother's song. A swarm of butterflies poured forth from the skeleton's gaping jaw, but the song stopped them. They were held back by the force of life within the melody and its words, swarming around Carmen and Yoltzi. The specters of Yoltzi's ancestors surrounded Luna. Even Carmen could see them now as the doorway within Luna had begun to open via the tzitzimitl within her, the borders between living and dead blurring. The spirits held Luna, trying to appease her and the vengeful spirit within. Its awful jaw hung from only one joint as it cried out, "Get away from me. Cowards! Of course, this traitor is your descendant, you who would rather rot in the afterlife forever, your memory and culture trampled on, than get revenge. I'll resurrect us. The world will be reminded of who we once were."

Carmen yelled out for her daughter.

"Luna! Please hear me! It's okay, I'm here! I love you! Please remember that we all love you!"

Yoltzi's guides closed in around the demon and it shrank away from them, lashing out with its bloodstained claws. Trailing behind it, Carmen could see a thick tendon of woven roots still connecting it to her daughter.

Outside, Izel had finally made it to the fire and, lifting the piñata above her head, she cast it down into the roiling flames. She heard the sound of cracking pottery, and the flames jumped higher, turning a beautiful multitude of green and red shades, but the leather casing of the piñata had kept it intact.

Inside she heard that otherworldly shriek again coming from the beast attached to her sister. She looked around for anything to push the piñata deeper into the flames, to break it open entirely, and grabbed a shovel from the side of the house. A crash came from inside as she brought the shovel down on the piñata with a loud crack. And again. And again. Sparks from the flame shot out with every strike as the shrieking and groaning in the house grew stronger.

The tzitzimitl crashed through the glass of the back door, dragging its host behind it as Carmen held on tightly to Luna's body. Izel looked in horror as it lunged for her and she brought the shovel down. The leather crumpled beneath the metal blade and the skin split open, spraying its insides across the embers of the fire.

Carmen held tight to Luna, refusing to let go even as the spirit that held her daughter thrashed about, heaving itself toward the fire to recover its heart. A sprinting blur, Yoltzi's feet crunched over the broken glass of the door as she leaped onto the demon goddess, wrapping her arms around it as it violently convulsed. Yoltzi was no longer chanting, but singing a calming song, practically cradling the thing as its claws scored the patio's concrete floor.

Yoltzi remembered the first time she had heard the words she now cooed to the goddess. Her grandmother had come into her room in the dead of night, having heard the young Yoltzi tossing about in her bed, calling out for help from the chasm of a terrible dream she couldn't escape. It was a frequent occurrence; Yoltzi had been a sensitive child, after all. When she'd opened her eyes that night, she hadn't been able to see her grandmother's face, but only the familiar shroud she saw around everyone. Within it had been the warmth and care of many, an entire family tree calling down through the simple song.

Now, looking down at the face of her people's apocalypse, a real manifestation of a culture lost and buried by violence and conquest, she saw the unconscious terror her people had felt centuries ago. The pain of erasure, the fury born from helplessness, and the grief of so much lost had twisted this powerful goddess, this woman warrior, into a demon of revenge. Yoltzi sang to it as her grandmother had sung to her.

The thrashing slowed to spasms, involuntary convulsions. Yoltzi and the Sánchezes breaths silently fogged in the cool air as even the tzitzimitl ceased screeching. Bone scraping against the concrete was the only sound besides ragged breaths as the creature feebly attempted to drag itself toward the ashes in the fire. Yoltzi looked within it and found that angry old woman looking back up at her. The woman from the woods who'd been hunted in the heart of her home. Yoltzi continued to repeat the refrain.

Yehua in Xóchitl
xiquiyehua ipan moyollo
pampa ni mitz tlazohtla
pampa ni mitz tlazohtla
ica nochi noyollo.

Within the contorted body of the tzitzimitl, Yoltzi saw a flash of recognition wash over the woman's face.

Yoltzi continued humming her song and looked down as the form of the black tzitzimitl separated from Luna, the tendrils of gnarled roots unweaving themselves from her chest. Luna coughed and sputtered onto Carmen's shoulder as she held her daughter tight. The tzitzimitl's eyes emerged from the darkness of its sockets and the flesh of its countenance reknitted into the worn face of the old woman from Yoltzi's nightmare. Carmen went wide-eyed. It was the woman from Tulancingo, from the train. Izel looked down at the old woman as well as she ran over to her mom, cradling Luna's unconscious little body between them, gently trying to shake her awake.

"Luna? Luna!" Izel called out to her, "Please be okay. I need another chance to keep you safe as a big sister. Please."

Carmen held her limp little girl's body in her arms as Luna's eyes finally opened. The darkness receding into the corners of her eyes, revealing the white underneath.

"Mom?"

Carmen, unable to speak, only clutched her daughter close to her chest, kissing her on the top of the head.

Luna turned to look at Yoltzi and the old woman, who in turn looked back at the mother and daughters holding each other and cried, reaching her hand out toward Luna as a voice like grinding bones echoed from deep within the fading body of the tzitzimitl.

"Ketzali," it croaked. "I came all this way for you, but I was too late."

Carmen recoiled, but Luna lifted a weak arm toward the woman. Their hands touched briefly, but the old woman's finger crumbled away as they made even the lightest contact. Her pale skin grew grayer and darker as she caved in on herself, dissipating into a heap of ash in Yoltzi's lap.

Carmen looked down at Luna. "What was that?"

"She wanted the same thing you wanted," Luna stared at the heap of ash before looking up at her mother. "She wanted her family back. She wanted their home to be returned to how it was."

"But we have to live among the living," Yoltzi interjected. "History moves with a swift cruelty. Fighting it is impossible. The spirits of the dead unable to leave their grudges behind poison the air for the living. Luckily many of my ancestors understood that more than others. Without them I would have never been able to stop the door from fully opening within your daughter."

"Thank you," said Carmen, her shoulders heaved into an uncontrollable sob. "Thank you so much."

She looked down at her daughter who'd once again lapsed into unconsciousness. "Luna?"

Carmen began to gently shake her again when Yoltzi placed a hand on her shoulder. "She only needs rest. She's been through more than any of us." Her eyes were glazed, almost unseeing as they looked straight through Carmen into some far-flung place beyond the space and time the two of them occupied.

A question quivered at the top of Carmen's throat as she looked into Yoltzi's lost face, but it caught there. Izel crashed into her as she buried her face in Luna's chest holding her mother and sister tight. Carmen finally rose, cradling Luna in her arms, and they stepped over the broken glass of the sliding door to go back into the house. Carmen laid Luna on the couch before going up the stairs to check her bedroom. All the crickets had disappeared and the house was perfectly normal once again.

When she returned downstairs, Izel was passed out on the carpet next to the couch her little sister was on. The two of them breathed slowly and deeply. Carmen watched the breath rise and fall in them for a while, feeling exhausted herself. She leaned against the wall and, not sure she'd make it to her room, thought about copying Izel and sleeping right where she stood before she remembered Yoltzi. The thought jolted her mind and propelled her off the wall toward the shattered back door.

"Yoltzi?" she called out, receiving no response as she drew closer to the backyard.

Snow blew in through the empty frame of the sliding door along with ash and faint wisps of smoke from the smoldering fire. Carmen called out again to an unseen Yoltzi, hearing only the gentle whistling of the wind in response. On the ground, among the ash, blood, snow, and glass, were crimson footsteps leading away from the edge of the remains of the bonfire that had clearly been disturbed. The steps, out-lined in blood, went toward the side of the house. Carmen followed them and ran out through the still open side gate onto the sidewalk where the footprints started again. More snow was falling, already cov-ering up the evidence of the night's battle and erasing Yoltzi's trail.

The wind whipped in Yoltzi's ears along with the whispers of the past. Thousands of years of history and ancestral memory was still thrum-ming through her mind. The deed had been done, catastrophe averted, but something still drove her onward. Yoltzi was only dimly aware of her body moving through the gray blizzard's gloom, like it wasn't really hers. She felt her own subjectivity slipping into the flood of the many within. They told her to keep moving, so she did. They told her it was all far from over.

The dead are never really gone, she thought. *They stick around. In the soil, the dust, in our stories and songs. Traces of them. All of those within me now. Traces. Shades of the past forming a picture.*

They responded, the voices in her head sounding eerily like her own, *Why would gods be any different?*

32

The next day, Carmen swept the ash from the patio onto the yard's grass where she picked up the shovel and buried it in the dirt. In the pile of ash, she found the jade bracelet. She picked it up gingerly and carried it to the far side of the yard to bury it deep. When she returned to the house, Izel ran down the stairs and into the kitchen.

"We have to go to the hospital!"

"What?" Carmen was startled. "Why? Is Luna okay?"

"Josh and Abuela are both awake."

Carmen swiped the car keys from off the counter and they jumped into the car. At the hospital they were greeted by the familiar Dr Müller. Josh's family was in his room when they arrived, so Müller brought them to see Alma first. The swelling in her brain had completely subsided and she was off of her painkillers. She was standing at the window with the support of a cane when they came into the room. She turned with a broad smile on her face.

"Ah! My children, my children! So glad to see you two. Where's Luna?"

Izel looked back at Carmen who looked in turn at Dr Müller who was standing just outside the door.

"We'll explain on the way home, Mamá. For now, let me pack all your stuff up for you so you can finally spend the night in your own bed."

Izel and Carmen gathered Alma's things and the three of them shuffled down the hall together, pushing Alma's wheelchair. They got her into the car, but before they left Izel stopped short of getting into the car herself.

"I just need to go say hi to Josh before we go. Make sure he's gonna be okay."

Carmen smiled. "Of course, hon."

Alma chuckled and looked at her daughter after Izel had shut the car door.

"I'm so glad to see you two all right after all this time. I had been having the most terrible dreams about you two while I was in there. Visions."

"We have a lot to talk about when we get home."

That night Luna came to bed with Carmen, not quite ready to sleep in her own room alone again. The two of them lay down next to each other in the dark, and the warmth of Luna's breath on Carmen's arm served as constant confirmation that she had her daughter back again. Luna rolled over and propped herself up on one arm, looking her mother in the face.

"Was I the one who did all those things? I didn't want to do any of them, but it was me in the end." She buried her face into Carmen's chest and sobbed, and spoke, muffled, "I killed those people didn't I."

"Luna, Luna," Carmen cooed, stroking Luna's hair, "of course not. None of what happened was your fault. I don't think Yoltzi would have come if she thought it was really *you* doing those things. I saw it with my own eyes too. That woman we saw was the one who did it."

"I know, but it's like she used my hands to do it."

Carmen grabbed Luna's hands and kissed them, pushing her face into Luna's palms.

"I don't think these hands could hurt anyone. We can talk about this as many times as you want, but I can see how tired you are still. You've been through a lot. Please, for now, for both of us, let's get you some rest. All right?"

Luna nodded and let her head fall against her mother's chest. The two of them breathed in and out in sync, slowly drifting to sleep.

For the first time since Mexico, Luna had a dream of her own. She was in a deep forest with the sun blazing overhead. In front of her a small girl trudged through the dense brush. Her body bruised and cut from days of traveling under the cover of the trees. Every once in a while, they would stop and the girl would go stock-still, listening for footsteps. Luna could make out a gray streak in the girl's dark black hair. They traveled together for days, the girl none the wiser to Luna's presence, until they heard the sound of running water. A river babbled through the trees up ahead. The girl broke into a sprint, vaulting over fallen trunks and bursting through the foliage into the bright light of the unobstructed sun. Her feet landed in the cold waters of the river, splashing droplets up into the air to glitter in the light.

Across the water and staring back at her was a group of Nahua tending to a fire and cooking what they had managed to forage from the surrounding area. Largely women and children, though there were some injured men among the group, the fellow refugees welcomed her with open arms to join them by the fire, offering her a shawl and a foraged hunk of fruit.

She sat down against a tree and leaned back as she bit into the fruit, finally able to rest after all that time running away. She looked up into the sun and began humming herself to sleep after a long night's journey.

> *Yehua in Xóchitl*
> *xiquiyehua ipan moyollo*
> *pampa ni mitz tlazohtla*
> *pampa ni mitz tlazohtla*
> *ica nochi noyollo.*

Hundreds of miles away, where home once was, small sprouts pulled from the topsoil by the rains already clung by their meager roots to the fallen, shattered stones of the houses and temples once clung to by their inhabitants. Underneath the girl though, beneath the shaded dirt and fallen leaves, the tree roots slithered down deep into the earth, branching into the soil's history, seasons and years and decades of old death teeming with life. Gnarled, searching tendrils wound their way through aquifers and ancient bones, knitting themselves into a network of catacombs. In the forest, pebbles and mortal detritus below find connection with the canopies above—remembered, if not completely.

In that remembering dark, under the shuffling feet of those trying to forget by the ever-changing creek, those roots wrapped themselves around and around one another as the layers of appendages twisted into a mangled fist, clenched around something only just beginning to grow.

ACKNOWLEDGMENTS

Gracias to the brilliant Lisa Gallagher, the greatest champion of impossible challenges.

Thank you with all my heart to all the incredible people that contributed to this wild ride: Naief Yehya, Kingsley Hopkins, Araceli López Mata, Gustavo Zapoteco Sideño, Matt Warren Bruinooge, James Handel, and especially to the magnificent Tor Nightfire team:

The wonderous Kelly Lonesome and Kristin Temple, my editors and heroes, and Jordan Hanley, Michael Dudding, Saraciea Fennell, Giselle Gonzalez, Esther Kim, Jeff LaSala, Devi Pillai, and Lucille Rettino.

Thanks to the fantastic jacket illustrator, João Ruas, and to the artist, Andres Rios.

Special thanks to my brother and partner, Everardo Gout.